MW00625039

The Devil Whispered

A Cyberpunk Detective Noir Story

Shawn Starkweather

Edited by Allister Thompson and Adam McLaughlin

Cover art by Jugoslav Stankin

ISBN Paperback: 978-1-7361864-0-4

www.shawnstarkweather.com

For my wife, who has been so incredibly supportive throughout this entire process. Her unshakable belief that I am capable of great things has been a driving force for my creativity, particularly during times when I have not believed it myself. This book could not have manifested without the never-ending supply of nourishment and encouragement that she has provided.

Table of Contents

Chapter 1

My consciousness snapped online with abrupt decisiveness. I had the acute feeling of being alone in a world that was wrongly serene, like the silence of the dead. I'd been dreaming of something horrifying, but the details were dancing just outside the boundary of my ability to recall. The panic I'd woken with was caught in my chest. It held me frozen to the sheets as my mind reconfigured to the safety and familiarity of my apartment. Though the context of the dream was faded and surreal, the fear was vivid and raw. It was a visceral terror, compounded by a deeply rooted aversion to vulnerability.

As I lay there, waiting for the sensation of cold dread to die away, the room was unceremoniously lit up by the glow of the wide monitor that comprised the wall opposite my bed. Shielding my eyes from the sting of the sudden light, I heard Ava, my virtual concierge, ask if I would like to receive a call.

"Who's calling?" I asked with what little energy I'd mustered.

"A Pavel Volkov is awaiting your response." Her voice was always the same, mildly empathetic with a touch of encouragement.

I wrapped the sheet around me and grudgingly pulled myself up to sit on the side of the bed. Looking out from the tall windows that constituted the eastern-facing wall of my bedroom, I saw that it was still deep in the night. The only radiance beyond the panes was generated by the city itself; from the broken lines of luminous code emanating from the trickling streams of traffic far below, and the windows of the high-rises that towered above them - light and dark, the ones and zeros of a binary skyline.

"Yeah, okay."

Then, Pavel's finely kempt visage was smiling keenly at me from my wall. He was standing on a rocky beach, and waves were lapping at the shore behind him. He wore a white silk suit and a bemused expression that seemed inappropriately unapologetic.

"It's late, Pavel."

"Good morning, Jacobi. My apologies for contacting you at this hour, but I thought you'd want to know that I've located the target."

"Where are you?"

"I'll send coordinates to your CUBE."

Pavel Volkov was a liar and a thief. He'd conned so many wealthy aristocrats that he'd become one himself, but he stayed in the game for the sake of his own twisted entertainment. He was an artist, who specialized in painting perfect illusions. Deception was his medium, but I'd worked with him for long enough that I trusted him when it came to getting the job done. Traces of malaise from my restless sleep were lingering, so the notion of lucid wakefulness was a welcome one.

"I'm on my way," I said. "End call."

Pavel's smirking face faded as the monitor went dark, and I was left with only my thoughts and the reiterating cycles of light from the softly glowing city outside. In the silence, I heard the faint percussion of fiery horse hooves falling away as the nightmare visiting me surrendered the assault and retreated to the depths of wherever dark dreams were designed.

———◆◆◆———

I'd been driving south from the city for long enough that dawn was preparing to break. After removing a dark, reflective cube from my coat pocket, I inserted it into a receptacle on the dashboard as the car wound its way along the high coastal road. The ocean below seemed anxious and dangerous, but I had a suspicion that it might just be a projection of my lingering unease. As the night began to evaporate into morning, a blanket of fog became evident, rolling in over the waves from the west. In the waxing light, the waves did, in fact, seem more violent than usual as they crashed over the rocks and smashed into the base of the cliffs as if searching for a weak spot to break through.

A holographic display came to life above my CUBE to alert me that I was approaching my destination. Pavel's location had remained static. Wherever they were, they were comfortable. He was very likely at someone's home or beachfront rental, and I had a feeling that whoever they were, they wouldn't be pleased to host unexpected guests at that hour. I turned off the road and parked at a scenic overlook from where I'd walk the rest of the way to the beacon he'd sent me.

Looking into the rear-view mirror, I was confronted by a reflection that accurately represented my state of exhaustion. My brown hair had grown too long and was starting to develop curls that looked as though they were trying to escape from my head. The green eyes staring back at me held an emerald sea in their depths, but they were tired. They'd seen too much to shine with any real luster. I felt the weight of the blame that they carried and held against me, for everything they'd been witness to. I had a recollection of having shaved recently, but a burgeoning shadow that hinted at negligence in that regard was beginning to grace my jaw. There were Israeli traditions that encouraged growing elaborate facial hair, but I'd always shied away from them due to the associated religious connotations. An ancestor from the other half of my heredity, and my namesake, Friedrich Heinrich Jacobi, had coined and promoted the concept of nihilism as the prime fault of the German enlightenment and would have certainly disapproved of my derision of faith.

I let out a deep sigh, chiding myself for my tendency to overthink everything, and said out loud, "It's just a beard, Jacobi."

I ejected the CUBE, which rose from the receptacle into my palm. It was cool to the touch as I unfolded it, revealing a gel screen that displayed an image identical to the dashboard projection that had terminated when I'd retrieved the device.

"Message Pavel: I'm here," I told it as I began hiking down the road toward the blinking red circle on the screen that indicated his location. The CUBE vibrated as I grew closer. I glanced at it to check his response, folded up the screen, and put it back into the pocket of my jacket. The thickening fog was moving toward the shore. It would be a blanket of cover, gifted by the gods of the sea.

There were mental exercises I'd been taught to prepare for this sort of engagement — techniques I used to clear my mind of excess thoughts that could impede a state of absolute focus. I'd visualize myself as an arrow in flight or a wisp of moonlight through the trees, elusive and ephemeral. Sometimes I imagined a black feather falling slowly in a white room. There was something serene and detached in that visualization to me; something that spoke softly of surrendering to the invisible currents that carry us.

I reached the driveway to the house, which snaked down through the trees toward the ocean. Above the beach, there was a modern, raised villa beyond a rotary, in which several cars were parked, near the main entrance. One of them, a cherry-red convertible, I recognized as belonging to Pavel. The morning light was growing in intensity, so I hurried forth to utilize the last bit of darkness the weakening night had to give. Pavel's message had suggested that we should meet on the beach below the house. As I neared, the trees began to thin, so I slowed my approach and took a wide berth around.

The west wall of the house was constructed from steel frames that supported massive glass windows, through which I could make out the shapes of people moving on the ground floor. From the back deck, a stone stairway led down a rocky hillside to the beach, but I kept my distance to avoid being seen, and backed down the steep hill using my hands to steady myself.

When I hit the sand, I scanned the shoreline for Pavel. A figure drifted toward me from farther up the beach. The cherry end of his cigarette glowed brighter for a moment when he raised it to his mouth, but any smoke he exhaled was lost in the heavy fog that had now reached the shore.

"Jacobi," he said in a moderately obvious Russian accent, before taking another drag off his smoke. Pavel Volkov looked to be in his late twenties, although I knew he was about a decade older. He had one of those irritatingly boyish faces that didn't age as quickly as everyone else around him. His short blond hair spiked out in all directions, and his white suit was freshly pressed and unmarred, but for the bottom of the pants, which had been dragged through the sand. His connections to the Russian syndicate had made him the ideal associate for this particular operation. Although he'd sworn off their activities long ago, his family was still deeply entrenched, and that had allowed him certain avenues of communication we'd taken advantage of to infiltrate this particular band of thieves.

"What's the situation?" I asked.

"Eight men, if you include Petr. Six women. I found his friends at the Nightflower, just like Lena said we would. Most are either fucking or asleep now. They brought me back here to where he's been hiding. At the moment he's still awake, getting high on Blu right off the deck in the living room. I left the door open."

"Okay. That's it for you. Go, and I'll transfer your payment."

He laughed and said, "*Moi droog,*" which translated to *my friend* in Russian, "you know it's not really about the money, right? I enjoy watching you work. If it's all the same, I think I'll stick around. Besides, I came with a lady. It's not very gentlemanly to leave without saying goodbye."

I didn't like it, but there was really no controlling Pavel Volkov. As I started back toward the house, he called my name, so I turned.

"This one is a real bastard. Be careful inside." Before resuming my hike to the house, I closed my eyes and took a deep breath.

Loose the bowstring and become the arrow.

Depending on how high he was, the Blu would either make this easier or much more difficult. It was a narcotic substance used to induce euphoria and mild hallucinations in small doses, but once enough of it was in your system, it also behaved like an amphetamine, granting increased strength and focus. Too far over the line, though, and you crashed pretty hard. They called it *riding the wave*. I crept up onto the deck, put my back to the wall of the house, and chanced a glance through the windows to get a sense of the situation inside.

Three men and two women were sprawled on a large white sectional couch at the center of the wide, open room, facing away from the deck. A glass table near the couch was littered with bottles and paraphernalia. A handful of empty glass vials coated with a bright blue liquid were haphazardly strewn about the table. Mixed in among the vials were several expensive handguns. From behind the glass, I could hear muted, operatic music — Anna Netrebko, from *La Bohéme*, around the turn of the century.

Two of the men looked mostly unconscious, but my target and both women were definitely awake, wildly entangled in a hedonistic amalgamation of injections, tongues, and arms. I moved carefully to the door in the center of the deck, which Pavel had left slightly ajar for me, and pushed it open far enough to pass through. The music washed over me as the door was opened, and I hoped it had drowned out any noise opening the door might have made. Keeping low, I crept to the back of the couch behind the threesome.

You are a wisp of moonlight, ephemeral and elusive.

Sensual groaning and eager giggling above me was occasionally interrupted by a soft *psssft*, the sound the Blu injectors made when you pressed them to your skin for a hit. A

8

gust of wind came suddenly from the beach and violently threw open the door to the deck I'd neglected to fully shut behind me.

"What the fuck?" I heard one of the men say as he sat up groggily on the couch. "Who leave this fucking door open?"

There was the sound of stirring from his direction, which had to be the second man, now conscious, sitting up. He groaned, then said, "My head hurts. I keep telling you, man, this shit is no good."

Their thick Russian accents were evident even over the volume of the opera. One of them rose from the couch, and I groaned inwardly with the realization that I was about to be exposed. I tensed as I heard the front door open and someone new entering the room but relaxed slightly when I heard the sound of Pavel's voice over the music.

"My apologies, Roman. It was me. I'll take care of it."

He came around the couch and closed the door to the deck, taking care not to look down at me where I crouched behind the sofa. Walking back, he glanced at the bodies grinding on the couch beside me and announced, "It appears our friend could use some privacy, comrades. Why don't you let me introduce you to someone? She's very lonely upstairs, but sadly, I must be on my way. Come! You should meet her and keep her company."

"What? Fuck it. You go, Andrei," said Roman. "My head is killing me. Petr won't give a shit if I stay. He doesn't even notice we're here. He's fucked up."

"Was that the one with the long black hair? The one on your arm all night, Pavel?"

"Indeed it was! Come with me, Andrei. I'm sure she'd like to meet you."

The soft moaning above me seemed to indicate Roman was correct in his assessment that privacy did not seem to be of major concern either for Petr or the women he was entangled with. Andrei and Pavel left down a hallway, leaving me to my work. I waited for about thirty breaths to give Roman time to relax back onto the couch then drew out a pair of patches from the front pocket of my suede jacket and peeled off the protective sheets. With a patch in each hand, I rose from my place of concealment and slapped them on to the skin of both women.

The fast-acting toxin activated almost immediately, and they both slumped into unconsciousness without a sound. With a confused grunt, the man between them looked up at me. I could see that his drug-addled mind was trying to work out what had just happened. The dulcet trill of Netrebko's soprano delivery rose to a high-pitched crescendo as we stared at one another.

"Who the fuck are you? Ey!"

His friend Roman sat up, holding his head. Upon noticing me, he immediately reached for one of the weapons at the table. I peeled my wrist back and a small, circular cartridge was deposited into my hand by a spring-loader attached to my arm under the sleeve. I hurled the cartridge at Roman as Petr threw the women off his arms and stood. The disc-shaped object hit Roman on the arm and stuck, releasing enough electrical energy to send him into stunned convulsions. As he fell back onto the couch, I spared him a moment of pity, because his headache was going to be a lot worse when he eventually woke.

While Petr was distracted by what was happening to Roman, I snapped my forehead forward abruptly into the side of his temple. His eyes lost focus, and he went limp then collapsed unconscious onto the bodies of the women. He was bigger than me, and heavy, so I cracked the knuckle of my left pinky finger.

That triggered a release of chemical endorphins from the enhanced pituitary modification I had installed. As a familiar rush of strength and energy surged through my body, I easily threw him over my shoulder and hustled toward the front door of the villa.

"Need a lift?" Pavel came out the door behind me, held up his key, and pointed to the sleek red convertible parked in the rotary.

I dumped the unconscious man into the back while the car was being started, hopped into the passenger seat, then pointed north toward where I'd left my car. Smirking, Pavel nodded, lit a cigarette, and drove.

You are a feather falling softly, aimlessly adrift.

"You're a dead man. Fucking dead."

The handcuffed Russian was in the passenger side of my car and understandably irritated. I'd wrapped a strip of cloth around his eyes to blindfold him, and his nose was broken with dried blood beginning to cake up beneath it. We were parked at the base of an immense building of darkened glass that rose from the earth and disappeared into the clouds above. It was a prince among the nobility of San Francisco's downtown mega-structures.

"Do you have any idea who I am? Who my father is? You are completely fucked, asshole."

Two hulking men with expensive sunglasses stood to either side of the double doors that made up the entryway to the building. One of them started toward us when I got out of the

11

car, presumably to tell me to move along, but he paused when I pulled the prodigal son from his seat onto the sidewalk.

"Walk," I grunted into his ear.

"What is this?" the bruiser asked.

"Contract, Petr Kamenev. Take me to your leader," I joked.

The man who'd confronted me raised a wrist-comm device to his mouth to check for orders while his companion fingered a concealed weapon inside his finely tailored suit jacket. Fortunately, the voice in his earpiece favored my advance, and I was waved inside. Once through the doors, I was met by an entourage of muscled suits who fell in beside us to escort us to the top.

The lobby was vast, open, and home to a variety of densely packed tropical trees. I caught a quick glimpse of a monkey of some kind, watching me from a full grown banyan before dropping down and disappearing into the brush. These eco-habitats were entirely artificial, but they were becoming increasingly popular throughout the city, particularly among the wealthiest denizens. They were expensive examples of bioengineering at the height of its ingenuity, which could be flaunted to impress the less fortunate. A fine mist permeated the lobby, which was humid and reeked of earth, like a greenhouse.

Petr had grown noticeably more silent, and beads of sweat were beginning to form on his brow as we all piled into an elevator. I wagered a guess he'd recognized the smell of the lobby and was beginning to contemplate the severity of his situation.

"Sorry about your nose," I said, glancing in his direction.

"Fuck you," he replied, but his voice had lost the conviction it had carried just moments before.

The elevator hummed as it shot skyward, and we reached the top quickly. When the doors opened, one of my escorts nudged me forward into the penthouse. The suite was bright. The tint had been lifted from the glass here at the top in order to allow in the sunlight, which fed an assortment of foliage matching the tropical biome of the lobby below.

In one corner of the room, an elaborate waterfall ran down a wall of cobbled stone, and into a decadent swimming pool. An older man with a thick gray mustache and beard pulled himself out from the pool and donned a towel about his waist. As he neared, I saw that the look on his weathered face was devoid of civility. I suspected his ill temperament was not directed at me, but rather toward the man he had hired me to retrieve, standing blindfolded at my side.

"Jacobi Slate. It seems it is true, what they say about you. I had not expected so swift a delivery, but you have my gratitude. You have done me a great service in returning my son."

Petr looked pale and nervous, and I couldn't blame him. Getting caught stealing from your own father made for an exceptionally awkward situation, particularly when your father was the head of the Russian syndicate Sokoly Zimoy, which translated roughly to the *Falcons of Winter*. Matvei Kamenev was not known for his compassion or forgiveness.

"As promised."

"I had expected to be waiting for some time, but you work quickly. It seems your reputation is well-deserved. The payment will be delivered, as agreed. Should I require this type of service again, you will be the first person we contact. For now, if you will excuse me, I have business with my son."

His kid had hardly been discreet, but that wasn't surprising. It wasn't in syndicate blood to stay under the waves. They often surfaced to feed, and you just had to know where to look for the dorsal fin. Even so, I wasn't going to belittle his high regard for my ability.

I nodded appreciatively and passed Petr and the release fob for the handcuffs into the tender care of the one of the muscled men who had escorted me up to this point. He accepted the man but shook his head slowly at the fob. The man yanked the blindfold from Petr's face.

"Get that nose looked at, bud," I jabbed, but Petr's fevered stare was already locked on a pair of cheap mechanical hands lying on a table nearby, where the ground had been covered in plastic. I wasn't sure he even heard. The goons parted ways behind me, and I left the way I'd come in. As the elevator doors closed, I heard Matvei Kamenev growl coldly for one of his men to fetch the doctor.

Dark storm clouds had gained purchase in the sky while I had been inside, and the opening salvo of rain was launched as I rushed to take cover in my vehicle. Thunderous cavalry charged somewhere overhead, and on the streets of the financial district pedestrians joined in the defense by raising their plastic shields to the sky.

I was tired, and traffic was moving slowly, like a stream of exhausted refugees. The rhythm of the wiper blades and the pounding of the water on the roof were seducing me into a semi-conscious, trance-like state.

"Command: takeover mode enabled. Destination: home" I

muttered to the car, which immediately responded by dimming the overhead display and disengaging the steering wheel to allow me more space. I decided to use the time to try to rest. I reclined my seat, crossed my arms over my chest, and fell quickly into oblivion.

I wasn't sure how long I'd been parked in the garage under my building, but I woke to a steady rapping on the passenger window. I opened my eyes to see a man in a trench coat, and the butt of his umbrella. Between his black trench coat, fedora hat, and black umbrella, he was color-coordinated and well prepared. He had me at a disadvantage in regard to both. His face was older, serious, and his lips were drawn and turned down at the edges as if he disapproved of naps. He placed an ID card up to the window. *Military, Division of….*

"Shit." I sighed. "Command: passenger window down." We stared at one another as the window silently descended. "Foreign and Domestic Crisis, eh? I'm guessing that isn't a coincidence."

"Mr. Jacobi Slate. I'd like you to come with me, please."

"Look, bud, I'm overtired and retired. What I need is a night off and a drink. Whatever it is, it's going to have to wait for the morning."

"It concerns Admiral Oaksley. There's…been an incident, and he's requested your assistance."

Suddenly interested, I sat up, feeling more alert. Old Oaks never asked for help. I had a hard time envisioning a situation in which that warhorse would even need it, and I thought I had a pretty good imagination. I tried utilizing it to imagine a way this ended with me getting some more sleep but came up short. I owed him, and there was no way around it.

"What happened?"

"I think it would be best if he were to tell you himself. If you would come with me…" He gestured at a nearby Cadillac. Black. At least this guy was consistent. I ejected my CUBE and noticed I'd missed several calls. I followed him to the car and situated myself in the passenger seat.

"So, where are we headed?" I asked him as he entered.

"Command: takeover mode enabled," he ordered the car as he turned to me, frowning. "Destination: Alcatraz Island."

———•••———

The sky darkened as night fell, and the rain was still heavy. Our Cadillac padded through the Chinatown streets like a predator — near silent, and direct with purpose. Strangers shared the shelter of food vendor awnings along the avenues, staring forward, down, and anywhere except for at one another. Steam rose from hot buns and noodle bowls. I cracked the window, and the sweet and sour smell of fried foods wafted in like an advertisement. Sharp yelps in Cantonese rang out, the dialect beautiful and arrhythmic to my untrained ears.

DFDC. The Division of Foreign and Domestic Crisis. I hadn't seen those letters together in over five years. The Department of Homeland Security had been under intense scrutiny heading into its fourth decade of policing American citizens with invasive and often legally ambiguous methods. The fear of being unprepared for terrorist attacks had edged out our nation's collective desire for privacy, but just barely. Then the Iran war began, and attacks on American interests worldwide had begun in earnest.

People had died by the tens of thousands, both here and abroad. There'd been a new major attack for the media to sensationalize every week. Hackers in North Korea and Iran used the interconnectivity of our systems as a weapon, derailing trains and crashing planes. The cyber-soldiers killed more people than the terrorists on the ground did. Every system had been a potential target before we started to figure out how to isolate our networks properly. Everyone had been afraid all the time. The roots of the Department of Homeland Security, fed by the fears of the nation, grew and dug deep down into American soil. The DFDC branch sprouted then quickly blossomed into Homeland Security's main arm for responding to crises both immanent and implied. It wasn't just *a* division anymore — it became *the* Division.

At first, the intelligence had been passed along to other branches of the military, but the time it took to move information along those channels had caused too many catastrophic delays — delays that had meant more deaths. Ultimately, a new special warfare group was formed to respond directly to the intelligence reports, and placed entirely under the jurisdiction of the DFDC. They were recruited from all branches of military Special Forces: Green Berets, Rangers, MARSOC, SEALS, and put through even more rigorous conditioning, making them the finest collection of operatives in the world. Formally, we were the FDEES, the Foreign and Domestic Emergency Event Specialists, but everyone called us Fades.

Benjamin Oaksley had been my commanding officer for three years while I'd served my first tour in the Navy SEALs. Later, he was promoted to rear admiral and assigned other duties, but when the FDEES were assembled, we were both recruited and spent another seven years on a team together. I'd been the captain of our unit in the field, but he'd been the one

17

calling the shots from headquarters here in San Francisco. I was the star player, and he was the coach. He'd been a great mentor to me and a good friend. Both he and his wife, Mary Oaksley, had been incredibly supportive when the war had ended and I'd experienced difficulty making the transition back into civilian life. Years ago, the admiral had tried to convince me that my over-analytical mind would make me a stand out private investigator. When I'd started hunting contracts for money instead, Oaks and I had grown apart. He called it "dark work" and didn't want anything to do with it.

He wasn't wrong, either. I'd once believed in what I did. Now, I worked to pay my bills and to keep myself from having too much time to think. I was proud of what we accomplished during the war, but I didn't want to dwell on many of the things I'd done.

Outside the car, interactive holograms of every color lined the sidewalk. A couple sharing an umbrella passed through a neon green dumpling and caused it to split into several mirror images of itself, all of which grew a pair of legs and began to dance in unison before collapsing back into one another, becoming stationary again. It must have worked on some subconscious level, because I remembered just then that I hadn't eaten all day. I whistled and waved to catch the attention of a server drone that flew over and hovered, pacing the car as we trudged along with the traffic.

"Yeah, sesame chicken," I said. Then, slightly embarrassed, I added, "Wait. And dumplings...pork." I passed my CUBE near its sensor and my device lit up briefly in response to indicate a successful transaction. The drone left to retrieve my goods.

"Supposed to be a long one, this storm. One for the records." It was the first time my escort had spoken since we'd left the garage under my apartment building.

"What's the record?" I asked. He shrugged, and I went back to watching holograms. The drone returned shortly, having tracked my location via the GPS of the device I'd paid with. I grabbed the bag of food it carried, and it hummed away into the night. It was good to eat, but the dumplings were overcooked.

"How'd you find me, anyhow?" I asked between bites, but almost immediately regretted it, remembering these were the people that trained me to find people.

"Just luck that I saw you in the front seat of your car," he lied. Division satellite networks could home in on anyone now. Infra-red thermography imagers could look right through a building. All he had to do was access the network address of my CUBE to track my precise location. It was relatively easy, but repositioning satellites was not inexpensive. I realized that Oaks must have pulled a lot of strings to track me down. He hadn't been active in the Division for years, but he clearly still had contacts among the existing brass there.

The bright lights and Chinese signs became less frequent, and the muted buzzing of voices faded as we moved north. A thick Pacific fog covered the wharf district. It reached out, grasping the street with finger-like tendrils. I could still see the Golden Gate in the distance. She rose, mountainous, from the fog beneath. A multitude of digital advertising along the base vied for the attention of passing seafaring vessels, while vivid azure lighting climbed her two spines to celebrate the towering summits above.

"When was the last time you saw Admiral Oaksley?" the driver asked.

"It's been a couple of years."

We passed several warning signs before the angle of the road dropped suddenly and took us down beneath the currents of the strait. Alcatraz Island had been reopened sometime around 2030, but it wasn't until about five years later that the tunnel had been built to connect it to the mainland. Strips of guiding halogen light pulsed past us in even intervals, the only light in the tunnel. *Woosh, woosh, woosh.* We rode the radiant underground waves of illumination toward our port of harbor in the distance, a well-lit gatehouse that blocked progress beyond that point.

"We are approaching a high-security zone," the car intoned without emotion. "Manual driving mode will be unavailable within the perimeter of the zone."

Beyond the fence, I saw automated turrets turn to lock onto the vehicle as we approached. We drove into a tube-shaped passage built into the fence and came to a stop before a wall painted in cautionary colors. A thin strip of light appeared on the floor of the tube and made its way up the wall in front of us before passing overhead to the rear and back again, checking clearance levels and scanning us for unauthorized weaponry.

Once we were cleared, the wall divided, retreating into the ceiling and floor, the car moved through the gate, and we followed the tunnel a bit farther before it opened up into a parking area crowded with vehicles. The Cadillac located the nearest available space and self-parked. As we exited the car, a pressure-activated guide light came on, which we followed. It led us to an elevator tube that took us from the tunnel to the facility above.

The elevator doors opened into a bright white lobby, mostly empty but for a few potted plants and some seats along the walls. There was a standing monitor in the center, broadcasting the news on both sides. A long window separated the lobby from a receptionist's cubicle in which a pockmarked orderly consulted a holo-display of fine print emitted from the tablet he carried.

"Slate, Jacobi," he announced as we approached the window. "Please place your firearm, boot knife, and the loading mechanism on your arm, all cartridges included, into the receptacle on your right." A drawer opened outward from the window. I unstrapped the weaponry and did as he had requested.

"I'll wait here, Captain," said my chaperone as he took a seat and began watching the news.

"I'm here to see Admiral Ben Oaksley," I addressed the orderly. "He sent for me?"

"Yes, Mr. Slate," he said. His voice had a nasal tone which I found anxiety-inducing. "I've been given instructions to allow you to enter the facility. Please approach the entrance." He motioned toward the corner of the room, where a door was set into the wall. A sign next to the door read *Alcatraz Island - Correctional Institute for the Criminally Insane.*

The orderly hit a button, triggering several bolts to disengage from the thick door, which opened inward with a loud hiss. A uniformed prison guard was there to escort me farther into the building.

"Exactly what capacity is Admiral Oaksley here in?" I called back to the orderly.

"He's been with us for nearly three days now, since the murder. Benjamin Oaksley is a patient, of course."

He led me down several corridors until we arrived at a small white room with a massive mirror that spanned the entire wall and a table in the center set with two chairs. Across the table sat Benjamin Oaksley, looking dejected. His hands were cuffed and chained to a ring. His beard was unkempt, and dark circles under his eyes suggested a desperate need for sleep.

"You have three minutes," the guard said, before shutting the door.

"Ben…" I sat down across from him. "What the hell is going on here?"

"I killed her." His eyes were heavy with remorse and pain. His voice was barely more than a whisper.

"Killed who, Ben?" I began to feel traces of the fear I had woken with the night before. It was a creeping dread that was slowly moving from my gut up into my throat.

He stifled a sob and took a moment to collect himself. "You don't know? Mary. Mary is dead. I killed her!"

I couldn't believe this. Ben loved his wife, deeply.

"Oaks, what happened?"

"I don't know…" He was crying now. Seeing him in tears was surreal. I'd never once seen him this shaken, and we'd been in some pretty horrifying situations. "I can't remember. I don't remember! But they showed me….on the cameras…they showed me. I watched it happen, Jacobi. I watched myself stab her to death! Over, and over…"

The pain in his eyes and the anguish in his voice left me speechless and stunned for several moments. I shook my head and tried to assert a counter-argument.

"Editing, maybe. They can do almost anything now. There are a lot of people out there who would want to frame you. Can you think of anyone who might go to these extremes?"

"No…no. It was me! I know it. I can feel that. I just don't know *why*? How could I possibly do that?"

"Were you fighting? Maybe an argument got out of control? Could there have been… someone else?" I was trying to make sense of an impossible situation with reason and deduction, but unnecessary violence was not something I'd ever actually expect from the admiral, and the idea of Mary having a second lover behind Ben's back was preposterous.

"No!" he shouted. "There was no one else. Don't be ridiculous! Listen to me, Jacobi. I did this, but I am *not* responsible for this. I can't tell you why this happened, and that's why you are here. I need your help."

I wasn't sure there was anything I could do. A man had killed his wife and had neither a reason, nor any memory of committing the act. "Oaks, I find people. I don't solve crimes. You know I'd do anything for you, but what can I do here?"

He wiped the tears from his face and took a deep breath before locking steel-brown eyes with mine. Then he growled, "Fine, you find people. Somewhere out there, someone is responsible for this, so find them for me. You find them, and you make this right."

"But how do you know there's someone out there?" I asked. If my friend had truly lost his mind, I could be out there chasing shadows to clear a perceived debt, owed now to a lunatic and a murderer. A guard opened the door.

Oaks stood up and raised his voice. "There is a note at the

house. I found it in my coat pocket, the night before…before…"
His words fell away, and I saw his remorse and the brutality of
his loss written on his once familiar face. "The footage…it's on
the network. My fish, understand?"

I didn't.

"Let's go, visit's over." The guard began escorting me from
the room.

"Ben, I'll try. I don't know…"

"My fish! Make this right! You're all I have now, Jacobi!
Please help me!" The door slammed shut, but my old friend's
desperate plea echoed hauntingly through the hall.

Help me! Help me! Help…

I sat there, helpless, with no idea where to even begin.

We rode out of the tunnel, and the unrelenting rain renewed its
assault on the windshield of the Cadillac in a sudden barrage.
The lack of sleep coupled with the sheer weight of what I'd just
learned was making it difficult to focus.

This was completely foreign to me. My strengths were in
threat analysis and direct, physical confrontation. My father was
a retired Mossad agent. He'd clandestinely become an Israeli
expatriate before I'd been born, and I never had learned why. As
a conscripted soldier, he was a firm proponent of maintaining
physical excellence and by the age of eleven I'd begun training
extensively in six different martial arts. By seventeen, I'd won
twenty-three competitions across the varied styles, but had

become more interested in honing my mind than my body. I'd begun practicing softer arts, such as meditation and Tai Chi.

In the early days of my navy career, my ability to retain a restful mind and comfort with the rigor of challenging physical activity paved the way for advancing quickly. I was quick to assess my options and disassociate myself from emotional distraction, which contributed to some advantage. Ultimately, it had been my ability to accurately assess others that had led to my rise in military status. I had an uncanny ability for reading people, which helped me manipulate them into favoring me.

Unfortunately, none of those skills were very relevant when it came to solving murders, particularly those in which psychologically unstable men had already admitted their guilt.

I rubbed my tired eyes and asked the man in the seat beside me, "You have a name?"

He looked up slowly with an expression of surprise on his face like he'd forgotten he had a passenger. After staring at me for a moment, he answered. "Sam. Sam Winston."

"Look, Sam, do you know what he told me back there? He seems to think that somehow, someone else is responsible for..."

"Slate, I don't know, and I don't need to know," he interrupted. "My job was to pick you up, get you to Oaksley, and take you home."

"You're aware of what happened, though," I said.

He looked at me intently, considering again. "I know enough to be saddened by it. Benjamin Oaksley was a good man and a great leader. Now he'll probably live out the rest of his life in a padded cell."

"So you knew him?"

"Not really," Winston answered, sounding bored. "But I've heard enough over the years at the department. People talk. You know how it is."

"Well, *I* knew the man, and I'm telling you, as sure as shit smells worse than honey, he wouldn't do that willingly. He loved that woman desperately and wouldn't ever have allowed harm to come to her, let alone kill her himself."

"People do all sorts of things they would never do otherwise when they..." He frowned and circled his ear with his index finger, making the universal sign for *lose their shit*. "Maybe all that pressure finally got to him? Being an admiral is no easy thing."

"He's been retired for half a decade. Unless you think making the choice between sunny-side-up and over easy every morning finally drove him over the fucking edge where hunting down and executing enemies of the state never did?" I asked, growing agitated.

Then, for a time, there was only the vibrating hum of the Cadillac and the sound of the storm outside, which allowed me to reflect on the outburst I'd just directed toward a complete stranger.

"Look, I'm sorry. I'm tired, and all this just has me rattled. You're only trying to get me home, and then you never have to think about any of this again, I get that. I just—"

"Do you have nightmares, Slate?" he interrupted.

The question caught me off guard. "Nightmares? What does that have to do with—"

"Bad dreams. The kind that wake you up at night and don't shake easily."

The persistent rain beat against the windshield as I

considered his question.

"I guess I do sometimes."

He was quiet for a little while, and then he turned and looked me in the eye. "Maybe your friend had them too. The shit he went through. The decisions he made? Maybe those nightmares ate away at him until he finally broke. Sometimes people break, and you don't see it right away. Sometimes they're broken, and *they* don't even know it."

I thought about that for a moment, and then shook my head. "I don't buy it. Not him."

Sam Winston raised a skeptical eyebrow.

"He's not the kind of man that held on to those sorts of things long enough for them to poison him. Sure, he made calls out of necessity, and some of them were grim, but I never got the impression he ever thought twice about whether they were right or wrong. He was a soldier to the marrow."

Winston smiled and nodded. "Hey, you're the one who knew him. I'm spit-balling here. Just hypothesizing. I'm sure you're right. But that man killed his wife of thirty years. He stabbed her thirteen times. That seems pretty broken to me."

He had me there. I turned to stare out the window and realized we weren't far from Ben's house in the Pacific Heights district.

"Listen, can we stop just up the way? I'm tired, and I'd rather not come all the way back out here tonight. His house is just a few blocks from here, and I need to look in on a couple of things for him."

"I'm not a taxi, Mr. Slate."

"Right. Sorry. No problem."

"That house is a crime scene. What sorts of things do you intend to look in on?"

"Need to feed the fish."

He raised an eyebrow in doubt. In turn, I gave him my most innocent smile. It was a rarely practiced look which appeared to only heighten his disbelief.

"You'd make me drive back out in this storm? I hear it's going to be one for the records."

Sam knew exactly where Ben's house was, because he navigated the rest of the way there manually and parked in front of the building.

"Ten minutes. I'll wait here."

I pulled the back of my coat up over my head, exited into the pouring rain, and ran up the stone staircase in front of the house. I was unsurprised to find a hologram stretching out across the door warding off intruders with an official police warning. The message "Crime Scene - Entry Prohibited by Law - SFPD" chased itself across the door repeatedly.

After the war had ended and the unit was disbanded, I'd stayed with Mary and Ben for some time while I'd gotten situated in the city. I held my CUBE near a rectangular panel over the handle and a display screen above it came to life, projecting an image of my face. The door clicked as the locking mechanism was released. I was still on the guest list, it seemed.

I entered, closed the door behind me, and found myself in a familiar mudroom with hooks for hanging clothing and a staircase that led up to the main floor. I took off my boots to avoid tracking water and footprints throughout the house, and hung my soaking jacket. It was quiet, and the smell of death and regret lingered in the darkness.

Upstairs from the mudroom, I requested lights, and began to look around for any sign of the note Ben had mentioned. The place seemed remarkably clean for having been the site of a brutal murder, until I arrived at the dining room and saw the bloodstains on the carpet. I looked away and shuddered. The blood was from a kind woman who had taken care of me.

"Command: access security records," I said out loud.

A voice similar to that of the concierge in my apartment responded. "Security records are not accessible to guests without an administrative passphrase."

Foiled, I reflected for a moment then tried Mary's maiden name.

"Command: access security records — administrative passphrase: Berkshire."

"Administrative passphrase unrecognized. You have two remaining attempts."

I recalled what Ben had said to me at Alcatraz, groaned at his lack of subtlety, and repeated the request.

"Administrative passphrase: Nautilus."

"Access to security records granted, Mr. Slate." The soft light of a holographic screen appeared in the air before me, displaying a number of dated folders. I selected the folder from three nights ago, the night of the murder.

"Send it to my personal device and close it out."

I wasn't sure I was ready to look at that footage. In fact, I didn't know if I *wanted* to be certain about any of this. During a final sweep of the remainder of the house, I located the note Ben had been convinced was somehow a clue to all of this. It was abandoned on the kitchen counter. Scrawled across the page was a list of names, some of which were crossed out. Neither mine nor Ben's names had a line through them. The list was made up of some of the people in our FDEES unit from over five years ago. I wondered if Winston had it right, and Ben had bent, then broken, under some great weight from the past, and written this in his madness. As agents, the names on that list were extremely confidential.

On my way out of the house, I stopped by a small tank in the living room, home to Oaksley's famed goldfish. The genetics of goldfish were simple enough that they'd figured out how to modify them in such a way as to effectively bring their aging process to a slow crawl. It was a rare experiment and had been gifted to him by a graduating class at the naval academy he'd overseen. He'd had it since before I'd known him. As far as I knew, the fish might live forever.

"But you still need to eat, don't you, Nautilus?" I said, sprinkled the tank with fish food, and then collected it to bring home with me. I put my boots back on, pulled my coat back over my head, and left, anxious to get away from the empty, lonely home I'd once felt so welcome in.

While exiting the vehicle back at the garage under my apartment, I thanked my chaperone for facilitating the meeting with the admiral. The tinted window came down as I walked away, and I turned back to the car when Sam called out my name.

"Take this card," he said, handing me a thin silver business card. "If you need me, reach out and I'll do what I can to help."

"Thanks, I appreciate that."

"Slate," he repeated. "Be careful how deep you dive into the madness of others. People aren't always as strong as you need them to be. Sometimes you get pulled down and drown right there beside them." Then he nodded at me, tipped his hat, and pulled away.

As the elevator climbed to the twenty-third floor, I tried to avoid falling asleep standing up along the way. Ava's hologram flickered into existence as I entered my unit and began to remove my coat and accessories.

"Good evening, Jacobi. You have several messages. Would you like to hear them?"

"No. Not now, Ava." The digital image of the young, professionally dressed Asian woman bowed briefly and disappeared.

I set the fish bowl down on a countertop and watched him hovering expressionless in the water. I needed to watch the footage from the apartment and to make sense of the list of names on the note I'd found. But all of that would have to wait until the morning, because more than anything, I needed to sleep. I felt tired to the bone, like I hadn't rested fully in days. *Tomorrow*, I thought as I removed my soaked clothing and collapsed into the bed, I'd reach out to some of the people on that list. *Tomorrow* I'd make some sense out of all of this. *Tomorrow*. Exhaustion carried me beneath the surface of the sea of dreams, and I slept below the waves, oblivious and blissfully ignorant of the deep emotional turmoil I'd been struggling to ignore.

Chapter 2

I woke to the absence of sound. The constant pitter-patter of the rain had subsided, though the sky remained overcast and dark. Memories from the night before were regurgitated by my hippocampus, sorted and delineated by my neocortex, subsequently packaged into neuronic data, and finally delivered to my conscious mind by way of theta oscillations. My heart sank with renewed sorrow as they arrived.

"Ava, bring up the local news." The concierge activated my wall monitor and tuned to an appropriate channel. A reporter was standing on Baker Beach, and the waves of the Pacific roiled and crashed onto land behind her. Her long brown hair danced wildly in the wind.

...not seen since March of 2035 when a record 7.2 inches of rain fell over the course of two days. High winds expected to reach upwards of fifty miles per hour will continue to contribute to extensive storm surge, which, coupled with the rising tide, could lead to severe flooding in certain areas of the...

I had been hoping for news about the murder, but in the immediate absence of that, my thoughts turned to making some progress on the investigation. I was a vehement believer that a good shower could wash away the grime of an ugly night, both literally and figuratively, and decided to put my faith to the test. The shower kicked on, and the surge of hot water and steam got to work on adjusting my dismal demeanor. I rested my hands on the glass and let it baptize me, hoping to be cleansed and reborn into something less cynical and odorous.

"Ava, transfer to augment display and bring up local news recordings from three days ago, specifically anything to do with the murder of Mary Oaksley."

A raven-haired anchor, seated at a desk beside her co-anchor appeared in front of me in the shower as the media was rendered onto the contacts that were permanently installed over my corneas. The audio came through the same speakers Ava used to communicate with me, which were installed in every room of the house.

A brutal murder took place late last night at the home of retired Navy Admiral, Benjamin Oaksley. Early reports indicate that Admiral Oakley's wife, Mary Lynn Oaksley, was stabbed to death in her Pacific Heights home by what evidence allegedly indicates was the admiral himself.

The broadcast shifted to footage of the scene of the crime, outside the house, where several police vehicles had cordoned off the area. It was night, and a drone camera zoomed in on two officers escorting a handcuffed Ben out of the house toward the cars. He looked confused, frightened, and extremely tired.

The rear admiral is a highly praised and decorated officer, who dedicated over twenty years of distinguished service to the navy.

There was another cut to a muscular young man wearing a white tank top and a backward baseball cap.

"I never heard anything from them, and I lived next door for twelve years. They were always real quiet. Then last night I heard the lady screaming like crazy, so I reported it. They showed up in maybe ten minutes, but she'd stopped screaming a long time before then."

"Ava, terminate broadcast." The broadcast disappeared from my augment lenses, leaving only the heated steam of the shower.

I'd ruined the process of cleansing by watching the news footage and felt more sullied than when I'd stepped in.

Frustrated, I threw a towel around my waist, and stepped out onto the balcony for some air, hoping it might breathe some inspiration into me or stimulate an idea of some kind. The occasional hum of a passenger drone flying by and the dull, muted sounds of traffic below were the only real deterrents to complete silence that high up. No shining bolt of wisdom or flash of insight struck me on the balcony, so I returned inside to search through the pockets of the suede jacket I'd worn the night before. I found the now somewhat crumpled list from Ben's house there.

There were seven names, three of which had been crossed out. The remaining names were Jacobi Slate, Wendell Hamilton, Cody Marshall, and Benjamin Oaksley. Ben said he'd found this list *before* he'd attacked and killed his wife. I hadn't heard from Cody in a while and wasn't sure what his current status was. Wendell, however, had stayed here in the city like me when our unit had disbanded. We'd gotten together to reminisce a few times since then, but I hadn't spoken to him at all over the last year.

I pulled out my CUBE and unfolded it to reveal the gel display screen.

"Command: contact Wendell Hamilton"

After a few moments, the CUBE vibrated briefly, and I had Wendell on the screen. He'd always been exceptionally burly, but from his neck muscles alone it looked like he'd spent the last year subsisting on a diet of protein shakes and punching bags.

"Damn, man. I didn't think you could get any bulkier. You look...healthy."

"Slate! How are you, brother? It's been a while."

"Not great, if I'm being honest. Have you heard about old Oaks?"

He pursed his lips and shook his overly large head. "Nope. What about him?"

"Listen, can we get together somewhere today? I could use an outside perspective, and there are some things you should probably be aware of. Are you free to meet up?"

"Today? Hm. I gotta meet up with my little brother down at Ares this evening. He's got his second fight. You could come down to the Mission and check him out if you want, though?"

"Fight?"

"Yeah, yeah. Remember last time we got together, I told you I got into some mixed martial arts bouts for the money? Well, I never really stopped. I guess it was the community, or the daily practice — something about it all really just clicked. Anyway, I guess he saw the impact it had on me, and then he wanted to try it, so I got him in touch with a trainer, and I've been helping him where I can. He won his first fight a few months ago, and he's headed back into the ring tonight."

"Ares? That on the map?"

He let out a brief burst of laughter, like the entire thing funneled through his throat at once and came out as a single sound. "Nah, not really. It's more of an underground thing. I'll send you the address. Hey, wait. You ever do that investigator thing you said the admiral was pushing? You ain't a cop now, are you?"

I shook my head. "No, not even close."

"Okay. I'll send you the location, and I'll put you on the list. I should be free to catch up a bit before the match starts. The fights start at 20:30. Ping me when you're onsite?"

"See you tonight."

"Hell yeah, Slate! My brother is a killer. You're in for a real treat!"

With the rest of the afternoon at my disposal, I had time to take care of some of the things I'd been neglecting. I started by bringing up the video messages I'd missed. The first was from Matvei Kamenev.

"I'm sorry we didn't have more time to talk after your delivery. I wanted to thank you again for bringing Petr back to me in one piece, although I must say, that didn't last very long." He coughed out a disturbingly sincere laugh and continued, "I sense a great future for our relationship! For now, we're even, but maybe I do you a favor down the road, then you do me another favor, like friends do, eh?"

The idea of working closely with the Falcons of Winter on a regular basis was not something I was at all comfortable with. While I appreciated Matvei's regard for my abilities, and having earned his respect, I trusted him about as far as I could throw one of his bodyguards.

"Hope to hear from you soon, Slate." The aging, scarred face, partially hidden behind his thick gray beard, broke into a gracious smile. It was a look reminiscent of one you might give a child you'd just handed poisoned candy. The message ended, and

37

a new one began.

I quickly sat upright on my couch with interest as the unexpected face of an old friend popped onto the screen. I immediately recognized her tension and distress which was accentuated by the urgency in her voice. Her usual slight, French accent always got a bit thicker when she was upset. It was coming through heavily now, though she wasn't yet mixing French and English, as she tended to do in the rare moments she was truly on edge.

"Captain, I think I might need your help. We might both be in danger. I know I haven't seen you in forever, and this sounds crazy, but please call me back as soon as you get this."

Another message from the same sender followed.

"Listen, Jacobi...please ping me so I know you're still good. I started looking into some shit that's been happening within our unit, and I'm worried. I'm not sure who I can trust. I heard what happened to Ben. Where are you? Are you okay? I've pinged you twice today already."

Her face faded as the message ended, but materialized back on the screen as yet another began. She wore a familiar, determined look I'd come to recognize long ago. Therisa Corbin was no stranger to fear. Our unit had been in some pretty terrifying situations over the years, but she'd always hated the feeling, and considered it weak. Whenever it started to get the better of her, she'd get the same look, before she'd turn on the fear and target it for eradication. Targets didn't last long in our line of work.

"Fuck this. I'm coming to the city. I'll find you."

I lay back on the couch and considered her involvement in

this. It wasn't at all surprising to me that our unit's former cryptologic analyst would be keeping tabs on us. She'd always seen the unit like a kind of family, a perspective I'd never fully shared. We were a team, of course. We helped one another in the line of duty to get the job done. While I cared about the people under my command in the sense that I was responsible for their safety, once the mission was over, I didn't necessarily need them around to remind me of the things we'd done to see it through. I couldn't deny the camaraderie that developed over years of being in tight spots with people you trusted to see you through to the other side, but I'd put that aside after the war ended in favor of privacy and anonymity.

I pulled out my CUBE and directed it to return the call. After several vibrations, I received a prompt to leave a video message. I put on a relaxed look, and patted my curls down in an attempt to discourage their unruly effort to evacuate my scalp.

"Risa, it's good to see a friendly face, even one as ugly as yours," I lied. Risa had a face so beautiful, it was hard not to stare, though it became considerably easier if you considered how easily she could kill a man with just two of her fingers.

"I'm okay here. I'm looking into what happened to Oaksley, and it's got me jammed up a bit. I'm meeting up with Wendell Hamilton tonight to let him know what's been going on, and I'd love to meet up with you as well. Would tomorrow work?" I ended the call.

With that out of the way, it was time to turn to the task I'd been intentionally avoiding, so I grudgingly brought up the video footage of Mary Oaksley's murder. If Ben truly had committed this act, I'd need to see it with my own eyes to try to determine the motive.

This was all insane. Insanity was the only answer I could come up with to explain how it could have come to this. My old friend had lost his mind. At some point, I'd need to surrender to that obvious conclusion, and abandon the idea that I could somehow get to the bottom of whatever happened between Ben and Mary. I didn't have the experience or the skillset for an investigation of this nature. I'd go through the motions and check all the boxes. I'd do the best I could to make sure I wasn't missing something and hanging the admiral out to dry. I owed him that much. I threw the video up onto the wall monitor and tried to harden myself for what was to come.

Concierge AIs, like Ava, were designed to observe and record every room of the house so they could watch for somatic gestures that might indicate potential commands. Ben and Mary's program was no different. I adjusted the view to show each room of the house and the area just outside the front door. I'd taken footage from the entire day, so I scuttled the feed forward to get closer to the time of death.

Mary was home alone. She was in the kitchen, cooking one of her famously hearty meals. Piles of vegetables were spread out across the cutting board, and water was boiling on the stove. I moved the feed forward to the point where Ben arrived but paused, uncertain if I could actually watch what was coming.

I knew I could just stop this and let this whole thing go right now. Ben had gone insane and killed his wife. It was a tragic story, and it would forever scar my memory of the man, but the imagery wouldn't be burned into my mind if I refused to go any further.

She smiled at him and asked how the meeting went. Ben replied that he didn't remember, and Mary gave him a strange look. He walked to the kitchen counter and removed a kitchen knife from a wooden block there. For no apparent reason, he shook his head. She laughed and asked him if he remembered if he'd already eaten. Again, he said he didn't remember, and started walking toward her.

No, Ben. Please, no.

He stopped suddenly, looked up and to his left, and then nodded. She told him he was acting bizarre, and asked if he was feeling all right. He replied that he was feeling well as he approached. She told him to stop, that he was making her uncomfortable, which he did briefly, then began advancing again. He kept turning his head slightly to the left, and his eyes seemed to lose focus on his wife as he continued walking toward her. She told him to stop again, which he did, then continued, after a brief pause. He lunged forward abruptly, too fast for her to evade, and the two of them fell into the dining room off the kitchen. There was violence and blood.

I gestured to stop the footage and put my head in my hands. I stayed that way for some time, trying to collect myself. There was more, but I didn't have the stomach to watch. I'd already seen more than I'd wanted to, and it sickened me. I wondered how anyone could do this to someone so dear to them, even in madness. Ben's remorse, and his lucidity during our meeting, further confounded that particular explanation.

There was a room in my apartment dedicated to the practice of movement and meditation that grounded me and helped me to feel centered. Desperately in need of both, I changed into some loose clothing and entered the makeshift dojo. I lit a sandalwood incense cone that was half burned in a sooty copper bowl on one of the four altars that surrounded a round, cushioned seat in the center of the chamber. Upon the cushion, I positioned myself in the style of the lotus and began to meditate on releasing the sadness and the shame I felt at my inability to help Ben. With my eyes closed and a deep exhalation, I cleared my mind, reaching out to the emptiness, devoid of earthly aspirations, to seek its blessing to walk within. I was no longer surprised by the ease with which I could attain this state of being. After thousands of journeys to this place of detachment, it felt welcoming and inviting, like a second home.

I never knew what wisdom, if any, I would emerge with from these visits. There are certainties, like the way we feel or how we react to adversity, which are often taken for granted. When observing those certainties from a place without self or ego, it sometimes opened the doorway for introspective insights that could lead to new, unique perspectives. When I fully let go, I escaped the restraints that my life experiences had forged. I rose above my emotional inhibitions and disassociated from my learned behaviors to view whatever I was struggling with from a place of compassionate detachment. From there, I could counsel my corporeal self with reasonable advice that was unmarred by subjective interference. Or, as was often the result, I would learn nothing discernibly beneficial whatsoever.

In this case, after an indeterminable amount of time in silence, I opened my eyes only to feel a renewed strength in the belief that I, so far, had done everything I could to aid my old friend. I refused to blame myself for not being able to change an unfortunate and horrific circumstance. Risa had mentioned problems with other members of our unit, though, and I couldn't help but wonder if they were somehow connected to the admiral. Though still conflicted, I was finally feeling rested. There was some solace to be found in the acceptance that there might not be anything I could do to help Ben. I'd look into these connections, but if there was nothing there, I'd tell him I'd done what I could and let it go.

When evening came, I threw on a loose, long-sleeved button-down shirt and a pair of jeans. As an afterthought, I grabbed a black cotton overcoat in case the Ares Arena had a dress code of some kind. I wasn't sure what to expect there, but I was looking forward to seeing Wendell again. I'd been solitary for quite a while, without much social interaction.

He wasn't the brightest bulb in the case, but it would be good to spend time with someone who was familiar with the older, lesser known version of me. He'd been there through most of the war and understood me on a level only members of that unit could claim to. That version of me had lain dormant for years now. As FDEES agents, our identities were completely confidential, and as such, couldn't be discussed with anyone that lacked clearance. Although Ben's list was opening a window into my past that had been sealed with dried paint, there was a part of me that had been feeling trapped behind it and was reveling at the opportunity to knock it open and let some air in.

The Mission hadn't changed much in the thirteen years I'd lived in the city. It still hid a heart of gold beneath a thick layer of grime. As culturally alive, and decidedly abundant with good food and music as it was, I often found myself wandering its streets on my emptier days. Tonight, as my car navigated the streets on its way to the arena, it felt dark and unfamiliar, like a stranger watching my every move.

Homeless men and women shuffled about in the alleys, hiding in tents, and under makeshift umbrellas constructed from just about anything that could provide protection from the rain, which had returned. My car drifted by, entirely unconcerned with their unfortunate circumstances, until it reached a cheap lot near our destination and self-parked.

The city lights reflected off the pools of water gathering on the street and sidewalks, shimmering madly and distorting with every drop of rain. I used the twisted light to guide me and passed several hard-looking vagabonds, sheltered under the awning of a closed antique shop along my way. They were engaged in what was no doubt some nefarious transaction and watched me for too long for my liking after I'd passed by. I checked my CUBE to make sure I was in the right place as I turned into a thin alley with minimal lighting. It looked correct, so I pressed on until the alley opened up a bit, and I noted the gated warehouse entrance ahead and to my left. There were several lit fire barrels out front with people standing around them. A pair of men that looked like they'd been directly injected with gorilla DNA stood on either side of a door that presumably led into the compound, and they watched me cautiously, arms crossed over their massive chests, as I approached.

"You know, that's a power stance," I said to the one on the left. He raised an eyebrow in curiosity.

"The way you're standing, with your arms crossed like that. It's called a power stance. It implies strength and dominance."

He gave me a silent stare that somehow spoke volumes regarding his interest, or rather the lack thereof, in my observation.

"What's your name?" He grunted out the question as he unfolded a CUBE and began scrolling through a list.

"Jacobi Slate."

He found me quickly and motioned for me to enter. The ape

on the right punched the door twice with his massive, meaty fist, which opened up, allowing entry into a dark room with a harsh halogen light emitting from behind the counter of what appeared to be a coat check. There were black ropes filing guests down a long, poorly lit, cement hall toward a pair of double doors, outlined by a thin red light seeping through the space around their outer edge.

A small handful of people congregated in the lobby, some handing their coats over at the counter, the rest queuing to be patted down by another bouncer, who appeared to be the final guardian of whatever dark paradise was on the other side of those double doors at the end of the hall. I waited my turn patiently and assisted the bouncer with locating both my primary sidearm and the combat knife in my ankle sheath. He took them both and carried them into the coatroom then returned with a ticket, which he handed to me before waving me through.

As I approached the doors down the hall, the sound of muted, industrial music grew louder. Pushing them open unleashed the full fury of the sound, which washed over me in a frenzy of sharp snare hits, synchronized drum and bass, and unintelligible vocals screaming out of furious lungs. The smoke was thick in the air, impeding my vision as I scanned the environment.

The outer edge of the arena was higher than the central floor, which hosted a caged ring. Inside of it, two large men attempted to pummel one another. Onlookers screamed their support for one or the other when the wild swings connected or went wide. Whenever one of the men hit the floor, gouts of flame blasted up from the corners of the cage, followed by the gloriously vocal approval of the crowd.

There was a wide variety of entertainment along the outer

walls. Half-nude pole dancers writhed synchronously with the music, fiercely catching the eyes of men and women alike, and daring them to look away with sultry glares that bespoke equal amounts of warning and invitation. A tattoo artist plied his trade at his booth. The glowing ink cut through the smoke, depicting demonic and angelic champions warring over the flesh on the back of a tall man with spiked, red hair who gritted his teeth in perseverance. I meandered through the crowd along the edge of the room and stopped to watch an arm-wrestling match between two men with cybernetic arms. Their faces were wracked with concentration and strain until one of the arms snapped off at the elbow in a sudden burst of sparks and flailing wires. With a victorious scream, the winner stood and raised two arms, his and his opponent's. The crowd cheered madly as the defeated man fell to the floor, desperately grasping at his broken investment.

I found a bar on the far side of the arena, pushed my way up to the counter, and stared blankly at the bartender until she noticed me. Her face was pierced in places that concerned me, but my fear for her well-being didn't take precedence over my desire for a drink, and I asked for a Scotch whiskey. She grunted affirmatively, and poured.

"Hey, man," I heard from a mouth much too close to my ear. The accompanying nudge on my shoulder confirmed the message was for me.

I turned to see an unkempt man with yellow teeth and wild eyes. His dreadlocked hair looked like it hadn't been oiled in months, and tumbled down away from his head at unnatural angles. He grinned wildly as I looked him over.

"You looking?" he asked, his fetid breath rankling my nose.

Confused, though hesitant to ask for clarification, I shook my head. "I don't think so."

Mistakenly sensing a lack of conviction, he pressed on, encouraged, despite my refusal. He rummaged through a pouch on his belt and pulled out a glass vial containing a substance I recognized. He looked up and grinned maniacally again.

"Cheap. Fifty a hit. One vial has four hits," he said and knuckled my arm again. Once more, he positioned his head too close to mine in an attempt to communicate over the music. "Fresh Blu! Straight from the depths of Neptune's playground! You can still smell the seaweed!"

"No thanks," I said, turning to down my whiskey. He grabbed my arm, causing me to lose about half my shot, which spilled out as I lifted it for consumption.

"You don't know what you're missing, man, this shit will rip your mind out!"

I bowed my head briefly to mourn the wasted liquor on the counter that I would have much preferred to have ended its days in my stomach, then turned and looked the stranger in the eyes.

"Fuck off."

"What'd you say to me, chum?" He squinted his beady eyes and crinkled his nose in a way he must have believed menacing. "What the fuck did you just say to me?"

The bartender must have had some kind of sixth sense for this kind of bullshit escalating, because she suddenly appeared between us, replaced my spilled shot, and pointed a finger at the dealer.

"The man don't seem interested. Gotta be a lot of other marks in here. Why don't you move the fuck along?" she asked, though it sounded very little like a question.

His face contorted like he was about to lash out, and I allowed my body to go slack in preparation to respond accordingly, but noticing the hulking men in power stances at both ends of the counter, he grinned unconvincingly and put his hands up before backing away into the crowd.

"Thanks," I said as I turned to address the bartender, but she'd already moved on and was busy pouring a drink for another customer.

I sent a beacon ping to Wendell to let him know I'd arrived and to specify my precise location in the building. The fight must have ended, because all four flamethrowers burst into life, and the crowd erupted into a cacophony of cheering and jeers that lasted longer than the others had. I maneuvered into a less crowded area of the outer ring where I could wait and have a better view of the cage.

Behind me, a horrific dogfight was underway. A pit bull was engaged with what looked like a mastiff of some sort. The dogs were holograms, and the outcome of the fight was based on statistics and mathematics. Whenever one or the other landed a bite, the images would flicker briefly, and numbers flashed above the circle of jeering fools who had gathered to watch, depicting remaining health values and adjusted victory percentages. I tried not to pay much attention. I didn't like visuals of animals in pain.

An announcer's deep, excited voice rumbled through the warehouse to declare the names of the next two fighters, their weights, and their fighting records. The men entered the cage from opposite corners and began an age-old dance of intimidation tactics, which took the form of flexing of pectoral muscles and practiced elimination of any trace of emotion from their faces.

I checked the time to make sure I hadn't missed my opportunity to meet with Wendell before his brother's fight. I wasn't overly late, and I hoped I would still have the chance to catch up with him beforehand, since I had little desire to stay any longer than necessary. My CUBE vibrated at that precise moment. I'd received a message from Wendell.

Fight cards are going quicker than expected tonight. Brother is up next. I need to be ready. Can we catch up after? Use the beacon invite I just sent to come find me ringside when his fight starts.

When the current bout began, it quickly became clear that one man's bravado was more deserving than the other, and the fight was nearly over in the first round. The man in blue shorts controlled the center of the ring well, and had his opponent on the defensive, forcing him to block quick jabs and take several kicks to his calf. As the end of the round neared, the man in blue faked another low kick but settled back into position as his opponent drew up his knee to block and landed a fierce haymaker square on the jaw. The fighter in black shorts hit the ground and looked barely conscious as flames jetted out from the corners of the cage above the roaring crowd. He was saved by the bell, though, and managed to pull himself up to get back to his corner.

The next round began, and within the first few moments, blue, the aggressor from the first round, threw a rapid combination that ended with a lunge and tackle. He landed atop the other combatant and rained blows down upon him that looked again as if they would end the fight early. Black slammed his elbows down into the upper thighs of blue and heaved upward with his groin, throwing his opponent forward, and forcing him to put both hands down onto the floor to brace. Next, he performed two rapid scoots in succession and slammed

49

his palm into blue's chest to throw him off balance. Recognizing his advantage, he followed up quickly, trapping one of blue's exposed legs between his own, grabbing his heel, and twisting hard enough that blue slammed the mat in surrender, ending the bout. The crowd went wild at the unexpected victory by leg-lock. Bells rang, and gouts of flame sent more heat and smoke soaring out into the huge room. I decided to go for another whiskey, both to help me cope with the intensity of the arena and to give Wendell and his brother time to make their way from the locker room to the cage.

I left the bar when the announcer began introducing the next contestants, and on my way back, I accepted the beacon that came through from Wendell. Once approved, the global positioning application on my CUBE coordinated with my augment lenses to digitally outline Wendell in the crowd. This approach would save the time I'd otherwise have spent navigating the sea of onlookers, since now I could see him regardless of what was between us. Back in the day, we'd hack into a target's hardware and approve unsolicited requests, which would allow the unit to track them easily. His beacon lit up ringside. The outline looked similar to viewing someone in infrared, but the lens didn't distort anything else I was looking at, and the edges were sharper and more closely aligned to the outline of the body.

Suddenly, I was shoved from behind. I stumbled forward into two men who spun me around to face my initial assailant and each held on to one of my arms. It was exactly who I should have been expecting but had been too distracted to keep an eye out for, and he was still wearing a stupid grin that showcased his yellow teeth unfavorably.

"Remember me, asshole?" he asked. From the following

cackle and the way his eyes refused to focus on me directly, I got the sense he'd been hitting his own product. "Fuck off, right? Is that what you wanted me to do?"

"Yeah. I'd still appreciate it, to be honest."

"I was trying to help you, man," he intoned piously. "I just wanted to sell you a couple hits on the cheap, but you had to go and disrespect me." He was holding a vial, and he came up close beside me.

"Just-a-couple-hits," he said, tapping the vial on my forehead to accentuate each word.

The man holding my right arm was looking around with wide, geeked-out eyes, justifiably nervous that the bouncers would see what was going down and come put an end to it. He happened to be just the right height that his head hung directly over my shoulder, so when I suddenly thrust it upward into his jaw, it had enough force to send him reeling backward, holding his face in his hands. My right arm, now free, lashed out to strike the kidney of the man on my left, who fell to his hands and knees, gagging. With my liberated left arm, I reached up and grabbed the vial from the dealer's hand while simultaneously grabbing his throat with my right hand and pulling him towards me.

I heard the crowd start to roar behind me and realized I must be missing Wendell's brother's fight, but I couldn't pass up the opportunity to rap the vial of Blu twice on his forehead while telling him to "Fuck-off."

"Yeah!" he croaked, looking visibly shaken by the sudden, violent turn of events. "Okay, man. I'm fucking off!"

I shoved him hard. He fell backward, and scuttled a short

distance on his hands and feet before getting himself back up to dart into the masses toward the nearest exit. The crowd was seething around me. I assumed I'd been the center of attention, but as I turned back toward the cage, I saw there was a commotion happening ringside, and no one had seemed to notice the incident.

From every direction in the arena, bouncers cut through the crowd in an effort to get from the outer edges to the cage in the center of the room. People were bunching together, crowding in on one another as they vied for positioning that would afford them a better view of what was transpiring. I began pushing aggressively through the crowd. I wasn't a huge man, but I had enough height and muscle to be forceful without much risk of reprisal.

Despite being unable to see the ring clearly, I could see the red, human-shaped digital beacon through my augment lenses. It was flailing about with intensity in that area. A bald bouncer with Celtic tattoos running up the back of his neck and onto his head passed me on the right, parting the crowd and screaming for everyone to get out of the way. I quickly moved into his wake and pushed along right at his back until I arrived ringside, where a horrific scene awaited me.

The mat inside the ring was covered in blood. The source was a fighter lying on the ground and bleeding profusely from a large gash across his neck. Bouncers were entering the cage to confront the red outline of Wendell, but he was wielding a knife and was having little difficulty throwing them aside or putting them to the ground as they approached him. There was another fighter in the corner of the ring, huddled defensively and trying to remain unnoticed. The bouncer in front of me reached the door to the cage, but I grabbed his shoulder as he tried to enter and spun him to face me.

"He'll kill you," I yelled. "I know this guy. Let me try to talk him down."

He was about to refuse, pointing for me to back away, but at that moment, one of the bouncers in the cage was thrown up against the wall next to us and let out a high-pitched wail that transformed into a wet gurgle as he was viciously stabbed several times from behind. The eyes of the bouncer I was speaking with grew wide, and he backed away from the door.

"It's just a job, man. Fuck this."

"Tell the rest of them to keep out of that cage," I said, pointing to indicate the other men that were approaching through the crowd.

I directed my CUBE to terminate the beacon signal so I could see Wendell clearly and stepped into the ring. He was emotionless as he dropped the body of the bouncer he'd just attacked, which slumped down the cage wall with lifeless eyes that stared blankly out at the crowd.

I held my hands up as he turned to me.

"Slate!" he said, smiling broadly.

I moved slowly toward the fighter in the corner, who I noted was also covered in blood, though it didn't appear to be his own.

"Hey. Hey!" I snapped, catching the fighter's attention. He looked up in shock. His expression mirrored that of a rabbit watching a diving hawk.

"Are you his brother?" I asked, hoping there was some kind of rational explanation for what was occurring here. I wondered if I'd missed something while I'd been distracted by the dealer, and if Wendell had just been defending his brother from an assault I hadn't witnessed.

"Wh…what?" he said shakily.

"Is that your brother?" I said, pointing at Wendell.

He shook his head and pointed at the man bleeding out on the mat.

"That's his brother."

I felt panic welling in my chest as I considered the list I'd found at Ben's house, and the similarity between what had happened to him and what was taking place in front of me. The chance that this was coincidental was too small to bank much hope on.

"You need to leave here right now," I advised, positioning myself between Wendell and the fighter as he bolted towards the cage door.

"What the fuck, man?" I asked Wendell, who was facing me with a blank expression. "What is this? What just happened?"

"I'm not sure," he said. He was still smiling, and it was unnerving. Briefly, I thought I saw something in his eyes that looked like a desperate plea for help, but just as quickly, it was gone, and they were dead again. He tilted his head to the side and seemed to lose focus on me, then nodded.

"Wendell, you just killed your brother. Why did you —"

I didn't have a chance to finish the question, since he suddenly feinted towards me with the knife, causing me to fall back defensively. He used the opportunity to bolt out of the cage door and knocked down a bouncer that tried to get in his way as he sprinted toward the nearby tunnel that led in the direction of the locker rooms.

About half of the crowd had dissipated during the chaos. The remaining occupants between Wendell and the doors parted before the giant, who was brandishing the knife dangerously in front of him as he ran. They found their courage once he was past, immediately falling in behind him with taunts, jeers, and to throw whatever they had on hand in his direction. While I commended their newfound bravery, they were making it difficult for me to catch up, since I had to push my way through the mob. When I hit the doors, I shoved them open and found myself in a poorly lit, cement hallway leading right and left, with no sign of Wendell in either direction.

"Command: reinitiate last beacon transmission."

My CUBE complied and traced a red highlight onto the outline of his position in the distance, which was running quickly to the north. I gave chase but was navigating an unfamiliar building, and forced to turn around several times after reaching dead ends that blocked my way to the beacon. Finally, I pushed my way through several strips of thick plastic onto a busy loading dock. There were a handful of confused men looking out the open docking doors. When they saw me running toward them, they pointed out to the street. I jumped down from the docking bay into a private parking lot that led onto a dark side street behind the warehouse.

I followed that street back to the main avenue and then paused to catch my breath. The rain was coming down harder now than when I'd entered Ares, and the street was mostly empty but for a few stragglers shuffling down the sidewalk. Wendell was still moving quickly, and the distance between us was growing. I sprinted up the road in his direction but couldn't close the gap until he finally slowed his pace to a brisk walk about three blocks away from the arena.

Behind me, there were no sirens audible. I supposed Ares was the type of place that cleaned up its own problems without assistance from the law. Wendell had left several bodies in his wake, and I couldn't help but feel partially responsible for it, since I might have stopped him if I hadn't let myself get waylaid. I needed to find him and get answers about what was going on here. If this had something to do with Mary's death, then pieces of this mystery were starting to fall together, but I was caught off-guard with nothing to catch them with, and those pieces were slipping right through my fingers.

Fifty yards ahead, the outline of Wendell's beacon had stopped moving, and its elevation had increased. It was higher up, but there was no hill in sight, so he was climbing something. Following, I turned down the next street. With eyes on the vicinity, I saw that he'd gone around the back of another enormous warehouse. There was an empty parking lot out front, and no light emanating from the building, but there were several holographic signs advertising *The Emporium* in fanciful, decorative lettering. Wendell had reached the top of whatever it was he'd climbed in the back. He stood and jumped back down to the ground level, inside the building.

The downpour had created a small river of overflowing water from the parking lot and it was funneling along the side of the building. I followed it, using the sound to cover my own advance to the back. There was construction underway there, and a scaffold was erected along the entirety of the rear wall. It didn't take long to spot the broken window on the second level that he'd entered through. I pulled myself up onto the rig and approached the window on my hands and knees to peer into the building. The light was poor, but I could see a lobby beneath me and a pair of massive double doors that led into the warehouse. I saw the highlighted form of Wendell farther inside the building, and could gauge the distance between us, but I had no way of knowing what lay beyond those doors.

I'd been told, frequently, that my overconfidence often led me to charge into the fray in situations where more caution was warranted. I briefly wondered if this was one of those times before jumping down into the lobby.

I landed as quietly as I could in the shards of glass from the broken window above. The large wooden doors were made to slide on rollers, and were already partially open from Wendell passing through. I slipped beyond them into what felt like an enormous, spacious area, though I could barely see past my hand now that I was inside. As I moved forward, groping through the dark, I tried to recall the various augmentation procedures Wendell had undergone to prepare myself for a physical confrontation between us, if it couldn't be avoided. He hadn't attacked me in the ring, and I was holding out hope that we could communicate rather than fight, but I wanted to be ready either way.

Our unit had all had the pituitary gland modification installed as standard issue, to be used for spikes of adrenaline in times of distress. A few of us had undergone the much more intense procedure of bone strengthening, but I had a memory of Wendell refusing, based on the fact that it left the agent out of commission for sixteen weeks. The meathead had said he couldn't imagine being unable to work out for that long. Once, north of Ahvaz, up to the hilt across the Iranian border without support, we'd relied on his night vision modification to guide us to an alternate extraction point when the mission had gone sour. I couldn't remember what we'd even been doing in Ahvaz.

There'd been so many that I lost track of the details, and the missions just started bleeding together.

Like the blood of the innocents that you left in your wake.

The dark and unexpected thought was a distraction I couldn't afford to ponder at the moment, so I shut it down and turned my mind back to Wendell's body augmentations. Abruptly, the warehouse came to life around me. Everywhere I turned my head, birds were flying through the darkness, bright and alive with a multitude of colors, twisting in unison, following patterns indiscernible to the human mind. On the floor, pieces of a luminescent walkway rose from the darkness far below me to assemble into a translucent, glowing path. Confused and off-balance, I fell to my knees to try to stabilize myself from the sudden loss of equilibrium. The walkway wasn't real, of course. The floor was just as solid on either side of it, but in the utter darkness my mind was having difficulty accepting the reality that I wouldn't fall off into a bottomless void.

Realizing what I was seeing was some form of augmented reality broadcast, I blinked twice in rapid succession to disable my augment lenses, and both the flock of birds and the walkway disappeared, leaving me in total darkness — a darkness in which I could no longer see Wendell's beacon. Given the aforementioned biochemically enhanced night vision, which he'd almost certainly have activated, this situation had all the ingredients for shit stew, and I could feel the water heating up. Wendell could rely solely on his ability to see in the dark to ascertain my location without distraction, whereas I was reliant on my lenses being active to track his beacon. I blinked rapidly to re-enable the lenses, and when the augmented images burst back into motion around me, I was better prepared. I shut out the distraction of the swooping flock of birds, and located the outline of his beacon about twenty meters through the darkness ahead of me, deeper in.

"Aren't they beautiful, Slate?" I heard his voice come through a speaker system and echo through the warehouse. At this point, I'd come to the conclusion The Emporium was some sort of AR funhouse where families and friends could put on cheap glasses or use their built-in contacts to come and experience the joy of augmented reality environment games together. There was a glowing scoreboard displayed near the ceiling in the center of the room, and anyone playing would be rated on their ability to navigate the lit pathway while avoiding the sporadic, diving flock of birds. I didn't care about my score, and now that I'd started to acclimate to the environment, I left the glowing path and began walking through the dark, directly toward the beacon.

Without warning, a new program began, running alongside the original. From every wall, neon blocks erupted, and began moving through the room — slowly at first, but picking up speed as they traveled. One passed through me, prompting a loud buzzer to erupt through the warehouse speakers. I looked up, and noticed my score had dropped into the red on the board above.

"You're not very good at this, Slate!" Wendell observed with great amusement from the distant security of what had to be a control booth on the far side of the room.

Spirals of purple flame began jetting up from small, round portals that opened intermittently from the darkness beneath my feet, but I tried to shut them out and concentrate on closing the distance between myself and Wendell. There was nothing but light now everywhere — pulsing, flashing, bursting into motion. As Wendell initiated each new program on top of the others, it was becoming increasingly difficult to identify the outline of his beacon. I felt discombobulated and overstimulated, but if I were to shut off the augment lenses, I'd be left in total darkness with no beacon to guide me in his direction. I realized then, that it had been the perfect trap, and I'd stumbled right into it.

A massive Chinese dragon was spiraling over my head, roaring. I was surrounded by treasure chests, erupting with golden coins. The overlapping audio of so many programs loaded at once was chaotic and disorienting. I'd completely lost the beacon in the madness now, but I kept moving forward through the augmented reality images in the direction I'd last seen it, hoping I'd find a way out of the main warehouse or a way to put walls between me and the augmented playhouse programs. The thought came to me that if he'd led me here intentionally, then he'd probably realized I was tracking him through the beacon all along, and if that were the case, he could rescind the invitation he'd sent and shut it off—

I was tackled by something with the force of a man-sized freight train. I hit the ground on my back and had the wind knocked out of me. A two-hundred-and twenty pound, muscled bull of a man was planted atop me in a full mount.

"I'm glad you came here," he said. "I need to give you something."

I struggled as my breath began to return, but to little avail under the bulk of the more experienced fighter, who shifted his weight and re-positioned with the ease of someone who'd spent the last year training.

"It's not a gun, by any chance?" I gasped with difficulty.

There was no response.

"What did you do to Oaksley?" I asked. "Why are you doing

this?"

"I'm only doing what I'm supposed to do. What happened to Oaksley?" He asked, sounding genuinely concerned.

"Wendell!" I shouted. "What are you doing? Get the fuck off of me!"

Surprisingly, I felt the weight lift from me immediately. With his beacon signal disabled, there was no reason for me to have my augment lenses enabled any longer, so I turned them off, leaving myself in total darkness. There were many places I would have preferred to have been just then than in the pitch dark with a trained killer augmented with biochemically engineered night vision who was behaving violently and erratically. I'd learned long ago, however, that sometimes we just had to play the cards we were dealt, even the losing hands.

"Tell me what we're doing here," I said to the emptiness around me. I adjusted my stance to one more appropriate for fighting multiple opponents, since if Wendell attacked I'd have no idea what direction he'd be coming from. I was going to have to rely on my hearing and intuition to avoid being blindsided completely.

"I don't know." The response came from directly ahead of me.

"Do you know how we got here?"

"No, I don't remember."

"Wendell, do you remember what you did to your brother?"

"I…no…I don't remember. What? Okay."

"You're not making any sense. Listen to me—"

"He says it's time for one of us to die."

The sound of his voice had been moving in a slow circle around me as he spoke. The hair on the back of my neck stood up, and my intuition was screaming now for me to run, to get away, that this was not a safe place. I felt the air current change ever so slightly, to my left and turned in that direction with my hands up defensively, only to feel a sudden burst of pain in my right calf. I'd been cut and could feel the wound leaking blood. I shifted my weight to the other leg but maintained my stance to the best of my ability.

A grunt sounded behind me, so I turned and struck out blindly, only to feel a similar pain erupt across my left shoulder. I grabbed the new knife wound with my other arm and gritted my teeth. He was toying with me. I tried to calm my mind and sought the place of stillness, which had been so easy to arrive at earlier in the afternoon, but the pain of my wounds was interfering, and it was difficult to focus. If I could just get one well-placed shot in, I might be able to—

Something slammed into the side of my face, and I fell to one knee, dizzy and nauseous. I spit out some blood that was filling my mouth and looked around me, trying to get a sense of where the next blow might come from. I reached out, feeling the space around me. If I could grab ahold of a leg or an arm, I could grapple him to the ground. Assailants were most confident when they had the upper hand and most vulnerable to sudden reversals of fortune.

Despite my instinct for survival, which refused to surrender, I knew I was beaten. The end had already come. I just hadn't been willing to acknowledge it. It would be one thing to be blind against one of the drugged vagrants who had attacked me at Ares, but this was an elite soldier with most of the same knowledge and training I'd had. He'd lured me into this place, and like a stupid fly, I'd buzzed right in and landed in the honey. I'd been an overeager fool in my effort to seek the answers I needed to make sense out of this insanity.

"Here it is, Slate, my gift for you." I heard his voice behind me, but this time I didn't bother to turn. Anticipating the inevitable killing blow, I sat, frozen, like a deer in headlights.

A deer in headlights. I grappled the sudden notion with the desperate hope of a thirsty desert nomad, lost in the dunes, who'd just spotted an oasis in the distance. I put my hand into my pocket and gripped my CUBE.

"I have a gift for you, too," I said.

"Oh? What is it?"

"It's here." I pulled the CUBE out of my jacket pocket, and held it above my head.

"What—" began Wendell, but I interrupted him with sudden instructions for my device.

"Command: illuminate. Maximum intensity." The device began to glow brightly, and gambling that the ploy had been successful, I took the opportunity to jump to my feet. I spun to face him and I could see Wendell now as we were both enclosed within the small bubble of light emitted by the glowing CUBE. He had backed off a few feet, momentarily blinded by the burst of light. Sudden bright light could overwhelm sight easily when the night vision enhancement was active due to overexcitement of the phosphors in the solution. His eyes were dead black from lenses that were infused with the CE6 insulin and dimethyl sulfoxide when the augmentation was being utilized. As I set my feet and assessed his readiness, he deactivated it, causing the solution to drain back into a repository in his tear glands.

Watching the process never failed to make me uncomfortable, which was the main reason I'd opted for the augment lenses instead when we'd been given the choice.

He'd been holding something in his right hand, but he dropped it when he began circling the outer edge of the light with his fists raised, gauging my strength and looking for cracks in my defenses. I briefly wondered where the knife had gone, but suddenly he was advancing with a combination of blows that took all of my concentration to counter. Not only was Wendell a larger man, but he'd also been training extensively over the past year, and was very likely the superior hand to hand fighter. To make matters worse, I had to hold the CUBE in one hand while I fought. I thought about tossing it on the ground to free my hand up, but it would only take one kick for Wendell to send it flying far enough away that it wouldn't benefit me, and then we'd be back in the dark where we started. Having been there moments before, I had a pretty good sense of how that would turn out for me, so I accepted my current disadvantage as a necessary one.

Wendell came in suddenly, and I narrowly avoided a blow to my temple by lowering my head and taking it directly to the top of my skull. I countered with two body shots, but felt like I was punching a slab of meat, and became concerned that my hands had taken more damage than his body. My wounds continued to drain blood as we danced in the awkward spotlight, and weariness began to seep into my bones. I knew I was quickly running out of the energy I'd need to settle this in my favor.

We circled one another, trading blows until he caught me off guard with an unexpected sweep, hitting my wounded calf right where it had been cut, causing me to fall on my back in pain. He took advantage of my compromised position and lunged forward to strike me. I raised both arms in front of my face to block the incoming blow, which bounced harmlessly aside.

The sound of the gunshot caused both of us to freeze and stare out into the darkness from where it had been fired. The shot reverberated through the chamber until at last it faded, and there was silence.

"You had better tell me what the fuck is going on here, *tout de suite!*" A woman's voice cut sharply through the silence, her familiar French accent triggering a wave of relief to flood over me.

"Risa?" I asked, bewildered, between heavy gasps for air.

Wendell stood and turned in her direction. As he rose, I saw his eyes begin to flush with black liquid, an indication he'd reactivated the night vision solution. He reached behind him to his belt, and drew the knife I'd been wondering about from its sheath. He turned his head to the right, and nodded slightly.

"Risa. He's not right. Something's wrong with him."

"Wendell, you had better put that fucking knife down. I swear to god I will shoot you, I am not in any mood to be—"

Wendell stepped out of the light, and slipped fully into the darkness towards Therisa.

"Wendell. Please don't make me shoot you. Wendell...Wendell!" Suddenly, the chamber was echoing with the sound of the gun once again.

"Stop!" Therisa yelled. "Please stop!" Another shot. And then another. And then, as the echo of those shots diminished, I heard a faint sobbing in the distance.

I pulled myself to my feet and began walking in her direction.

"No! Don't come near me!" she shouted. I stopped, and raised my arms.

"Risa—"

"What the fuck is going on?" she yelled, still sobbing. I pointed the CUBE in her direction and saw that her own eyes were black with night vision insulin. She had her gun in both hands, and it was pointed directly at me. Wendell lay face down on the floor in front of her. His hand was still gripping the knife, and blood was beginning to pool on the floor around him.

"I don't know," I said softly. "But we should leave."

Her face was a battlefield of emotions warring for dominance. I watched confusion struggling with anger, fear, and sorrow, but the battle was ultimately won by prudence. She lowered her pistol and held her head in her hands.

I turned back to where I'd been fighting Wendell, remembering he had dropped something. I ran the light from the CUBE over the area until it came to rest on a small, square piece of thick paper with an image on it. It took me a moment to recognize it for what it was, because I hadn't seen one since I'd been a child. It was a physical photograph depicting a young man in military fatigues. I picked it up and studied it. He looked hauntingly familiar, but I couldn't place him.

"We need to go," I said as I walked over to Risa to help her up. She took my hand and rose to her feet. As our eyes met, I saw that the solution had drained.

After one last look at Wendell's body, we turned and walked away. We passed through a set of double doors identical to the ones I'd come in through in the back and into the front lobby of The Emporium with the light from my CUBE providing guidance. From there, we left through the main entrance, through which Risa had broken in, and escaped into the parking lot. It was empty except for a sharp-lined, silver Mustang, the lights of which came to life as Risa remotely started the engine.

I raised an eyebrow at her. She shrugged and said, "What? It's a rental."

"I'm not complaining," I replied. "Just get me home."

Chapter 3

The Mustang was blasting water from the streets onto the sidewalks as it sped out of the Mission on autopilot toward my apartment downtown. I was pretty sure I already knew the answer, but I asked anyway. "So, how'd you find me?"

"Your Control Unit Biometric Executor. I hacked it."

A forlorn sigh escaped my chest. I'd put all the right measures in place to prevent that sort of intrusion into my CUBE including encryption, multifactor authentication, and a robust onboard IPS, but Risa was one of the best systems penetration experts in the world, so I wasn't terribly surprised. During the war, I'd seen her hack enterprise systems that had been locked down like chastity belts.

"But if I'd known you were going to be warehouse hopping for death matches tonight, I might have just stayed home," she quipped.

"You know about what happened at Ares?"

"That's where I found you first. I saw what happened. Your message mentioned you were going to meet Wendell. I was trying to catch you together so that I could talk to you both at once. But I was too late." She looked away, ashamed, and then continued. "I had to watch you both first, to see how you behaved, because I needed information. I don't know what is going on or who I can trust right now, so I just waited and watched. And then he…who was that, in the cage?"

"His brother."

"*Merde!*" she exclaimed. "Jacobi…" Risa began, but she gasped, and her eyes grew wide as she looked in my direction. "You're hurt, man! You're bleeding all over the rental!"

"I'll be okay when we get back to the apartment. I have a kit there."

We rode in silence for a time before Risa looked in my direction with sympathy.

"I'm sorry about what happened to Mary and Ben. I know how close you were."

"Ben's still alive. If any of this has something to do with what happened, I need to figure out how and make it right."

I took the photograph I'd picked up at The Emporium from my pocket to have another look at it. Risa leaned over to study it as well. She smelled like honey and amber. It was a warm, earthy fragrance that further enhanced her allure, distracting me from my observation of the photograph.

"It's Robbins," she said. "Is this what you picked up from the ground as we were leaving?"

"Robbins," I mused. "Mason Robbins." I looked closer at the photograph and realized she was right. The picture had been taken when he'd been much younger than when he was a part of our unit, but it was definitely him.

"Hang on." I fished around in my jacket pocket, which caused my shoulder to scream in agony and my head to swim, but I persevered and pulled out the crumpled list from Ben's kitchen.

"What's that?" Risa asked.

"It's a list of names I found at Ben's house. He said he didn't make it, that he'd found it in his pocket the night before the murder. It's some checklist of people from our unit. Mostly names from the later years, except…" I read through the list to be sure. "Robbins isn't on here."

"I think Robbins died a few years ago. I remember hearing that." She took the paper from me and ran her finger down the list, checking each name. "I'm not here either," she said, breathing a sigh of relief. "There are names missing from the list. It's not complete." She studied the paper for a while longer then added, "All of these names are people who were there at the end, just not all of us."

"I think Wendell was trying to give this photograph to me. He kept saying something about how he had a gift for me. I can't make any sense out of it…I…" My concentration was wavering. I felt my thoughts growing more distant and unfamiliar by the moment. The process of coherently forming groups of words into relevant tools for communication was breaking down completely.

"Captain, we gotta get you patched up soon." Risa enabled manual driving and pushed the wheel forward to accelerate our journey back.

"Jacobi," I said without a choice as the delirium took full control of my motor capabilities. "Earlier, you called me…Jacobi. I liked that…"

She studied me with concern, and I felt the car speed up again as I succumbed to the darkness welling around me.

My waking was a slow, resentful process, hampered by an almost abnormal desire to keep my eyes closed and remain in whatever dream I'd been having. The very moment I acknowledged that waking had, in fact, occurred — even in the barest sense of the word — the process of slipping back into consciousness became tragically inevitable. I barely recalled there had been a problem of some kind, and that fact nagged relentlessly at my semiconscious state with tiny shocks of warning that made it impossible to return to my blissfully ignorant slumber.

When I finally surrendered to opening my eyes, I first recognized that I was in my bed and that a sudden change in the light was what had woken me. Next, I ascertained that a beautiful woman was standing by the window. Her brunette hair was loose and untidy as it tumbled down past her shoulders about half the distance to her shapely waist. My eyes wandered slowly back up her slim, muscular frame, and arrived at her face, which was watching me with a scowl. The sun streaming in through the windows outlined her silhouette and shot out from behind her in glowing rays, an image that was comically religious.

"My guardian angel," I said.

Memories were sporadically returning in brief, confusing jumbles of data from the night before. After we'd left The Emporium, I had the memory of getting into the car and discussing the photograph of Mason. After that, I recalled only brief moments of lucidity as I half walked and was half dragged by Risa from the garage into the elevator, then into my apartment.

"You've been asleep for about fifteen hours. You probably need a lot more too, but we need to talk."

I sat up, not without pain. Putting a hand to the shoulder Wendell had cut, I felt a bandage covering the area. I peeked under the covers and saw that the same was true of my calf.

"Thank you," I said.

"You were like a complaining child. Six stitches on your calf, and you would think I had to cut your leg off from the groaning."

"I can't really be held accountable for something I don't remember."

Risa had a forlorn look in her eyes as she said, "I wish that were true."

"Did you sleep?"

"Yeah, I crashed on the couch. I ate some of your granola too. I hope that's okay."

"I'd call that a fair trade for rescuing me from a psychopath, dragging me up to my twenty-third-story apartment, then cleaning and bandaging my wounds."

"It wasn't *that* good." She said, laughing. But the laughter was short-lived, and her face took on a concerned expression. "What's going on here exactly, Cap? Why is this all happening?"

"I don't know," I answered, shaking my head. "Let me put some clothes on and eat something, then you can fill me in on what you know."

She didn't bother to give me privacy, choosing instead to patiently wait, staring at my bare ass as I dressed. Any insecurity I might have once felt about nudity had been sufficiently pummeled into submission by my time in the armed services. I'd lost a considerable amount of blood, and I hadn't eaten since before leaving the house the day before, so my first priority was getting some nutrients and energy back in my body. Afterward, I was ready to convene our discussion. Risa joined me at the kitchen table as I finished eating.

"Okay," I began, "you called me. What prompted you to do that?"

She took a deep breath. "Every few months I like to check in on people. I just like to know everyone is doing okay."

"Everyone?"

"Mostly. I get nostalgic. I'll have a memory or something makes me laugh, and then I'll call whoever it was I was thinking of. There's a few, people like Mason, who never really had any interest in making memories you'd laugh about, if you know what I mean."

I did. Mason Robbins had been extremely introverted and had never really formed a solid bond with any others from the crew that I'd been aware of.

"So yeah, the ones that I connected with the most, I guess."

"I don't remember getting a call every few months."

She rolled her eyes. "You're the captain. You were the boss, man."

I stared at her, expecting a better answer. Her face became serious.

"I mean, come on. I just...didn't think you wanted to remember."

She was right, of course. I'd never really put much energy into staying connected after we'd disbanded. The occasional call or night out on the town was all the effort I'd given. She looked concerned that she might have given offense, so I smiled apologetically and waved it away.

"That's on me," I said. "I should have reached out more. I just—"

"It's okay," she interrupted. "I get it. So anyway, there I was, working for this big market research corporation over in Texas. I'm waiting on the results of a static analysis with my feet kicked up on the desk, absentmindedly fiddling with some lever on the side of the chair, when the chair just drops all the sudden, and the whole thing tilts backward. My legs are up on this desk, and my ass is like three feet underneath it, my coffee spills all over my shirt..."

I chuckled supportively, wondering where this was going.

"And it reminds me, for whatever reason, of that night in Kuwait City when we got called in from leave at like two in the morning because…because.."

I laughed and did my part to contribute to the reminiscing. "Because Jaabir el-Faris had supposedly been sighted in Basrah, and we were the closest Fades."

She nodded. "Right. But Watts was so drunk he couldn't land the chopper to pick us up on the roof. And the ass-end was hanging off the side of the fucking building with just the front wheels on the roof."

I wiped my eyes. "Oh, man. Yeah, that wasn't good."

"Anyway," she said, sobering, "so I thought of that, and I called him up, but a woman answered instead. It was his mother, and she said he'd passed away. I asked her what happened, but she didn't want to talk about it. So I started doing some research to find out, searching the Evernet, bringing up local broadcasts

— it turned out Watts had shot someone named Phillip Holsted during broad daylight at a shopping mall in Vancouver. Then he just sat down on a bench until the cops arrived, and when they did, he fired on them and was gunned down."

"Jesus," I said, sitting upright in my chair.

"So I started contacting people that knew him, trying to understand what happened, and I find out Phillip Holsted was Watts' best friend from childhood. No one could offer any explanation for it."

My mind was racing with possibilities concerning how this news related to the actions of both Wendell and Oaksley. I could feel my blood turning cold as the suspicion that this was all connected took root within me. Those roots grew and sprouted tendrils that spiraled upward and wound into knots that constricted around my brain as I tried to make sense of it. I got up, poured a glass of water, and took a couple of headache pills while I continued to listen.

"I remembered Watts and Turner were pretty close, so I thought I should let him know what happened. When I called Turner, I just got a terminated line. I looked him up on social media to try to get a message to him there, and his page was blowing up with testimonials. *I'm so sorry. You'll be missed. I just heard. How could this happen?* He was dead."

Watts and Turner. Both dead. The news hit me right in the gut. I'd helped to train them and been on dozens of missions with them both. We'd counted on and come through for one another time and time again. They were both dead, and I hadn't even been aware of it.

"When was this?" I asked.

"I found out about Turner a couple of days ago. I think he's been dead for a couple of weeks, though, judging by the timestamps on some of those testimonials. Watts died just about a week ago. When I heard what happened to the admiral, I started calling you."

I took out the list I'd found at Ben's house and put it on the table.

"They're both on here. Hang on." I grabbed a pen and crossed out both the admiral and Wendell's names. "It's just me and Cody Marshall left. We need to let Cody know."

Risa nodded and pulled out her CUBE to make the call.

Analytically, I understood that at least three members of our unit had killed someone close to them for no obvious reason. The number was probably higher, if the list in front of me could be directly correlated. I had no idea why, or how any of this made sense beyond those facts. I did know that with only two of us remaining, I'd need to take measures to protect myself while I tried to figure it out.

"Cody? It's Therisa. I'm here with Captain Slate."

I broke away from my thoughts to follow Risa's conversation.

"Risa! What can I do for you?"

"I wish I had better news for you, but we called because there's a strong chance that members of our unit are being targeted. Watts, Turner, and Wendell Hamilton are each confirmed dead, and Oaksley's in Alcatraz awaiting a trial. He believes he was framed somehow. This has all happened within the last couple of weeks. The captain found some evidence that indicates a possibility the two of you might be targeted next."

She gave him a moment to process the information.

Watching the screen over her shoulder, I saw him reel from the hit then wrangle his emotions, but his gaze remained distant. He'd always been skilled at being able to compartmentalize in a crisis, but finding out that your brothers and sisters in arms, people who were like family, had been killed, and that you were also in danger, was a jagged pill.

"Have you heard from anyone else recently?" Risa asked.

"No. No, I haven't," he responded, but his words sounded hollow, and his eyes were distant.

I stepped beside Risa and joined the conversation. "Marshall, you need to go dark for a while. Do you have something in place?"

"I have a wife and kids now…" he argued.

"There's a possibility they're also in danger," I countered.

Cody put his hand to his forehead then sighed deeply and nodded. "Yeah, we can disappear."

"Cody," said Risa, "I'm going to send you my secure connection. When you're safe, contact me on an encrypted line. I can give you all the information we have."

"Roger that."

"Watch your six, Marshall," I warned. "I don't know what this is, but it's ugly. We're going to figure it out, though."

He nodded again then terminated the connection. I looked to Risa, who had her elbows on the table and her face buried in her arms.

"You should do the same," I said.

"What?" She looked up. "No way. I'm with you. We're going

to figure this out together."

"Risa, we have no idea what's happening here. I could be a danger to you. I think you should consider disappearing as well."

"No. Fuck that. I didn't fly out here to turn around and run away. I owe it to all of them. I'm staying with you."

I'd have argued more, but I recognized the futility of doing so when I looked into her eyes and saw the emotion burning there. Instead, I shrugged and put my hand on her shoulder.

"I might not have made it out last night if you weren't there. If you want to ride this out, it's your choice. Honestly, I'll be glad to have the backup."

"I'm glad to see you're coming back to your senses, *Jacobi*." The way she smirked when she said my name triggered a vague memory of the night before, but at that moment my subconscious mind decided it preferred ignorance to embarrassment, and I quickly moved on.

"I'm going to put a friend of mine on our people," I said, pointing to the list. "His name is Pavel. He should be able to confirm their status and get some background on each case."

Risa nodded.

"We need to know how this is all connected," I continued. "Wendell specifically wanted me to have that picture. There has to be a reason why. We'll follow up on the photograph. I'll reach out to someone I know at the Division and see what he can tell me about Mason Robbins."

"And me?" she asked.

"Can you drop me off at Ares so I can get my gun and my car?"

"I'm a chauffeur now?"

"No one rents a Mustang who doesn't want to drive."

She looked as if she'd respond indignantly but then shrugged and conceded the point.

"After that, I need you to see if you can find someone here in the city with your *research*," I said, referring to the illegal hacking she was prone to term as such. "I need you to see if you can get us an appointment with a man they call The Blacksmith."

We arrived back in the Mission, which looked far less menacing in the daylight, despite the overcast sky that hinted at more rain to come. The shadows and threats that had lurked in waiting down every alley the night before had evaporated, leaving only plain streets and avenues littered with trash and partially flooded with rainwater. I opened the door to get out of the Mustang, which had come to a stop on the side of the road near the entrance to the Ares compound.

"The Blacksmith?" Risa asked. "That's it?" She eyed me suspiciously.

"That's it," I answered as I exited the vehicle and closed the door. The window came down slowly, and I leaned down to meet her irritated glare.

"Where did you even hear about this guy?"

I'd done a job a while back for a corporate executive who'd been trying to track down his business partner. She'd cleaned out their piggy bank right after they'd hit paydirt on a deal, and disappeared. Totally invisible. All of her accounts had been terminated simultaneously. Even her CUBE identifier, which was impossible to reassign, had been severed.

Fortunately, her boyfriend hadn't been too pleased about being abandoned and volunteered that he'd heard her referring to someone called The Blacksmith over a call. I'd hit up anyone who'd owed me a favor for information on who he was and gotten the same answer from anyone who knew anything about him. She was gone, don't bother looking. I never did get paid for that job.

But I'd learned other things, too. He was discreet and reliable. He was some kind of purveyor of gadgetry and cybernetics. He was the kind of man you went to when you wanted things done right, and he could almost certainly do whatever you wanted. For what I had in mind, he was exactly what I needed.

"The circles I work in aren't always exactly on the level. You hear things — ways of getting what you need through alternative channels. I think this guy can help us."

Risa scowled and let out an unconvinced grunt.

"I've added you to the guest list for my apartment," I continued, disregarding her lack of faith. "It should be equipped with everything you need. I won't be long here."

"You sure I can't track down anyone else while I'm waiting? The Tailor, or maybe The Cobbler?"

I chuckled. "If either of them can do for us with what I'm hoping The Blacksmith can, then you're welcome to try. I'll take help from just about anyone at this point."

I walked over to the entrance I'd used the night before as Risa pulled away. It wasn't the kind of place that had a lot of day traffic. The doors were shut tight, and there was no one out front. I slammed on the entrance a couple of times. When no one responded, I wrapped around the building until I reached the private lot with the loading dock I'd chased Wendell through.

The docking bay doors were open, and a couple of tired-looking workers were busy loading pallets of supplies. I jumped up into the dock like I belonged there and walked straight back into the hallways that I knew led to the main arena. The open warehouse where the fights had taken place the previous night was empty, except for a snaggle-haired kid on his hands and knees in the cage, frantically trying to scrub the bloodstains from the mat.

I passed through the double doors that led to the coat check area and was pleased to find it was unoccupied. Once I'd slipped into the back office, I pulled my ticket from my pocket and checked the number. The back wall was made up of numbered storage cubes, and I riffled through the one that corresponded to my ticket and reclaimed my pistol.

"Hey! You can't be in here," I heard from behind me. Turning, I saw that one of the bouncers had entered the room behind me. I recognized his balding head and the tattoos on his neck from the previous night. He was the one I'd stopped from entering the cage.

"Oh. It's you," he said, relaxing somewhat. "What happened to Wendell? There are a lot of people around here looking for him. And not in a good way, you know what I mean?"

"Dead," I said. "You should be able to confirm that on the news today; his body was probably discovered this morning."

He looked at me suspiciously. "You a cop?"

I shook my head. "Nope."

"Damn. You killed him?"

"He killed himself," I answered, deciding a half-truth would serve me best here. He'd died brandishing a knife at someone with a gun pointed at him, yelling at him to stop or they'd fire, so technically I wasn't lying.

"This is mine," I said and tapped my weapon. I handed him the ticket.

On my way out, I was struck by a sudden curiosity, so I turned and asked, "Anyone else die last night besides his brother?"

"Yeah. One of the guys on my crew. But Wendell's brother is alive, if you can call it that."

"No shit?"

"We wrapped up his throat, and some of the guys got him to the hospital in time. He's in critical condition, but he's alive."

The gentleman was kind enough to open the front door for me. From there it was a short journey to the lot where I'd parked. As I walked, I considered what I'd learned from the bouncer. I didn't have any evidence to back it up, but my intuition led me to believe that Wendell would be happy to know his brother had survived, wherever he was now. I doubted very much it was any kind of heaven.

Men like us have little business there.

I found my car and paid the exorbitant cost of having parked it overnight on my way out. The sky was growing dark again as storm clouds billowed over the ocean, rolling steadily inland.

"Command: contact Pavel Volkov."

Above the CUBE, seated in its onboard receptacle, a blue

holographic circle spun as the connection was attempted. It was accepted almost immediately, at which point the circle disappeared and Pavel's face appeared on the built-in display above the device.

"Ah, Jacobi! What a pleasure to hear from you. And so soon!" Pavel was seated at a table in a smoke-filled room, which was poorly lit by paper lanterns. Behind him, several elderly men were smoking cigarettes, playing Mahjong, and swearing loudly at one another in Cantonese. There were also several chickens parading shamelessly around the room.

"Did I catch you at a bad time?"

"I'll always take your call, my friend. You are the most interesting person I know."

Opposite the side of the table Pavel was seated at, two roosters suddenly erupted into battle. Several of the old men, who were more agile than I'd have given them credit for, sprang into action, reaching for various implements with which to break it up. One found a straw broom and started flailing it wildly in the direction of the birds on the floor. Pavel ignored them completely.

"Right. Well, listen, I have a job I think you could help me out with. I've got a list of names, and I'm hoping you can investigate each of them then get back to me with a report. I suspect several might be deceased, but I'd like to understand the circumstances surrounding their deaths."

A rooster, fleeing the broom, jumped onto the table, knocking over money and pieces of the game in the process, much to the dismay of the men, who renewed shouting at one another. A short man with no hair pushed a taller, gray-haired man with a finely manicured mustache, who fell back into the

83

table, making a worse mess of the game.

"I'd be pleased to do this for you, for the usual amount, of course," Pavel said, unaffected by the chaos ensuing behind him. "You can send me the information I need to begin via our secure channel. Is there a deadline?"

"As soon as possible, but do it carefully. Is everything okay there?" I asked, growing concerned about the rapidly developing conflict.

Pavel waved a hand dismissively.

"This one is personal for me, Pavel. Stay low on this. Whoever is behind what's happening to me has gotten to some highly trained people. If you think you're in danger at any point, I want you to shut it down, and just get me whatever you've dug up."

"Always looking out for me, *moi droog*. I'll stay as quiet as I can."

While the two men fought, rolling clumsily around the floor, others began picking up the game pieces and money that had fallen to the ground. One of the gamblers, who had thinning white hair and a wrinkled face, hadn't moved from the table. He laughed hysterically between long drags on his cigarette.

"I'll send you the names later today. I appreciate it."

"*Dasvidanya*, Jacobi."

He turned and shouted something angrily in Cantonese at the men fighting on the floor as the connection terminated. Shaking my head, I wondered — not for the first time — at how my life seemed at all interesting to Pavel Volkov when compared to his own.

I reached out to Sam Winston next. I'd given Mason's name to Pavel, but since Wendell had gone through a good deal of trouble to give me Mason's photograph, I thought it might help to find out if the DFDC had any additional insight into Mason's death. Sam had offered me assistance when we parted ways, and I was being honest with Risa when I'd told her I'd take help from just about anywhere, including the Division. The screen abruptly displayed the man, who seemed hard at work at a desk in a busy office space. His shirt was neatly pressed, and he was wearing a brown tie that perfectly matched the color of his neatly cropped hair.

"Mr. Slate. To what do I owe the pleasure? Do you have an update on your investigation?" He was behaving amiably enough, but he looked tired, and his words were tight, like someone doing their best to conceal their irritation at being interrupted.

"Sam, I appreciate you taking my call. I'm sorry to bother you. I'll try to make this quick. I was hoping you might be able to look into something for me. There's someone who was a part of my unit for a couple of years, from about '46 to '48, named Mason Robbins."

"I see. What sort of information are you hoping for?"

"Actually, I heard he died a while back. I'm looking for anything surrounding his death, and maybe some contact information for kin."

"I might be able to get you what you're looking for. I'll admit to being curious, though. What does this have to do with Admiral Oaksley's situation?"

I wasn't ready to divulge the details of my investigation to someone working for the DFDC, especially since I didn't yet understand how these things were connected and had no reasonable answer to his question. I had a gut feeling it was and that somehow Mason Robbins' death was the next lead I needed to follow. Someone still connected to the DFDC could potentially have direct access to the agent profiles I knew, without a doubt, were retained and updated regularly there. I wasn't sure exactly what role Sam played there, but based on the fact that they'd sent him to escort me to Ben, I thought he might be some sort of liaison between the agency and the public, with access to those profiles.

"I'm not sure yet. Probably nothing, but I'd be doing Ben a disservice if I didn't at least look into it. Do you think you can help me out?"

"All right, I'll see what I can find out."

"Thank you," I said and terminated the call.

The car slid under my building and into the garage just as the skies opened up again. Upstairs, Risa had unpacked all of her electronics onto the kitchen table. There were control tablets, holographic displays, and wired devices I didn't even recognize spread haphazardly across almost every available surface in the room. She didn't look up as I entered. As such, she was unable to appreciate the effort I put into crafting a look that thoroughly represented my state of absolute disapproval upon seeing the chaotic jumble of machinery in my otherwise orderly home.

"Comfortable?" I asked.

"Mmm," she replied as her fingers danced across her keyboard, entering commands into an open console window.

Despite the limited counter space, I managed to make us both sandwiches and placed Risa's down beside her as I took a seat at the table. She picked it up and took a bite without looking at it.

"This Blacksmith," she said between bites, "has me confused."

"What do you mean?"

"Well, he doesn't exactly want to be invisible, since he advertises his services on unindexed sites. But he doesn't leave any way to contact him, and he's taken some pretty extreme precautions when it comes to leaving any sort of residuals on his activity."

"So he can't be traced?"

Risa took another bite out of her sandwich, looking perplexed. "I'm still using the decryption tools we had access to when we were working. I've peeled back each layer and found an identifier, but everything I've traced so far leads back to a private network service that doesn't log connection data. That means I can't associate his actual identifier to the one he's been allocated. It's impossible, since there aren't any logs. That's the point of the service."

Looking at one of the displays, I saw one of the unindexed sites she had referenced — sites that wouldn't come up when searched for but that third-party applications could find and access. She'd browsed to an article posted by someone with the moniker of The Blacksmith. It listed *weapons, wet-wiring, neural enhancements, augmentations, cybernetics,* and several other services as available.

"I might be able to hack the private network service directly to get access to the deployed identifiers in real time. Then I'd be able to see their leases. If we can catch him live and grab his identifier, I could translate it on the spot and attempt to pinpoint his location from there."

"No," I said as I studied the listing. "This isn't the kind of guy you want to show up to see uninvited. What are these numbers around the edge of the post?" I pointed to a border made of ones and zeros erratically arranged along the outer edge.

Risa grabbed the tablet from me, and after staring at it for a moment, she began to laugh.

"What?" I asked.

"Good catch. It's a message, in binary."

"You can read binary?" I was impressed.

"Read it and translate it into ASCII text, yeah."

"Is that normal?" I wondered out loud. She didn't respond for a minute or so as she concentrated on the binary octets, then looked up.

"It's an Evernet contact address."

The Evernet was a massive conglomeration of media. As technology had evolved, the need for separate sources of delivery had diminished until major broadcasting networks, the film industry, and the titans of technology in Silicon Valley had all begun working under the same single umbrella to deliver content, provide search engines, mail, television, news, and other entertainment through one unified source. Contrary to the ways in which people believed it would stifle capitalism, it had actually encouraged it. With everyone on the same platform, it was solely the quality of the content that had driven consumer interest, which had encouraged development of only the finest and most useful applications. It had been a bit of a Darwinian approach to consumer satisfaction, and the level playing field had ensured only the strongest survived.

A few minutes later, Risa had successfully requested a meet. Twenty minutes after that, we received a response. It was another series of numbers, this time indicating GPS coordinates, which she input into a map to reveal the location of the meet.

"That can't be right," she said and transferred the image from the tablet she was using to one of the holo-displays. The image of the map popped up on the display. A small red dot was blinking out in the Gulf of the Farallones, a couple of miles offshore to the west of Golden Gate Park.

"Can you access a live satellite feed of those coordinates?"

"Maybe," she said as her fingers resumed attacking the keypad. "There are some older polar orbiting imaging services from before the war that I've accessed in the past. Let's see if there are any currently in the neighborhood."

I waited patiently and finished my sandwich.

"Hmm. This one might work," she mused as she attempted to connect. "If this vulnerability was never patched…"

Another display came to life and showed the feed Risa had just taken control of. As she typed in coordinates, the image zeroed in on San Francisco, then closer, to the waters west of the city, where a small black dot could be identified.

"Get closer," I said.

"I'm trying. Hang on," she muttered.

The satellite zoomed in closer, but whatever we were looking at was too blurry to make out until Risa worked her magic to bring the focus in line, revealing what appeared to be a medium-sized cargo vessel, stationary in the ocean.

"It's a ship," I deduced.

"Very good, Jacobi. Did you learn that in the navy?"

Ignoring her, I began to contemplate our options for the ingress of the ship. I was a recluse and admittedly terrible at maintaining my relationships, but I thought I still had a connection or two that might be able to help us in this case.

"I think I can get us a boat. Are you up for this? It might be a little rough out there with that storm." I remembered that she'd never liked being on the open water due to a bad experience on a boat as a child.

"Is this necessary? What do you even want from this guy?" Risa protested.

"I'd prefer to tell you later."

"Why not tell me now?"

"Because you aren't going to like it, and if I tell you later, it will be too late to say no."

"You're really something, you know that?"

I stood up and flashed my most charming smile, which was mostly ineffective, judging by the frown she gave me in response.

"Look, Risa," I said, growing serious, "the truth is I'm fucking scared right now. If this really is someone coming after me, I don't understand how or why they are doing it. I've seen people I love turn on their family for no reason I can explain. I can handle threats that make sense, but this…this is insane. The last thing I want to do is hurt the people closest to me."

"I'm scared too," she acknowledged.

"I have an idea that might help, and this is the guy who could make it happen. Right now, I don't know if what I have in mind is even possible. Just trust me, okay? We'll meet with him, I'll run the idea by him, and we can discuss it then."

Honestly, I didn't think there was any chance Risa would go along with what I had in mind. If she knew what it was, she'd definitely try to talk me out of it and would probably refuse to come with me, in protest. I felt like having her there, watching my back, would make this whole thing a lot easier. And perhaps more importantly, her presence was comforting. Having someone I could trust at my back was something I hadn't experienced much of since our unit disbanded, and it felt good. She bowed her head in acquiescence and started packing up the things she planned to bring along. I gathered my own equipment, and together we ventured out into the storm.

Chapter 4

Immediately upon getting out of Risa's rental, we were buffeted by the heavy wind and rain. The sun had nearly set, and we were parked in a lot above a series of small piers, just north of Sausalito. There was a rundown building at the edge of the lot with a sign swinging madly in the wind out front. It had the name Boatopia printed in bright red on both sides. All of the lights in the building were out. When we arrived at the front door, we found another sign hanging in the window that indicated the shop was closed. Risa and I huddled under the stoop in an effort to avoid the rain, which was mostly ineffective since the wind was whipping it at us laterally.

"Looks like we're waiting until tomorrow after all!" she shouted. I pointed to another building down the hill toward the water, which had lights on inside. I felt cornered. Something dangerous was closing in on us, and I didn't want to wait for anything if we didn't absolutely have to.

"Come on!" I shouted. We ran toward it with our hands above our heads in a vain attempt to shield ourselves from the downpour. The building was even more beat-up than the shop. There were stacks of sheet metal and piles of assorted wood dotting the yard out front. We passed some sawhorses holding up a plank and a wire mesh fence surrounding a pile of compost and hay. It looked like the kind of place where manual labor was conducted frequently, but from what I could see, not much of it was dedicated to home or yard improvement.

When we arrived, I rapped solidly on the door a few times and shouted, "Gray! You in there? It's Jacobi!" The light from the windows dimmed as someone passed in front of the source within.

"Who is it?" came a shout from inside, barely audible in the storm.

"Gray! It's Jacobi!" I repeated, a little louder than before. The door didn't open immediately, and Risa gave me a skeptical look, which struck me as comical on account of how pathetic she appeared. She was completely drenched. Water was streaming from the brim of her Boonie hat like a fountain, and her expression insinuated both frustration and regret at having been coaxed into accompanying me. I managed to keep a straight face, held one hand up placatingly, and knocked again. The door opened abruptly, and we were greeted by the barrel of a black, pump-action, twelve-gauge tactical shotgun with ghost ring sights and a non-glare matte finish.

I instinctively raised my hands. Risa's instincts were more aggressively oriented, as indicated by the sidearm she'd unholstered and leveled at the head of our assailant, almost faster than I was able to observe.

"I think we all might need to relax here," I said. "Gray?"

"Slate?" he said, finally recognizing me. "Shit, man. What the fuck are you doing here?" He lowered the barrel. We clasped wrists with one arm and wrapped our free arm around each other's backs.

Risa holstered her weapon and muttered, "Sorry. We've been a little on edge here."

Gray shook his head, chuckled, and then waved us inside. "It's all right. Come on in."

The house was rundown to the point that it struck me as more of a dilapidated shack. Water trickled in through multiple leaks in the roof, and in some instances it was being caught by buckets on the floor. It smelled like cigarettes and unwashed socks. Dead soldiers were standing at attention on most of the surfaces of the room, and crushed aluminum cans littered the floor.

"Place has seen better days, Gray," I said, looking around. He put his weapon down in the corner, and as he fell backward into a ratty reclining chair against the wall, I could tell from his body language that he'd been drinking.

"Business ain't been great," he confided. "You just come by to insult my current living situation?"

Studying Gray, I saw dark circles under his eyes. He had about a week or two's worth of stubble, and his dirty blond hair was unwashed and greasy. In the navy, he'd openly flouted hygiene standards when he could get away with it, but this seemed excessive even for him.

"No. Sorry. Just worried about you, man. Everything okay?"

He let out an exaggerated sigh. "Been all right. Making ends meet. Some fancy new shop opened up a couple of miles up the road. They got newer boats, pretty people at the counter. I been working on my vehicles, trying to get 'em into better shape, to try and keep up, you know? Who's this?" he asked suddenly, looking at Risa.

"Therisa," she said, walking over and offering her hand, which he shook.

"Navy?" he asked, looking at me.

"Army," she replied.

"Slate, you're bringing Army to my house now? I thought I could trust you, man," he said, grinning. "Either of you want a beer?" He rose from his chair and made his way past us to the far side of the room. There was a miniature fridge there, and a ramshackle sink that barely fit the dishes that were piling up inside.

Risa declined with a shake of her head.

"I'm good. I gotta drive," I said.

"Drive?" he called out from behind the open refrigerator door. "Them cars can drive themselves now. You know that, right?" He closed the door overly hard, and I heard several items fall over inside.

"Not a car, a boat," I said. "I need a boat, Gray."

"A boat?" He laughed. "Have you looked out there? Not an optimal time for a boat ride, Slate."

I nodded. "It's not my first choice. But I wouldn't be here if it weren't important."

"You're serious? You want to go out in this, with one of my boats?"

"Yeah, I'm hoping so."

"What's this all about? What's out there?" My request seemed to have sobered him somewhat. The glaze over his eyes had lessened a bit, and his words were less slurred.

"I know you're not going to like this answer, but you're better off not knowing or getting involved."

"Well, shit, Slate, now I'm fuckin' interested. I ain't seen you in prolly five years. Then you show up in the night, in the middle of a goddamn thunderstorm, talkin about takin' one of my boats off to some mysterious situation I'm better off not knowing about? I mean, what did you think I was gonna say? 'Oh, hey man, no problem, here's the keys. Hope I see my boat again'?"

"I *was* hoping for something like that, honestly, yeah."

"Well, fuck you, man! No! You ain't just takin my boat."

I had wanted to avoid giving Gray any details that might endanger him or involve him in whatever we'd gotten into, but in retrospect, I could see I'd been naïve in that regard. We went back a long way, but it was a lot to ask out of the blue. I had to give him something.

"You remember Admiral Oaksley?" I asked.

"Oaksley? How could I forget? That bastard had it in for me. He always liked you, though."

"Well, he's in some shit. I'm trying to help him out. I need to meet some people that might be able to help with that, on a ship out in the Farallones. That's the best I can do, bud."

"Help the admiral…" Gray said. I could see the wheels turning upstairs as he tried to reason out the connection. "This is all to help that cranky old son of a bitch? I just told you he couldn't stand me. Why should I help him?"

"He's not asking you. I am."

"Look, Jacobi, you done a lot for me over the years, I know that. But there are favors and there are *favors*, you know what I mean? I lose a boat, and that's it for me. If I can't bring people out, I can't pay my mortgage. And honestly, I don't even know what I'd do if that happened. Things ain't been too great for me lately, far as money and some other things, too."

I looked over at Risa, who'd been standing patiently near the door. She gave a slight shake of her head, meant to indicate her silent opinion that we weren't going to make any progress here. I was struck by how easily we communicated without words. It had been a long time since I'd had anyone in my life who knew me as well as the members of my FDEES unit did. And out of all of them, Risa had always been particularly empathic.

Turning back to Gray, I said, "I wouldn't ask if it weren't important. And we need to move quickly. There's more to the story that I can't tell you, but here's what I will do. I'll transfer fifteen thousand credits to your account right now. Ten thousand as a deposit on the boat, and the remainder goes to you, for interrupting your evening and for your discretion."

"If you're thinking about taking the Zodiac, that boat is worth over seventy thousand credits."

"Fuck! Really?" I said, shocked and demoralized.

"Color radar, chart plotter, digital sounder, onboard GPS, headset intercom with night vision...she ain't no joke, Slate!"

"What about a different boat? A cheaper one."

"Nope. She's the only one I got that can handle that surf out there as it is."

I felt confident in my ability to get the boat where we needed to go and back, even in this storm. Zodiacs were commonly employed by both the SEALs and the FDEES, and I'd piloted my fair share of them, but I'd had no idea they were that expensive. I didn't have that kind of money to leave as a deposit. Deflated, I put aside my concern about lice and sat down on the couch.

"Look," said Gray after a moment, "if you're serious about paying me five thousand credits, you can have the boat. Lord knows I need the money. But I know these waters better than you, and I'm not gonna gamble my livelihood on your piloting skills still being sharp. You want the boat tonight, I'm driving it. There ain't no other way this goes down."

Risa rolled her eyes and followed up with a wide-eyed stare in my direction that seemed to ask, *Are you fucking serious right now?* with a delicate French accent.

"Give me a second," I said and walked over to consult her.

"This guy can hardly walk right now," she whispered.

"He's a great boat pilot. He knows the area, and he knows what he's doing out there. We're only going a few miles. He could probably do this blind."

"How about blind drunk?"

"Hopefully," I offered, feeling optimistic.

Risa said nothing. She just blinked and stared at me.

"I'm missing the days when you couldn't question my orders without risking a court martial," I said.

"These aren't really orders. It's just a series of bad ideas I'm going along with for some reason."

"So, you're good?"

She shook her head but said, "Let's just get this over with."

"We're good," I said and turned back toward Gray. "Give me your CUBE. I'll authorize the transfer."

He spent some time looking around under piles of clothes and other debris, trying to locate the device. During that time, I stared at my feet, knowing Risa was glaring at me. I got that I was coming at this too aggressively, and she had every right to be frustrated. I knew we could wait until tomorrow morning to give the storm time to die down and that we'd probably be a lot safer for it. But earlier in the afternoon, when I'd told Risa I was scared, that wasn't entirely accurate. I was terrified. The deeper we got into this mess and the more it became clear that our friends had probably been acting against their own will, the more I felt the dread welling up inside me.

The notion of not having control of my own actions or thoughts triggered something deep within that I didn't fully understand. I was taking a play out of Risa's playbook and turning on that fear. We were going to do whatever we had to in order protect ourselves while we hunted down the answers I sought. If that meant getting drunk-taxied out into the bay in a severe thunderstorm, I was willing to take that risk, because we had no idea how or when this thing might come down on us. I hoped Risa understood that and was just venting her frustration at her own feelings of fear.

"Damn. Here it is," said Gray, holding up his CUBE. He'd been digging through the mini fridge. I chose not to question it, since some mysteries were best left unsolved. I issued a command to initiate a transfer for the amount I'd promised him and held my device next to his until they both lit up.

"Okay, sailor," I said. "You're up."

Gray's personal life might have been dysfunctional, but when it came to his work, he was an absolute professional. He was clearly going through something emotional, but he was still a

Navy SEAL. Things might have gone nonlinear for him, but he knew how to choke it off. He went about his business with the focus and alacrity I'd expected he would when it became necessary.

He'd provided each of us green plastic ponchos with hoods to help with the rain. Then he'd brought us down the hill from his dwelling to a boathouse floating out on the water next to the pier. Inside, the Zodiac and a few less impressive boats were chained up to some posts along a wooden walkway.

The ocean was angry, and you didn't have to be a sailor to feel its furious energy. That much was evident on Risa's face as she stood on the pier, looking out into the darkness with trepidation, fully aware she'd soon be subjected to its mighty tantrum. I approached and put my hand on her back.

"It will be a short trip, and I meant what I said about this guy earlier. We're in good hands. These Zodiacs are as tough as nails. It's going to take a lot more than what I'm seeing out there to put us in any real danger, but you know all that, since you've done all this before."

"I'm fine," she said, forcing a smile. "It's just been a while."

"You kids ready to ride?" Gray asked. Having finished checking the instruments on the boat, he was busy disengaging the chain from a post on the walkway and nodded toward the passenger seats.

We walked over and boarded the vessel. Before he followed, Gray pulled some floatation devices off the wall and tossed them to us. We put them on over the ponchos. Then he jumped into the boat, unlocked a storage compartment, and riffled through it for helmets. Both Risa and I were familiar with the equipment, and we switched the headsets on to bring communications online while Gray input the coordinates Risa had given him into the ship's navigation console.

"Radio check. Over." Gray's voice came clearly through the headset.

"Roger," I replied.

"Loud and clear," said Risa.

"It's a beautiful night!" Gray yelled. As the engines kicked on and the boat moved out of the garage through the spray of the waves that were kicking up against the pier, he cried, "Giddy-up!" The boat lurched forward with a speed I'd forgotten it was capable of, and I felt myself pressed back against the seat from the inertia.

And just like that, I was back in a comfort zone I hadn't realized I'd been missing. As the vessel shot out into the darkness, cresting heavy waves that came at us head-on with unsettling ferocity, the feeling of lingering dread was gone. I felt like a rookie SEAL again — a son of Poseidon, riding the waves like I'd been born to do, heading into the unknown, overly confident I'd been prepared with the skills to conquer whatever awaited us.

"Tell me you don't miss this!" I heard through the headset and looked over at Gray, who was wearing a wide grin. The feeling of the wind whipping over us as we flew south out of Richardson Bay was both exhilarating and comforting. Whatever malaise had been looming over my old friend earlier in the evening appeared to have evaporated for now. Even Risa cracked a tight smile when I looked in her direction.

As we came around the corner of Yellow Bluff, I could see the soft blue glow of the Golden Gate Bridge towering over the edge of the San Francisco Bay in the distance. Its two spires were guarding the portal to the Pacific Ocean like a pair of battle-hardened sentinels. South of us, lights from the city's skyline could be seen in their multitudes, in stark contrast to the emptiness of the ocean void we were traversing.

I could also see the lights of Alcatraz Island to the east. Knowing Ben was in there alone, with nothing but the knowledge of what he'd done, reminded me of what I was doing out here, crashing across the bay toward an unknown purveyor of biocybernetics. It lent fuel to the fire welling up within me, an anger that up until now had been mostly masked by confusion. Someone was attacking the people I cared about. Although it remained undefined, the threat felt less ambiguous now, more imminent, and I knew that no matter what shape it took, I'd do whatever was in my power to end it.

We passed under the bridge like ghosts and into the waiting embrace of the open Pacific. The waves were even higher now that we'd broken free from the bay, but Gray didn't slow the Zodiac, which skipped over them with grace, and before long we'd left the bridge far behind. As we sped toward our destination, I found myself being lulled into a trancelike state by the darkness, the wind, and the rhythmic cresting of the waves. I was pulled from my reverie by Gray's voice over the radio.

"We're not far now. You sure I don't need a situation report before we arrive?"

"Just be cool, man. There should be no reason these guys will have any problem with us," I said. "If everything goes smoothly, you'll just wait in the boat for us to get back then drive us home."

"Roger that. We're approaching something on radar ahead."

I peered into the night but saw nothing. We slowed as we neared the precise coordinates. A red searchlight came on from about a hundred yards away. Gray navigated the Zodiac toward the light, and as we neared, the cargo coaster we'd seen from the satellite image came into view. Up close, with its clean lines and pristine condition, it looked more like an enormous yacht than a tanker. The hull was pitch-black, and the vessel's name, *The Forge,* was painted in silver lettering along its side. We pulled up beside it. Crew members loosed a rope ladder from the deck above, which rolled about ten meters down the side of the hull. Gray secured it to the Zodiac.

"Good luck, boss," he said as I removed my helmet and handed it to him. Risa did the same. I motioned for her to take the ladder first.

"You okay here?" I shouted to Gray over the rain.

"Oh, just peachy! I'll be here," he yelled back. As he did, he made a barely noticeable nod in the direction of his right side and pulled up his poncho enough to reveal the muzzle brake of the kinetic carbine he was hiding there.

"That won't be necessary," I hollered.

"I'm *mostly* sure you're right," he said. I nodded, appreciating the wisdom of having a backup plan, violent or otherwise. I'd come fully loaded myself, so I was in no position to criticize the sentiment.

Once Risa reached the top of the ladder and disappeared over the side of the ship, I began my ascent, climbing up over the railing and onto the deck. There I was greeted, in Japanese, by a man wearing a loose, flowing white cloak. His fine, tailored clothing was also all white underneath the cloak. A woman with long, straight black hair stood at his side in an identical outfit.

103

They were each carrying clear plastic umbrellas sporting solid white lights that ran down the spine from the center to the tips, offering multipurpose functionality as both protection from the rain and a source of light. The deck was empty and dimly illuminated by a series of rectangular, red-tinted lights that marked the boundary of what appeared to be an empty helipad. One of our escorts set off in the direction of the bridge, which rose from the deck about thirty meters away, toward the bow. The other held out her hand, indicating we should follow, and fell in behind us when we did.

We passed through an open metal doorway onto a platform with ramps on either end. One led up toward the bridge, the other down, where it disappeared into a dark hallway. The two closed their umbrellas in almost perfect unison and set them down against the wall as we passed through the door. I'd assumed we would be taken to the bridge above, but instead we were led down the ramp into the hallway. It was dark, but rings of blueish-white light pulsed along the ceiling in brief intervals. The rings traveled simultaneously along several tubes encased in black, braided nylon sleeving, about half a foot in diameter and running the entire length of the passage. As we approached the end of the cramped hall, the density of the tubes on the ceiling increased as more emerged from circular ports near the top of the walls to either side then crawled upward to merge with the others. We finally reached a steel door with a large wheel on it. The man in front rotated it a full circle, unsealing the portal, and motioned for us to pass through.

I followed Risa through and tried to make sense of the room on the other side. We were in a huge chamber. I guessed it had been used for storing and transporting liquid at some point in the past, but it had undergone extensive renovations, which had removed the container walls and completely opened up the space. From nearly every direction, the dark, pipe-like shapes we'd seen on our way in were feeding into the room from ports in the walls and collecting on the ceiling, which was almost entirely blanketed with them. In the center of the room, they coalesced into a dark, jumbled mass before consolidating into a column comprised of dozens of twisted tubes, which hung down about two meters from the ceiling, where it connected to the top of a large, hanging sphere. The sphere itself was roughly two meters in diameter and entirely dark inside, despite the fact that the outer layer was constructed of a transparent material of some kind.

Besides the occasional pulses of light emitted along the tubes, there were strips of bright blue light along the perimeter of both the ceiling and the floor. The outer edge of the chamber was occupied by a dense collection of consoles, monitors, holo-displays, and machines that were beyond my ability to identify. There were medical stations set up in intermittent intervals as well — gurneys with cables and wiring connecting them to the computer equipment. I noticed a particularly insidious-looking chair with ominous sharp instruments on metal arms hovering to either side of it and shivered involuntarily.

Our escorts moved to stand at attention on either side of the door we'd entered through as Risa and I assessed the room. The breathing rhythm of the pulsing blue light made the entire place feel somehow alive. Looking into the swirling emptiness of the lightless sphere, I felt unnerved, as if something were looking back out at me. In the awkward silence, I noticed a faintly audible *whoomph* occur each time the rings of light cycled along the tubes.

Through the doorway, a shape was moving toward us, intermittently visible as the pulsing rings passed rapidly along the ceiling. It was low to the ground, and parts of it were glowing red. The lights were moving too quickly for me to fully assess exactly who or what was approaching us, until it had nearly reached the door. It was an elderly Asian man, seated in a wheeled chair, the metal of which was aglow. The colors of fire swirled within it and gave the metal the molten appearance of having just been drawn from the flames. The man looked to be in his seventh or eighth decade. His white hair was short, straight, and neatly combed. The sharp, piercing gaze from beneath his glasses belied any assumption that his advanced age might have dulled his mind. For a few moments, he quietly studied us, and I had the sense we were being compared to a preexisting expectation.

I bowed then, timing it as I deemed appropriate to reflect the proper amount of deference, since I was a guest on this ship and had come seeking his assistance. Risa followed my example.

"*Kangei Shimasu*," he said in Japanese, bowing his head respectfully. "Be welcome, Jacobi-san."

"You know my name," I said, unsurprised.

He paused for a moment, as if to consider how to answer, and then nodded. "I do. I know a great many things about both of you, but before you ask, I am unwilling to fully explain the methods we use to gather our intelligence. We should use the limited time we have to share with one another this evening to focus on less complex matters."

"You are The Blacksmith?" asked Risa.

"Yes. Welcome to the *Forge*, Ms. Corbin. You, of all people, might appreciate the room in which we stand now. Do you understand what you see, I wonder?"

"I think…" she said, looking slowly around the room, "if I had to guess, considering the amount of power you have being routed to that sphere, it's probably the central processing unit for some sort of massive neural network. AI, perhaps?"

"Not just any artificial intelligence. Certainly nothing along the lines of those ridiculous programmed concierges you see installed in every home now. The Anvil," he said, nodding in the direction of the sphere, "is the foundation of all of the work we do here at the *Forge*. I began developing it more than five decades ago, and it has since evolved into what you see before you now, a fully functioning example of the potential of machine learning."

"What does it do?" she asked, walking closer and running her hand along the surface of the sphere.

"It manages complex medical procedures and data-mines the Evernet with astounding speed and accuracy to provide me with information. In many ways, it functions as an assistant of sorts for me, without which the work I do would take an extraordinarily increased length of time to complete."

"And what is that exactly?" she asked. "The work you do, I mean."

"You contacted me. That seems a great deal of trouble to go through without knowing what you seek."

"It certainly does," Risa said, giving me a poignant glare.

"Well," he continued, "we do a great many things here in the *Forge*, mostly in the field of biological cybernetics. Our moral inclinations tend to be much looser than the places where this work is performed legally. And with the assistance of the Anvil, we can perform it in a fraction of the time it would take otherwise."

"Why out here? Why on the ocean? A ship hardly seems the ideal place for a man in a wheelchair," I said.

"Well, ship stability technology has made some leaps forward in the twenty years since you were in the navy, Mr. Slate. Advances in the field of magnetic internal stabilizers, as well as wave pattern recognition and prediction, have given way to a new era of onboard motion control. As you can surely see, there is a powerful storm raging outside yet barely the slightest hint of movement here within the hull."

I hadn't been paying too much attention, distracted as I'd been by the strange environment and the neural network, but he was correct. I bowed my head in concession to his point.

"To answer your question, it provides some amount of security, and the mobility we need to maintain our privacy. The ocean also provides a consistent, natural source of coolant that we utilize in maintaining our operation. Additionally, we have systems onboard that harness both thermal energy from the sun's heat and mechanical energy from the tides and waves. Water, Mr. Slate, is a powerful tool when properly manipulated."

My curiosity was sated, and I was impressed. The Blacksmith's chair rolled forward past us, seemingly of its own violation as his hands were neatly folded in his lap. It repositioned to face us when it reached the Anvil.

"So, let us not waste any more time. Tell me, what service do you hope I can provide?"

I looked at Risa, who was watching me expectantly, and drew a deep breath.

"I need a kill switch for my head."

"Meaning?" he asked.

"Can you program my brain to shut off on command?"

"I assume what you mean is, your consciousness? You're looking for a way to lose consciousness on demand?" He looked intrigued.

"Sure. Consciousness. I'd like to be able to turn myself off."

I'd assumed there would be some amount of consideration, or at least posturing, while The Blacksmith determined if such a thing were possible, so his immediate response came as a bit of a surprise.

"Certainly. This is not a difficult thing to accomplish."

"No?"

"No. It would be a simple procedure, easily performed this very night if you were to choose to move forward."

This was going much easier than I'd imagined, so I prepared myself for the catch.

"And the cost?"

"The cost is subjective in that I would request a trade and will leave it up to you to determine the relevant value."

"Trade," I said, confused. "What could I do for you?" I was beginning to wonder just how much he knew about me and my past.

"I'm currently faced with a situation that you might be uniquely suited for resolving."

This was starting to feel familiar. It sounded like the beginning of every opening conversation I had with a prospective employer.

"You need someone brought in," I stated.

"Brought in or eliminated, yes."

"I'm not a killer. I retrieve people."

"Whether or not you are a killer is debatable, Mr. Slate. However, I respect your work ethic in this regard, and as I stated before, retrieval would be a perfectly acceptable resolution."

I folded my hands behind my back and began walking along the perimeter of the hull, inspecting the equipment. I wondered what the Anvil was busy computing, noticing almost all of the monitors and holo-displays were actively broadcasting permutations and executing commands.

"Do you have a deadline? When does this need to happen?" I asked.

The Blacksmith's chair began following me as I roamed, and Risa kept pace behind him. "By whenever you plan to execute the procedure we discussed. Tonight, presumably."

I stopped walking and turned in frustration. "Tonight? I can't make that arrangement with you. We're in the middle of our own crisis. I'm afraid I don't have the time to resolve someone else's issues. These things take research, information gathering, and if he's in hiding, we might need to spend time staking out locations. There's no way—"

"Jacobi-san," he interrupted. "I concede that for your usual cases, this is how you are used to working. However, as I mentioned to you before, we have a great deal of information at our disposal here. I know where the target is right at this very moment and would be able to update you on his approximate position in real-time."

"Why not send your own men to bring him in, then?" I

wondered.

"The chance they would be killed in the process is too high. You must understand that finding qualified men and women who are willing to spend the majority of their time on a sea-faring vessel with an old man and his machines is not a simple thing. The members of this organization that you see are not hired muscle. They keep this ship functioning and assist me with my work. They are recruited from among the most exceptionally talented scientists and engineers and then undergo additional, extensive training on self-defense, decorum, computer science, cybernetic theory, and other aspects of the work I do. We are a family here, tightly knit and indispensable. No, people like you, Mr. Slate, are a much more appropriate solution for situations like this."

"People like me?" I asked, slightly offended.

"Yes," said The Blacksmith as his chair rolled past and turned to face me. "People like you and your friend here, Ms. Corbin. People who have seen more combat than most men and women will likely hear about in their lifetime. People who can perform a task like the one I am proposing without breaking stride, because success has been the only option they've ever had, the alternative often being unthinkable. To put it more bluntly, Mr. Slate, precision tools, expertly honed by the fires of chaos and warfare, or in a word, Fades."

"Now, that is impressive," I said, matching the intensity of The Blacksmith's gaze directly. "Those service records are not easy to obtain. Hell, I've known Gray outside for almost twenty years, and even he doesn't know about what I was involved in after the navy. It's not the kind of thing that's readily accessible, even in the darkest recesses of the Evernet. I know that because we used to scrape it regularly."

"As I said before, I'm not willing to delve into an explanation regarding the specific methods we use for obtaining information. Suffice it to say, we *do* know a great deal about you both."

"Look," I said in an attempt to move away from the uncomfortable subject, "I'd prefer to pay you for the service. Give me a reasonable figure, and I'll pay it."

"Look around you, Jacobi-san. The things you are seeing here come at an astronomical cost. There is nothing you could pay me that would equal the value of even the short amount of time I would spend on this procedure. No, I do not work for money. We operate on a strict trade-only policy here, so if this is important to you, I have told you what the price will be."

Something he said earlier came back to me, and I asked, "You said you believe whomever you sent after this guy would be killed? Who exactly do you want us to bring back here?"

"A mistake. We put our faith in someone who has chosen another path. His name is Himari Okada, but I fear he is barely the same man who was given that name. He is more a machine than a man now. Himari was a member of our family here who benefited immensely from the technology I am capable of providing to those that advance through our ranks into the inner circle."

"What happened? Why did he leave?" asked Risa.

"I'd prefer not to delve heavily into the details of our affairs. Himari had a change of perspective that caused him to become volatile, and he behaved violently toward several of his brothers before he left the organization. As it stands, he owes a great debt to us and refuses to pay it, despite the stain it leaves upon his honor. He is *rōnin* now, and dangerous."

"Like a machine, you said. What sorts of augmentations and modifications does he have?" I asked.

"Too many to list," snapped The Blacksmith. "He's enhanced in just about every way you could imagine. And he's ready for a fight. He knows I'll be sending someone to collect the debt he owes."

"I'm sorry," I said. "But if we do this for you, it's important I have any information that could give us an advantage or prevent a surprise. You'd need to tell me exactly what you've done to him."

The old man sighed and nodded. "Of course. Please forgive my frustration. I did not mean to direct it at you. When I consider everything I've done for him, I am reminded of the extent of his betrayal."

I waved away the apology. "No offense taken."

"So, do we have an agreement then?"

"I'll need to discuss it with both of my associates before I commit to anything."

"Very well," he said. "My apprentices will escort you back to the deck. After you decide, let them know whether or not we can expect you to be returning to us this evening. If so, I will send you the list of modifications, update you with his location, and await your success. If not, then it was a pleasure to make your acquaintance, for we are not likely to meet again."

The apprentices stationed at the door each bowed their heads and held out a hand, suggesting we should lead the way down the hallway. The Blacksmith turned his glowing chair, parked it at one of the nearby consoles, and began typing at the keypad.

When we reached the top of the ramp we'd initially come

down from the deck above, Risa took the umbrellas that had been left in the corner and handed one to me. We opened them up and made our way back across the deck to where the Zodiac was tied off. The white-clad assistants seemed content to wait on the platform, out of the rain.

Upon reaching the rope ladder that connected the railing to the Zodiac, I shouted down to Gray, who was huddling in his poncho below. He looked up immediately and waved. I beckoned him up, and before long he had reached the top and stood in a tight circle with Risa and myself, under the protection and light of the umbrellas.

"What's up, boss?"

"What's *up* is that this night just got a lot longer and more complicated," said Risa.

"I need to get to the city and back, tonight," I said. "Are you up for making more credits? I'll double what I paid you already."

Gray nodded. "Yeah, you got it, whatever you need."

"Okay. Head back down and prep the boat, we'll be down in a minute."

Gray disappeared back over the rail to do what I'd requested. I looked up at Risa, who was staring at me expectantly.

"Look," I said. "I know this is coming out of left field. I'm just trying—"

"I get it," she broke in. "I understand."

"You do?" I was suspicious.

"I mean, I'm nervous about it. A kill switch? You're making yourself pretty vulnerable with something like that, but yeah, I get it. Let's just do what we have to do and get back to finding the assholes who are putting us in this position."

I nodded. She hit the ladder, and I went to inform the pair waiting inside on the landing that if all went well, we'd be back later that night. They both bowed respectfully in response. The woman reached out, and when I returned the gesture, she dropped something into my hand. I opened my fingers to find a bullet, the caliber of which appeared to match my sidearm. It was silver, with a glowing blue ring around the center.

"This stick in," she said in broken English, pointing at her own shoulder, "and make space with no power." She finished the explanation by holding her hands out about an inch from her body and shaking them. I accepted it with a nod of thanks, though I might have been more appreciative if it had included clearer instructions. She wished me luck in Japanese.

I responded with a proverb I'd been taught by an old friend. "*Koketsu ni irazunba koji-o ezu.*" To which they both smiled, and nodded agreement.

If you do not enter the tiger's cave, you will not catch its cub.

Chapter 5

As the Zodiac hummed through the storm on its way back toward the city, I received the information The Blacksmith had promised. I swore out loud when I noted the location. The comms picked it up, and both Gray and Risa turned to look at me. "Bring us south of the Bay Bridge. We'll dock at South Beach."

"Where's he at?" asked Risa.

"He's in the Night Market," I answered.

Gray swore.

"The Night Market," she said. "What's that?"

"The last place we want to be," said Gray.

South of the Bay Bridge, there was an area along the coast, about a half a mile long, which had been hit hard by an Iranian tactical warhead that had slipped through our antimissile defense system during the war. Tens of thousands had died, and the area was horribly damaged. Many of the structures that remained intact were burnt and unstable. Since the majority of city funding was being funneled directly into support for the war effort, resources had been scarce for years after the strike, and efforts toward reconstruction were hampered and limited.

After nearly a decade of war, San Francisco's already vast homeless population had only increased, both because of the toll it had taken on the economy and because of the many soldiers returning home faced with the adversity of trying to function in society while simultaneously processing the horrors they'd been exposed to. Over time, they moved from the streets of the Tenderloin, the Mission, and other neighborhoods where they were regularly harassed and treated as pariahs to stake claim to territory in what they called the Quiet Zone, where they were generally left alone. The criminal underground was soon to follow, recognizing the potential of an unpoliced area of the city that was, more or less, forgotten and abandoned. Before long, it became known as a lawless and unsafe area, trespassed upon only by the brave or heavily armed.

That had been over eight years ago. The SFPD would organize a raid and sweep the area once every few months, but there was nothing of any real value to protect, so it was mostly to stir things up and keep the residents of the QZ from getting too comfortable. They just didn't have the manpower or motivation to maintain a presence that could deter everyone from coming right back. It had changed somewhat over the last couple of years as the criminals began to realize they could profit more from letting people in and selling them what they needed than by robbing and killing them. The area had slowly transformed from a place that offered near-certain death into somewhere you just didn't want to go without people watching your back. If you were willing to take the risk, you could find black-market vendors for weapons, drugs, sex, and just about any other vice imaginable. To make it easier than wandering broken buildings and dark alleys, a loosely organized central market was established in the skeletal remains of the city's old baseball stadium, which had come to be known as the Night Market.

As we traveled, I studied The Blacksmith's list of Himari's augmentations to get a sense of what we were going up against, and had to admit it was comprehensive. I was concerned and a little impressed. I passed my CUBE to Risa so she could have a look, and she started reading it out loud.

"All limbs replaced with Haiku VII prosthetics, with hydraulics — expect massive increase of power and mobility. Right eye capable of thermographic vision and magnification. Left eye equipped with augment lens. Enhanced aural spectrum capable of audio filtering and sound segmentation. Motion sensor and radar display for monitoring tagged objects and broadcasting to HUD via augment lens. Increased oxygen reserve. Enhanced viral and toxin resistance and/or immunity. Targeting system — pairing of right limb with ocular HUD for near-instantaneous fire upon locked targets. Desensitized pain receptors. Interwoven graphene skin shield on back and torso — protecting vital areas from most kinetic attacks—"

"Right now, I'm *really* hoping that you ain't reading off a list that has anything to do with someone we're about to meet," interrupted Gray through the comms.

I looked over at Risa, who had closed her eyes and was taking a deep breath.

"I want you both to stay on the boat," I said. "I don't want either of you getting caught up in this any more than you already have."

Predictably, Risa's eyes shot open and were filled with an intensity I'd anticipated.

"This *thing*," she spat the word out, "is going to kill you. You're in over your head." She crossed her arms over her chest and turned away.

"Boss, I ain't one to question your badassery or nothin', but

I'm forced to agree with Army on this one. If you're fixin' to pick a fight with that, I'd like to be paid that second half of what you owe me before you go."

"Don't worry, you'll have it." A part of me had meant what I'd said about wanting both of my friends out of harm's way. There was an equal part that wondered how I was going to get to this mark alone without getting myself killed in the process. Risa wasn't wrong; I was in over my head.

The Bay Bridge, in contrast with the Golden Gate, was not brightly lit. There was a scattering of holographic advertisements along the base for boat traffic, but she was nothing like the shining beacon her sister was. Tonight, passing beneath her felt cold and foreboding, as if crossing over the boundary she represented had somehow committed us to whatever dark fate lay ahead.

From there it was a short ride to the piers at Old South Beach, which had been reconstructed from materials scavenged from the wasted Quiet Zone and reached out like skeletal hands from the shore. I could see lights in the Night Market. There were bulbs powered by generators and assorted colors of holiday strings for marking territory and bringing attention to the makeshift storefronts. There were scattered groups of people congregating in the shadows under whatever protection from the rain they could find. The storm would work in my favor here, since it was keeping the crowd minimal. The fewer people in my way there while I hunted, the better the odds to resolve it quickly.

Gray managed to grab hold of a post as we docked at a series of charred wood planks strapped to floating traffic barrels that were masquerading as a pier. As he tied off the boat with a chain, I transferred the funds I owed him to his CUBE, which was parked in the boat's dash receptacle.

"That should settle us," I said.

"Settles us for the money," he agreed, "but I think it's time you told me what we're doing here, since I'll be coming with you."

"We already agreed you'd stay," I argued, shaking my head.

"No, you said *you'd* like me to stay, and I said I wanted to get paid first. We didn't agree on nothing. Ain't no way I'm sittin' on my ass while you're out there getting yours kicked. That's not how we do things, Slate. You know that as well as I do. And ten thousand credits? I don't know what you've been into these last years, but where I come from that buys a lot more than a boat ride," he finished and patted his side where his rifle was strapped.

Risa stood up. She removed her helmet and the flotation device then stored them both in the central compartment. Pulling the poncho hood down in order to allow for more peripheral vision, she exited the vehicle onto the floating pier.

"I'm coming. Are you going to tell him what the plan is?" she asked. "Because he thinks you have a plan."

I didn't bother arguing. I'd never truly believed either of them would actually stay on the boat. I'd given them an out, which I'd felt ethically obligated to do, and they'd made their choice. Despite my concern for their safety, I felt a surge of relief knowing we'd be hunting as a pack tonight. I stowed my gear in the cabinet and went over my inventory on the pier. I had my gun, extra magazines on a pouch on my belt, a mysterious bullet, my knife, and was wearing the cartridge loader on my right wrist. I had two stun patches in my front pocket, but I doubted they would be effective, since Himari was enhanced with resistance to toxins. My CUBE was broadcasting the tracking dot The Blacksmith was transmitting to me on a heads-up display that I viewed via my augment lenses.

"Damn, Army!" I heard Gray exclaim. "Is that CE6 insulin? Vison mods? You got any more surprises?" I looked over at Risa, who stared back silently with pitch-black eyes, having activated the night-vision solution.

"Yeah, I do," she answered.

"Who is this woman, Slate? And why haven't you married her?"

I grinned. "She's too good for me."

Once we were situated, Gray locked the central cabinet and activated the silent alarm system, which would alert him remotely if someone tampered with the boat. Approaching the others, I prepared to lay out a plan I hadn't even begun to formulate.

"Okay. The signal is being muted somehow and isn't precise. If I had to guess, there's probably equipment installed somewhere in this area that's purpose is to interfere with tracking signals of this kind. Right now, the beacon is indicating an area a bit larger than the stadium. That means he's in there somewhere, but we'll need to split up to try to get eyes on the target."

"Back up a second. What or who are we looking for here, exactly?" asked Gray.

"Extremely augmented Japanese male, late thirties, early forties. My height, at around six feet...here," I said, and unfolded my CUBE to show them an image The Blacksmith had included in the information he'd sent to me. "His name is

Himari Okada."

"And what's the objective?"

"We need to bring this guy back to the *Forge*. Objective is capture only. The target is to remain breathing."

Gray nodded, satisfied.

"Try to keep low. I don't want to stir up the rabble here. Things could go sour pretty quickly if the locals decide we're acting against their interests. If you see him, don't engage. Send me a message, and we'll coordinate to approach him together. And keep an eye out for any communication from me," I said, holding up my CUBE. "I'll do the same."

"He's going to be on alert," added Risa, speaking to Gray, "since according to the contact, he's expecting trouble. Make sure he doesn't see you first."

"Easy to say when you can see in the dark, lady," Gray muttered.

We set off in the direction of the Night Market. It was farther down the promenade, which was really just an area that had been mostly cleared of debris. The walls of the stadium were relatively intact in most places, but there were areas where the outer wall and seating stands had collapsed completely. Those areas had been cleared and turned into entrances to the park and were lit up to indicate as much. We chose the nearest one and then filtered through individually over a short period so as not to attract undue attention by arriving as a group.

The sound of generators and the smell of machinery greeted me as I passed under a hanging strip of lights and entered the stadium. A village of sorts had been erected on the ancient baseball diamond. Shoddily constructed stalls were haphazardly positioned across the field. There were fire barrels lit where paths intersected, providing sparse illumination and casting shadows with jagged edges that danced wildly in the rain.

Hooded figures stood beneath canvas awnings, warming themselves near the barrels, all casually taking note of the presence of an outsider. Their distrust was evident in their expressions. I went out of my way to avoid lingering eye contact out of concern it would be taken as a challenge. I wandered past a canvas tent with clouds of smoke occasionally billowing from the entrance and was propositioned by a scantily clad, skinny teenage girl with long black hair. She wore a collar that was attached to a post outside the tent by a thin chain.

"Put some clothes on, you're going to catch a cold," I said as I walked past. "Your parents are worried about you."

"My parents are dead, you fucking asshole," she said and spat in my direction.

It was a good reminder that I needed to keep my mouth shut or I'd quickly end up in a situation I was going to regret. I wasn't there to judge anyone or change anything. I just needed to stay focused on finding Himari. As I neared the center of the field, I saw a wooden structure that stood out on account of the holographic image being broadcast above it. It depicted a nuclear explosion expanding outward in a cloud of smoke and fire, repeating on a loop. There was a wide piece of plywood leaning up against the front of the establishment, which looked like the words *The Atomic Drop* had been originally spray-painted onto it but had since had a line sprayed through them and been replaced with *Billy's Place* underneath. There were a few wooden boxes out front under an awning that looked like they could substitute as seats. It dawned on me that this was some sort of bar. A strip of yellow lights ran along the underside of the bar itself, the corner of which had several bottles on it, grouped up next to a stack of questionably utilized plastic cups.

Thinking it might be a safe place to try to get some information without attracting too much attention, I walked over. There was a man standing in the shadows behind the bar. He made his way into the light as I took a seat on one of the boxes. He had a scarred, leathery face and a ragged brown beard so large it popped out from the front and sides of the hoodie he had pulled up over his head.

"You Billy?" I asked.

"Nah," he said. His voice was low and gruff. "Billy don't run this place no more."

"Fair enough. What's on tap?" I said, nodding toward the bottles.

"Tap? We got booze."

"Perfect. I'll take booze," I said, yielding to his expert salesmanship.

He hesitated, looking me over, before grunting and emptying the contents of an unidentified brown liquid into a plastic cup, which he put down in front of me.

"Fifty," he said, which was almost certainly the price for strangers only. I realized my mistake as I reached for my CUBE to pay. The likeliness that he carried his own biometric executor was pretty slim, since the devices were expensive. Even if he'd found or stolen one, it was even less likely that it would be linked to an account that could accept payment properly.

"Sorry. Fifty what?" I asked, embarrassed.

"Dollar bills, asshole."

The US dollar had been practically eliminated in the early forties when the existing system had been replaced by a global, credit-based alternative. There had been a period in which physical money could be exchanged at full value, but within a decade the dollar was completely devoid of any worth. It was almost never carried anymore, and as such, I had no way to pay. I supposed it made sense that a community of people existing outside the boundaries of typical society would still be making use of it as a functioning currency.

"I'm looking for somebody. If you take a minute to look at a picture and tell me if you've seen him, I'll pay for that and the drink with this," I said as I reached down to unstrap my ankle sheath then laid it on the table. The combat knife inside was military issue and easily worth several bottles of the booze he had in stock.

He pulled the knife out of the sheath and looked it over before asking, "You a cop?"

I was getting that a lot lately. I sighed, shook my head, and said, "Just a guy looking for a friend."

"Show me," he said.

I pulled out my CUBE, unfolded it, brought up the image I had of Himari, then turned it for him to have a look. I watched his eyes, which flashed briefly with recognition. He looked up and seemed like he was about to say something but fell silent, a look of fear crossing his face.

"Nah. Sorry," he said then grabbed the knife and began to walk away from the counter. I caught his wrist as he did. He tugged futilely in an attempt to free himself from my grasp.

"I feel like you are not being honest with me," I said. My

voice had taken on a cold, practiced edge that I liked to employ when I wanted to insinuate immanent violence.

I'd been too focused on gauging the man's reaction and hadn't been paying enough attention to my surroundings or to exactly what he'd been reacting to and was therefore surprised to hear a soft voice suddenly near my ear.

"Perhaps I can help. Let me have a look."

I turned to identify the speaker and saw Himari Okada standing immediately behind and to the right of me. He reached down with one hand and turned the gel screen of my CUBE back around to face us so he could have a look.

"Seems like a very handsome man," he said appreciatively. "Although I'd say he looks quite dangerous."

I let go of the booze vendor's wrist. He fell away and immediately vacated the structure.

"Okada," I said. "Have a seat, let's chat."

"I'm comfortable standing. Are you alone?" He kept his voice quiet, but there was a strength behind it that exuded confidence.

I nodded and replied, "Just came to talk."

"I doubt that very much. Tell me, did the old man send you to kill or capture me? I'm curious about the lengths to which he's willing to go to cover his shame."

"How'd you make me?" I asked, genuinely impressed but more to avoid having to answer his question.

"You don't exactly fit in here. And when I scanned you, I detected the metal used in the bone-strengthening procedure for your arms and legs. You move like military, and you look like exactly the kind of man he'd send after me."

"Oh, yeah? What kind of man is that?"

"One both brave enough to come here and dumb enough to think he'd survive."

I needed to stall for time. I was no match for Himari alone and without the element of surprise. My best chance was to try to draw the conversation out long enough for either Gray or Risa to spot me. I thought back to what he'd said earlier and attempted to bait him into further conversation with the subject matter.

"The Blacksmith told me that you were the one who's behaved dishonorably. What did you mean when you said he was trying to cover his shame?"

Himari studied me carefully then said, "There are others here. You are stalling."

My hand balled into a fist and shot out to strike him in the ribs with inhuman speed. I'd cracked my pinky to activate my pituitary enhancement when he'd first spoken, and I was crackling with the boosted adrenaline it provided. I hit something hard beneath the loose, cloak-like garment. Whatever it was, it had protected him from having multiple broken ribs, but he did fall backward several steps before dropping to one knee in the mud.

I jumped up from the box I'd been sitting on, drew my pistol, and leveled it at Himari. "Don't get up," I said. "I don't want to shoot you, but I won't hesitate to if you stand up."

I could see that the residents of the Quiet Zone were beginning to take notice of the conflict. They hovered just out of the light, undoubtedly assessing the ways in which this situation could be used to their benefit. Himari's head was bowed as he gathered himself and shook off the blow. One metal arm and one knee were still on the ground, but his body looked tensed and poised to strike. The hood of his cloak was drawn, and the cowl hung low, concealing his face. Slowly, he dropped his other knee into the mud and raised his torso. He raised both hands and pulled the cowl of his cloak back from his head, revealing his face. His augmented eyes blazed with unnatural light, and I saw that he was grinning.

"Very well," he called out to me over the sound of the storm, "*Anata wa anata no unmei o erabimashita.* You have chosen your fate."

He threw his cloak to the right side of his body and placed his hand on the pommel of a blade sheathed on his left. As he drew the blade forth, I could see it was a katana sword, the dull back edge of which was glowing with the same molten intensity as had the metal of The Blacksmith's chair. With the cloak out of the way, I saw what I had punched earlier was a lightweight layer of black fabric Himari wore, protecting his chest. It was stylized to appear similar to a traditional Samurai cuirass in design, with overlapping segments attached to the bottom that protected the abdomen and upper legs. Contrary to its soft, lightweight appearance, I was sure it had layers of either graphene or Kevlar within it, and possibly metal plating of some kind based on the resistance my fist had met.

Between that and the graphene skin shield augmentations I knew he had installed over his vitals, I knew that shooting him anywhere but the head wasn't likely to kill him, but I hoped it might slow him down. As he began to rise, I fired three rounds, all of which landed squarely in the center of his chest. He stumbled with each impact. The final bullet launched him backward through the air. As he landed, he rolled and came up slowly, coughing and holding his free hand to his chest.

"I've got a whole magazine here," I yelled. "Drop the sword and lie down on the ground."

"You seem to want me alive," Himari croaked, still holding his chest. "That's going to make this very difficult for you."

He darted forward and suddenly to the right, then launched off of his metal right leg and was propelled by hydraulics into the air toward me. I fired off another two rounds, but he was moving too quickly and my shots missed the mark. He hit the ground at about half the distance between us, ducked, and used both legs to spring directly at me with the sword raised over his head in both hands. The adrenaline boost was still surging through my body, but even with my speed enhanced, I barely rolled away in time to avoid the blow.

Himari was moving toward me before I'd even had time to recover from my roll. The sword was already in motion, and I knew I didn't have time to stand and defend myself. Instead, I threw myself backward out of the way. Undeterred, he let the momentum of his strike carry him forward and raised the blade for another blow. I rolled onto my back, lifted my gun in both hands, and fired another three shots directly into his torso, sending him reeling backward once again. This time I didn't hesitate, and as he recovered from the impact, I snapped my wrist back, loaded a charged cartridge into my hand, then threw it at him.

He was clutching at his chest where the bullets had impacted and barely looking up but still somehow managed to bat the cartridge away with his sword. The impact activated the disc, causing electricity to surge around it visibly as it landed harmlessly in a puddle several feet away.

"Parlor tricks from a man with no honor," growled Himari. "I hope you have something more impressive than that up your sleeve."

The discouraging truth was that I didn't, but it hardly felt advantageous to share that information with him. The cartridges had been my best hope for taking him down reasonably unscathed. The situation darkened further when Himari sheathed his katana and reached his hand into his cloak, which came out grasping a massive revolver. No words were spoken, but the look in his eye silently promised death as he raised the weapon. I thought about trying to run or take evasive action but knew it would accomplish little, since Himari could lock on to moving targets. The link between his targeting system and his cybernetic hand would allow his onboard computer systems to control both aiming and firing. Time slowed as our eyes met. When the shot rang out, it took me several seconds to piece together what had happened.

The gun in Himari's hand was gone. The weapon itself had been struck by an unbelievable shot from Gray, who had stepped out from around the corner of a pile of melted plastic arena seats on the field nearby and was advancing with his rifle at his shoulder from about ten meters away. Gray rapidly fired several more shots at Himari, and I heard the clink of metal as bullets ricocheted off his limbs.

The circle of onlookers had been tightening slowly around us since our fight had begun, but with the arrival of another armed outsider, the crowd quickly dispersed. Himari began reaching for his katana once more, but when I renewed firing shots in his direction, he opted to retreat rather than continue to take fire from us both.

With uncanny speed, he turned and sprinted into the rain. Gray and I both set after him immediately, but Himari used the structures on the field to his advantage, blocking our view of him whenever he could, and it became increasingly difficult to keep eyes on him as the distance increased. He was heading west, into the unlit Quiet Zone. By the time Gray and I arrived at the western wall of the Night Market, we'd lost sight of him completely.

I tensed as I suddenly felt a presence beside me but relaxed when I recognized Risa's voice as she pointed into the darkness and whispered, "There."

We let her lead the way with her thermographic vision. She couldn't detect his heat behind structures or barriers, but she did catch sight of him occasionally as he slipped between buildings or traveled straight along the road. We moved as quietly as we could. Despite the noise cover provided by the rain, I was concerned that his ability to filter and segment audio could alert him that we hadn't abandoned the pursuit.

The buildings around us were mostly collapsed. Debris had tumbled away from many of them, and it cluttered the road. The ones that were still standing were in terrible condition, and many of them looked unstable. I could see small fires attended by denizens of the zone in some of the more intact structures, but they did little to provide light for us. Instead, they interfered with my vision adjusting to the darkness and kept me reliant on Risa to guide the way.

As we navigated the maze of burned and rusted cars along the road, Risa held her hand up, signaling a halt. She scanned the area for several moments then looked back at me and shook her head, communicating she'd lost sight of him completely. She motioned for us to continue forward, and as one, we began moving quietly toward the location where she'd last had eyes on him.

When she finally stopped, we were in a large, open area that appeared to have once been a commuter train yard. Overturned train cars littered the yard at odd angles, looking as if they'd been scattered in frustration, like toys, by some enormous child's hand. Weeds and other plant life had emerged through the cracks in the cement platforms between the sets of tracks, reclaiming the once-bustling station in the name of a natural order that rejected the consequences humankind had brought upon itself by its efforts to subjugate and control. The echo of that truth resounded vividly in the bones of the dead city around us and in the whispers of the ghosts of those who had once walked there. If they were with us, observing our violent intentions and trying desperately to warn us against making the same deadly mistakes, we were too arrogant to pay them any heed.

We moved in silently, weapons drawn and eyes scanning systematically for any sign of movement or evidence our prey was near. A few minutes later, we'd reached a platform between two trains, one standing upright and one that had been blown onto its side when the bomb hit. Risa stopped to look through the broken doors of the upright train car to see if she could spot Himari's heat signature. I turned to wave Gray past me, only to find he was no longer behind me. I put my hand on Risa's shoulder. She turned and immediately recognized the cause of my distress. We hustled into the train car and took cover on either side of the doorway. When no threat presented itself, she leaned out to scan the platform and then signaled it was clear.

Leaving the cover of the car behind, I crossed the platform and climbed up the undercarriage of the train on the opposite side. It took several minutes, since the metal was rusted in some places and incapable of supporting my weight without breaking, forcing me to attempt the ascent at multiple points along the length of the car. When I finally reached the top, I was rewarded with a much better view of the yard. I reached down to grasp Risa's wrist and lifted her up beside me. From our elevated position, we scanned the area for any sign of Gray.

"Jacobi," Risa said and pointed below us. There was a body collapsed face down on the ground on the far side of the train car we'd climbed up.

I hopped down and stayed low as I approached it. The poncho it wore matched our own. I rolled him over to check the pulse on his neck. As the body rolled onto its back, one of the arms shot forward to grab me by the neck, and I found myself looking into the glowing eyes of our target. Himari's other arm grabbed my wrist as I brought my gun in line with his body and easily held it to the side where the weapon couldn't threaten him. His metal hand squeezed tighter on my neck, restricting my ability to breathe. I knew it wouldn't take much more pressure to crush my windpipe altogether. I began lashing out with my free hand, striking at his face, but had no leverage from my position with which to put any real weight into the blows. I tried to shout, to alert Risa to what was happening, but it came out as a strangled gurgle.

I was losing focus and tried to calm myself and consider the tools I had at my disposal. Despite my inability to level my gun at Himari, I still had my finger on the trigger and fired several shots with the pistol to get Risa's attention. He rolled, came up on top of me, and slammed my hand down onto the cement several times until I lost my grip on the weapon, which he swatted away. As my vision began to blur from lack of air and

Himari's weight on my chest, I heard several shots ring out. The weight lifted from my body as he fell to the side and released his grip on me. Air rushed back into my lungs, and I grasped at my throat, wheezing.

Risa jumped down from the train car and landed crouching in a puddle of rainwater, her pistol trained directly at our assailant's chest. Her black eyes showed no emotion, revealed no fear. Himari stood beside me, breathing heavily. The bullets couldn't penetrate his armor, but it was obvious he could feel the impact of every one. His dampened pain receptors would help him ignore the pain, but I hoped his body might be slowing from the damage and the bruising that taking so many shots must have been inflicting.

As if to answer my curiosity, Himari leaped toward the train car on our right, and moving almost faster than the eye could follow, he jumped up and ran along the side of it toward Risa. There were more shots fired, which must have missed, because as he neared, he pushed off of the car and flew through the air then struck out with a kick that landed on her arm and caused her pistol to fly from her hand.

Risa cried out as she fell to the ground but immediately kicked out to sweep at Himari's legs. The strengthened cybernetic limbs barely moved when her sweep connected and didn't stop him from reaching down to grab her by her poncho then lifting her from the ground. Still coughing, I got to my feet and looked around unsuccessfully for my pistol.

Once again, Himari drew the katana at his side from its sheath, and its soft orange glow cut through the darkness of the train yard. I snapped my wrist back to load another disc-shaped cartridge into my hand then launched it as hard as I could in Himari's direction. His reflexes were too quick. For a second time his precise motion tracking detected the movement, and the disc was easily batted aside by his blade. I loaded another, and threw it anyhow. Then another. It was a desperate attempt to keep his attention on me to prevent him from harming Risa. While those cartridges were being deflected, I scanned the area to try to locate anything I could use to combat his blade.

My eyes landed on a long piece of rebar steel sticking out from a chunk of concrete that had cracked off from the main platform. I continued loading discs into my hand from the device on my wrist and throwing them at Himari, who continued to deflect them with little effort. I only had so many, and they were going to run out soon. To stand a chance against him in hand-to-hand combat, I'd need to crack my knuckle again for the chemical release, but using it twice in such rapid succession was going to lead to an extreme hangover when the effect wore off. That would leave me with limited time to bring the conflict to an end, or I'd find myself at even more of a disadvantage than I already was.

Risa was still being held in place by Himari's left hand, but while he was distracted deflecting the cartridges I was throwing, she unsheathed a combat knife on her waist. She raised her arms and ducked, slipping through the poncho he had a hold of, and came up brandishing the weapon. His attention was split, and realizing an opportunity, I put the series of events I'd been visualizing into action.

Himari used the poncho in his hand as a weapon, snapping it around Risa's arm when she attacked and then yanking her forward and off-balance into a punch delivered by the same arm. At that same moment, I cracked my knuckle for one final burst of the energy it would provide and then took hold of the rebar with both hands and heaved the chunk of concrete into the air. I smashed it down onto the platform with all of my strength, and the remaining concrete crumbled away from the bar, freeing it completely.

Turning back to Himari, I saw that Risa had collapsed. Her face was covered in blood as she lay in the water collecting around her. He stood facing her and raised the katana to strike. I loaded one of my last two discs, releasing it as I ran at him. As I hoped, he turned away from her, knocked the cartridge away, and then braced himself to meet my wild rush.

My first swing had the momentum of my charge behind it, but instead of blocking it, Himari moved gracefully aside, turning the momentum against me. I had no choice but to follow through and was left unbalanced. He punched my side, sending a shock wave of pain up my ribcage. He followed up with an overhand strike from the katana, but I managed to throw the rebar up to block it at the last instant. I took another swing, which he effortlessly knocked aside. He kicked forward suddenly, catching me right in the gut. I fell to my knees, winded and gasping for air on the ground in front of him.

"I take no pleasure from ending your life, but you have given me little choice," he said, standing over me and raising his blade. "You should never have come here."

"You should never have let me get so close," I said as I snapped my wrist back to load the final cartridge into my hand then slapped it hard onto Himari's leg.

The disc immediately activated and released a wave of electricity into him. He fell to the ground, convulsing from the voltage. In a testament to his unnatural constitution, he didn't lose consciousness completely. He was stunned and unable to move his body but tracked me angrily with his eyes. I took his katana from him and used the light it emitted to search the area for my gun, which I found in a dark recess under the train car we'd fought next to. I took a spare magazine from the pouch on my belt, knocked out the bullet on top, and replaced it with the one I'd been given by The Blacksmith's apprentice. Then I emptied the bullet in the chamber of my pistol, loaded the weapon, and pulled the slide to reload the chamber while walking back to Himari, who remained stunned but conscious.

"I'm sorry for this," I said, standing over Himari. "But you, my friend, are extremely dangerous. I don't think we'll get you back to the ship without this." Then I kneeled, lifted his stolen poncho, pulled back his armor, and fired the hollow point round into his left shoulder.

Himari's eyes filled with pain and rage. I truly did feel shame for shooting a defenseless man, but with what he was capable of I couldn't rely on that last shock cartridge to keep him stunned throughout the entire trip back. The thin lines of visible energy running along his limbs went dark as the power terminated, and he collapsed completely. As I had hoped, based on the limited explanation I'd received, the bullet The Blacksmith's apprentice had given me was emitting a repeating electromagnetic pulse. It had completely shut down Himari's cybernetic limbs, which would effectively paralyze him until the bullet was removed or the energy within it was depleted.

"This stick in, and make space with no power," I repeated appreciatively, remembering the description I'd been given for the bullet. I went to check on Risa, who had come around and had rolled up onto her hands and knees.

"Are you okay?" I asked, kneeling beside her.

"I think so," she said while poking and prodding her facial

features to test for fractures. "Just a bloody nose."

"Can you walk?"

She nodded and began wiping her face with her shirt. Even covered in grime, I was struck by her beauty. It was her quiet strength that so impressed me, evident in the sharp and defiant edge she had honed herself to. I was certain it could cut through anything.

"We need to find Gray," I said with trepidation in my chest. We searched the immediate area but found nothing. Considering the scope of time that he'd been missing, I knew Himari hadn't had long to hide the body. I was struck by a sudden inspiration and climbed back up onto the train car, much to the consternation of my ribcage, which was still extremely sore from the blow I'd received. I backtracked along the train until I reached the place where Gray had disappeared initially and finally saw what I'd been looking for below me.

Gray had been dropped through a broken window on the side of the car and was tangled amid a set of passenger seats below. I kicked away the remaining glass, lowered myself into the car to check the body for a pulse, and let out a relieved sigh when I felt it thumping softly beneath my finger. His hair was damp and matted with dried blood on the right side, where it looked like Himari had struck him with something blunt. I shook him lightly and called his name. When that failed, I repeated the process, harder and louder, but he remained unresponsive.

I employed Risa's help to lift Gray up and out of the train car. His rifle was lying on the ground where he'd landed, so I collected it and passed that up to her as well. I felt weak and nauseous as the adrenaline drained from my system and had some difficulty climbing out myself. We rested him on his back and elevated his head slightly. I wasn't sure how much time we had before the EMP bullet stopped emitting charges into Himari, so despite my training, which suggested I should wait for Gray to wake on his own, I took more direct measures. I began gathering rainwater in my cupped hands then throwing it onto the side of his face, careful to avoid getting any up his nose. Between that, shaking him lightly, and calling his name, he eventually came to. His eyes fluttered open slowly, and he sat upright, confused.

"Gray," I said, thankful to see him regaining his faculties. "We did it, bud."

"What's going on?" he asked. He was groggy, and he probably had a concussion, but compared with the alternatives I'd been considering, I was grateful for his condition.

"We're heading back to the Zodiac now. We gotta get you a bandage and mend your head. You're wounded. Can you move?"

He needed a few more minutes to break free from the daze of returning to consciousness, which I was happy to allow. My body was completely depleted from having overused the adrenaline enhancement, and I welcomed the rest. Afterward, we carried Himari, thankful to discover his cybernetic limbs were extremely lightweight, and returned to the South Beach pier by traveling around to the north of the Night Market to avoid the unwanted attention we would get from lugging a body through it.

Gray agreed to let me pilot the vehicle on account of his head wound. Upon arriving at the boat, he retrieved a first-aid kit from the central compartment, which Risa used to tend to his injury. She cleaned and wrapped Himari's bullet wound as well, since it had been bleeding significantly. It felt good to leave the

Quiet Zone behind us and to be back on the open water. The storm had lessened somewhat, but even in the less volatile bay, the waves were still aggressive as we returned to the *Forge*.

Himari was leaned against the wall of the boat behind me. He was still completely immobile but was no longer stunned from the cartridge I'd hit him with and had regained the ability to speak. He raised his voice loud enough to be heard over the sound of the engine.

"You know he'll kill me when you bring me in. That means you are killing me."

I tried to ignore him. I felt justified in my actions. Like many of my contracts, he had made bad choices, and they had led him to the wrong side of a powerful man. It was something I ran into frequently in my profession. I'd rejected any job that had involved retrieving people who hadn't done anything wrong. Like I'd told The Blacksmith, I had no intention of being responsible for harm coming to an innocent. But he'd told me this man had refused to pay a debt he owed and attacked others, which was enough for me. The way I saw it, whatever happened to him back on the *Forge* was a result of the poor decisions he'd made.

"Are you so sure you know the truth?" he asked, as if reading my mind.

I didn't respond, but the seed had been planted, and the figurative wheels were turning in my mind. I began to wonder if I had been as thorough in getting the full story as I might have been if I hadn't been quite so desperate to get the procedure I was trading for. The more I thought about it, the more I realized I hadn't been given very specific information in this case. I tried not to ask, but guilt can be a heavy weight, and before long the question slipped out without my full consent.

"So what happened then?"

"What do you know about the organization? Let me guess. You need tech, and they can provide it," he croaked out a laugh, "and that's about it, am I right?"

"I know he takes on apprentices and teaches them what he knows. He said there are ranks or circles and his students benefit from advanced tech as they rise through them," I said, remembering what The Blacksmith had told me about Himari being a part of his inner circle.

"That's true," Himari agreed, "but do you know why they do it?"

I didn't, but I took a guess. "He said you are scientists and engineers. You do it to learn from someone as smart as he is. He's like a sensei."

"No," Himari said, shaking his head. "It's more than that. It's a religion. Everyone on that boat believes the next great evolution of humankind will come when we are fully merged with machines. We call it the Singularity."

I'd heard of this before. Singularitarianism had been around since before the turn of the century, but it had never gained much popularity outside of the societal groups that had the resources necessary to afford the kinds of enhancements it would take ever to approach that kind of an evolution. Besides which, neither the science nor the technology had evolved to a point where it was even possible, as far as I knew.

"I was one of his later apprentices, but I moved through the circles of knowledge and technique quickly until he agreed to bestow the ultimate honor upon me."

"The ultimate honor?"

"Yes," Himari said. "Integration."

I considered his response. "You're saying The Blacksmith has engineered the technology to merge a human mind with that of a computer."

"That's what I thought. That's what he told us."

"What do you mean?" I was genuinely curious now.

"The Anvil. I'm sure you've seen it, since he goes out of his way to show it off. It is the most advanced artificial intelligence human beings have managed to produce thus far. He told us those who made it to the final circle would have the honor of integrating our consciousness with that of the AI — that we would undergo a procedure in which we would be allowed to host it within our bodies. But that was a lie."

I said nothing, silently prompting Himari to continue explaining.

"It was just two days before the ceremony in which I would evolve. There was an incident on the *Forge* — an electrical fire. I came to let him know and happened to interrupt him while he was performing a simulation of the procedure. When he left to deal with it, I lingered behind, curious about the results. The simulation finished, and I discovered his lie."

"So it wouldn't work?"

"No. The integration would be successful. But over time, the Anvil would become more and more dominant as it replicated and infiltrated my neural pathways. The results showed that the machine intelligence would view my consciousness as competition and ultimately gain full control over my body and behavior, slowly taking control until finally there would be nothing left of me at all."

Fuck. It was a selfish thought. My preconceived justifications were on the run, but Himari was shining a spotlight on them, preventing them from escaping back into the shadows of ignorance, where this worked out for everyone but him.

"I confronted him. I asked him about the results and how they showed the integration failing over time. He told me I was mistaken and that I hadn't understood the data, but that was just another lie. I know what I saw. When I threatened to expose him, he told the others I was a coward and that I had changed my mind about going through with the integration ceremony. He told them I was going to run away with all of the enhancements he had given me, without paying my debt to the group. I knew I had to leave, and I did not want to have to hurt my colleagues, but several of them tried to stop me on my way out. I was forced to incapacitate them in order to escape, but no one died. I had hoped it would serve as enough of a warning for him to let me go, but here we are."

Himari had certainly had opportunities to kill each of us during our encounter. In Gray's case, he had gone out of his way to leave him alive. I needed this kill switch procedure, but there was no way I could justify delivering an innocent man to his execution on account of protecting myself.

"So he'll force you into this when we're back on the ship?" I asked.

"No," he replied. "The procedure needs to be consensual. Every test we've run indicates that the mind is too capable of resisting the initial integration. The process won't work unless the patient willingly allows the merge. At this point, he just wants to eliminate the threat I pose. The information I have could decimate the organization if the other apprentices believed the work they were putting toward attaining integration would only serve to expedite the eventual annihilation of their own consciousness."

"And now I know as well," I said.

Himari nodded. "Yes, and I would be very careful if I were you."

We were approaching the GPS coordinates of the *Forge*, so I wasn't surprised when the red spotlight once again came on to guide us toward the vessel.

I waved Risa up to the front of the boat, and she came up beside me.

"How are you holding up?" I asked.

"My nose hurts. I'll live."

I smiled. "Listen, I can talk to The Blacksmith about getting one of these installed for you as well. I know you aren't on Ben's list, but what if you're targeted for helping me?"

"A kill switch?"

"I know it's crazy. I'm nervous about this too. But if whatever happened to the others happens to you..." I looked into her eyes.

She looked away, ashamed. I knew what she was thinking.

"Risa. What happened with Wendell wasn't your fault. He might have been in there somewhere, but it wasn't him who attacked you. When he looked at me in the ring at Ares, I swear I saw terror behind his eyes. For a moment, it was like he was trapped inside himself. It was like someone else was controlling him. If we could shut ourselves down somehow, we might be able to avoid something like that happening again. I know it's not much, but it's the best plan I've got right now."

I could see her weighing her horror at the possibility of assaulting a loved one against the vulnerabilities born from having a hidden key to her consciousness installed.

"Just think about it, all right? I'd feel a lot better if I knew there was an alternative to shooting you in the face if you happen to try to kill me."

She laughed. "In the face? If it comes to that, shoot me in the heart. It would break anyhow if my beautiful face took any more punishment."

I cringed. "You may want to find a mirror if you think your face is beautiful right now. Maybe under all that dried blood that's caked on it. Listen, you don't need to do anything you don't feel good about. We'll figure this out either way. I just wanted you to know you had the option."

She smiled then put a hand on my shoulder and squeezed. "I appreciate the offer. But I'm not as comfortable as you are with people playing around with things up here." She tapped on her head. "We'll just have to find whoever's doing this before they get to me. Is that okay?"

I returned the smile. "Of course. Yeah, of course it is."

Our gazes stayed locked for longer than I felt comfortable with, and I looked away awkwardly.

Turning back to Gray, I yelled, "Things might go a little sideways this time. Are you up for coming on board with us?"

He looked tired but nodded amiably. "Let's see this thing through to the end, boss, so I can get home. I'm out of smokes."

Before we arrived, I slowed the boat and huddled up with Risa and Gray to pass along the information I'd gathered from Himari and discuss what I intended to do about it. They both expressed concerns, which I shared, but when neither could offer a better alternative, they agreed to back me on the play.

The spotlight directed us to pull up on the starboard side of the ship, close to the bow. A ladder was dropped, and Risa and I boarded while Gray stayed in the boat to assist with Himari. We were met by the same two apprentices in white who had originally greeted us. They bowed respectfully.

The woman threw a harness down to Gray. Following the rope attached to it with my gaze, I saw that it connected to a large winch nearby. Gray secured the harness to Himari, and once the winch was activated, he was pulled up to the railing, where we lifted him onto the deck. Two men wearing an outfit similar to that of the other apprentices, but black, came and took hold of him. As they began dragging him away, he turned his head and met my gaze, a last look to remind me that his fate was as much my responsibility as those to whom we'd turned him in.

"Where are they taking him?" I asked.

The man in white said, "To the brig, where he'll await punishment for his betrayal."

Satisfied he wouldn't be executed immediately, I waited for Gray to finish climbing the ladder and board, at which point we allowed the apprentices to guide us onto the bridge, where The Blacksmith was waiting for us in his glowing chair. I prepared myself for a difficult and potentially violent conversation and shared a glance with both Risa and Gray, searching for encouragement, but saw only trepidation in their eyes.

The bridge matched the rest of the vessel in appearance and

style. It was sleek, sporting modern lines and dim white perimeter lighting, and was filled with instruments that were illuminated by the blue glow of holographic data. There were several apprentices there as well, working at the consoles or standing at the ready with their heads forward and their arms folded behind their back.

"Jacobi-san," said The Blacksmith, "You have met my expectations and surpassed them."

"You've got a well-greased machine here," I said, looking around appreciatively. "But at the risk of dampening your opinion of me, I'm afraid I might have to throw a wrench in it."

The Blacksmith frowned and prompted me to continue with a raised eyebrow.

"I think you'll want some privacy for this conversation," I suggested.

He looked at me suspiciously but must have ultimately decided it would be in his best interest, because after a moment he clapped his hands and snapped, "*Hottoite!*" This prompted the apprentices to drop what they were doing and quickly exit the bridge. The entire exodus took less than fifteen seconds, and just like that, we were alone.

"So, tell me what troubles you," he said.

"I told you before, I'm not a killer. You sent me to retrieve an innocent man."

"Oh? What lies did he tell you?"

"One thing you do learn quickly in my business," I said, looking directly into his eyes, "is when you're being lied to. I gave Himari the chance to describe his side of the coin, and I didn't get that impression. I'll give you the same opportunity now. Tell me about how the integration fails over time?"

"Give *me* an opportunity, Mr. Slate?" he said, his voice rising. "It was you who came here looking for my assistance. This was the cost I demanded and that you agreed to."

"I agreed to retrieve a man who owed you a debt and who had harmed members of your organization. I retrieved a man who was deceived, who nearly had his consciousness overwritten, and who defended himself while trying to escape."

"If you do not wish to move forward with our arrangement, you are welcome to leave now."

"My concern," I continued, pointing to Risa and Gray, "is that now we know your secret. And what's stopping you from treating us the same way to prevent the knowledge from spreading?"

"First," he practically spat, "you know nothing. I have no secret! The results Himari saw were accurate, but I am developing a way to resolve the partitioning issue. Even if he had lost himself for a short time, I am certain I would have eventually been able to bring him back online. But I need to work with the actual mind and body. I can't complete the work in a simulation! Second, your word will suffice. If you agree not to speak of this, I will accept that and let the matter drop, provided none of you return here and you stay out of contact with my people."

"Would Himari's word not be sufficient as well?"

"No. Himari must be punished for attempting to abandon us."

"I know the eyes of a killer. You are a driven man, I can see that. You want to protect your operation. But you aren't a murderer, and I don't believe you truly want to see one of your protégés dead. There is another way."

"Himari betrayed us!" The Blacksmith yelled, finally losing his composure. The fire was burning brightly in his eyes now.

"No," I said. Cold iron and my frustration at being deceived were creeping into my tone. "You betrayed him. You lied to him, and he caught you in that lie. But even then, he kept it to himself. He could have told everyone on this ship, but he came directly to you and gave you a chance to explain. But rather than telling him the truth, you lied to him and called him paranoid. And now his faith in you is gone, and all he wants is to be done with you."

"He...I..." I saw the flames burning out, extinguished as he acknowledged the truth behind my harsh words. He sank lower in his chair, deflated, and muttered, "What do you suggest?"

"Exile," I said immediately. "You part ways and never look back. It's true you have given him a great deal of your time and technology, but you also threatened his very existence. I'd say that makes you even. And if it's true you'll soon have a way to integrate a human consciousness with that of a machine without it taking over, then I'd suggest you try being more honest with the next apprentice you work with. I think you'll find their faith in you is stronger than you give them credit for."

"And what of our arrangement, Mr. Slate?" he asked, beginning to regain his composure.

"Nothing changes. You complete this procedure for me, then we leave. And you have our word that this stays between us."

The Blacksmith folded his hands on his lap and closed his eyes, considering. "And what if Himari does not live up to this agreement? What if he seeks revenge?"

"I haven't known him long," I said, "but he seems like the kind of man that keeps his promises. Do you think he'd shame himself by going back on his word?"

"No. I don't," he said, hanging his head. "He is…a good man."

I stayed silent to let him consider all the variables until eventually he lifted his head and nodded.

"But if he does, that stain will be upon your honor. And it will be on you to clean up the mess you have made. Are we in agreement on this?"

If Himari ever broke his word, then he wasn't the man I thought I was fighting for here. I didn't believe that would be the case, and I was willing to gamble on it.

"Agreed."

"Very well, Jacobi-san. I also agree to these revised terms. Himari will swear an oath of silence and vow never to return here. For that, he will have his life and his freedom. You will have your kill switch, on your word of honor that the information goes no further."

I bowed low.

"And as for your concern regarding the safety of my other apprentices…I am an old man," he said, sighing. "If I don't find a way to resolve the issue Himari became aware of, then I will not be able to integrate myself. Therefore, you must believe me when I tell you I will do everything in my power to do so."

"Tell that to your lab rats," I said. "Religion is a funny thing. They'll probably be willing to sacrifice for the greater good and all that."

"Lab rats," he scoffed. "If I believed that, then Himari would not be spared. They are...important to me." He looked up, wearing a distant, sad expression.

Meeting his eyes, I believed him and saw that Himari would be missed.

I was taken to the brig to convince the rōnin to agree to the proposed terms. The only access to the room acting as his cell was through a thick steel door locked by several cylinders bolted into the wall, which needed to be individually released before I could enter. Once it opened, I saw that he'd been discarded on the ground in the small, brightly lit room. His face was on the ground when I came in, but he turned his head to look in my direction.

"I'm sorry for this," I said, saddened by the way he'd been treated.

"The last time you said that, you shot me."

I chuckled. "Not my finest moment."

He grunted.

"I'm here to talk about a deal."

I proposed the solution I'd discussed with The Blacksmith. It didn't take much to get Himari to agree. He'd already tried to impose an exile upon himself, and the alternatives here weren't particularly appealing. Once he'd agreed to take the vow, The Blacksmith entered the room. The distrust and tension between the two was palpable, but Himari grunted the words out, and the old man rolled away, satisfied.

With that resolved, we carried Himari to an operating table in the area of the hull where we'd originally met The Blacksmith. The dark sphere of the Anvil's central processing unit stood silently by while several apprentices removed the bullet in Himari's shoulder and twisted it to deactivate the thin EMP field it had been emitting. The power returned to his limbs, and he didn't immediately strangle anyone, which I took as a positive indication I'd made the right decision in trusting him. They patched up the hole when they were done.

For me, the operation was a bit longer and more involved. Much to my dismay, I was directed to sit down on the metal chair with the sharp objects surrounding it that had caused me anxiety when I'd seen it for the first time earlier that night. Fortunately, it was more comfortable than I'd expected, and after I'd been strapped in and injected with an anesthetic, I slipped into oblivion.

Though it was invasive and complex, the technology and experience The Blacksmith and his apprentices commanded enabled the surgery to take place quickly and without issue. True to his word, the procedure was completed within hours. I woke with nothing more than a bandage on the back of my neck and a slight sore spot. While I'd been under, he'd also seen to it that the wounds of my comrades were properly tended.

Light was starting to appear in the eastern sky as Risa, Himari, and I regrouped on the deck. After getting his head wound looked at, Gray had chosen to return to the Zodiac below and get some sleep rather than watching me undergo the surgery.

"Jacobi?" asked Himari. "I heard you called this earlier."

I nodded and extended my hand, which he clasped.

"I owe you a great debt," he said with sincerity.

"I'm only trying to repair the damage I caused here. There is no debt owed, Himari."

"We have a difference in perspective, but I will honor yours, if that is your wish."

"Where will you go?" I asked, suddenly realizing he would be leaving behind everything he'd known for years.

"Into the city, for now," he answered. "I was an engineer, before…this. I have resources and enough money to survive comfortably for a while."

Again, I nodded, glad to hear he wouldn't be returning to the Quiet Zone.

"Can we offer you a ride back to shore?" Risa asked.

He breathed a sigh of relief. "Yes, please. I was beginning to think I might have to swim."

I started to laugh then stopped when I realized from his expression that he'd been serious.

The Blacksmith, accompanied by several apprentices wearing cloaks of varied colors, rolled out onto the deck of the *Forge* and came to a stop when he neared our congregation. Himari looked away, refusing to meet his eye, and then left to board the Zodiac.

"Our voyage together ends here. I have…learned much from your visit. I've sent you an application that can be utilized to alter the passphrase for triggering the kill switch I installed. You will also be able to determine whether or not it is active or disabled there."

"Thank you," I said.

"Remember our agreement," he said with a stern look of warning. "Farewell."

We exchanged bows with his entourage before finding our way back to our vessel, where Himari had woken Gray, and they were both preparing for departure. We were silent as the craft pulled away, each appreciating the sunrise and our relatively intact condition in light of the night we'd shared.

As we raced the waves home, the physical stress of everything we'd experienced began to break through the barriers I'd erected to try to ignore it. Despite the pain and exhaustion, I was overwhelmed by a feeling of gratitude for having been blessed with such skilled and devoted companions. Risa looked up and caught me staring at her, and this time neither of us looked away. We were in this together now and would see it through to the end. It had been a long time since I'd felt that level of camaraderie, and longer still since I'd felt the other, less familiar emotions that were welling up as our eyes made contact.

I didn't know what the next step was, but I felt a strong sense of relief in knowing I now had a way to shut myself down to avoid harming anyone I loved, if it became necessary. While the nature of the threat still wasn't clear, and I wasn't convinced it would even be an effective solution, it was nonetheless a light in the darkness that provided some small hope against the defenselessness I'd been feeling. We could only wait now and hope it was enough.

Chapter 6

We said goodbye to Himari at the pier downtown. He had told us where to find him, given us a way to contact him if he could be of service in any way, and then bowed to each of us before departing. Without his cloak and armor, which he'd removed and now carried folded in his arms, he looked less the superhuman out of a comic book that had nearly singlehandedly defeated three highly trained special operatives. He'd even thrown on some respectable clothing that he'd taken from the *Forge*, which covered his metal limbs and almost allowed him to blend in with the early rising pedestrians of the wharf. If it weren't for the fluidity and grace with which he carried himself, or the way in which he subtly moved his head to observe and understand every detail of his surroundings, he might have passed as just another Japanese businessman on his way back to the hotel.

As for Gray, he was grateful to us for including him in our escapade. After docking the boat back at Boatopia, he wished us well and told me he was glad I'd come to him. From our limited conversation on the ride back, I gathered he'd been late on his mortgage to the point of nearly losing his shop. On top of that, his wife had recently left him, which accounted for the general lack of hygiene and the excessive drinking. It also explained why he'd turned what had once been his workshop into his living space when he'd been kicked out of their shared home.

He called our visit a "multifaceted gemstone, sparkling in the shit." Between the credits that would allow him to keep his shop, how the excitement of the entire affair seemed to have breathed some life back into him, and the fact that he'd gotten bashed on the side of the head by a cybernetic samurai, I sympathized with his description.

On the drive back from Sausalito to the city, I thought about the extreme divide between those of us who lived in the lofty towers I could see in the distance and the residents of the Quiet Zone, for whom danger and the fight for survival were a daily reality. I didn't know if I'd have the kind of strength it must take to live each day not knowing where your next meal was going to come from or if you'd be attacked in your sleep. Frequently, I imposed judgment on those in less fortunate situations, presuming that if they had made better choices, they could have avoided their dire consequences. But after what had happened with Himari, I felt less certain that our presumptions about the lives of others could be trusted with any degree of accuracy. I couldn't change their fates or the cruel ways in which the world often handed us each our lot in life, but I could appreciate the difficulty they must face and at the very least respect them for their ability to press on through the adversity. The strong kept marching where the weak collapsed, regardless of their address.

The tension that had been building between Risa and me finally exploded when we arrived back at my apartment. We'd spoken very little on the drive home, but each time one of us caught the other quietly watching, something meaningful had been communicated and understood. The moment I'd closed the door behind me, I was thrown against the wall as she wrapped her arms around me and locked her mouth on mine. I'd like to call what happened there that morning making love, but it was more furious, more primal. It was the wild desperation of animalistic beings, high on the ecstatic rush of touching death

156

and clinging savagely to life to bring the balance back. It was a sudden release of pain from recent losses that we'd pushed aside out of a need to continue functioning efficiently. It was a scream of denial that the fear we'd been fighting to keep at bay would not succeed in keeping us from feeling fully alive.

With that shared understanding vibrating through our bodies like electricity, we became interwoven in an intense carnal celebration of our metaphysical elevation. It was not making love. It was a rebellion against the fragility of our mortality. It was a futile but defiant rejection of an awareness born from proximity to our own demise, that we were but momentary creatures, temporarily cognizant of our own sentience, and tomorrow was uncertain. And so we lost ourselves in the ephemeral absolutes of the shared pleasures that our corporeal shells could offer one another that morning, and it felt familiar and right. When it was over, we collapsed, drained and exhausted, and did not wake for the rest of the day or most of the night that followed.

When we finally began to stir, it was still dark. We lay awake with one another, naked and sprawled across my bed, until the reflections on the windows from the lights of the glowing advertisements on the buildings around us were lost to the light of the rising sun. I stretched excessively and groaned then slipped out of bed to shower. The cleansing ritual was deeply satisfying, made even more so when Risa's body pressed against mine from behind. It felt so familiar that I turned with a confused look, which she took as a sign I had wanted to be alone and began to apologize. I grabbed her and brought her lips to mine, allaying her fears that she was at all unwelcome.

Pulling away, I said, "It's just that you feel so familiar. I feel like I've been here with you before."

She lowered her eyes.

"What is it?"

"It's nothing. It's…" she said. Her voice was soft and distant. "It's just ridiculous."

"Yeah, I know. Sorry."

She shook her head and smiled. "Got any more of that granola? I'm starving."

When she mentioned food, an alarm went off in my stomach, and I realized I hadn't eaten in about a day and a half. We finished bathing, and I went about the process of preparing a meal to match our voracious appetites. After we'd eaten, I started cleaning the kitchen but was interrupted by Ava's voice informing me that I was being contacted by Sam Winston.

Risa took over the cleaning as I walked to the next room and threw the call up on my wall monitor.

"Good morning, Sam. How can I help you?"

"Good morning, Mr. Slate. I'm calling to give you the information I was able to find regarding the associate you'd asked about. Do you have a few minutes?"

"Absolutely," I said then sat down on the end of my bed. "What do you have for me?"

"Well, like you said, Mason Robbins died about three years ago."

"Right. Any idea how it happened?"

"There was a fire. We don't have a lot of information, but based on the records we have here at the DFDC, his wife died that night as well. It happened in a small town west of Boulder,

Colorado, on some land owned by his father, a man named Richard Robbins."

"You said this happened three years ago?"

That was a long time ago for this to be connected to current events.

"That's correct."

"Is the father still alive?"

"He is. Runs some sort of private military company by the name of Phoenix Coalition. They've been active down in Colombia on and off over the last several years. I'll send you what I have."

"Please, and thank you for looking into this for me. I really appreciate it."

"In return, perhaps you'll keep me informed of any new developments in your case. I'd like to know if you discover that there's anything tangible in the admiral's claim that someone else is involved in this."

"I can do that. If I get anything solid, you'll be the first to know. Thanks again, Sam."

"Ah, Mr. Slate. Before you go...Wendell Hamilton was recently discovered deceased in an augmented reality theater in the Mission district. You wouldn't happen to know anything about that, would you?"

"No," I lied, "I'm afraid not."

"Of course not," he said. "I just figured I would ask, since he was a part of your unit, and the DFDC logged a phone conversation between you and him on the same day of his death."

"Right," I said. "I talked to him the other night. We were going to get together to discuss the admiral's circumstances. He never showed. I guess now I know why."

"Indeed. However, since it seems members of your old unit are experiencing tragedies at an alarming rate. I would be particularly cautious moving forward."

"Yeah, sure. I'll keep my eyes open. Thanks."

"Take care, Mr. Slate."

I ended the call and sighed. So the Division had more of an interest in this than I'd realized. I had an uncomfortable suspicion I might still be working for them, minus the paycheck. That they were aware of the recent deaths of their former agents shouldn't have surprised me, but I hadn't even considered they might have a stake in the game. It didn't matter. I was doing this for Ben, and if they ended up benefitting from my discoveries, I didn't have a problem with that. If we came out the other end of this thing with an explanation that somehow vindicated the admiral, legal assistance from the DFDC could even be vital in helping clear his name.

My CUBE vibrated when Sam sent me the information he had on both Mason and his father. I reached out to Richard Robbins immediately, but the connection was refused. Giving up, I wandered back into the kitchen.

"You're right. Mason Robbins is deceased," I told Risa. "He and his wife died in a fire a few years ago."

She looked up from her computer with a frown. "So we're at a dead end?"

"I reached out to Richard Robbins, his father. I'm hoping he might be able to give me more information on the circumstances leading up to it. He rejected the call, though."

"That's pretty thin."

I nodded. "I'm open to suggestions."

"I wish I had one for you."

"I'd rather be doing something than sitting around waiting for this asshole to make a move. How would you feel about flying to Colorado?"

"What's in Colorado?" Risa asked with a dubious expression.

"The father, according to the information I just got from my contact at the Division. I'm thinking this might be the kind of conversation it's better to have in person and that maybe we could get a better picture of exactly what happened there if we're onsite."

"So we fly there just to talk to him and see where it happened? I don't understand. Do you really think that's necessary?"

It was difficult to put the anxiety I was feeling into words. Risa was making sense, as usual, but I was having a hard time with the idea of just sitting and waiting, or even worse, hiding, and that was what I felt I'd be doing if we stayed in San Francisco.

"Wendell gave me that photograph for a reason. Whatever's going on here, I have to believe it has something to do with Mason. Why else would he go through so much trouble? Those cuts Wendell landed on me that night — they weren't just missed shots. He easily could have killed me."

"If you think it's our best move, then let's go," she said.

"Thanks," I said, appreciative of her flexibility. "I just...want to keep moving right now."

"You're buying the tickets."

Risa booked us a flight from San Francisco to Denver for later that afternoon, and I paid. It was a paltry sum to part with for the comfort of having her along. We packed our things and set out for the airport.

The streets were filling with water. It had been raining for almost four days without much respite. Between that and the storm surge wracking the coast, the city was beginning to strain under the impact. Cars were moving sluggishly along flooded roads and trying to avoid city crews that were desperately scrambling to reroute the overflow. Pedestrians were practically wading as they traversed the sidewalks and street crossings, which were completely lost under water that came up to people's calves in some cases. It never ceased to amaze me how humans would do anything to try to normalize extenuating circumstances to perpetuate the regularity of their daily routines. As I watched them struggle, I wondered if some pending catastrophe drove each of *them* out to face the developing chaos rather than staying safe at home, or if I was the only one with a story so complex and bizarre.

After arriving at SFO, we checked our luggage and declared our weapons then boarded a small, solar-powered aircraft with about fifteen other passengers. The engines kicked on. Soon, the plane rose from the ground and shot into motion. We were jostled by the high winds as we rose through a pocket of turbulence and the lightweight aircraft shook violently.

"You think these things fly all right without sunlight?" I asked, looking around nervously.

"Hydrogen reserves," she answered. "We'll be fine. The solar power assists in the process of creating the hydrogen for the fuel cell, but they have alternative ways of charging it. How else would they fly at night?"

"I never really thought about it much until I felt like I was about to crash in one."

"The great Jacobi Slate, afraid of flying!" she exclaimed, clearly amused. "We've taken hundreds of flights together. How could I never have noticed?"

"I'm not afraid, exactly. I just don't like situations I'm not fully in control of," I answered. "If I'm going to die, I want it to be of old age or because I fucked up, not somebody else."

"I can appreciate that. Though technically, it would be your fuck-up for having gotten on the plane, so it could still meet your criteria," she said, smiling playfully. "Me, though, I could live up here in the clouds. So quiet, and calm. It feels safe."

Before long, we'd left the storm-besieged city behind us and were comfortably coasting. The flight lasted for about an hour, and Risa and I used the time to catch up on the last several years. She'd been working as a freelance intrusion countermeasure specialist in the corporate sector. She'd stayed single, since she focused on her work to the point of obsession and didn't have the additional bandwidth or attention span it took to keep a committed relationship healthy. She owned a home that overlooked the coast in Oregon but was rarely there since she was almost always traveling for work.

I filled in my own blank spots. I told her about how difficult the transition away from operative work had been. I spoke about my relationship with Ben and how it had taken a turn when I'd started taking money for retrieval contracts. I wanted to tell her how alone I'd felt without the unit and how I often felt lost without the sense of purpose the job had given me, but I didn't want to darken the conversation any further. It felt good to pretend at normalcy for a time and to have the type of conversation two moderately normal adults might have.

Once we landed, it felt like we'd entered another world. The skies above Denver were clear, and the sun was shining brightly. The oppressive weather and constant violence we'd been experiencing in San Francisco felt distant and removed, as if a weight had lifted. Outside, Risa smiled and turned in a circle with her arms outstretched, fully embracing the contrast. Watching her, I was nearly able to forget the danger we were in.

Before leaving the airport, we retrieved our weapons and luggage. Since we weren't sure what types of roads we'd encounter on the way to Mason's father's residence in the mountains, we rented a large gray truck with four-wheel drive. We drove north for a time, took a short detour into Boulder, where we stopped for food and water, then headed west into the foothills of the Rocky Mountains. On the way, I tried contacting Richard Robbins once more, but again there was no response.

Our destination was a set of coordinates northeast of the Rainbow Lakes, high on the side of the range at an elevation of about ten thousand feet. The mountain was steep, but we wound our way along the deep forest roads without incident until we arrived at the unnamed but well-maintained dirt road we believed would lead us to the property. After about a quarter of a mile, we reached a large, closed gate that blocked further progress.

I turned off the vehicle and got out to find out if the gate was locked. As I approached, I was taken completely off-guard when several men appeared from behind the trees around me. They wore black and green uniforms and were armed with rifles. A man around my own age with a neatly trimmed graying beard stepped forward and spoke gruffly.

"Raise your hands, both of you. You," he said, pointing his gun at Risa, "exit the vehicle, slowly."

We both did as he asked. "I'm here to see Richard Robbins," I said. "I came to talk to him about his son, Mason."

Two men, both younger than the one who'd spoken first, came forward and patted us down, looking for weapons. They located and confiscated our pistols, then motioned for us to move down the road, beyond the gate. There were four of them in total. I was surprised by the speed and skill with which they had executed the ambush, which had been elegant in its efficiency. I made a mental note that whoever had trained these men was almost certainly dangerous and wondered if it had been Richard Robbins himself. I'd been told he ran a private military company, but I hadn't realized they'd be here on the land with him, so far from civilization.

The man with the gray in his beard took out a hand radio and stepped away from us to speak in private. Afterward, he returned to the head of the column and began leading us down the road. We trod down it for at least a mile before the heavy forest around us began to thin and opened up into a large field. There were several structures arranged in a semicircle at the edge of the tree line on the far side of the field, and we were headed in their direction. As we approached, the structures became more defined, and I realized they were dwellings. The main road ended in a roundabout in front of them, but two smaller roads departed from it and fell downhill to either side, just before the rotary.

They circled around like arms behind the houses to a group of even larger buildings that could have been barns or warehouses.

The smell of animals and fresh earth was growing more pungent. In the enormous field surrounding us, there were dozens of raised bed gardens. There were wire mesh coops, cattle grazing, and goats that wandered aimlessly. Men and women were sparsely congregated about the land, laboring at tasks like gardening and cutting wood. We even passed a woman who was defeathering hanging poultry. In a dirt lot at the distant southern edge of the field, I saw a line of parked machinery that included dozers, loaders, and a few power shovels.

The houses we passed had been constructed with identical layouts and materials. There were slight variances, but they appeared to each have a cement foundation, aluminum walls, and shingled roofs that were angled slightly toward the back. The design looked comfortable and efficient. There were about fifteen homes in total, which could easily have each housed three or four residents each. At first I assumed it was a barracks of some sort, but we passed several children playing in the field. They were quickly rounded up and ushered inside by women wearing expressions of concern. Down the hill, outside one of the large buildings behind the houses, there were several parked trucks. The doors to the barn-like structures were all closed.

In the center of the semicircle, one building stood out from the others. It was painted more elaborately: red walls with yellow trim, and nearly twice as large at two stories. We came to a stop in front of that house, and the man with the gray beard relayed the message that we'd arrived over his radio. We waited in awkward silence until the front door opened and a grizzled man who looked as if he'd spent half his life in the sun stepped outside. His white hair was shaved on the back and sides but blended longer on the top. He wore a short-sleeved black and green outfit and had a pair of dark shades over his eyes. He looked older but was in such good physical condition that it was difficult to assign a precise age.

He approached with a grimace smeared across his face. Then in a low, gravelly voice that sounded like it had been dragged through tar he asked, "Who are you?"

I cleared my throat, which had become extremely dry. This had not been the situation I'd anticipated when I'd decided to drop in for a surprise visit. I felt unprepared.

"Mr. Richard Robbins?" I asked. He didn't respond. He just continued to stare at me, expecting an answer to his question.

"My name is Jacobi Slate. This is Therisa Corbin. We served with your son, Mason Robbins. I came here hoping to talk to you about Mason."

"What about him? He passed away some time ago."

"Yeah, I found out about that only recently. I'm sorry. I was hoping we might be able to discuss the circumstances leading up to his death and to get your opinion on some things that have recently transpired in regard to our unit."

"Slate," he said. "Yeah, I know that name. He talked about you a whole lot."

It wasn't clear whether that worked to our benefit or not, so I chose to simply nod. He waved his hand in a dismissive motion, and the four men who'd escorted us from the gate saluted then departed in the direction we'd come from.

"Walk with me," said Robbins. He put his hands behind his back and began to stroll after them. Risa and I fell in on either side.

"So you served with Mason. You were his captain, isn't that right?"

"Yes, sir, that's right."

"Terrible thing what happened to my boy," he continued, "and Rose."

"Rose. Was that his wife?" Risa asked.

His forehead crinkled, and his eyes turned down at the edges. He looked away, frowning, as if the memory irritated him, but nodded. "These," he said, indicating the semicircle of homes around the rotary, "all got built in the last few years. Mason's house was one of the original structures on the land when we bought it almost…" he paused as he assessed the duration, "almost twenty-five years ago now. It was right over there." He pointed out into the field, but I didn't see any discernible structure or foundation there.

"That's all gone now," he said. "We cleared the burnt remains of that place away, foundation and everything. The field's grown back over it, which is just as well, because I didn't want that memory staring me in the face every time I walked outside."

"I can understand that. And I'm sorry we're here to dredge those memories up now, but I wasn't sure who else to turn to for information."

Richard turned and directed a brief, inquisitive stare at me. "Exactly what information do you think I can give you?"

We walked as I explained the events of the last several days, hoping he might have some insight into why the photograph of his son was given to me in the fashion it was. He led us off the central driveway and down toward the larger buildings behind the houses as I relayed the story. I told him about the admiral and about the list I'd discovered. I spoke of Wendell and his brother, which led to an explanation of how the photograph of his son had ended up in my possession. I thought being fully transparent could contribute to whatever chance Richard Robbins might have at understanding Mason's involvement.

Outside the barn-like structures I'd seen from the road above, Richard stopped walking and busied himself with organizing some tools that had been left on the ground. As I finished the story, he looked up, shaking his head.

"Like I told you, Slate, my son is dead, going on three years now. Some whack job gives you a photograph, and you think he must be involved in all of this somehow?"

"I just hoped that maybe you might know about something going on in Mason's life from before he passed that might have tied him to anything I've described. I know it's a long shot, but like I said earlier, I really just wasn't sure where else to turn for information at this point."

"Well, the truth is," said Richard, "my son never liked you much. In fact, he often blamed you for what happened. Me, I don't care personally. People aren't generally worth a lick of salt, so I say put them down when they need to be put down. It won't matter much soon anyhow."

"I'm sorry, I'm not following," I said. "Blamed *me* for what happened?"

"Slate, do you know what we do here?" he asked. It was an abrupt change of subject, and I couldn't help wonder if it had been intentionally done to avoid my question. "Do you know what this," he said, indicating the houses and the land around him with a wave of his arms, "is all about?"

169

"I was told you're in charge of a private outfit. From what I understand you've been working mainly out of Colombia. You all live here together?"

"That's part of it," he agreed. "But that's just what we do to finance our operation."

"Operation?" asked Risa.

Richard walked over and slid the doors open on the structure then threw a light switch on a nearby wall. Track lighting on the ceiling came to life, illuminating the barn. Inside, there were rows upon rows of shelving, stocked to the brim with just about everything imaginable. Canned foods, filters, medical supplies, blankets, and hundreds of other items lined the shelves.

"Preppers," I said under my breath.

"Survival, Slate," said Robbins. "This here is the overstocked nonperishables, and next door we…"

He was interrupted by the radio at his belt, which came alive with a beep, followed by static.

Richard walked out of the barn then held the radio up and said, "Go ahead."

There was a response, but he was too far away for me to make it out. On the far side of the field, I could see black smoke beginning to billow up from the edge of the tree line.

"Goddammit," he growled then waved down a man who was walking along the driveway up the hill from us. The man had been working out in the field and was covered in dirt and sweat. He wiped his face with the shirt he held in his hand as he approached and extended his other hand, which I shook. He had kind eyes, a friendly smile, and short, black, curly hair matted with the sweat and grime of hard work.

"This here's Jack. Jack, I'd like you to take Jacobi and Therisa here on a tour of our facilities. They came all this way to visit us at our private retreat; least we can do is show them what we do here. I need to take care of something. When you're done, bring them up to me at the house."

Jack bobbed his head. "Sure thing."

Richard turned to me and gave me another scrutinizing stare. He seemed frustrated and torn. I ascribed the cause of his agitation to the sudden appearance of unannounced guests on his private land and to the quickly spreading brush fire in the distance.

"We can finish our talk about Mason once I've taken care of this. Maybe I might have something that could help you out, so you come right up once Jack's through showing you around, all right?" Then he turned and started stomping up the hill without waiting for a response. Robbins was clearly used to getting his way.

I turned back to Jack and said, "Look, it's really okay. We don't need a tour. We'll just wait here for him to do whatever he needs to and get back."

Jack shook his head while putting his shirt on. "Sorry, sir, but I have my orders. If I don't show you around the place, he'll take it out on my hide." He let out a nervous laugh. "Come on, this way."

We followed as Jack led us to the next closest barn and slid the doors open. Inside, work benches were placed at even intervals and overflowing with what I recognized to be the tools for making ammunition. Gunpowder, brass casings, reloaders, lube pads, primers, and machines for casting lead were prevalent at every station. On the walls of the barn were hanging guns of every type imaginable, covering them to the point that you could barely see the wood behind.

"Well, as you can see, in here we keep the weapons we aren't using. We regularly make ammunition here at these stations and—"

"So this is about the end of the world?" Risa interrupted.

"No, I wouldn't say that," said Jack. "I'd say it's more about an end to the way of life most people have gotten comfortable with. We don't trust that the people in charge are going to stop fucking up any time soon, and when they do…"

"When that happens, and the world turns upside down, you'll be prepared. Up here in the mountains," said Risa.

"Something like that," Jack agreed. "Follow me. I'll show you the best part."

We followed him out of the barn, but instead of leading us to the next building in the line, he took us farther from the houses toward the southern tree line. When we reached the top of a low knoll, several cement circles became visible along the base of the other side. There were at least five, and they were spaced out at a distance of about a hundred feet. We walked down the hill toward the closest one. I estimated it was about fifteen feet in diameter, with a square hatch in the center. Jack bent down and opened the hatch, revealing a ladder leading down a tube into darkness.

He grabbed the rungs and started heading down. As he did, lights on the walls of the silo that had been dug into the earth lit up, activated by the motion of his descent. I gave Risa my best sarcastically enthusiastic smile.

"Down we go!" I said.

"What the fuck are we doing out here, man?"

"Surrendering to the current that guides us," I answered then began climbing down after Jack. Risa sighed heavily but followed close behind me.

When we reached the bottom, the silo-shaped tube opened into a spacious, rectangular cement chamber with an arched ceiling which had been painted white. There were hanging gardens on many of the walls, fed by halogen lights that filled inserts in the ceiling above them. The construction wasn't complete, but the extensive work that had already been done on the walls and floors indicated the final product would be ornate.

"They're all connected," said Jack. "It's one giant complex. Follow me."

We left the room through an empty doorway into a tunnel that was also painted white and had an arched ceiling matching that of the room behind us. The entirety of the hallway's walls and ceiling were covered by enormous screens that stretched from end to end and depicted a cohesive scene of a canopy of trees, creating the illusion that we were walking down a forest path.

"How do you power all of this?" I asked.

"You'll see," answered Jack.

We passed through a room that was dimensionally similar to the first but was furnished with bunk beds and chests for personal storage. The walls had been painted with vivid colors depicting a stunning field of wildflowers.

"Rose painted this room," Jack said as we passed through.

"Mason's wife?" asked Risa.

He didn't respond but continued leading us through the facility. Some rooms had several tunnels leading away from them, making for a maze of interconnected chambers. There were rooms for storage, recreation areas equipped with gear for exercising, composting toilets, and countless tunnels leading to areas we didn't explore. Similar to the first, every tunnel connecting the chambers was plated in monitors that displayed varied scenes of natural beauty. I was truly impressed. In the twenty-five years that Richard Robbins had owned the land, these people had built a veritable underground fortress.

We were led down a tunnel different than the others in that it was completely rectangular, without the arch in the ceiling, unpainted, and had less headroom. I heard running water as we approached the door at the end of the tunnel, which was thick steel and securely bolted with multiple locking mechanisms. Jack entered a code into a panel beside the door, and the bolts withdrew with a hiss. The door popped as it opened, and we passed through it into a wide, natural cavern.

The side of the cave that we stood on had been fortified with a structurally sound platform and ceiling that merged with the natural rock of the cavern farther in. From the platform there was a cement pathway leading to the far side of the room, where a quickly moving underground river cut through the cavern. There was equipment on the ground along the walls I didn't recognize, but I took a guess it was part of a system for converting hydraulic energy into electricity.

"The snow melting from the mountains must keep this river flowing strong," I yelled above the sound of the rushing water. It was brilliant, really. They'd built up against a natural source of constant power and were harnessing it to provide energy for the entire facility.

Jack walked over to stand between Risa and myself. His eyes were wide, and he looked distressed. He held a finger over his mouth then leaned forward to talk directly into our ears.

"What is it?" I asked, imitating his action.

"What is it?" he said. "What is it? What the fuck are you doing here? Are you crazy?"

Risa's baffled expression gave me confidence that the complete lack of understanding I was experiencing was warranted.

"Do you have any idea where you are, man? You're in the fucking lion's den. If I hadn't lit that brush fire, you'd be dead right now. Why would you come here?" He was shifting his weight and looking around nervously, signs of extreme agitation.

"What are you talking about?" I asked. "Do you know who I am?"

"I know enough," he said. "I know you're on Mason's list."

"His list?"

"The list he made, for the tests Richard put him in charge of."

And in that moment, I understood. The heat of excitement mingled with the chill of dread as the implications of what Jack was saying burned coldly in my chest. "Mason is alive."

"Yeah, Mason is alive, but more importantly, his father is about to kill you for sniffing around this ranch. Why did you come here?"

"Tell me what's happening," I demanded.

"Why are you helping us?" said Risa at the same time.

Jack shook his head and looked desperately frustrated. "There's no time right now. Listen to me. You need to get out of here. If you go back up there, you're both dead. This is a private operation, and there is no way Richard lets you see everything we're doing here and then lets you walk. He didn't have much faith Mason wouldn't screw this up to begin with, and I'm pretty sure his patience just ran out."

"I don't understand." I was confused and thirsty for more information.

"It doesn't matter," said Jack. "All that matters is that you leave here. Now. The turbines are downstream, and the water is dammed up before that. You're going to have to follow the river upstream. There are parts where you'll have to swim under the surface, but just keep going and it will open back up. You'll come to a grate that can be opened from this side. Open it, get out to the surface, then head east to get back to the road and your vehicle. You stopped at the gate, right?"

"Yeah, we were stopped there," said Risa.

"They'll be posted up watching the driveway and won't expect you to come from the road."

"I can't leave yet," I said. "I need to make sense of all this. It's why we came here."

"Did you listen to me at all? If you go up there, you are one hundred percent dead. I'm trying to save your life here, man. And in return, I need you to get me the fuck out of here. I have to take care of a few things and pack, but I'll meet you when night falls. There's a campground southwest of here. You'll find it on any map. Wait for me there, and then we'll talk. I don't know much, but I'll tell you what I know once we're away from here."

"Let's go, Jacobi," Risa said. "It won't help us to know what's going on here if we're killed. We have no weapons, and they have home-field advantage."

Frustrated, but seeing the wisdom of her logic, I nodded.

"Hit me," said Jack. "Make it good. I'll tell them you came up behind me and—"

Risa lashed out suddenly, struck Jack in the carotid artery on the side of his neck with the side of her open hand, then caught him as he crumpled to the floor and laid him carefully down. We looked at one another for support then began wading upstream in the river. I used my CUBE to light the way, grateful the device was completely waterproof. The rock ceiling had been carved out enough to allow us to remain standing for the first part of the exodus but sank lower and lower as we progressed until we were eventually forced down into the water. We continued to swim upstream, keeping our heads above the surface since there was just enough room to come up for air. As Jack had warned, we came to an area where we were forced to go under as the ceiling of the cavern met the water. Risa went ahead of me, and I filled my lungs then plunged into the river in pursuit. Even with the light from the CUBE to guide me, the murky water was too dark to see much of anything. Fortunately, my navy training had greatly expanded my lung capacity, and they'd barely begun to burn before I felt the cavern open up above my head. I rose from the current and took in a gasp of air, thankful Jack's assessment of the distance had been accurate.

At last, we arrived at the grate he had described. Steel bars had been put in place across the entire river, running from the rock above into the ground beneath the water. The grate was centered in the middle and had a thick handle, which we turned together to open it up.

Once beyond the grate, we continued up the river, which had become much steeper and more difficult to traverse. Between that and the thin air at this altitude, exhaustion was beginning to set in, but we pushed one another into keeping a strong pace. Finally, natural light began to invade the darkness ahead of us. It crept in from above to define the boundary between the subterranean world from which we'd arrived and the familiar terrestrial surface I'd begun to long for. We pushed our way up through the falling water and scaled a rocky cliff to escape into the light of day.

We were in a large pool of white water rushing quickly through a sandstone canyon around us. Carefully, we helped one another to shore at the base of a cliff that looked as if it would be the easiest to climb from. Using the rock itself, the vines hanging from the ridge above, and the roots protruding from the earth, we managed to reach the rim of the canyon. I looked down into a maelstrom of water that tumbled away into the darkness we'd emerged from and couldn't help but grin foolishly at Risa, who laughed.

"Never a dull moment with you," she said. Maybe Pavel was right and I was more interesting than I gave myself credit for.

We headed east along the ridge of the canyon, which became even forest ground before we'd traveled far. About a half a mile in we found the road, which we stumbled onto from the forest, filthy and wet. The sun was beginning to sink, and I estimated the time to be around four or five o'clock.

"How do you want to do this?" asked Risa.

"Don't kill anyone. I'm still not sure what's going on here. We'll need their guns, though, in case they follow us."

We both took our shoes off before turning onto the dirt

driveway; our truck was parked farther along, in front of the gate that had blocked our way earlier. The first thing you learned in FDEES training was how to be invisible. We'd spent hundreds of hours on woodland stealth alone with instructors that had drilled us on things like how to plant our feet into the earth to avoid breaking branches or crackling leaves, centering our balance for moving quickly with purpose and intention, and using natural sounds like the wind to camouflage forward progress.

Like specters, we moved off to either side of the road and disappeared into the trees. Cautiously, we crept forward, scanning the rocks and trees for any sign someone might be lying in wait. We passed the truck, and before long we'd identified two targets. The men were facing cover and looking toward the property with their backs to us, as Jack had expected they would be. Risa signaled she was ready, and we coordinated our timing to move forward and strike simultaneously. I heard a strangled noise from off to my left, and the sound of leaves rustling. The man I'd moved in behind turned to investigate, but I'd anticipated his reaction and positioned myself to his right to remain out of his line of sight. Before he could call out, I sprang up and wrapped my arm around his neck, bringing him to the ground and cradling him there while he struggled until he went completely slack. I held him for a bit longer to make sure, then unstrapped his rifle from his shoulder, took an extra magazine from his belt, and made my way back to our vehicle, careful to stay low. Risa had made it back before me and recovered our footwear, which we threw in the back with the rifles we'd absconded with.

"Ready?" she asked.

"Let's go."

"Can you push? I think I can get us out of here quietly."

We were on a slight hill, so with me pushing, Risa was able to build some momentum rolling backward without turning the engine on. I caught up to the truck and jumped in as we rolled. We managed to reach the main road before we started the vehicle, and when no one began shooting at us immediately, we each let out a sigh of relief.

I popped my CUBE in the dash receptacle and navigated to a list of nearby facilities, from which I was able to quickly identify the campground Jack had directed us to meet him at.

"Well," Risa said, "that was fucking interesting."

"Not exactly how I pictured that visit going. I'm sorry," I said, putting on my boots.

"So, Mason is alive," she observed. "I still don't see how he's connected to what's happening."

"Me neither. Hopefully Jack will be able to fill in some of the missing pieces."

"If he gets out of there alive."

Since we still had a couple of hours until our rendezvous at the campground, we decided to pull off onto an old, weed-covered logging trail. Risa parked the truck far enough back that it couldn't be seen from the road, and I got out and waited behind the cover of a large boulder to watch for any sign of traffic from the direction we'd fled. About a half hour into my vigil, two trucks flew past the trail. I recognized both of them as ones that had been parked on the land. There were a couple of armed men in each vehicle. About an hour later, as the sky began to darken with the coming of dusk, Risa came up beside me and let me know that it was almost time to go. Suddenly, she crouched and took cover as headlights appeared on the road below, heading back in the direction of Richard's property. One of the trucks that had passed us before was returning home.

"One still out there," I said. Risa gave me her hand and helped me up from the ground. "Let's go get our guy and get home."

The road got progressively worse as we neared our destination, and I appreciated our foresight in choosing the truck we had. From where we'd pulled off the road, it took about fifteen more minutes to reach the campground, which looked like it hadn't been visited in decades. There was a sign welcoming visitors, but it was ancient and faded. A small cabin that might once have been an office had been ransacked. Its windows were broken, and nothing remained inside but dust. There were picnic tables surrounding the parking area, many of which had rotted and partially collapsed. In the distance, I could see one of the Rainbow Lakes through the trees. The bright orange rays of the setting sun danced over the water as it passed beyond the mountains to the west. It would have been a romantic place to have explored with Risa if we weren't being hunted by armed militia.

Once again, I made an effort to hide the truck by driving it far enough into the trees away from the main lot that it wouldn't be seen immediately by anyone pulling up. They'd find it if they drove farther into the campground, but we'd have time to get prepared and the element of surprise. We left the truck, and Risa collected our stolen rifles from the back. She tossed one to me then wandered off to watch the entrance.

We waited there for at least another hour. It was nearly dark by the time I heard someone tromping through the woods to the north. I trained my rifle in the direction of the noise and didn't lower it until I recognized Jack's curly black hair.

"Over here," I called.

He jumped in surprise, since he hadn't seen me crouched in the darkness ahead of him. He was wearing a large backpack that was packed to the brim and had a rifle strapped to his shoulder.

"You bring enough underwear?" I asked, motioning toward the backpack.

"Seven years of my life in that place," he said. "This is the bare minimum. We need to go."

Risa had activated her thermal vision and noticed his arrival. She moved closer and took up a position within earshot but continued to watch the road.

"Not yet," I said. "We're going to need some answers before you get in that truck with us."

"Can't we just talk in the truck, man? The sooner we're out of range from here, the safer we'll be."

"I don't know you," I said. "I don't even know if what you told us back there is true. Start elaborating, or you can hike down the mountain for all I give a shit."

Jack sighed, exasperated. "All right. Jesus. I told you I don't know everything, just pieces. What do you want to know?"

"Why are you helping us?" asked Risa for the second time.

"Rose," said Jack. "She and I...we were...we wanted to leave that place."

"You were having an affair?" Risa asked.

"We loved each other. We were young when we got involved with the Coalition. Richard paired her off with Mason pretty quick, or at least he made it clear that was what he wanted. That's kind of how things work around there. She never loved him, but there were benefits to being married to the boss's kid. We…we kept seeing one another. Can I sit?" asked Jack, pointing to one of the few picnic tables that had endured the years of abuse from the harsh Rocky Mountain winters.

I nodded and joined him at the table.

"Anyway, Mason…Mason is an evil son of a bitch. He knew she didn't love him, and he hated her for it. He'd hit her. I'd see her with bruises, and I wanted to kill that asshole every day. But you can't touch him. He's protected by Richard. Rose got pregnant. But she'd stopped being with Mason, she hadn't been intimate with him, so when she started to show, he knew it wasn't his. He went into a mad rage; everyone could hear him screaming at her from that house, and he set in on her. I couldn't do anything…I wanted to…"

Tears began streaming down Jack's face as he relived the horror of that night. He wiped them and gathered himself.

"I'm sorry. I haven't talked to anyone about this since it happened. I've just been trapped there with those sons of bitches. They'd kill me if they knew it was me who got her pregnant. They'd kill me if I tried to leave. I didn't have an out until you came along."

"What happened to Rose?" I asked. "You never finished."

"He killed her. He hit her so hard, she never got up again. And those motherfuckers burned the house down around her to make her death look like an accident. And that night, Richard saw something in his son. He saw the monster that he'd become. And you know what? I think he was proud, that sick fuck. So he tells Mason to pick someone he thinks got his wife pregnant.

Now, Mason had no idea. We were always too careful. So, he points at whatever poor fucker pissed him off last, and Richard shoots the guy in the head, right there in front of us."

Risa shook her head, her face full of sorrow.

Jack nodded. "They took him and threw him in the fire next to her. Richard turned to Mason and told him he was free now. That it was him in that fire. Said that was the nature of the phoenix, to rise from the ashes and be reborn stronger. But really, what he meant was with everyone on the outside world thinking Mason was dead, he'd have someone without accountability to execute all his insane plans."

"What sorts of plans?" I asked. I could feel the excitement rising in my gut as we began to approach a possible connection to our own investigation.

"Like that list you're on," he said. "The tests he talks about. This one was big. I wasn't a part of it. Only Richard, Mason, and a few of the lieutenants know. But Mason was thrilled. He kept talking about how you'd all finally understand and about how you couldn't run from yourselves. And man, he hated you. Jacobi Slate, he'd talk about you all the time. He said you made him the way he was, blamed you for 'hiding from yourself like a coward.'"

Risa looked at me, but her black eyes revealed nothing of her emotions. My head was humming as I tried to process all of this new information. It grew louder, and I realized it wasn't in my head at all but was an actual whirring in the sky above us. The three of us each began to look around, searching for the source.

"Time to go," said Risa, darting toward the truck.

"Drones!" yelled Jack as he scrambled after her.

I ran to the vehicle and jumped into the driver's seat. We were under the cover of the trees, so it was possible whatever was out there hadn't spotted us yet. I didn't want to turn on the engine until it became absolutely necessary. Risa had the passenger window down and her rifle at the ready. We waited like that, my hand on the ignition, hers on the trigger. Jack had jumped into the bed of the truck and was tucked down in the corner. If it was a drone, it was very likely it would be equipped with a thermal camera, so I was thankful he was staying as low as possible. What seemed like minutes passed as we held our breath, frozen, waiting for a sign we'd been spotted.

Just when I began to wonder if it had passed us by, a loud rattling broke the silence from ahead in the direction of the parking area we'd passed through. The telltale sound of projectiles striking metal rang around us as the drone unleashed a flurry of bullets, and I could see flashes of muzzle fire from midair, about thirty yards away. I immediately started the truck and took over manual driving then slammed the wheel forward to accelerate quickly. The truck soared out from under the trees and into the lot.

"Can you see it?" I asked Risa.

"Now that it's firing," she said, leaning out of the window and taking aim. She took several shots then slid back into the vehicle. We hit the dirt road beyond the lot, and I drove as fast as I was comfortable with, considering the conditions of the road.

"It's down," said Risa, "but there could be more."

I slipped the window open behind us and yelled, "Jack, can those drones keep up with us? How fast do they travel?"

"They'll be all over us!" he yelled back. "These can hit speeds of ninety miles per hour. That one must have been after me, from the ranch. But now that they know where we are, they'll send more. We need to get out of range as fast as possible."

"How far?" I asked.

"Around fifteen miles."

They'd be on us in minutes. Traveling fifteen miles on mountain roads would be impossible without them catching up, since the drones wouldn't need to follow the road.

"We'll need to hide. Do you know anywhere we can pull in to get off the road?" I yelled back to Jack.

"Maybe. There's an old ski lodge about a mile south of here. It's been abandoned for years. They might assume we'd keep driving straight down the mountain and pass it by."

"Risa, see if you can get it up on the map," I said. She took out her CUBE, spent a few moments locating the facility, and then deposited it in the dash receptacle. A map came up, highlighting a path to the lodge.

I accelerated, and the truck raced down the treacherous mountain road. We couldn't be sure how quickly they might have reacted to locating us at the camp. There was a chance it would take them more time to deploy additional drones, but I generally made a habit of assuming worst-case scenarios, and since I was still alive it was a habit I had no reason to break.

We were approaching the turnoff the map indicated I should take to reach the lodge. Risa abruptly sat up straight and pointed toward the intersection.

"Jacobi, headlights," she said, but I'd already seen them. They were approaching from farther down the mountain, and I had a sinking suspicion I knew who they were. They had to have already seen our headlights as well, which removed the option of hiding at the lodge from the table. We had no choice but to try to make it down the mountain as quickly as possible.

"Jack!" I yelled. "Hold on tight!"

The two vehicles were going to reach the intersection at about the same time. We were going so fast, it was difficult to keep control of the truck. As we neared, I engaged the emergency braking mechanism and moved the wheel toward the inside of the turn. The truck's rear end continued to swing in the direction we'd been traveling, but I accelerated and flicked the wheel into the slide, regaining control of our momentum. As the drift leveled out, I released the brake I'd engaged, and we shot toward the vehicle in our path, which had turned sideways to block the road. I aimed for the back end, prepared to use the momentum we'd maintained to push them out of the way. As we collided, I caught a glimpse of the gray-bearded man in the driver's seat, who stared back with eyes wide with disbelief at the unexpected vehicular assault. Our truck sent theirs spinning out of the way, and we sped past through sparks and the cloud of dirt that was kicked up from the collision.

I checked behind us to make sure we hadn't lost Jack, who was there, desperately clinging to a handle by the window with both hands.

"Jesus, Jacobi!" he yelled. "You're a lunatic!"

Behind us, I saw the other truck recover from the collision and right itself in our direction to give chase. I pushed the wheel forward to try to put as much distance as possible between us without losing control at one of the sudden hairpin turns and plummeting over the edge. The other driver knew the roads better than I did and used that advantage to steadily gain on us.

He was able to drive more recklessly on the straightaways, since he knew when he'd have to slow to turn, whereas I was forced to maintain some amount of caution. I heard gunfire as his passenger fired shots from out of his window.

"Jack?" I called out. "Can you fire that weapon?"

"I'll try!"

He hooked his arm through the hand bar he'd been holding and managed to get his rifle pointed in the direction of the truck while keeping himself stationary. He returned fire, and our pursuers backed off slightly. I heard bullets hitting the car and saw more muzzle flash from what must have been a drone in the distance, to our left. It continued to fire, easily keeping pace with us.

"Risa?" I asked, my voice tense with concentration.

She nodded and threw open the moon roof of the cab then stood up through it and brought her weapon to bear on the drone.

"Keep us steady," she called down. I did the best I could to maintain our velocity, but the winding road was making it difficult. Risa and the drone traded fire repeatedly as we progressed down the mountain. Thankfully, we were granted a brief respite as we dropped behind a line of trees that blocked its line of sight.

"Keep us steady, man, I can't hit it!" she yelled.

As we turned a corner, our headlights landed on another drone that had taken position in the center of the road, at a height level with the truck's grill. It began firing at us immediately, and I accelerated to ram it. Having heard the shots, Risa turned to train her weapon on it and pulled the trigger. The shot clipped it, causing its right side to dip slightly from the impact, which gave me just enough time to connect with it before it could rise up out of the way. Our grill slammed into it, sending it flying to the ground in a burst of sparks beneath us.

The truck behind us had gained ground since I'd slowed to try to keep us steady, but I didn't notice until our cab brightened suddenly when the headlights neared.

"Jacobi!" yelled Jack, firing at the windshield of the oncoming truck, which accelerated into our rear. The impact shook us, but I was able to maintain control. Risa turned in their direction and unloaded several shots into the grill, but their vehicle didn't slow.

"Where are we at with not shooting these assholes?" she called down.

"I'm over it. Shoot him!" I yelled.

They accelerated to ram us again, but as they approached, Risa took aim and fired several rounds at the driver. One must have hit, because the truck braked, veering back and forth on the road before coming to a stop behind us.

The gunfire commenced again as the remaining drone cleared the trees. I pulled back hard on the wheel, and our truck screeched to a sudden halt. Bullets exploded into the road in a line in front of us as the drone overshot the mark.

"There! We're steady!" I yelled up to Risa.

Risa unloaded on the drone, which tried to take evasive action, but not quickly enough. I saw the sparks of several shots hitting their mark before she slid back through the moon roof, breathing heavily. I put us back into motion. Adrenaline was coursing through me, and I couldn't help but let out a cry of relief at having fought our way free of danger for the moment.

"Well done," I said. "Thank you."

She let out a deep breath and nodded, smiling. "Let's get the hell out of here."

"Can you book us on the next flight out?"

"I'll see," she said, retrieving her CUBE to go about the task.

"You okay, Jack?" I called through the window.

"I think so," he said. He was shaken but uninjured.

The moon was on the rise. It came up bright in the distance over the treetops and cast a fiery orange glow down onto the valley we were passing through. As the tension of our escape began to die away, I took a deep breath and slowed to acknowledge the beauty of the vista. It was too easy to forget that those moments, though fleeting, were what we fought so hard for. Survival meant nothing if we didn't take time to appreciate those gifts when offered.

The weight that had lifted when we'd arrived earlier that day had returned with the setting of the sun. But what had been a masked oppression, vaguely hovering at the edge of the darkness, now had a face and a name. The danger was solidifying, beginning to form the shape of something tangible — something I could understand. I wasn't sure why Mason had targeted our unit or what sort of sick game he was playing by handing me breadcrumbs to follow. It was the unknown I feared. This was just another man, who'd soon discover he'd picked a fight with a pack of wolves. Where I'd been grateful to have escaped San Francisco just hours before, now I smelled blood in the distance and burned with the desire to return and resume the hunt.

Chapter 7

We'd have gotten away clean if the next flight hadn't been three hours away. Instead, we were forced to wait at the airport in Denver, hoping Richard Robbins would be careless enough not to send men to the most obvious place we'd be. Jack assured us he would not be and that we should expect company.

"He'd kill you just for having seen what I showed you at the ranch. As for me, I might not know everything, but I know enough that he'll keep trying to disappear me until I'm in the ground."

"Why?" I asked. "What have we seen? An underground bunker and a group of people who think the world is going to end. What's it matter that we know it's there?"

We were seated at gate 88 in terminal B. Our flight was still an hour away. Risa had wandered away to find something to eat.

"You've got to try to understand the minds of these people. They don't just think the world might end — they think it's a foregone conclusion. That means anyone that isn't ready is already dead. Whatever they do to others, it's justified because it doesn't make a difference," said Jack.

"You don't agree with them? You lived up there for over half a decade. You must have similar beliefs."

"Me and Rose, we weren't ever really sure. When they killed

her, any remaining resolve I'd had about it cracked and fell away. I started to see them for what they were, and all of Richard's dogma started sounding like a bunch of bullshit. But I had nowhere to go and knew they'd kill me if I ran. When I saw you and they told me your name, I knew it might be the last chance I'd ever have to escape. You're a Fade, like Mason. You *can* help me, right? You've got to hide me. I'll tell you anything you want to know."

I wanted to help, but I wasn't sure how I could. I felt sorry for him. To watch someone you love burn and then live with her killers for as long as he had was unimaginable. It must have taken an incredible amount of self-control to maintain the mask he'd worn on the ranch.

"I haven't worked for the Division in years," I said. "But whatever I can do to make you invisible, I will. It will take some time. I'll need to reach out to some people. In the meantime, we'll put you up somewhere in the city."

He nodded enthusiastically. "Whatever you can do. I'll take whatever help you can offer. Thank you. Thank you so much!"

"You were explaining to me why it matters that I've seen Robbins' operation up close," I reminded him.

"He's got big plans. You knowing anything about what goes on there could compromise them. I don't know what they are, exactly, but I can tell you this," said Jack, looking at me intently for emphasis, "it's got something to do with the government. I think he's trying to start a war."

"Start a war? I think he's giving himself more credit than he deserves, if that's his plan."

"You don't know this guy, Jacobi. He's hell-bent on bringing the end down on all of us. He's scary smart, and he's been planning this for a long time. And you're part of that somehow."

"Me?" I asked, incredulous. "This gets even better. How am I a part of the plan?"

Jack shrugged. "Like I said, I don't know for sure. But it has something to do with the tests I told you about earlier. Richard put Mason in charge of them, and it's the first stage of something bigger. You being at the ranch means Mason fucked up somehow, and Richard wouldn't have let that slide. He would have cleaned up his kid's mistake, like he always does. That's why you were in danger."

"We've got company," I said and nodded at the three men I'd just noticed coming down the terminal hallway toward our gate. They were dressed in the same green and black outfits we'd seen the Phoenix Coalition mercs in earlier.

"Damn it," Jack hissed, tensing.

"Relax," I said. "They can't shoot us right here in the open at the airport. They wouldn't have been able to get in this far with their weapons anyway." We'd taken the firing pins out of our own stolen rifles and ditched them in a dumpster before we'd returned the truck. "They're probably just here to confirm we're heading back to San Francisco so they can track us."

They'd noticed us now and were heading our way. I watched them carefully as they approached, looking for hidden weaponry and studying their body language for any sign of aggression. They passed by as they walked to the opposite side of the gate and waited against the wall there, staring malevolently at Jack.

Jack took a deep breath and tried not to stare back, but I could tell his emotions were running wild within. I could only imagine what he must have felt, but I thought it was likely a mixture of shame for having betrayed the people he'd worked so closely with for so long, fear, and anger at having been forced to endure what he'd had. Since no one at the Coalition knew about his relationship with Rose, they probably saw his betrayal as one without reason.

"Don't worry," I said. "I've got your back here. You're doing the right thing."

He seemed to relax and nodded his thanks. I spotted Risa approaching, carrying a tray with sandwiches and drinks. As she neared, she gave the men on the far wall the middle finger.

"What are they doing here?" she asked, setting the tray down for us.

"Probably just tracking us," I said, picking up a sandwich and unwrapping the foil.

"Should we ask them?" she wondered, looking at me hopefully. I knew what *ask them* meant in this case, and I shook my head.

"We can't afford to miss this flight. We'll be boarding soon. Let's just get on the plane and get home. We can worry about Richard and his men once we're back."

"What if they get on the plane?" she asked.

"We'll worry about that if it happens," I answered. Risa shrugged.

The next half hour went by slowly, as if it were dragging the heavy awkwardness of our situation behind it as it crawled. When they finally announced it was time to board, we were ushered down a staircase to the platform outside where the plane, which looked identical to the one we'd flown in on earlier that afternoon, was waiting to depart. The men had filed in behind us and looked as if they intended to board as well. As we neared the entrance to the aircraft, I looked behind me and saw that they had stopped about halfway across the boarding platform. Two of them embraced the third and clasped him on the shoulder before he continued toward the plane.

"That can't be good," I said.

"What is it?" asked Risa.

"Those two guys just said goodbye to their buddy like they'd never see him again."

Risa raised her eyebrows. "Boom?"

"Can't be sure, but I think we might need to revoke his ticket."

"What's he doing?" asked Jack, who had turned and seen the Coalition mercenary approaching the plane behind us. "Is he boarding the plane?"

"How committed would you say your friend back there is?" I asked. "Do you think he's willing to die for your cause?"

"It's not my cause any more, man! I told you that. And I don't know. Maybe. His name is Justin, and he's young and stupid, like I was. Would he do it if Richard told him too? Maybe. Probably. Why, do you think...oh *fuck!*" stammered Jack, his voice dropping to a whisper. "You think he's *going to blow up the plane?*"

"We're not going to let that happen," Risa cut in. "Jacobi..."

"What's up?"

"I'll see you back in the city," she said, leaning up to kiss me softly on my cheek. She pushed the key fob to the Mustang into my hand.

"Risa…" I said as she turned to walk away. "*Risa*," I hissed when she ignored me. She turned back and raised her chin defiantly, daring me to tell her not to go.

"Be careful," I said instead. "Please." Then I turned and ushered Jack toward the door of the plane. "Let's go. She'll take care of it." I spared one more look across my shoulder as Risa strode with violent purpose toward Justin and the other two Phoenix Coalition mercenaries.

Once we'd boarded the plane, I was frustrated to find that our seats were on the opposite side of the aisle than the one Risa was engaging the mercs on. I parked in an empty seat on the other side and peered out to make sure she was all right, but it was difficult to see anything in the darkness beyond the window. After a short while, the real owner of the seat arrived, and I excused myself to cross the aisle and rejoin Jack. In the distance, I saw the flashing blue lights of a squad car racing by and thought I heard sirens, but before long it was silent.

Jack watched the door like a wide-eyed rabbit, expecting Justin to board at any moment, but I knew he wouldn't. Shortly after, the door to the plane closed and we rose straight up from the boarding platform, leaving the ground, and Risa, behind us.

As we climbed, I could see the flashing lights of several police cruisers, unmoving and parked in a half-circle as if they'd pulled in to surround someone a short distance from the terminal we'd departed from. Suddenly, the cars were rocked by an explosion at their center and tumbled away from the epicenter. The flames of the blast grew smaller beneath us as we continued to rise. I closed my eyes and prayed to an unspecified higher power that Risa was unharmed.

Jack had his eyes closed and hadn't seen, which was good because it would only have added to his nervousness. I needed him calm so that over the hour to follow I could pick his brain for every detail he could remember about both Mason and his father.

"Wake up, Jack," I said. "We need to talk."

The most relevant piece of information that came out of our conversation was that Mason was scheduled to meet with one of the other members of the Phoenix Coalition at some point during the next couple of days. Jack wasn't sure where or when they planned to meet, but he was certain one of the lieutenants had departed for San Francisco the day before we'd arrived on the ranch. I was on edge as we landed, knowing at least two trained soldiers were already positioned in the city and were most likely lying in wait for us.

Without Risa at my back, I felt tense and exposed. I'd given Jack my word I'd protect him, but that began with getting him to safety, and I wasn't sure I could do that alone. We exited the plane, and I hurried him across the boarding pad with my jacket up above our heads. It wasn't overly conspicuous, since the rain was still beating steadily down on the drenched city. Once we reached the top of the stairs and entered the terminal, I led him straight to the public restroom. Because of the large terminal windows and the airy, open atmosphere, it was one of the few places that wasn't vulnerable to a potential sniper perched somewhere outside the airport. I needed to make a few calls to see what I could put into place before we went any farther.

My first call was to Matvei Kamenev. I didn't feel good about owing the Sokoly Zimoy organization any favors, but he had something I needed now, and I decided I'd worry about the consequences down the road.

"Jacobi," said Matvei with an affectation of affection as he answered the call, "I see you came to your senses. What can I help you with so late in the evening?"

"Mr. Kamenev," I said in greeting.

"Matvei!" he insisted.

"Matvei. I apologize if I'm disturbing you. I'm calling because if you were serious about discussing further opportunities for collaboration, then I could use your assistance with something."

"Go on?"

"Do you own a building in the city that I could put some people up at for a while? I need to keep them off the grid. I'd be staying with them as well."

His eyes sparkled as he considered the value of my request, and, more importantly, what he might be able to extract from me in return for providing the safe harbor I needed.

"Trouble at home?" he asked wryly with the venomous humor of a man who played with his kills before he ate them.

"Nothing I won't have wrapped up quickly. Within the week, I'd estimate," I replied, pulling the timeframe from the ether with no reasonable evidence to support it whatsoever.

"Hmm," he mused. "Fortunately for you, there *are* several people I'd like the pleasure of speaking with face to face. And you, Mr. Jacobi, are just the person who could make that happen. We don't need to talk about the details now, but if you were to agree to…say…fly to Moscow when this is over…?"

"I'm sure we can work something out," I acquiesced to the devil's bargain.

"I take you as a man of your word, since you have not given me any reason to doubt you yet," he said. The warning was evident. "So that is good enough for me. And I am currently out of the country, which means you are free to use the suite we last met in. I will alert my staff to expect you and your entourage, and to treat you with the same respect they bestow upon me. For this, you will be in my debt, and we will convene when your ordeal is at an end to discuss the details of the arrangement further. Are these terms acceptable?"

"More than acceptable," I said honestly. I hadn't expected anything quite so lavish. "A lesser apartment would be fine, I don't want to trouble—"

"Nonsense," he interrupted. "You will stay in the penthouse. Enjoy yourselves. Relax. We will talk soon." He terminated the connection. My skin crawled, and I felt unclean, like I'd fallen into a pit of vipers. What I'd meant was I didn't want to incur that much of a debt, but at the moment it was a viable solution with repercussions that were manageable down the road. I'd have to be content with that.

"One more call," I said to Jack, who bobbed his head. I reached out to Himari, and the call was answered immediately. I gave him a brief explanation of our situation and asked if he'd be willing to help. When he agreed, I let him know what I needed specifically and apologized for getting him involved.

A toilet flushed, interrupting my call, then a middle-aged man came out of a bathroom stall with a panic-stricken expression, washed their hands, and left quickly without looking at me. In retrospect, I realized I'd foregone subtlety in favor of alacrity.

Given the nature of my discussions, it would have been wiser to have made sure we'd been alone beforehand, if only to have avoided terrifying the locals. I thanked Himari and terminated the line. We waited a bit longer before leaving the bathroom to throw anyone off who might have been watching for us. In that time I reached out twice to Risa, with no response in either case.

Once we left the restroom I led us back to the gate we'd arrived at. The door that led outside and down to the landing pad was closed but unlocked. After a look around to make sure we weren't being observed, I opened it and we slipped through. I left the landing bay with Jack close on my heels, and we stayed in the shadows along the edge of the building as we moved toward the end of the terminal.

If there was anyone lying in wait for us, I couldn't be sure if they would confront us here or follow us to wherever we were going before making their move, but one was just as bad as the other. In either case, the most likely place they would look for us would be at the main entrance. Jack seemed reasonably skilled at staying hidden as we moved with stealth to avoid the attention of airport employees going about their business on the pads we passed. When we finally reached the end of the terminal, we cut around the side and hurried toward the front. We were still some distance from the main entrance when we reached the road. I waved over an automated transport vehicle and told Jack to get in the back.

"When will you get there?" he asked, his voice panicked.

"Jack, I'll be right behind you. When you arrive, get in the lobby and tell them you're with me." I gave the destination address to the vehicle's computer and closed the door. As it pulled away, I turned and walked toward the main entrance of the terminal. I ducked in the first set of rotating doors I came across then wandered through the main lobby several times, trying to appear as if I were looking for someone. I was keeping an eye out for threats, but more importantly, I wanted to be seen. Eventually, I made my way out front, hailed my own transport, and gave it instructions to bring me back to the car. I arrived without incident.

The Mustang departed the airport slowly on automatic piloting until it hit the highway. If Mason was out there somewhere, I didn't expect he'd fall for my antics. He understood my capability when it came to remaining unseen and would undoubtedly recognize I was going out of my way to be spotted. If it was the man who'd come to meet him in the city, then there was a chance I'd catch him off-guard, since he might just assume I was an idiot. However you sliced it, if anyone had been waiting for us, they wouldn't have any choice but to play along if they wanted to find out where I was going or why Jack wasn't with me.

I wanted to understand what was driving Mason to do this. I needed to know how I was connected and if there was any truth to what Jack had said about the Phoenix Coalition using the people on that list as test subjects for some unknown experiment. I had so many questions, and it was becoming clearer that the only way I'd get any more information would be to get my answers directly from those responsible. I smiled grimly, because if things went the way I hoped, that was exactly what was about to happen. The car parked itself under my building, but I waited, unmoving, until the lights shut off. About five minutes later, my CUBE vibrated and I pulled it out to answer the call. It was Himari.

"You were right," he said. "There was one. He slowed down when he drove by the building you pulled under but kept going.

I'm on him now. I'll send a beacon for you to follow."

The beacon invitation came through shortly after the call ended. To be on the safe side, I moved from Risa's Mustang to my own vehicle. Then, keeping my distance, I followed the signal out of the financial district and into the Tenderloin and drove south until we landed just north of the Mission. Himari's vehicle had stopped. As I came up behind the signal, I spotted Himari in what must have been his rental car. It was a Nikola Panther with curves in all the right places and high-tech motion lighting that accentuated its elegance. Somehow, it suited Himari perfectly. I parked behind him and approached the driver's side window, which lowered as I neared. He was wearing a casual suit, similar in style to the one I'd seen him in last at the docks when we'd dropped him off. One metal hand gripped the wheel and the other extended in greeting. We clasped hands, and I leaned down to hear him over the sound of the rain pattering onto the car roof.

"This is the spot then?" I asked.

"*Hai*," he answered. "He pulled into that garage three minutes ago and hasn't yet come out."

"I appreciate you helping me out with this tonight. I can take it from here."

Himari nodded. "Are you sure there isn't anything else I can do? The debt between us remains significant, regardless of what you say about it. I would be grateful for the opportunity to continue repaying it."

"Well, I don't know about all that, but how would you feel about a babysitting gig? And a room upgrade?"

"Certainly. If you are in need, you can rely on me."

"Okay. I can fill you in on all the details later, but for the time being, I'll send you an address. There's a man in the penthouse named Jack. I need someone to keep an eye on him over the next several days. I'll be staying there as well, but I'll be coming and going, and I'm concerned for his safety."

"Understood," said Himari. "I will protect him."

"Tell the men in the lobby of the building that you're with me. They'll bring you up. Try not to scare Jack too badly. He's a little on edge."

Himari smirked, rolled up the window, and pulled away. After sending him the location of Matvei Kamenev's apartment, I ran across the street into an alley that overlooked the garage to wait for whoever had been trailing me. It was around the corner from a seedy-looking hotel called the Starlight, at least according to the neon sign that hung vertically on the side of the building, advertising rooms that were rented by the hour. It was the kind of place that didn't even give the impression it had seen better days, and had likely been dispassionately maintained since its inception. I imagined the closest thing to affection that had ever graced those walls was the fake moans of the Tenderloin whores who frequented the thirty credit rooms, selling their loving devotion to lonely souls with about as much authenticity as whoever had the nerve to call themselves the *caretaker* of the establishment.

A man came out of the garage, looking down at his CUBE as he walked. He was tall and lanky and wearing a thick, buttoned, flannel shirt that hung down over jeans. He sported a baseball cap with the logo of the Boulders, Denver's professional heliosphere team. It wasn't Mason, which was not entirely unexpected. Up to now, he'd stayed completely in the shadows. I hadn't really believed he'd allow himself to be exposed quite so easily. If this man could tell me where to find Mason, though, it would be a worthwhile consolation prize. He put the device in his pocket and hustled across the street toward the entrance of the hotel.

Once I was just outside of his peripheral vision, I slid from the alley and quickly jogged up the sidewalk to peer through a window. Even with the rain pouring down onto them, the windows were filthy and difficult to see through. I used my coat sleeve to rub away some of the grime. Inside, the light was dim, but I saw the merc walk past a receptionist who was asleep behind a counter protected by thin steel bars. He reached a wide staircase at the back of the lobby and started heading up.

I moved to the entrance and opened the front doors carefully to avoid making noise. The fat man behind the bars snorted once as I entered, but after repositioning his head on his arms, he went back to snoring immediately and didn't stir again. The lobby was decorated by a torn red carpet that covered almost the entire floor. Parts of it were sticky, and I preferred to attribute the mess to the reek of stale beer that permeated the hotel rather than several less appealing alternatives. There were planters with skeletons of shrubbery in them that had gone unattended and starved to death. Movie posters were framed along the walls, but with only one bulb working in the center of the room, it was difficult to read them. The light flickered occasionally, as if it wanted only to expire, join its allies in death, and leave the lobby in total darkness. It refused to extinguish, however, out of what must have been a civic sense of responsibility that at least one thing in this place would hold the line against total apathy.

The staircase hit a landing and wrapped back in the other direction at every floor. I moved up quickly to try to cut the distance between me and my target but listened intently for any sign that I was getting too close. After I'd made it up five floors, I heard someone open a door and pass through it two floors above me. I hurried to catch up. I pushed the door open slightly and looked through to see the Phoenix Coalition mercenary stop several units down the hall. As he stepped into the room, I bolted from the staircase to his door. It was almost fully shut, but I'd reached it in time.

I ran into the door with my shoulder and was rewarded when it met the resistance of his unsuspecting body on the other side. He fell to the floor, giving me time to enter the room and close the door behind us. His back was to me as he rose to his hands and knees. I wrapped my arm around his neck and pulled him upright. He reacted quickly, much quicker than I'd anticipated, and shot an elbow backward into the same side Himari had bruised badly with a punch two nights before. I gasped and relaxed my hold somewhat, which he took advantage of and twisted out from under my arm.

Once free, he spun to face me, lifted his flannel shirt, and reached for a belt holster to unstrap his firearm. I closed the distance and kicked him in the hand that was fumbling for the weapon. Forced to abandon the attempt to arm himself, he brought both hands up, and we began to slowly circle one another in the cramped quarters.

He threw a kick, which I blocked easily, then followed up with a series of punches that I moved away from. A look over his shoulder revealed his desire to put distance between us. I knew he wanted time to draw his weapon, so I moved in closer to stay within reach to trip him up if he tried. I blocked another jab aimed at my midsection then feinted forward with my left shoulder, causing him to throw his arms over his face in defense. With his vision hampered, he was slow to react when I pivoted to my right then dropped and swept his legs out from under him. Once we were on the ground, I wrapped one arm around his neck, clasped my elbow with my other arm, and then rolled onto my back so that he was above me. His fate was nearly sealed when I wrapped my legs around his lower body for leverage and began to squeeze.

I felt his arm drop to his side and realized that he was trying to draw the gun again while both of my arms were wrapped around his neck. I saw his arm come up with the gun in hand and was forced to release my elbow with my right arm to grab his wrist. We struggled in that position, but eventually his strength gave way and I slammed his hand down onto the floor several times until the gun finally came loose and slid away. He bucked and tried to break free again, but I brought my right arm back to secure the hold by grabbing my left elbow before he made any progress. He flailed a bit, grasping at my arms to try to pull them away, but my body was completely tensed now, and the hold was too tight. With no leverage to strike at me and no way to break free, it wasn't long before he ran out of strength to fight and fell unconscious.

I pushed him off and rolled out from underneath him, breathing heavily. Afterwards, I undid his belt and removed the holster on his waist, then attached it to my own belt and retrieved his gun from the floor nearby. There was a sensor on the wall, and it triggered the lights when I ran my hand near it. They were neon green and accompanied by a buzzing I couldn't imagine trying to fall asleep to. The room was small, and riffling through it revealed nothing of interest. The bed was unmade, and some clothes were strewn about the floor. I took a quick look out the window at the back to see if there was a staircase or ladder of some kind but found nothing.

Determined, I picked him up by his underarms and dragged him out of the room into the trash-littered hallway. Some guy at the end of the hall was peeking out from his doorway. He looked half asleep or high as hell on some kind of downer, but that didn't stop him from slamming the door with alacrity when I started dragging the body in his direction. There was an exit onto the fire escape at the end of the hall. It descended along the side of the building for four flights before ending at a platform above the alley I'd waited in earlier. I kicked at a release mechanism on the platform that would lower a ladder to close the last ten feet to the ground. Since I couldn't climb with the mercenary, I lowered him as much as I could toward the ground and dropped him. If I'd been a better person, I might have been more concerned for his well-being, but his friends had chased me down a mountainside and nearly blown up my plane. With Risa's status unclear to boot, my stores of civility were almost entirely depleted.

Before climbing down, I called my car over remotely. It pulled into the alley from the main road and came to a stop. On the ground, the merc was starting to come to. He opened his eyes and looked around, confused.

"Now," I said as I grabbed his ankles and started dragging him toward the car, "it's a little cramped in here. I haven't had a lot of opportunities to clean or organize this week since I've been busy trying to figure out why my friends are all killing people they care about."

He started kicking as the gravity of the situation he was in began to come back into focus, but I held on and continued dragging him.

"But it's comfortable enough for a trunk," I continued. "You're a bit tall, but I'm sure we can find a way to cram you in there."

I dropped his legs and grabbed him under the arms, then heaved him up toward the back of the car.

"And then," I said, trying to control his squirming and maneuver his upper body into the trunk, "we're going to have a nice, long chat about the Phoenix Coalition, Mason Robbins, and what the *fuck* it has to do with me and my unit."

He started laughing as I pulled up his legs. It wasn't a healthy laugh but rather one that rang of desperation. It sounded sick as it bubbled up through his throat, and he coughed violently as if he was drowning in the delusions he'd been swimming in.

"You think you're special?" he asked between bouts of the hideous laughter that were intermingled with coughing fits. "You think this is all about *you*?"

I said nothing, because I was focused on the white foam that had begun to form in the corners of his mouth.

"You're a guinea pig. You're a fucking lab rat—" he was interrupted by another fit of coughing. The foam was bubbling up more intensely in his mouth, and he started convulsing.

Somehow, the son of a bitch had activated some sort of suicide contingency. For all I knew, it could have been a false tooth or just a pill he'd taken when I'd hadn't been looking. In either case, it was quickly ending his life, and I had no way to stop it. I removed his CUBE from his pocket and used his hand while it was still warm to turn the device on. Using his finger, I went into the management settings and selected the option to add an additional administrative user for the device then input my own identification code. My CUBE vibrated in my coat, and I took it out to acknowledge I was being added to an unknown device. Once I'd confirmed, the other CUBE prompted me for voice verification to continue.

"So, the world is doomed?" I asked him, holding his CUBE in range to acknowledge his response.

"Yes," he said through clenched teeth, "once you realize…"

"That'll do," I said, interrupting him. The verbal confirmation had been successful and completed the process of adding me as an administrator for his device. I dragged him out of the trunk and dropped him in the alley. He wouldn't live much longer, but I needed to be sure. I waited for the poison to finish its job, then, without looking back, I got into my car and left the Starlight behind.

After a brief drive back to the financial district, I exited my vehicle in front of Matvei's building. As the car departed for the lot nearby, I stood, staring up at the towering, dark glass building. I'd been standing in this same place when I'd delivered Petr Kamenev earlier that week. Life had seemed much simpler then. It was astonishing how quickly the illusion of normalcy could be ripped away. And underneath the façade, all that truly remained was a reminder that control was a concept, never a guarantee.

Matvei's goons, four of them in total, were standing inside to avoid getting their expensive suits wet. The heat of the bioengineered jungle climate in the lobby was a welcome contrast to the cold storm raging outside. I looked around for any sign of the monkey I'd seen on my first visit, but he wasn't in sight. I wasn't sure if the bioengineered animals needed sleep, but I knew I did. One of the men approached me and extended his hand. I gave it a firm shake.

"You are, Jacobi Slate, yes?" he said with a heavy Russian

accent. "I remember you from the other day."

"That's me," I said. "Did my friends arrive?"

"Yes, one arrived shortly after the other. Are you expecting anyone else?"

"A woman," I said, "hopefully."

He laughed and gave me a knowing nod.

"No, I mean...hopefully, once I let her know...forget it. Can I head up?"

"Come, this way." I followed him past the large fountain in the center of the lobby and under the hanging leaves of the banyan trees into the elevator.

On the way up he let me know Mr. Kamenev had indicated we were to have the run of the place and could come and go as we pleased for the remainder of the week. He had me press my hand against a tablet for biometric analysis and then told me to say a few words out loud to calibrate voice recognition so I'd be able to make full use of the penthouse facilities.

"The concierge will be able to assist you now with whatever else you need," he said. "If she can't help you, then you can reach me on this," he said, holding up his CUBE. I held mine over his until they both flashed then confirmed the contact request on my device. "You can repeat this process with all of your guests to give them the same level of access."

"You should know," I said hesitantly, unsure how he would react to the news, "it's possible there are people looking for us. People who want to harm us."

He erupted into laughter. "People are always looking to hurt Mr. Kamenev. Most know better than to try to do that here. This place is equipped with the finest security money can buy. And the best guards," he said with a wink.

I tried to think of something clever to say that might further endear myself to the guard but decided I was too tired and was more likely to miss the mark and offend him. When we reached the penthouse, the doors parted to reveal a familiar scene. The massive entry hall's appearance matched the temperate eco-habitat of the lobby downstairs. A waterfall in the corner tumbled down into a large pool, and the room was filled with tropical trees and other vegetation. Walkways of stone pebbles weaved between the trees and shrubbery. The entire room jutted out away from the building, seemingly suspended in the air. The ceiling and walls were all transparent, and the penthouse was currently engulfed by a cloud. The light of neon advertising could be seen piercing up through the fine mist sporadically, hinting at the city's expansive sprawl beneath us.

As the elevator doors opened, I heard the sound of Himari's katana leaving its sheath from down a hallway that circled away from the lobby and out of sight.

"It's me," I called out and entered the luxurious apartment. "Thanks again…uh…" My voice fumbled, as I was unsure how to address the guard.

"Boris," he said as the elevator doors began to close.

"Boris. Goodnight."

"Goodnight, Mr. Slate."

Himari entered the room and waved a greeting.

"Where's Jack?" I asked.

"Asleep," he answered. "He was almost out already when I arrived."

"Think you can make it a few days in this place?" I said, impressed by the surroundings.

"I'll survive." Once again, I found myself wondering if Himari was joking. "Tomorrow I'll need to return to my hotel to check out and gather my things. Will you be here in the morning?"

"I should be. I won't leave until you return. I really appreciate you keeping an eye on him for me. I'll feel a lot better knowing he has you here looking out for him."

"It is my honor to have the opportunity to repay the kindness you showed me, Jacobi-san."

I began walking as we spoke, curious about the rest of the suite.

"Feel free to get some sleep yourself. I think we're probably okay up here based on what Boris said about the building's tech. No one even knows we're here in any case."

"Boris?" asked Himari.

"One of the guards. This place is owned by a powerful man. A criminal. I'm going to owe him pretty big for letting us stay here for the week, so make sure to take advantage of it. Eat all his food, swim in the pool, use the best sheets, that sort of thing. Maybe it will have been worth it when all's said and done," I said, chuckling.

Himari nodded stoically.

"You deserve to know what's going on here, too. Tomorrow, I'll go over everything with you and catch you up on what's been happening."

"It is not necessary—" he began, but I interrupted.

"I'd like to. I could use your insight. An outsider's perspective could be helpful."

He bowed his head. "As you wish."

It turned out there was no shortage of rooms to claim for sleeping. The apartment was a masterpiece of engineering. From the entry lobby the elevator opened into, a tunnel-shaped hallway led away in both directions and circled the entire outer edge of the penthouse. The floor and outer wall were made from a transparent material, and it took me a moment to adjust to the feeling that I was walking on air. It felt like glass but could easily have been a polycarbonate with similar qualities. I nearly scratched it to find out but remembered who it belonged to and chided myself for even considering the foolish notion.

The central apartment was accessed via multiple entrances off the outer tunnel. It was a large, open-concept area that consisted of a kitchen, living room, and dining area. There was a deck connected to the apartment with two massive sliding doors that opened onto it. It was also entirely transparent. I placed my hand on a biometric sensor, and the doors slid open silently. Stepping outside into the cloud with only the see-through material beneath my feet was exhilarating. The rain had died away to a light drizzle. Despite my exhaustion, I spent a few minutes enjoying the experience of being immersed in the mist before returning inside.

Staircases on both ends of the central living space spiraled up to a circular platform, which had doors along it that led to more rooms, the majority of which seemed to be for sleeping. I picked the least lavish looking quarters I could find and fell backward onto the bed. Every muscle in my body was screaming for me to stop moving and go to sleep, but I couldn't do that yet.

I pulled the dead mercenary's CUBE out and began scrolling through his messages. There were a few back-and-forth from over the last couple of days with a contact labeled MR. The first series of communications went as follows:

(4/29/59-14:45:07) TC: Landed. I'll be camped at the Starlight. Requesting details for delivery.

(4/29/59-15:02:36) MR: 1:00pm – Thursday. Row F Seat 37. Sending ticket.

(4/29/59-15:04:45) TC: Confirmed. Ticket received.

Then several more, from earlier this evening.

(4/30/59-23:15:04) MR: Contact RR. You're needed tonight.

(4/30/59-23:49:17) TC: I'm in position.

(4/30/59-23:51:15) MR: Exercise extreme caution. Recon only. Contact me directly with results.

MR and RR. Mason and Richard Robbins. I thought about the timeline the messages had transpired along. If Mason had activated TC for recon of the airport at 11:15 p.m., then that had occurred after the explosion at the Denver airport. If he'd thought the plane had exploded, he wouldn't have needed anyone on the ground in San Francisco. That meant there was a good chance someone had gotten the information back to Richard that the bomb hadn't been successful. There was no way it would have been reported by the media within fifteen minutes of when we took off. I couldn't help but worry about what it meant for Risa's safety that someone had been able to reach Robbins and let him know they'd failed. If she'd successfully gotten to them all, they wouldn't have been able to report back to him. Maybe one ran in terror and escaped. It didn't necessarily mean she'd come to any harm. Lack of sleep and concern for her well-being were beginning to interfere with my ability to stay focused.

I had a date, a time, and a location Mason would be at tomorrow. I needed to rest and get my head straight for a direct confrontation with him. I checked TC's applications, identified a ticketing service application, and verified a ticket existed for an event with tomorrow's date. It was a heliosphere game at a stadium south of the city. The Denver Boulders would be playing San Francisco's team, the Fog. There was a chance I could surprise him there, but he'd be on guard with everything that had happened. I'd need to plan my approach with caution.

I removed my wet clothing, hung up my jacket on the door, and put the rest into a dryer I found in the bathroom connected to my quarters. Before I retired, I tried one final time to get through to Risa. I was holding on to hope that she'd been too occupied with chasing the mercs, running from them, or getting back to the city to answer my earlier calls. The sound of the call attempting to connect carried on until I was prompted to leave a message. "Hey. Please call me as soon as you can. I saw the explosion and…I'd just like to know you're okay. I have some updates on our situation. I hope I have the chance to share them with you soon. Oh…I stood in a cloud tonight. I thought of you. Goodnight."

I was restless, and I tossed and turned through the remainder of the night. By the time the light of dawn started seeping through the thick clouds outside, I'd probably managed only an hour or two of actual sleep. I heard Himari leave quietly to take care of the affairs he'd mentioned but lay in bed for a while longer, struggling to capitalize on the possibility of additional rest. I wasn't exactly in ideal condition to be confronting another Fade, but if it meant an end to the mystery of this conflict, I would have crawled to the stadium. Bested once again by the strong arm of necessity, I sat up with a tired groan and prepared to struggle through another long day.

Chapter 8

I walked out onto the second-floor landing and was once again astounded by the beauty of the suite. It was overcast, so the light was dim, but what little there was brought the room alive with splendor. Jack looked up from a plate of toast and eggs on the floor below.

"Jacobi!" he said with his mouth full. "This place is incredible! Who did you have to kill to get us in here?"

"I'm not sure yet," I replied, feeling distinctly uncomfortable about the subject. Jack didn't seem to notice.

"Seriously, though, this is amazing. When you said you'd put me up somewhere, I figured I'd be in some hole in the ground. I thought I'd be fighting dope fiends for breakfast bagels, you know what I mean? You, sir, are a class act."

"I aim to please." I walked down one of the spiral staircases and opened the sliding glass doors to the balcony then fumbled with some buttons until I managed to find one that extended a roof that would protect me from the rain.

"How'd you open that?" he asked. "I tried earlier and had no luck."

"Oh right," I said, returning inside. "Concierge?"

A sultry-looking hologram appeared between us and offered a greeting in Russian. She was dressed in a maid's uniform that was entirely inappropriate for those types of responsibilities. I couldn't fathom a reason you'd need thigh-high stockings to wash floors or clean toilets.

"Switch to English."

"Of course, Jacobi. What can I help you with this morning?" Her tone hinted at something entirely different than what I'd had in mind.

"What's your name?"

"Annika."

"Annika, go ahead and configure Jack here for guest access to the suite."

"Mmm," she cooed. "Right away, sir."

She glided over to Jack, who was sporting a shit-eating grin, asked him to hold out his hand then proceeded to scan it. I left them to finish up the procedure and made my way outside onto the balcony to stretch and try to meditate. Maybe it was the fact that I hadn't slept well, or being up in the clouds with the wind rolling past me, but I found the place of nothingness easily and was quickly lost in timeless contemplation. At some point, Jack opened the doors and joined me.

"She's something," he said.

"Annika's an illusion. Cheap artificial intelligence, Jack. She'll break your heart," I said, rousing from my reverie.

"Not her, Jacobi. I meant Risa." He looked away. "She's okay, right?"

"I'm not sure," I answered honestly. "But if I had to gamble, I'd put my money on her."

"I'd just…I'd hate to be the reason something happened to her. I'm sorry. I hope she contacts you soon."

I stood up and patted his shoulder, nodding. "Thanks, Jack. Whatever happens, I'm sure she'd tell you she was responsible for her own decisions, not you. Her fate is in her own hands."

"Yeah?"

"Yeah. Then she'd probably scold you for making it all about you."

He laughed. I smiled, but thinking about her was too distracting right now.

"So what's next?" he asked.

"Nothing for you. Go for a swim, spend the day in the clouds here. You gave me a good lead. If it pans out today, I'll get some answers. Himari tells me the two of you were acquainted last night?"

"Himari, that's the metal guy? You've got some crazy friends, man. Yeah, we met. Is he going to be staying here too?"

"Himari is your new bodyguard. And believe me when I tell you they don't come any better. Consider yourself fortunate to be in his care."

"What are you going to do?"

"I'm going to find Mason. He's supposed to meet someone at a heliosphere game today around one o'clock. I'm going to be there instead."

"Mason is dangerous. Don't underestimate him."

"I won't," I said, thinking back to the time we'd shared in the FDEES. "There aren't a lot of Fades out there, but every single one of them is dangerous." I'd spent quite a bit of time helping with his training. He'd been a Marine Raider, and he'd been frustrated at having been transferred out of his regiment. Our unit had been working together for nearly five years by the time Mason joined. We'd had people come and go during that time. Some had died, some had been transferred. It usually didn't take long to form a bond, since we got thrown into the field with one another quickly and were forced to look out for each other. In his case, we never found that glue. He'd been reserved and on edge, resentful he'd been recruited rather than considering it an honor to serve like the rest of us. At one point, it had gotten so bad I asked the admiral to transfer him out because I wasn't sure he'd be there for us when we needed him to be. Ben had told me to give him a chance to adjust. He'd been convinced Mason had what it took to make the transition.

"It's just…" said Jack, interrupting my recollection, "he's got this anger. He's filled with rage, like all the time. And when it comes out, it's frightening."

"I'll be careful. Thanks for your concern."

"Concern? Shit, man. If you die, I'm completely fucked. I was only thinking about myself." He laughed then sobered and said, "I'm serious. Watch your ass out there, for both our sakes."

It was a good reminder that there were more lives on the line here than my own. As much as I wanted answers, I'd need to move cautiously, especially now that I'd be going after someone with similar training who could potentially anticipate my actions. I'd underestimated Wendell the last time I was in this situation, and I didn't plan on making that mistake again.

Himari returned shortly thereafter, carrying a small suitcase. He brought it upstairs to the room he'd chosen. Jack had taken my advice and decided to go for a swim. I could hear him whooping and laughing from down the hall. Himari raised an eyebrow as he wound down the staircase.

"He's just letting off steam, I think," I said. "We had a rough day yesterday."

"When I let off steam, something is malfunctioning," Himari replied.

"Okay. That was definitely a joke. I'm on to you."

The corner of his mouth turned upward slightly, but that was the only confirmation I received. I motioned for him to take a seat at the table with me.

"Everything go okay at the hotel?" I asked, though in retrospect I regretted having done so. The man could probably single-handedly topple a government, and I was making sure he didn't encounter any problems picking up his clothes and checking out of a hotel. Nevertheless, he nodded and sat.

"The outside world moves at a much different pace than what I've become accustomed to. In some ways I struggle to remember what my life was like before," he said. "Returning to what is normal out here might not be as easy as I'd hoped."

"I get that," I said, nodding in understanding. "When I got out of the service, I saw functional people all around me, but I couldn't sink into a rhythm. It was like everyone was dancing but I didn't know the steps. I felt completely alone. But I had a friend who was there for me, and he and his wife took care of me while I adjusted."

"Maybe you will teach me to dance?" asked Himari. Now that I knew his tell, I looked for the slight curl of his upper lip and confirmed he was fucking with me.

"I wouldn't presume to teach you anything, since I know for a fact you're smarter than I am. But I can tell you that you aren't alone. One crazy old man on a boat doesn't make the world a bad place. Just don't lose sight of that. It'll all start coming back to you. Coffee?" I asked, getting up to fill my cup.

"Tea?" he asked hopefully. I didn't take Matvei Kamenev for a tea guy, so I was surprised to find a shelf fully stocked when I looked. I threw some water on for Himari and sat back down.

"So," I began, "that friend I mentioned earlier..." I proceeded to tell Himari the entire story, from Sam Winston tapping on my window with his umbrella through how it was we were now sitting here in the lap of luxury. Jack had wandered in, wearing a towel, about halfway through the recap and sat, listening intently while I finished.

Himari sipped the last of his tea and stood to prepare another cup. I was struck by the grace with which he managed to move with cybernetic limbs. Every motion seemed to have intention behind it, never faster than it needed to be. I knew how fast he could move when he wanted to, so it must have taken great restraint.

"So you will confront this man alone, today, at the stadium?" he asked, retaking his seat at the table.

"I hope so," I said, unsure. "He's a smart man. I don't know if I'll be able to catch him off-guard, but I'm going to try."

"We could come with you, work together," offered Himari.

"Negative. I appreciate it, but no. He's too dangerous, and I need Jack out of harm's way. You being here guarding him is already helping me immensely."

Himari agreed reluctantly. I knew it couldn't be easy for a

man of his ability to be relegated to a babysitter, but I didn't know anyone more qualified to make sure Jack remained safe in my absence. In addition to that, I wasn't willing to put anyone else at risk until we fully understood the method Mason was using to accomplish the violence that he had so far.

"Good, because I had no interest in that whatsoever," Jack chimed in, laughing. Growing serious, he added, "Don't get me wrong, I want that son of a bitch, too. Probably more. I know my limitations, though."

"Jack, tell me more about Mason," I said. My memory of the man was vague. I hadn't had as many interactions with him as I had with other members of our unit, since he'd intentionally distanced himself. And a man could change a lot in five years.

"Well," said Jack, "I didn't know him before the war. I joined the Coalition later. People say he was kinder, less inclined to violence then. I don't know what happened to him, but by all accounts he came back on the edge."

Jack adjusted his towel and continued, "I can't imagine being raised by a man with as little regard for humanity as his father. I don't suppose it was easy hanging on to a shred of decency. His mother died when he was young, and the one guy he looks up to is constantly telling him we aren't worth a damn."

Jack looked thoughtful for a moment and then grew somber. "The night he killed Rose, I think he just broke under some invisible pressure. Maybe it was the war, maybe it was his father. I don't know. The night she died, Richard told him he died too, and in a way, I think he did. A light that was already dim left that man's eyes, and I never saw it again."

Jack rose from the table. "I'd better get some clothes on," he said, excusing himself.

The morning was growing late. It was nearly time for me to depart for the Loop transport that would bring me to the stadium. I wanted to stop by my apartment to pick up some additional weaponry and other useful gadgets, but I couldn't be sure it wouldn't be watched. Richard might easily have sent reinforcements to San Francisco from his private army during the night, and if he had, they would absolutely have eyes on the place. I wouldn't jeopardize our relative anonymity now that we were secure. I'd have to go to the meet with nothing but the sidearm I'd relieved from the man at the hotel the night before. After saying farewell to Jack and Himari, I took the elevator to the lobby.

There was another group of guards assembled around the front desk who were laughing at something as I passed by. I didn't see Boris, but the guards must have all known who I was, because they waved and let me pass without incident. Matvei had definitely kept up his end of this bargain. I'd do what I could to honor our agreement as long as the people he wanted me to bring in were criminals and had earned whatever sick punishment he had in mind. It felt good to have a safe house and know that Jack was protected.

I'd called my car, which was waiting for me when I exited the building. After a short drive, I stepped out at the Loop station, and the vehicle departed to park itself. The station was normally a bustling metropolis crossroads, but the intermittent storm and the flooding streets were keeping many people home. A wide, half-hexagonal stairwell led underground from under a massive holographic arch at the entrance. The plaza leading up to the stairs was flooded by at least two inches of storm surge. I'd never seen the city hit this hard before, and I wondered if the game would be cancelled, spoiling the one chance I had to get eyes on Mason. I hadn't received any notification that the ticket had been refunded, so I hoped for the best and made my way underground.

When the stadium had been built, about thirty miles south of San Francisco, deep in the forested hills outside of San Jose, the Loop transport had been installed as the primary method for transporting ticketholders. Utilizing maglev technology, it could shuttle a pod to the game in just over three minutes. They'd chosen a remote location beyond a large swath of preserved woodland for the site, both because of the cost benefit of building it outside the most expensive city in the world, and because it allowed the arena an element of privacy. It took advantage of that privacy to deploy holographic explosions, fireworks, and other elaborate and extremely loud displays of enthusiasm that would have been frustrating to many city dwellers. Out of necessity, an agreement had been made with the state to avoid a large amount of overland traffic that would have been destructive to the environment. The Loop transport had been the most agreeable solution, since it had been successful in other areas of the country. You could now take a Loop transport from Boston to New York and arrive in less than twenty minutes, and new tunnels were being constructed every day, slowly replacing solar and hydrogen fuel-celled trains and flights as the primary source of transcontinental travel.

At the bottom of the stairway the station opened up into a large hall. An illuminated walkway built into the mosaic floor indicated the path toward a central booth for purchasing tickets, and other paths broke away in various colors, each directing travelers toward departure points that varied based on the destination. Flickering holographic advertisements played in the open air above, vying for my attention with carefully vetted phrases designed to pique my interest.

"Tired of one night stands?" asked a voluptuous redhead with a sultry voice. *"Why stand at all when you could just lie there and let me do all the work? Download the Virtually Erotic app today."*

"The Tesla Deuterium," boomed an invisible voice from somewhere near a lustrous sports car that spun horizontally, showing off each perfect angle, *"She's the hydrogen, you're the neutron. It's only natural."*

I ignored them all, intent on the confrontation I was heading into and trying to relax under the pressure of its outcome. I felt unsettled, and I knew part of that was because I still wasn't sure where Risa was, or if she was okay. I trusted her and believed in her ability, which was why it was frustrating me that I couldn't seem to let it go. I felt a strong connection with her, but I'd been separated in the field from my team many times before, and I'd never let it distract me to this extent. I missed her presence and the confidence I felt when she was near. Something about our relationship felt so familiar. It was unsettling. Since it was outside the boundaries of anything my conscious mind could currently define, I let the thought fall away and concentrated on finding the proper boarding zone.

A map hovered above the booth in the center of the station that suggested traffic for the heliosphere stadium should follow the tiles that lit up purple. The station wasn't busy, but there were small, sparsely scattered groups of people, and most were heading in that general direction. I fell in behind an excited group of young adults with an outrageous amount of San Francisco Fog paraphernalia. They wore jerseys, hats, and had just about every other imaginable way of supporting the team via merchandise protruding from their bodies. They had clearly started the party early. The smell of alcohol was heavy in the air, and several of them were being supported by friends as they caroused their way through the station. I was actually impressed by the way the group managed to maintain a synchronized swerving approach to the boarding area rather than a straight line. It was not unlike watching a flock of inebriated birds, confused but somehow graceful in their herd mentality.

We passed through an arched entryway from the station's main hall into the boarding zone, a platform that extended about fifty feet to the left and right. A white pod arrived. It was completely smooth, ovular, and had a translucent strip along the center that formed a window of sorts. Two panels on the side lifted and sunk into the ceiling and floor, respectively, creating a portal for entry, which the revelers quickly took advantage of and seated themselves inside.

The group was now clamorously singing a song I didn't recognize, and based on the sound their collaborative effort emitted, I hoped for the song's sake that they weren't doing it justice. I decided to wait for the next pod. Within seconds of theirs pulling away, another had arrived, and as luck (or decision making based on observational data) would have it, I had it all to myself.

Inside the pod there were three rows of three seats, all facing forward. They were each equipped with a harness that was designed to drop down over the head, securing the torso, to keep the passengers in place. A woman's voice came through the speakers on the ceiling.

"Welcome to the Loop! In moments, your pod will be shuttled at a fantastic speed to the Davenport Coliseum. Please lower the harness then slide the fastener at your waist to the right in order to begin your journey. The doors of the pod will not close until each passenger is fully seated and their harness has been locked. We hope you enjoy the game!"

Once I'd clicked the harness into place, the panels on the wall closed and the pod departed. It reached its max speed within the first few seconds, at which point I was being magnetically propelled through the rings that made up the track of the Loop transport at around seven hundred and fifty miles per hour. Through the transparent strip along the side of the pod, I watched the brilliant, glowing blue rings flash as the pod passed through them. I didn't feel any inertia pressuring me back into my seat; in fact, if it weren't for seeing the rings flash past, I wouldn't have known whether I was moving at all. Just as I was settling in and getting comfortable, the intervals of light representing the rings we were passing through began to slow, and we glided to a halt at the destination platform.

"We've arrived at Davenport Coliseum. Slide the fastener to the left until you see a green light. The harness will lift automatically. Please remember to behave responsibly and report any suspicious or inappropriate behavior to the nearest member of the security team. Thank you for using the Loop! We'll see you on the way back!"

A ramp led up and away from the track, and before long I'd left the underground and was proceeding down a wide thoroughfare with glass walls. Behind them, a dense forest was all that could be seen to either side. The digital advertisements sprang to life around me as I walked to remind me that I could find whatever I needed at the nearby refreshment stands, rent magnification goggles for enhanced viewing of the action, upgrade my tickets to box seats, or have my needs met in a variety of other ways, all of which I automatically disregarded.

The stadium rose up out of the trees ahead, massive and looming. I passed the group I'd walked behind back in the city; they had stopped to help one of their members that looked as if they'd fallen. In helping, several of them had also fallen and were now laughing hysterically on the ground. One of them looked up at me as I passed. It was a skinny girl with a pair of goggles, the lenses of which were displaying an animated San Francisco Fog logo.

"Hey! Sir, can you help us up?" she asked between bouts of tear-inducing giggling. I walked by without looking, which caused them all to laugh even harder.

The thoroughfare finally terminated at the entrance to the stadium itself. People held their CUBEs over a sensor and passed through a turnstile once their tickets were accepted. I did the same and entered the outer ring of the stadium, where an active world of commerce awaited. Drones hurtled through the air above the crowd, taking and delivering food orders. Shops and services made up the inner section of the ring, and short lines of consumers waited to acquire their goods. There were lights everywhere, from floor lighting to indicate directions to the various sections of the coliseum to the outer walls that were alive with video of historic game highlights.

I circled around, looking for a map to identify my seating section. I found a group of people surrounding a slowly rotating holographic layout of the area that responded to somatic input and waited for my turn to access it. When the others had backed away, I approached and dragged the image to zoom it out, rotated it until the blinking light indicating my current location was aligned with the direction I was facing, and took note of the path I needed to take to reach my seat, which was on the opposite side of the arena.

I walked to my section, but instead of heading right up, I waited near the bottom of the ramp that led out of the lower ring and into the stands. It took three separate attempts of approaching a single man and offering to pay them to exchange seats before someone agreed. The first had looked at me like I'd just thrown up on his shoes then walked away. The second was part of a group who was already seated and wanted to remain with his friends. The third was hesitant, but when I upped the offer to two hundred credits, he accepted immediately.

Afterward, I found one of the stores in the outer ring that was selling the magnification goggles I'd seen advertised earlier. With those in hand, I made my way up the ramp and out into the stands. The stadium roof was closed due to the storm, but the energy in the air was still electric as I emerged into the coliseum. It wasn't full, but there were enough fans to create the constant murmur that hummed in a way only thousands of people congregating together could sound — distant but intense.

The field was white turf designed to create a modest and inconspicuous background to film against for all of the drones that would be broadcasting the game to the Evernet from above. In the center, about thirty meters up, was suspended the enormous spherical framework that allowed the spinning plates guarding the heliosphere at the center to operate.

Along the edge of the field on both sides, stations for the controllers were established but currently empty. Soon, the controllers would enter the field to glorious fanfare and introduce the bots they'd be entering into this night's contest. The controllers were the real stars, since they'd be the puppeteers, guiding their respective bots to victory with unbelievable feats of precision and reaction time. Nonetheless, the bots themselves often had a significant fan following despite the fact they were simply tools being manipulated. Human beings never had much difficulty assigning personality to inanimate, unthinking objects. We saw ourselves in the icons. We ignored the greed, violence, and stupidity so common to human nature. We saw only the aspiration, hard work, and commitment that every bot struggling for victory glorified. It was almost impossible not to root for something that conveniently embodied only the best parts of us.

The seat I'd traded for was about twenty rows or so above the one I would have had if I hadn't exchanged it. That gave me a better vantage point to try to observe Mason. At the moment, the seat next to the man I'd traded with below was still empty, so I waited. I strapped on the magnification goggles, which would help me confirm Mason's identity when he arrived and served the additional purpose of covering my face in case he was scanning the crowd. I couldn't think of any reason he'd suspect his meet with TC had been compromised, but I also knew how careful we'd been trained to be.

The crowd erupted as light burst out from around the perimeter of the stadium ceiling. Holographic fireworks were accompanied by loud, booming audio, and the visual of residual light from the explosions trickled down into the crowd.

"*Are you ready, San Francisco?*" asked the announcer through hundreds of speakers positioned throughout the coliseum, to which the crowd responded by throwing their hands into the air and shouting even more enthusiastically.

The announcer went on to introduce the controllers for the Denver Boulders, who each emerged from their team's tunnel with their fists raised above their heads. The screens surrounding the walls above the stands came to life with videos introducing the bots they would each be piloting from their stations on the field. I kept my eyes on Mason's empty seat below and waited. The Boulder controllers connected wiring to their suits at their stations and donned the helmets that would allow them to see through the eyes of their respective bots. The sensory stations

231

they were connected to would allow them to run, twist, turn, and jump, and every action would be imitated by the robot they controlled.

I was starting to get nervous and wondered if Mason was going to show. I tried not to get too tense about it and reminded myself that the game hadn't even started yet. The San Francisco Fog entered the field, and the aforementioned fanfare ensued to the effect of much revelry among the crowd. Once the controllers had wired up at their sensory stations, the bots themselves began to arrive from the dark tunnels that led back to their team's respective locker rooms. They glided out on hovering discs and lined up on either side, awaiting the signal to begin the match.

The crowd grew still, and the noise levels dropped dramatically while they waited anxiously for the opening signal. Then the deep toll of a gong rang through the stadium, and the bots burst into action. The discs they rode shot up toward the maze of wall-like plates, which had begun to rapidly shift and slide along the spherical frame near the ceiling. In near unison, they leapt from their discs and latched onto the plates at whatever entry point they had decided to begin their journey. The displays on the walls of the stadium showed different perspectives from the eyes, or cameras, really, of the bots on the field. This allowed fans to follow along with their favorites and see exactly what the controller was seeing.

The bots began to fight their way toward the center of the sphere, dodging plates that were collapsing from above or sliding into one another with a force that could easily crush them. There were several layers to the labyrinth, and each bot did everything in its power to hamper the progress of the others. Each consecutive layer had plates that moved faster than the one before, and in the center of it all, the heliosphere waited to be claimed. Occasionally, one of the bots would either be pushed from the contraption or leap off by choice to avoid being crushed by a rotating plate. When that happened, their hoverdisc would rise up quickly from where it waited on the field below, and in most cases, the falling bot could catch hold of it, pull itself up, and ride it back up into the fray. Sometimes they simply hit the ground and were deemed out of the contest, requiring the controller to swap out with a second-string teammate waiting in the wings.

With Mason still absent, I was distracted by the action long enough to see Perseus, a crowd favorite, breach the final layer of the sphere. The black case surrounding the heliosphere separated to reveal a flaming orb. He leapt off a plate in motion and landed on the circular platform at the center. Preparing to *steal the sun* and claim a point for the Fog, he reached for the orb but was suddenly tackled from the side by Avalanche, and both of them fell from the platform, ricocheting from several plates as they spiraled downward. Avalanche entwined himself around Perseus, who was unable to reach out for his hoverdisc when it rose up to break his fall, and both of the bots hit the ground with a resounding crash. The crowd went wild.

"*Sacrifice!*" boomed the announcer as the fans celebrated the carnage.

I returned my attention to the seats below and saw a man in a black coat making his way along the aisle. He was wearing a baseball cap and facing toward the field as he slid past the other seats, so I couldn't make out his face. He paused as he neared the empty seat and got a look at the man in the seat next to his but continued advancing after a few seconds of consideration. When he arrived, he tapped the shoulder of the man I'd traded seats with then leaned in to ask him a question. They spoke back and forth until the man I'd traded with turned and pointed upward, directly at my seat. The man in the cap followed his finger and looked directly at me.

I didn't know if he could identify me from that distance, but with the goggles on I could see Mason Robbins clearly. His straight, black hair was just long enough to creep out from under his cap. He looked older than he should, as if the years since we'd seen one another had harried and beleaguered him with pain and doubt. It was his eyes, wrinkled, with dark bags beginning to form beneath them that struck me the most. They were the intense, calculating eyes of a predator, but there was something familiar there as well. It was the guilt and self-loathing I saw in my own eyes whenever I looked in a mirror. His lips broke into a thin, false smile as our gazes met, then he turned, and began to leave the aisle the way he'd come in.

I ignored the shouts of protest and the insults as I leapt into action, jumping onto the top of the chairs beneath me and running along them toward the main aisle. Mason hit the stairs before me and casually descended to ground level. When I finally reached the aisle, I ran down the stairs after him, but by the time I reached the ground floor, he'd reached the bottom of the ramp that doubled back under the stairs toward the outer ring of the stadium. He looked back over his shoulder. Seeing me at the top of the ramp, he dashed to the right and disappeared around the corner.

I gave chase. When I reached the bottom of the ramp, I saw Mason weaving through the crowd and pushing people out of his way as he progressed along the ring. I set out as quickly as I could, maneuvering through the thin crowd as I ran. There was only one way back to the city. Even if he found an exit from the stadium, we were surrounded by dense forest on all sides for miles, and if he chose that option, I'd eventually catch up. I just needed to stay in visual range to make sure he didn't disappear into the crowd. He was heading directly for the Loop departure zone, and I kept on him doggedly, making slight progress as we raced along the outer ring. Once he reached the thoroughfare leading out, the crowd thinned considerably, and any gains I'd made were lost as he raced away unimpeded. By the time I'd arrived at the entrance to the thoroughfare, he'd put enough distance between us that I doubted I could catch up to him by the time a pod arrived.

I pushed myself and ran as hard as I could down the ramp. As I burst through the arched entryway onto the platform, the panels of a pod were closing, and Mason, seated inside, stared emotionlessly at me, panting heavily on the platform as I watched the pod pull away. Before I'd caught my breath, another pod arrived. I boarded quickly, pulled the harness down, and slid the lock in place. As I traveled along the Loop, I looked down and realized my hands were shaking. It wasn't fear or adrenaline causing the shaking. It was anxiety at the notion Mason might so easily escape the trap I'd set and what that might mean for the safety of those I cared about.

When the pod finally glided to a halt, I unlocked the harness and stood at the wall of the pod in a position to dash out of the portal when the panels opened. The woman's voice came over the speakers, thanking me for using the Loop. The panels opened, and Mason, standing directly in front of the exit, blew a fine powder from his open hand into my face.

I blinked in surprise and immediately tried to rub the dust out of my eyes. Backing away, I drew the pistol at my side and aimed it in the direction of the portal, but he was gone. I ran out of the pod onto the platform and looked to both sides to see where he'd escaped to. Seeing nothing in either direction, I realized there was only one other way he could have gone in the short amount of time I'd been distracted by the dust. I spun, but he'd already jumped from the roof of the pod he'd mounted and connected with me before I could bring my weapon to bear.

The tackle toppled me onto my back. I cushioned his landing and took the brunt of the impact. Mason took advantage of my being winded by the collision and batted the gun out of my hand. He stood up and backed away, and as I rose to my knees, he drew a pistol and aimed it at me. I froze and put my hands in the air.

"Looks like you finally get whatever it is you wanted, Mason," I said, searching his face for any hint of what might have motivated the assaults. It remained expressionless, and I felt sorrow and a great sense of disappointment knowing I was going to die without even understanding why.

"Not quite yet, Jacobi," he said softly. "You've got some work to do."

"What is this all about?" I asked. "Why are you doing this?"

He laughed dryly. "It wouldn't matter if I told you. You're not going to remember this conversation." His lips curled into a snarl, the first real emotion I'd seen from him. "You don't understand any of this because you're a fucking coward."

I felt a fog beginning to pressure the outer edges of my conscious mind, pushing softly and closing in. That's when I made the connection. The powder. I wouldn't remember.

Oh, god.

"You got sloppy," he said, moving in and kneeling in front of me.

I wanted to reach out and grab the gun from him, or just grab him by the throat, but I couldn't. The fog was thickening, and I was losing myself with every passing moment.

"So desperate to be in control," Mason continued. "You haven't changed at all."

I stared helplessly into his blue eyes as he moved his face directly in front of mine.

"Pick up your gun. You're going to need it," he commanded.

With horror, I realized I was doing exactly that. Walking over to where it lay, I picked up the gun and returned it to the holster. I wasn't sure how much longer I had, so with a desperate surge of mental focus, I drew on the last vestiges of my willpower to blink my eyes in a specific sequence meant to initiate the recording feature of my augment lenses.

As the fog closed in around me, I felt the nightmare arrive. I could see it stomping flaming hooves from deeper into the mist. Its fiery eyes locked with mine, and I stared in horror as the black, equine demon let loose a terrible baying and reared. Then it was charging, and the night was moving with it, ripping the fog away and leaving only darkness in its wake. As it passed through me, and my control was ripped away completely, I screamed and knew nothing more.

I woke and had the acute feeling of being alone in a world that was wrongly serene, like the calm before the storm. I'd dreamt of something horrifying that haunted me, writhing just outside of my ability to recall. The terror held me frozen to the sheets as my mind reconfigured to the safety and familiarity of my apartment. The context of the dream was faded and surreal, but my panic felt real enough as I tried to catch my breath.

Finally, the feeling began to fade, and I sat up and threw my legs over the side of my bed. It was late in the night, but dawn would be breaking soon, if I were judging the light outside accurately. I was overcome with a feeling of urgency but couldn't recall what I was supposed to be doing. I had no memory of going to sleep and no clear recollection of what I'd been doing in the time leading up to that. I felt dazed and was finding it difficult to remember specifics. When I tried to concentrate on anything from the day before, it was like my mind was a starving wolf, scattering the memories like a flock of sheep whenever it neared.

I got up and walked into the kitchen, poured myself a glass of water, then looked around and noticed the computer equipment scattered over all of the surfaces.

Risa.

The thought of her was like an anchor. It allowed me to begin pinpointing related memories and slowly reconstruct the events of the previous week. Eventually, I'd placed enough puzzle pieces to form a mostly intact picture of what I hoped was the day before. I remembered talking with Jack and Himari and heading to the game. I remembered taking the Loop to the stadium, the image of Mason's fake smile as he spotted me in my seat above, and giving chase. Beyond that there was nothing. I walked back into my bedroom and noticed my jacket and clothing had been thrown onto a chair nearby. Thinking perhaps I'd find a clue about the events from the night before, I picked up my pants, which were still damp from the rain, and noticed a dark stain on the leg.

"Ava, put the lights on," I said. The lights came on, and I dropped the pants, disgusted. They were covered in dried blood. I riffled through the other clothes and found the same was true for my shirt and jacket. I checked myself for wounds, but other than the ones that had already been dressed and cared for, I didn't find anything new. A cold feeling seeped into my chest as I realized the blood could belong to anyone. I backed away from the soiled clothing, sat back down on the bed, and covered my face with my hands, trying desperately to remember and not knowing if I even wanted to.

"Think, Jacobi," I said, my voice shaking. "What the fuck did you do?"

With my eyes closed, I noticed a blinking red light in the corner of my right augment lens. I dug my CUBE from out of the pocket of the pants on the floor and opened the user interface for the modification. I touched the help button and asked, "What does a blinking red light mean?"

"*A blinking red light on your lens indicates that a video recording was interrupted. If you would like to resume recording, please perform the standard function for initiating a recording. The standard function to initiate a video recording is to blink both eyes three times, holding them closed for one second between,*" droned the audio response, but I'd stopped paying attention as I frantically searched the interface for the area where recordings were saved.

I found one, and the timestamp lined up with what I believed to be the previous night. I reached down to start the video and my hand froze. It felt so similar to what I'd felt when I'd been preparing to view Mary's murder, but then it had been Ben, and I'd thought he'd lost his mind. I wasn't sure I had the strength to watch myself harm someone I cared about, but I had to know. I transferred the video to the augment lens display and asked Ava to shut the lights off. In the relative darkness, there was little to interfere with the broadcast on the lens display, and through my eyes I watched the scene on the platform of the Loop station play out from when I'd begun recording.

"Take this," said Mason, handing me what looked like a small circular piece of metal. "Clip it on your ear."

I reached up and did so.

"I wish you did know," he said. "I wish you knew exactly why you deserve this. But since you're too much of a coward, it will have to do that I remember. And that will be enough."

I nodded stupidly.

"Stand here," Mason said and walked to the far end of the platform.

I raised my arm and waved, and he walked back over.

"Could you hear me clearly?" he asked.

Again, I nodded.

"Good. Listen to me. You're going to go back to wherever you have Jack hidden, and we're going to take care of him. Do you understand? We're going to take care of all of your friends. Go."

I left the station and waited in the flooded plaza for my vehicle to arrive. The wind was blowing wildly, and the rain was becoming more intense, but I made no effort to protect myself from the downpour. When my car pulled up, I got inside and input a destination.

"I understand. No problem."

The recording wasn't picking up Mason's voice in my

earpiece, but I assumed I was responding to something he'd told me.

"Command: contact Himari Okada."

The CUBE attempted the connection, and Himari answered.

"How did it go?" he asked.

"I'm not sure," I replied. "I need to talk to Jack."

"He's out on the balcony, hold on."

I waited while the display the CUBE was generating above the receptacle showed Himari in motion then knocking on the glass doors of the balcony and motioning for Jack to come inside. Jack started and came in.

"What's up?" he asked.

"Jacobi needs to talk to you."

Himari's stoic face swapped out with Jack's cherubic countenance on the display.

"Well, you're alive," he said. "Did you find him?"

"Yes," I said. "Jack, I need you to meet me downstairs in the garage. Come alone."

"What? Why?"

"I need you to meet me there alone. I'm pulling in now. Come down immediately." I ended the call.

The car pulled into the garage and found an available parking spot. I exited the vehicle and leaned up against the hood of the car to wait for Jack.

Sweating and unable to stand the tension of waiting, I fast-forwarded the footage until I saw Jack approaching.

He waved from the stairwell and began walking toward me. I left the car and walked in his direction. We were about one hundred feet apart. He put his hands out to both sides with his palms up and asked, "What is this, man? I thought you wanted me out of sight. Is this even safe?"

"I'm not sure," I called out to him. Eighty feet.

"Then let's go upstairs! Come on, Jacobi. What are we doing here?" Sixty feet.

"I don't know," I answered. Jack stopped moving toward me.

"You don't know? What the fuck, man? Are you okay?" Thirty feet away. I kept walking directly toward him.

"I'm good," I said. At a distance of ten feet, I could see from the look on Jack's face that he was trying to decide whether or not to trust my response. I reached to my side and unholstered the gun. Jack began backing away, and I broke into a run toward him. He let out a strangled cry and turned to run, but it was too late. I raised the weapon and fired twice. Both shots hit him directly in the back, and he lost his footing and fell forward onto the ground.

"Fuck!" I yelled, fumbling with the interface for the augment display to stop the playback. "Goddammit. No. No, goddammit!"

I finally managed to stop the playback just as I watched myself walk up and stand over Jack, weapon aimed at the back of his head. Falling to my knees, I let out a primal shout of remorse and rage and slammed my fist on the ground next to me. I stayed that way for a time, the guilt over what I'd done coursing through my body, feeling a boiling rage at having lost control, at having been used like a puppet, and at feeling as helpless as I did in that moment. Very slowly, the fire inside died down to embers until I was eventually left feeling only the cold, hard certainty I would make Mason pay for what he'd done. Picking myself off the floor, I forced myself to resume the footage. I had to know everything.

Jack rolled over onto his back and looked up at me with a shocked expression. Coughing blood, he held his hands up and muttered, "Wait...wait...please."

I waited.

"Come here," he said quietly, beckoning for me to come closer. I kneeled down next to him. "You don't want to kill me, Jacobi," he managed to mutter. "Come here. It's okay." I knelt down closer, and he put his arms around my neck. "Help me up."

At least one of the bullets had passed directly through him, because he was bleeding profusely from the front. I helped him stand, and he leaned into me. "Come on," he said. "Come on." He was delirious and confused.

Tilting my head slightly to the right, I nodded and said, "I understand." I dropped Jack onto the ground beneath me and brought my weapon to bear at his chest. I fired, but the shot went wide. Someone had grabbed hold of my wrist and pulled my arm to the right, causing me to miss. Spinning around to face my assailant, I caught a brief glimpse of Himari before I went flying backward from a straight kick into my midsection. He held on to my gun as the momentum carried me back, disarming me.

"Himari," I said, sitting up from the floor.

"You are not yourself, Jacobi. You need to go, now. Leave this place."

I looked over at Jack, unmoving on the ground. Blood was beginning to pool beneath him.

"Yes, he's dead," I said, presumably responding to Mason again. "Okay."

The puppet master pulling my strings must have ordered me to attack, because I ran at Himari with my fists raised.

It became difficult to track specifics from the footage as I engaged him, since we were both moving very quickly. From what I could deduce, Himari had blocked several blows before grabbing my wrist and twisting me around so that my back was against his chest. Since I let out a few strangled gasps, I guessed he'd wrapped his arm around my neck and was choking me out. My eyelids slowly shut, and the camera went dark. I heard Himari swearing in Japanese and the sound of what must have been him lifting Jack's body and dragging it away.

There had to be more. I'd woken up in my apartment, not the garage at Matvei's building. I put the footage on fast-forward once again, until sometime later when my eyes began to flicker open.

I pulled myself up from the garage floor and looked around, seemingly confused. Eventually, I returned to my car and got inside. I just sat there, unmoving, for a while, until my CUBE vibrated, breaking the silence abruptly. I accepted the call.

"Jacobi?"

A cold, dark feeling expanded from my stomach into my chest as Risa's face appeared on the display, where it collided with an equally intense feeling of warmth and relief that she was all right.

"Yes?"

"It's Risa…are you okay?"

"Yes."

"Uh…good. Great. I would have called you sooner, but my CUBE was broken when I went after those men. I've been completely dark. I know you were probably worried, I'm sorry. Listen, we have a lot to talk about. Can we meet up?"

"Okay," I said without emotion.

"Where are you?" she asked. "You're not at your apartment."

There was a pause before I answered, in which I was almost assuredly receiving instructions from Mason, because I'd tilted my head slightly again, as if it had been surprising to suddenly have a voice in my ear. I'd seen the same behavior from both the footage of the admiral and with Wendell at the Emporium.

"I'll meet you there," I said. "I'll be there soon."

I scrubbed forward through the recording until I was riding the elevator up to my suite.

I opened the door to my apartment. The lights were mostly out but for a few motion-detecting night lights that dimly lit the kitchen, which I walked through until I stood in the doorway to the bedroom. Risa looked to be asleep atop the covers on the bed, in only her underwear. She didn't stir at all as I stood in the doorway, watching her. I walked back into the kitchen and rummaged through the drawers there until I found a large butcher knife. Returning to the doorway with the knife in my hand, I stopped. Risa was awake and sitting up in the bed.

"Jacobi?" she asked nervously.

"Yes," I answered, walking slowly toward her.

"What are you planning to do with that knife?"

"What he told me," I said.

"What who told you? Jacobi?" she snapped as I neared, then sprung to her feet, crouching on the bed.

I raised the knife and rushed at her.

"Jacobi, activate your kill switch."

The feed ended, and everything went dark.

Chapter 9

I sat on my bedroom floor, feeling anxiety and sadness after what I'd just witnessed, but also gratitude that it hadn't ended differently where Risa was concerned. Exhausted, I leaned back against my bedframe and let out another emotional shout, which emerged sounding like something between a bark of laughter and a strangled cry. I had nothing now. I'd killed the man I'd sworn to keep safe. I'd been beaten by Mason, dominated. He'd used me like one of the bots at the game. What little control I'd thought I had had been ripped away like torn paper. I'd been turned into the very thing I'd feared the most. I'd been used as a weapon. That thought triggered emotions buried deep within me. I was struggling to make sense of them when I heard the front door of the apartment open and close. I didn't bother to rise. I didn't care.

Fortunately, it was Risa and not someone with more villainous intentions who entered the room. She walked over, sat beside me, and put her arms around my neck. She held me for a time, and the scent of amber and honey soothed me as I buried my face in her arm. When I finally pulled my head up, my eyes felt swollen and sensitive. Outside, the light had arrived and I felt cornered and revealed, incapable of hiding from what I'd done. The morning was indifferent to my desires, but Risa must have recognized my pained expression.

"Ava, please tint the windows," she requested. The panes

darkened softly until they were semi-translucent, shading the light significantly.

I cleared my dry throat and said, "You don't have to say please, you know. She won't take offense."

Risa smiled down at me, her face having somehow grown even more beautiful in the mere day we'd been apart. She ran my hair from off my forehead with her hand and leaned down to kiss me. It was a small bit of warmth in the sea of ice I found myself treading, but I was desperate for something to hold on to, something to keep me afloat, and I savored the moment. If it were possible to freeze a moment in time, I'd have done so then. Not to capture it, but to take refuge in it so as not to have to face what I'd done. But time would not negotiate. It had other obligations. We both did.

"I'll kill him," I said quietly.

"How will you find him?" she asked. I had no idea. "We need to understand what's driving him before we can try to get into his head and out-think him."

"I had a chance. I thought I had him. And now…Risa… Jack's dead."

"I know," she said, her voice soft and filled with compassion.

"How?"

"Himari. After you called him, he followed Jack downstairs and tagged your car for tracking. He showed up here a little while after you did. He was following you to make sure you stayed safe and told me everything that happened. How do *you* know what happened? I thought you wouldn't remember."

I tapped my eye. "Recording. I threw it on right after Mason hit me with some sort of powder at the game. I don't remember,

247

but I saw it all. Fuck," I said, palming my forehead, "I saw all of it. What happened to you?"

"Things got out of hand," she answered.

"I saw the explosion. I wasn't sure…"

"I know. I'm sorry. I was nowhere near it, though. I dragged Justin away, or at least that's what Jack called him, and left him with a broken ankle. Some people watched me assault him, and the alarm went up pretty quickly. I left him there and went after the two men he'd come with. Then I heard the bomb go off a few minutes later. I think he tried to drag himself away, but the police confronted him. It was all over the Evernet. There was footage of him triggering a device and taking out all those cops."

"Jesus. I'm glad you're okay," I said.

"So glad that you tried to kill me when you saw me," she quipped.

I lowered my head.

"I'm sorry," she said. "That was low. Really, I'm fine, Jacobi."

When I didn't raise my head, she grabbed my chin and lifted my face to look directly into my eyes.

"I'm fine because of you. Because of what you planned for. I know you. You're sitting here thinking he beat you, but you beat him. You didn't do what he wanted you to do to me, or whatever else he had in mind, because you had the foresight to protect us from it."

"And Jack?" I asked.

Risa looked uncomfortable. I could tell she wasn't telling me everything. "Jack was an unfortunate casualty in this fight. What happened wasn't your fault any more than it's my fault Wendell is dead. You told me that."

"I told him I'd protect him. He helped us, and I shot him," I argued.

"No. No, Jacobi. Mason shot him." Risa set her jaw, and her voice took on a tone of finality. "And we're going to find that son of a bitch and end him."

"So, what happened?" I asked, moving away from the difficult subject. "Did you catch up to the men who came to the airport with Justin?"

"I caught up. We had a talk outside the airport. One of them had a club or something, and I caught a pretty good hit on the side, right into my CUBE. *C'est mort.* Dead." She mouthed a silent poof and mimicked an explosion with her hands.

"Bad luck," I said.

"Bad defense," she countered. "But *oui*, there I was. One of them didn't make it. The other one I threw in their truck. I drove out into the hills until I found an old barn I could pull into so we could get more familiar with one another."

"Should I be jealous?"

"Definitely not," she said, smiling. It took a special kind of person to find a woman smiling about torturing someone for information so attractive, but I did. "He was pretty good. Richard Robbins trained them well, but he caved. He was a lieutenant, and he knew about the powder. He told me Mason was using a drug to control people. He doses them and puts an audio transmitter in their ear to direct them from a distance."

I sat up from the bed frame and put my hand to my ear. I hadn't considered Mason could still be listening to us and berated myself for being so foolish. Risa held out a hand and showed me what had once been the transmitter I'd been given. It had been sufficiently smashed and was clearly incapable of operating effectively.

"Looking for this?" she asked. "I pulled it from your ear after you collapsed."

Relieved, I leaned back into Risa's arms and asked, "Did he tell you why?"

She shook her head. "No. Either he didn't know or he's trained better than I gave him credit for and managed to keep it from me. Eventually, I stranded him there and drove his truck farther west. I found a small airport where I could charter a private flight. That was a few hours ago. I came straight here and contacted you through Ava. You were acting strange on the phone but I didn't imagine he'd gotten to you already. I thought maybe I'd woken you, or you were upset I hadn't answered your calls. I took a shower, and thought I'd make it up to you, but I was so tired I passed out for a few minutes."

I sighed. So now we knew the *how* but not the *why*.

"Jacobi, I have a guess as to the reason for all of this," she said cautiously.

I sat up. "A guess? What is it?"

"I can't say yet. Not until I can confirm it."

"You can't say? I don't understand. Risa, if you know anything about why I'm being targeted, you have to tell me."

"It's complicated, Jacobi. You have to trust me right now. If we can verify my suspicion, then I'll tell you what I think, but not before. I'm sorry. I know how frustrating that must be."

"How do we verify it?"

"You won't like it."

"Risa, don't use my own tricks against me."

"The Division. I need to hack the DFDC."

"Okay? Why would I..."

"From inside," she interrupted. "I need to be on-site, on the network."

I groaned and stood up.

"We can do this," she argued, standing up with me. "I'm going to call Cody. We'll need his expertise to get inside, but we all know the building, and I know the network."

"I don't know, Risa," I said, beginning to pace. I was already calculating, weighing the various strengths and weaknesses of what I remembered about the security at the DFDC primary headquarters. It had been over five years since we'd worked there. I could only imagine how much things had changed.

"What's to know? Listen, Jacobi. If you want to catch Mason, we need to understand his reasons for doing this. If I'm right, and we can get in, I think I can get that information."

"I'm not sure. Maybe I can reach out to Sam. I have a contact at the Division who's been helping with the case. Maybe he can get us access." Our odds of infiltrating the headquarters of one of the most well protected organizations on the west coast weren't ones I was comfortable shoving my chips all in on.

"If I'm right, there is a good chance this goes way beyond his access," she said.

"What is it you think you know?" I asked, spinning to face her in frustration.

She looked at me sympathetically and shook her head. "Please, trust me."

The unfortunate truth was that we didn't really have another move to make. Mason was in the wind now, and I didn't know where or when he'd lash out again. If I couldn't understand what was motivating him, I had little chance of predicting his behavior or finding him. And I did trust her.

"Do we really need to bring Cody in on this?" It was just one more person I'd have to consider the safety of. With Jack's death, my credibility for coming through in that regard had plummeted significantly.

"He's the best we know. I think it would improve our odds considerably," said Risa. It was true. Cody Marshall's knowledge of intrusion countermeasures and perimeter security was unrivaled and could potentially be the difference between success and disappearing into a dark hole somewhere, never to be seen again.

"And you're sure this is necessary? If there is any other way…"

"Well, we could just ask Mason if we see him again," she said coyly. "But I'm not sure he'll be interested in cooperating."

The mention of his name stirred the embers of the fire in my chest that had slowly been dying. As the flame roared back to life, it brought with it a renewed sense of purpose and commitment. I nodded firmly.

"Okay. We'll do it."

Risa smiled tightly and embraced me, then leaned back and looked up into my eyes. "Are you okay, Jacobi?" she asked sincerely.

I took a moment to consider her question. "No, I'm not okay," I said, shaking my head. "But I will be. Let's just focus on finding out what's happening here, and I'll work it out when I find Mason and make him pay for what he's done to me. To all of us."

She nodded slowly and leaned back into me. We stood there for a time as the light of dawn fought to breach the clouds of the overcast sky outside. Eventually, I pulled away and began to pace again.

"Take everything you need from here. This place is compromised. We can't stay here any longer." Risa began packing up her electronic equipment, and I was grateful to have the opportunity to gather some clothes and gear of my own. I didn't recall telling Mason where we'd been holed up in the footage I'd watched earlier, so as far as I knew, the safe house remained secure. In either case, we'd be a lot better protected there than in my apartment. We gathered everything we might need and packed it up. I wasn't sure how long we'd be gone, so I grabbed the fishbowl, too. Nautilus gave no indication he cared much about what lay beyond the glass wall of his domain, but I wasn't going to abandon him. We departed in our respective vehicles, separated as we turned out of my garage, and drove randomly through the city until we were convinced we weren't being followed before reconvening outside of Matvei's building.

The guards in the lobby tensed as we approached, their hands not so subtly reaching into their suit jackets. Boris was there, and he stepped out in front of the others.

"Mr. Slate," he said with a welcoming tone. "I trust everything was taken care of to your satisfaction?"

I wasn't really sure what he was referring to, but I nodded

slowly.

"Excellent. And look, your dreams have come true. A woman arrives at last. And it seems you have a fish. What a happy family."

I chuckled and said, "Boris, this is Therisa. Therisa, Boris and these other fine gentlemen will be watching out for our safety while we indulge ourselves in the audacious glory of Mr. Kamenev's apartment upstairs.

"It's a pleasure, Boris," she said, extending her hand. "Thank you for keeping us safe."

Boris took her hand, bowed slightly, and gently pressed his lips to the back of it. "You are most welcome," he said, rising. The guards behind Boris snickered. He turned and began to berate them in Russian as we continued on our way through the lobby to the elevator.

"What is this place?" asked Risa, admiring the dense tropical environment. "Is that a monkey?"

"We have them all over the city now. Eco-habitats that can be biologically engineered to imitate any environment you can think of. It's just another way the ultra-rich get to wave their money around. This place, though, it's a favor from someone I'd rather not owe."

She seemed to accept that and didn't press for more information, either because she didn't want to push on a sore spot or because she was entirely fascinated by the monkey who was staring at us curiously from a nearby tree as we boarded the elevator.

When it opened, we stepped out into the hall, and Risa's eyes widened, impressed. I gave her a tour around the outer circle, then we made our way into the main living space, where Himari was resting comfortably on one of the couches.

"Himari…" I was ashamed and embarrassed, and I wasn't sure where to begin my apology.

"It's okay, Jacobi-san. I know what happened was not your fault. You were as much a victim in that situation as Jack. I am only sorry I could not better protect him. I failed you both."

"It's a complicated situation. I don't think anyone could have been prepared for…that. If I hadn't allowed Mason to get the better of me, you wouldn't have been put in that situation. Please, forgive me."

He shook his head. "There is nothing to forgive. But I assume there is no purpose for me to remain here?"

"Actually, I'd really appreciate it if you stayed. Having you here is like having an additional layer of security, and that puts me at ease. We might have another joining us, but there's plenty of room. If you want to go, I understand. But this isn't over, and I could use the support, if you're willing."

He gave a tight nod and said, "*Hai*. I was hoping you'd say that. I haven't used the pool yet."

I reached forward and clasped his forearm. "Thank you. And thank you for what you did in the garage." Struck by a sudden curiosity, I asked, "Where is Jack's body? What happened after I left?"

Himari shot a quick glance at Risa, but she didn't seem to take notice.

"The security in the lobby," said Himari. "I told them that Jack had been attacked and that we needed to get him to a hospital. They refused. They said it would be unacceptable to connect Mr. Kamenev's building to the events in any way."

"What?" I said, growing angry.

"They had an alternative solution," he continued. "They called for a man employed by their organization. He works off the grid, underground. He came and did what he could for Jack, but it was too late. Some cleaners came in as well, a small team of people who went through the garage and removed any trace of what happened."

I sighed. Jack deserved better. He'd had a tough run of things, and it ended badly for him, but I'd learned enough in my time to accept that life wasn't fair and people rarely got what they deserved. I'd be no use to anyone if I stayed lost in mourning or distracted by contemplation of karmic injustices, so I tried to stay focused on our agenda.

"I need to sleep," said Risa. "I've been awake for two days. Where do I park?"

"I'll show you," I said, standing up. I led her upstairs to the room I'd stayed in. "With me, unless you want your own room?" She removed her boots, took off her outerwear, and collapsed into the bed without answering. I walked over and knelt beside her. Her eyes were barely open.

"I have a secure connection to Cody. Wake me in a few hours and I'll contact him, then we'll get started," she said, her voice losing strength. I nodded, but her eyes had closed.

"Goodnight, Risa," I whispered and then stood and left the room, closing the door behind me.

I badly needed to wash the night before off, so I gathered a change of clothes and hit the shower. A local Evernet broadcast came alive on the shower wall monitor while I desperately tried to scrub the filth and shame I felt away. It was an emergency broadcast, and I turned up the volume to hear it better.

"...are asking that all San Francisco residents prepare to evacuate inland away from the expected storm surge. Officials are citing dangerous levels of flooding that will drastically impact travel in and out of the city over the next several days. Many seawalls have already been breached, leaving the downtown area increasingly difficult to traverse. Flood warnings have been in effect for several days for the Napa, Guadalupe, and Russian rivers, and the city warns that atmospheric rivers contribute to a high likelihood of increased mud slides throughout the bay area. Those who are able to leave the city should do so at the earliest opportunity. For those who are unable to do so..."

"Annika, turn off the broadcast."

The concierge materialized next to me in the shower, and I jumped in surprise.

"I'm afraid I can't, Jacobi," she said with an exaggerated melancholy. "Protocol demands emergency broadcasts are transmitted fully via all available devices."

I sighed heavily. "I think this device is malfunctioning. I saw sparks earlier. Let's just assume it's broken for now. You can keep broadcasting on all of the other monitors in the house. Okay?"

"Mmm," she purred affirmatively in a way that made me uncomfortable. "If that's what you want."

"Yes, please. Thank you. That will be all for now. Thanks."

She giggled and disappeared as quickly as she'd arrived, but looking up at the ceiling, I couldn't help but feel as if the holographic transmitter installed there was watching me. Fortunately, she'd done as I requested and terminated the broadcast, and I was able to enjoy the rest of my shower in peace.

Once I was clean and had changed into a new set of clothing, I was beginning to feel more grounded. Maddeningly, though, whenever I'd start to think I was getting it together, the unwelcome thought of Jack bleeding out on the floor of the garage would spring to mind. The shame would come flooding in, casting me back into a battle against a depressed and anxious state of self-loathing.

There was no way I could sit around the apartment until Risa woke up. I needed to get my mind off what had happened and try to be productive somehow. I could see Himari through the huge doors in the living room that led out onto the deck. He had his eyes closed and was practicing a complex *kata*, moving fluidly across the deck, whirling and occasionally striking out at the air around him. I decided to reach out to Pavel, who answered after a few vibrations.

"Hello, my friend. I was expecting your call." Behind Pavel, I saw several glossy animals with poles emerging from their necks, rising and falling. He was on a carousel somewhere, and it was in motion. A gorgeous blonde in a white dress blew a kiss as she laughed and bobbed up and down on a zebra several animals behind him.

"Pavel, are you at the Pier?" I asked, recognizing the buildings in the background.

"I am indeed! It's completely abandoned here. The water hasn't exactly reached dangerous levels yet, but it's gotten bad enough that they've shut everything down. A few well-placed coins to grease the pockets of the right people and here we are. We had our own private playground all night."

Shaking my head in wonder, I said, "The city is being evacuated, and you bribed your way into a restricted area for a date."

"Yes!" he exclaimed. "It's shaping up to be an amazing weekend. There are many places I look forward to exploring."

"I know you're probably looking to get some sleep, but is there any chance you might have time to meet up with me today? If you have an update on that list I sent you, I'd love to get together and talk it over.

"Absolutely," he replied. "Should I come to you?"

"No," I said a bit too sharply, but Pavel showed no sign of having taken offense. "Not here."

"I know just the place," he offered. "I have a friend I believe will be able to provide for us. Do you like noodles? Let's meet in Japantown. It shouldn't be hit too hard by the flooding yet."

"That works," I said. "Noon?"

"Excellent. I'll send you the address. See you then."

The call ended, and I was glad for it, since the constant rising and falling of the carousel had made it difficult to focus on the conversation. Alternatively, my general lack of focus could have been attributed to having just recently recovered from executing a kill switch that had shut my consciousness down with an electrical signal, prior to having had an involuntary, drug-induced lapse of memory and willpower.

I spent the rest of the morning working on regaining my strength of mind and body. I ate, meditated, and spoke with Himari about his life before becoming a part of the Singularity community. As a young man, he'd been a talented software engineer in Tokyo but had spent much of his free time

259

fraternizing in underground cabals of rebellious youths, intent on changing civilization as we knew it. They'd been neon souls, wandering the invisible grid of the Evernet in search of societal evolution and justice by means of anarchy, dissent, and outright rebellion when necessary.

When the war began, Himari and many of the more skilled hackers he'd associated with had been forcibly recruited by the Japanese government to assist with tightening the national defenses against cyber intrusion. He'd been something of a shining star in both worlds, which had earned him the attention of The Blacksmith, with whom he began a long-running dialogue regarding the merits of human evolution by way of bio-cybernetic improvement, before ultimately being convinced to come and participate himself. He hadn't even spoken English then, but eight years ago, he'd flown to America and been inducted into his new family. The more I learned about Himari, the more impressed I was, and I counted myself fortunate to call him an ally.

As noon approached, I left the apartment and cautiously navigated the waterlogged streets toward Japantown. As Pavel had guessed, the flooding hadn't made it quite that far inland yet. Japantown was on enough of a hill that the water pouring out of the city's overfull drainage system was mostly passing through rather than getting stuck. Despite the limited flooding, there were very few pedestrians walking through the plaza when I arrived.

Many of the digital cherry trees that lined the central plaza were flickering intermittently due to a technical difficulty with the wiring somewhere underground. The transmissions displayed huge pink trees in full bloom. The blossoms danced in a preprogrammed pattern as they floated from their boughs on their way to being scattered over the ground beneath the tree. *Glitch*. Nothing remained but an empty planter box, the electronic foliage unpowered and dispersed. *Glitch*. The tree was back, but the illusion had been spoiled, the mystery lost. Immersion was the water nourishing the roots of our fantasies, and without it they decomposed, rotting and forgotten. I hurried through the square as the intensity of the rain increased, leaving the struggling digital forest fighting to survive in my wake.

I could see lightning flashing across the sky and heard peals of thunder rumbling distantly as I reached the doors of the boutique mall where the restaurant was located. Surprisingly, they were unlocked, and I entered a large mall with a second floor open to the one beneath it. Many of the shops that lined the walls of both the first and second floors were closed and had security panels blocking entry, but strips of neon lighting illuminated the gardens, and the moving ramp that led upstairs was powered on, hopeful signs that I wasn't currently trespassing. The ramp took me up a level, and I made my way farther into the deserted building, looking for the restaurant Pavel had indicated. I finally found it tucked into a corner at the other side of the building. The outer wall had a pop-out awning, which was open, revealing a small but comfortable space. There were a few simple tables inside, lit by candles burning in small red jars. Pavel was seated at one of them. I entered and took a seat across from him.

"Pavel," I said as I sat.

"*Moi droog!*" he replied. He looked tired, but it was no surprise, since he'd been up all night, carousing about the abandoned San Francisco piers. He ran his hands through his hair and shook his head to try to wake up. "I'm sorry you find me in such a state. I'd expected to be lying in the arms of the beautiful woman you saw behind me on the pier by now. Sadly, though she tastes complex and smells of elderberry and cinnamon, her heart is fickle, and she lacks the patience of the finer wines I prefer."

"I'm sorry," I said. "I didn't mean to interfere with your plans. Things have been a little hectic as of late. I just wanted to tie this off to make sure you didn't end up uncovering anything we don't already know."

"Jacobi. I have many vices, and I won't lie to you and tell you that women are not high on my list of favorites. But even they pale in contrast to my love of intrigue! And that is what makes you so exciting."

A young woman in a traditional Japanese kimono approached, greeted us warmly, and placed a beautiful porcelain teapot at the center of the table before bowing her head and departing.

"So," said Pavel. "Your list. Shall I begin?"

"Tell me what you learned."

Pavel took out a pair of reading glasses from the breast pocket of his suit and put them on. He unfolded his CUBE and began scrolling through his notes.

"Aaron Watts," he began. "Army Green Beret...Black Hawk pilot. Two tours, Distinguished Service Cross, honorably discharged 2043. Nothing on record during the war, but he pops back up in 2049 when he purchases a home in Maple Ridge, Canada. No wife, no kids. Nothing out of the ordinary until about two weeks ago, when he puts a bullet into a Phillip Holsted in a mall in Vancouver, then fires at police who arrive on the scene. He is shot and killed. I've got footage from the incident if you want to see it, sourced from the local media, who got a hold of the mall security recording."

I nodded and leaned over to take a look at the recording, which showed Aaron and Phillip walking together, laughing. For seemingly no reason whatsoever, Aaron unholstered a weapon from under his jacket suddenly and fired into the back of Phillip's head.

"Wait," I said. "Go back to just before it happened."

Pavel reversed the recording and hit "play," and there it was. Aaron turned his head and looked suddenly to the left, seemingly at nothing, just moments before drawing his weapon. The expression on his face showed surprise, and I thought I knew why. I'd have wagered my last nickel he had an earpiece in and had just received instructions from someone on the other end.

"The media reported Phillip and Aaron had attended elementary school together and been life-long friends. No motive has been established for the murder. Jacobi, the list goes on here. Elliot Ivers, captain in the 82nd Airborne Division, US Army. Highly decorated, leaves service right around the start of the war and goes dark until it's over. One DUI two years ago and otherwise nothing until three weeks ago, when he's arrested in Chicago for stabbing his girlfriend, who remains in critical condition. He claims no memory of the assault. Is any of this helpful?"

I sipped my tea, lost in contemplation. "I'm not sure yet," I said absently. "Go on."

"Wendell Hamilton. The night before you contacted me and asked me to do this research, his brother arrived at a hospital here in the city, stabbed near to death. Wendell is in the wind, can't find him anywhere, but he has a similar history. Highly decorated Marine...absent for the duration of the war...back on the grid afterwards. Jacobi, are you seeing a pattern here?"

"Which pattern?"

"These were all extremely skilled soldiers, and their expertise would have been highly crucial during wartime. There's no chance they were all just let go at a time when they would have been needed the most. From what I'm looking at, these men were recruited into a deeper agency, the kind that doesn't put their agents on lists."

"Let's ignore that part," I said, "and focus on the timeline and the killings."

Pavel gave me a slow nod and smirked, then said, "As you wish." Sometimes he was too smart for his own good.

"Benjamin Oaksley..."

"Skip Oaksley," I interrupted. "Tell me about James Turner and Tucker Rogers." They were the only two names on the list I didn't have the full story for yet.

"Tucker Rogers, similar military background, blah, blah, blah, why did I bother with this part if you didn't need it...oh, this one was interesting. He threw his wife and child off of a tall bridge into a river in New Hampshire. He was on the run for a few days while the police tried to find him, then he goes back and jumps off the same bridge, kills himself. This was the oldest incident of violence. It took place over three weeks ago."

I sighed heavily. Tucker had been a good man and a close friend. I'd suspected his story wouldn't end well, since he'd had a line through his name on the list I'd found, but I'd been holding on to hope he might still be alive.

"James Turner. Found dead about a week and a half ago at

his home in Louisville, Kentucky. No clear cause of death; it was ruled undetermined. No accompanying crime, so far as I could tell, at least not one that was connected in any way by the authorities. I looked into the local obituaries to try to identify anything that might have been related, but nothing jumped out."

"What about Mason Robbins?" I asked, hopeful Pavel's team of *researchers* might have uncovered something more substantial than what I'd learned from Sam.

"He's a strange case. At first, all we could discover was a death certificate claiming he died in a fire in Boulder County, Colorado. That was about three years ago. It seemed pretty obvious someone had wiped any other information, because there was nothing else. No birth certificate, no military service like the others. One of my guys kept digging into data nodes of deleted information on unindexed sites, or the *voidspace* as it's more commonly referred to now."

"Deleted?"

"When you scrap your data, it's not necessarily gone permanently. Not immediately. It's just compressed and set aside until space is actually needed. There are repositories of deleted data that can be reconstructed with the right tools. A deep scrape of one of those repositories pinged a data package that made several references to Mason Robbins."

"What was the nature of the repository he located it in?"

"It was a record of a series of conversations that had taken place at a private communication hub. People tend to use them when one or more of the parties are looking to remain anonymous. The strange part was when we started reconstructing it, the data started to corrupt. Someone was watching us and didn't want that information seen."

"Do you think you were compromised when the alarm was triggered? This is important, Pavel. These people are dangerous."

"Doubtful," he replied. "They would have to have been incredibly skilled and had access to next-level software to track his identifier through all of the countermeasures he had in place. The only thing he managed to salvage in time was one compressed file, but he wasn't able to crack it open. There was some sort of locking mechanism in place that wouldn't even let him extract it. I left instructions with my guy to get it over to you. Maybe you'll have better luck."

An elderly Asian man shuffled out of the kitchen in the back wearing a large smile and an apron depicting a heron standing in the water. He bowed as well as he was able to with his crooked, aged back that looked stunted and bent, like he'd been in the back cooking over a cauldron for centuries.

"Kama-san, thank you for having the courage to keep your establishment open despite the catastrophic environmental conditions, and for allowing us to dine here," said Pavel respectfully as he stood and returned the old man's bow. I rose and did the same. Upon meeting my eyes, Kama seemed to take interest in something about me that caused him to grin even wider.

"Ahh," he said, his voice soft but enthusiastic. "You are of the way."

"The way?" I asked, uncertain. "I don't think so…"

"There are many ways. I'm sure you are of at least one." He laughed and motioned for us to sit back down. "But…" He looked unsure suddenly and bent to study my face. "You ate too much."

Having eaten nothing since breakfast, I was sure he was mistaken.

"May I join you?" he asked.

"Of course! Please take a seat," said Pavel, smiling. "Kama's eyes are shining like they do when he wants to tell a story. Settle in, Jacobi."

"No," said the old man as he sat, "no story today. But I would speak with Jacobi."

"Ah, I see. Kama fancies himself as something of a witch doctor or spirit priest. If you let him, he'll tell you what he saw in the tea leaves this morning or what the ghosts haunting the mall have to say about you. If anything is talking to him, it's probably the voices in the rice wine he keeps in that flask at his side," poked Pavel.

Kama grinned graciously and chuckled. "Pavel is still young enough to behave as if everything in this life is a joke," he countered. "A man who takes nothing seriously cannot be taken seriously, so we will speak as men while the boy prattles for attention."

"By all means," said Pavel. "I'm getting a call anyhow. I believe it is Bethany, from the pier. If I had to guess, I'd say she realized how dull life is without me and has called to beg me to rescue her from the monotony of solitude. I'll be right back." He stood and left the restaurant to speak more privately, leaving me with Kama, who was looking at me intently with a concerned expression.

I sipped my tea uncomfortably, unable to meet his penetrating stare. He said nothing, so in an effort to break the awkward silence, I eventually asked him why he had chosen to keep his restaurant open despite the flooding and the orders to evacuate.

"Pssh," he spat. "Have you ever been to Nihon?"

"I've spent some time there," I answered.

"We are a country of islands. Rising sea levels and climate change over the last several decades have not been kind to us there. Here, some water touches the precious streets and they run and hide. When a tsunami comes, my daughter and I will move. Until then, I will serve fish soup and noodles. This is all probably just an Ameonna, lost somewhere in the city."

"An Ameonna?" I asked, curious.

"An old *yōkai*. A spirit. A rain woman, cursed with rain that follows her wherever she goes."

I was silent for a time and then said, "What you asked me earlier...did you mean the Shinto religion? The way...of the *kami*?"

Kama's comforting grin erupted back onto his face, and he nodded.

"I don't practice, but I am familiar with some aspects of it," I said.

"I can see the spirits at war around you. You bear many scars left by the wake of their battles. You might not have decided it, but you are *of the way* because you are playing a part in their story somehow."

"Well, that explains a lot," I said, smiling.

Grinning and pouring himself a cup of tea, he asked with an exaggerated tone of mystery, "Have you heard of the Baku, Jacobi?"

I shook my head.

"Another *yōkai*. The dream-eater. He descends when summoned and eats the nightmares of others so they do not have to endure the fear. But eventually, he grows fat with the suffering of others inside of him, and if he is not careful, the darkness will consume him, for even one as strong as the Baku can only endure so much darkness."

I said nothing, considering his words.

"You have eaten too many nightmares. You have taken on too much of the pain and suffering of others, and you must be careful. Your cup is full. And there is more."

"What else?" I asked with a whisper.

"You are not whole. You are wandering lost through this world like a *yūrei*. A ghost. You must find what you have lost, for only then will you overcome the darkness inside of you. Do not let it linger unattended or, like the Baku, you will be consumed."

We stared at one another intently until a peal of thunder outside rattled the roof. I started at the sound, and Kami wheezed out a burst of jovial laughter. It was infectious, and I couldn't help but join him.

"But then what do I know?" he said, opening his flask and pouring the contents into his teacup. "I'm just an old drunk. I say whatever my rice wine tells me to!"

We laughed even harder at that until Pavel arrived back at the table, looking confused.

"Well," said Kama, standing, "I'll leave you to more *serious* conversations. But remember what I've told you, Jacobi."

"I will, Kama. Thank you for your insight." I stood and

bowed briefly. Smiling broadly, he returned the bow before departing to the kitchen.

Pavel sat down across from me.

"He's a character. Seems like a good man," I said. "How did it go with Bethany?"

"I'm not sure," responded Pavel.

"Oh? She didn't beg you to save her from her monotonous solitude after all?"

"No."

I raised an eyebrow. One-word responses from Pavel were like an eighteenth syllable in haiku.

"You all right?" I asked but then froze when he looked up suddenly and to the side with an all-too-familiar expression of bewilderment and surprise.

"I'm all right," he said. As he responded, he reached inside his coat, and his hand came out holding a 9mm pistol, which he pointed directly at my forehead. I slowly put my arms into the air.

"He says to tell you that when your dog digs up bones buried in someone else's yard…"

"Pavel, listen to me carefully," I said quietly as the blood in my veins turned cold. His head twitched to the right slightly, and he knocked back the hammer on the gun. "Pavel, I want you to reach up and take the earpiece out of your ear."

With his free hand, he began reaching toward his right ear but stopped about halfway there. "Take it out, Pavel," I reiterated. He became anxious and confused, caught between conflicting instructions.

"…you should have kept them on a leash," he finished, his voice strained and cracking.

"Pavel, take the earpiece out!" I said, more forcefully. The hand holding the gun began to shake as his other hand reached his ear. I saw the same thing in his eyes I'd seen in Wendell Hamilton's. It was distant and far removed, but there was a definitive and horrified plea for help swimming in the ether of his blank expression. Then, suddenly, it was gone. His gaze became vacant and emotionless, and in that moment he lifted the gun to his own temple…

"Pavel! Take—"

…and pulled the trigger.

A woman screamed behind me and the residual echo of the shot was accentuated by the sound of a tray of dishes falling to the ground, but I couldn't look away as my friend collapsed. His blood covered the wall next to us, slapped on like a coat of crimson paint, but even that couldn't convince my mind that this was really happening. It desperately clung to a reality in which I hadn't been responsible for the death of another innocent.

"Pavel…" I croaked, dropping to my knees. "No…no…no…"

"What?" I heard Kama's frantic voice say behind me. "Pavel! No! Jacobi, what have you done?"

"No…" I tried to argue that I hadn't done this but couldn't, because I had. I had brought Pavel into this situation and asked him to look into those murders.

Kama was hitting my back as I knelt, weeping. His daughter had recovered from her initial shock and was pulling at her father, yelling at him in Japanese that Pavel had done this to himself. But I knew that wasn't true.

"Himself? Oh god," cried Kama, who stopped hitting me and collapsed onto his knees beside me. We stayed there together for a time, him mourning Pavel and me coming to terms with the fact that this was actually happening and not just a terrible dream, until Kama looked up at me with bloodshot eyes and said, "You must go. Leave here. We will say he came alone."

"I..." I tried to find the appropriate words to refuse...to thank him...to explain, but was capable only of silence and regret. He was right, of course. He needed to report this, and I couldn't be there when he did. Kama was trying to do me a favor. I reached out and turned Pavel's head to the side then removed the audio transmitter from his right ear.

"Go," he said, softly. "I will pray for you."

I spun away from Kama and his weeping daughter and put the earpiece into my own ear as I departed.

"You'd better fucking kill me the next chance you get," I snarled. "Because I will find you, and I won't waste my time with games."

"How will you find me?" said Mason through the earpiece. "You won't find me, Jacobi. I'll keep using you, and your friends will keep dying around you until I'm done playing with you. Then you'll die."

"What the fuck do you want from me?" I yelled. "Why are you doing this?"

"Because you can't just escape from the decisions you make. You can't just pretend that the choices you make don't have consequences. There are always consequences, Jacobi."

"You're a psychopath. Before this is over, you're going to

understand consequence intimately, in the biblical sense, you piece of shit, because I'm going to shove it up your ass."

He laughed casually. "You used him to pry into my affairs. You knew the risks if he was discovered. Did he, I wonder? And Slate, whatever I am, you made me this way. So in a sense you could say you did all of this to yourself."

"How? How did I make you this way? I don't know what you're talking about."

"And that, Captain, is exactly the problem. Watch yourself out there; it's an unpredictable world. And oh, say hello to Risa for me."

"Fuck you." There was no response. "Mason? Fuck!" Outside, in the plaza, I took out the earpiece and threw it onto the ground then crushed it with my boot. The storm was full-blown now, but I paid it little regard as I collapsed to my knees, holding my head, and released a scream of frustrated rage. The cherry trees surrounding the plaza flickered mockingly, as if asking, "*Are you immersed? Is this real enough?*" And I wept.

Chapter 10

The elevator doors closed behind me. I dripped rainwater through the apartment as I walked to my room. Risa stirred as I entered but remained asleep while I changed into something dry. Afterward, I lay on the bed beside her, staring at the ceiling, lost in thought until she eventually rolled over and opened her eyes.

"Did I sleep long?" she asked.

"Probably not long enough," I answered honestly, "but we should get started."

"Are you okay?" She sat up.

"Yeah," I lied. "I'm okay. We've got a lot of planning to do." I got up to retrieve a bag from next to the door where I'd dropped it when I'd entered then handed it to Risa. She dug inside and pulled out an unboxed CUBE. "You should be able to link your old service to the new device, right?"

"Yeah," she said. "This is great. Thank you. Jacobi?" she asked as I turned to leave, "Are you sure you're okay?" I offered her a thin smile and nodded, then left the room to escape her doubting, intuitive stare.

When she arrived downstairs shortly thereafter, she'd already transferred service to her new device and secured an encrypted connection with Cody Marshall. Risa placed her CUBE on the table between the couches we sat on.

"Are you there, Cody?" she began.

"Yeah, I'm here."

"Is your family safe?" I asked.

"They're safe. Thanks, Captain."

I filled Cody in on the details of our situation. I told him everything we knew to get him fully up to speed.

"Mason. I never liked that piece of shit," said Cody when I'd finished. "I'll leave this afternoon. It's going to be a little difficult with the evacuation. They probably won't be allowing inbound commercial flights, but I'll figure something out."

"Ping me when you reach the city. We can pick you up or send you a beacon to where you'll be staying if you end up driving in."

"That sounds good. I'll let you know when I'm close."

After terminating the call, the three of us prepared a meal together and spent the rest of the afternoon and evening enjoying a peaceful interval in which no shots were fired and no one was bleeding. Himari finally got his swim in, and Risa and I slipped away to enjoy one another's company privately for a time. Once again, we lost ourselves in an ecstatic, sublime entanglement of the physical and the spiritual. Our bodies danced a prayer of devotion, our eyes locked like the missing pieces of a puzzle, and the shared energy between us expanded exponentially until it was all around us, holding us. It heightened into a frenzied maelstrom of writhing passion that grew hungrier and hungrier as it built, its voracious appetite sated only once we clung to one another, gasping and convulsing synchronously, our bodies physically spent.

It was the only thing that had so far been successful at

distracting me from the dark, emotional state I'd been in since Pavel's death, but I was left feeling guilty that I'd used our lovemaking as an escape. I wanted to believe the self-serving diversion from my negative thoughts wasn't something that detracted from the authenticity of what we'd shared. The hiatus from pain and guilt had been much needed, but I didn't want Risa to believe it wasn't meaningful to me in other ways as well.

When we rose from the bed, it was dark and had been for some time. Risa's new CUBE began to vibrate. It was Cody calling. He'd flown into Palo Alto and driven north to the city. She sent him the address for the apartment and gave him instructions to mention my name to the guards below. We dressed and rejoined Himari downstairs; he was tactful enough to ignore our extended absence.

It turned out he was something of a chef as well and was busy preparing another meal. He'd managed to find fresh fish somehow and looked more focused and intent on stirring the stew in front of him than when I'd seen him fighting for his life. His brow was intensely furrowed, and he kept dipping a metal finger in the pot to taste his creation then shaking his head in frustration and adding more seasoning. I wasn't sure what it was about the taste that was frustrating him, but it smelled amazing, and I was immediately hungry.

I received a call on the wall monitor from Boris, asking me to confirm Cody's claim that I'd invited him and looking for approval to allow him up to the apartment. Soon thereafter, we heard the elevator doors open and Cody whistle appreciatively at the view. I called him over, and he found his way to the main living space. He smiled widely as he entered and removed his backpack, dropping it to the floor. Risa embraced him in a tight hug, and when she let go I jumped in and grabbed him, picking him up off the ground in a bear hug. He laughed loudly until I set him back down on the floor.

"It's fucking good to see you, man," I said. "Let me look at you. You look civilized. Domesticated." I laughed and clapped him on the arm.

Cody was about the same height as me, slightly less muscular but still in excellent physical shape. He had brown skin, short, black hair, and a warm smile that exuded safety and kindness.

"Married, isn't that what you're trying to say, Captain?"

I laughed. "You said it, not me."

He looked at both of us and shook his head. "It's been too long. I wish we were here under better circumstances."

I nodded solemnly. "I'm glad you're here. Hey, come meet a friend of ours."

We walked to the kitchen, where Himari was still working on perfecting the fish stew.

"Cody, Himari. Not only does his stew smell amazing, but I'm seriously wondering if he jumped into the freezing ocean and caught those fish with his bare hands. It would honestly not surprise me."

Himari stopped stirring for a moment and bowed deeply. "Jacobi exaggerates, of course. The water wasn't that cold. It's a pleasure to meet you."

"Cody, on the other hand," I said, "he'd find a net and engineer a secure, automated system the fish couldn't bypass. And maybe throw in a dynamite failsafe to take out the entire school if one managed to slip through."

Cody reached out and shook Himari's hand then said, "I'm

no demolitions expert, but honestly, nitroglycerine is pretty unstable underwater. You'd probably want to use EPX-1 or some other polymer-bonded explosive to be certain."

"Listen, Cody," I said, "why don't you go upstairs, find a room without messed-up bedding, and stake your claim. Once you're situated, we'll all sit down to eat this delicious stew and start coming up with a plan."

By the time Cody returned, Himari had declared the stew complete and was pouring it into bowls at the dining table. I was famished, and the smell was practically making me delirious. Once everyone was seated, I set into the meal like I'd never eaten. Himari proved himself a more than capable chef, his multifaceted talent delivering an extraordinary culinary delight. Looking around the table, I laughed inwardly at three Fades and a half-metal man breaking bread and sharing stories. Through their companionship, my faith was being slowly renewed that we would come out of this victorious. I wondered how Mason and Richard could possibly hope to combat the capability, intelligence, and integrity of the people at that table. More than anything, it was their willingness to dive into the storm just to do what was right that made them so unique. They'd each cast fear and concern for their own safety aside to join me in getting to the bottom of this insane situation, never questioning what was in it for them, simply doing it because it was necessary.

We stayed up late into the night, drinking wine and discussing our options for getting into the DFDC headquarters so Risa could connect directly to the network. Cody thought that with the evacuation in place, the building would be more vulnerable than usual, since many of the staff would have left the city. After a long debate, we decided we'd move forward in two nights. It would give us the following night to stake the building out, try to identify any patrol patterns, and get a sense of how many people were coming and going, which would help us determine the most appropriate time to infiltrate. It would also give us two days to make sure we had all of the equipment we expected to need and let Risa and Himari dig in online to find out if changes had been made to the building layout or security in the years since we'd left.

They'd give whatever information they could find to Cody, who would incorporate it into the security assessment that would ultimately determine each step of our approach. I'd handed the reins to him on this one, happy to be directed for a change with all the pressure I'd been feeling lately. While Himari wouldn't be breaching the building with us, he'd offered to act as a switchboard of sorts from back at the apartment, monitoring audio channels and locating then sending any additional information that might become integral to the success of the mission as it progressed. Once Risa had secured a connection onsite, she'd be able to open a conduit and provide Himari with a backdoor into the internal network. With that access, he'd be able to assist her in scraping the network for the information we were after. I still had no idea what that information was, since Risa wasn't yet willing to share her suspicions with me. I wasn't sure how I felt about that, but she'd asked me to trust her and I'd agreed, so I landed on just trying to avoid thinking about it.

Cody had brought a considerable amount of his own equipment with him. Most of it was specifically oriented at creating and taking advantage of holes in perimeter security, but he had some other tricks up his sleeve as well. If this were any other building, Risa would have simply walked in, found a corner somewhere, and brute-forced her way on to the system, but the DFDC's sole purpose was to prepare for and prevent those types of attacks both here in the States and abroad. Cracking the countermeasures they had in place on their own network was going to be a challenge worthy of her and Himari's combined ability.

My role would be to manage any patrolling guards and to intervene if either Risa or Cody's positions became compromised. Although I had a considerable amount of technical ability when it came to cybersecurity and network intrusion, my knowledge paled in comparison with theirs, so it made sense that I'd stick to being a body-blocker for them. Cody's responsibility would be to control and bypass systems like perimeter defenses, electrical, and observational. To do that, he was going to need to get into the operation center. That would be our first and most difficult objective and the one we'd spent the majority of the day discussing.

That evening, Cody and I drove north to Mill Valley to get eyes on the target and do some reconnaissance. Keeping our distance, we skirted the perimeter of the grounds, which were protected by a tall cement wall. The goal was to look for weak spots in the surveillance that could be taken advantage of, but we were unsurprised to find that the cameras were evenly distributed and fully functional along the entire length of the barrier. We tucked in deep within the tree cover, and Cody deployed a remote drone to collect intelligence from beyond the wall, making sure to keep it safely above the view of the cameras. As he'd expected, there was very little traffic in or out of the building. There was a shift of the guard at midnight and a couple of dedicated staff leaving who'd worked late into the night. Beside the incoming security staff, no one else had entered the building. We were further encouraged that the lot outside of the building was nearly empty. Cody directed the drone to do a complete assessment of the grounds and recorded the footage for us to reference once we were back at the suite.

When we returned, Himari and Risa gave us a breakdown of everything they'd discovered on the Evernet. We had updated blueprints for the facility and records from Mill Valley's Department of Public Utilities with information on the generation and deployment of electricity, water, and gas. Risa had spent hours looking through publicly available financial records and had been fortunate to run into a wealth of documentation referencing the budget for system upgrades. We'd made good progress, and based on the information they were able to provide regarding the existing security mechanisms and models, Cody felt confident we could bypass and overcome them with the proper approach.

We spent the following day scouring the details of the operation, looking for holes in the plan and coming up with contingencies for when things inevitably stopped proceeding in an ideal way. Satisfied that we'd planned as sufficiently as we could with the information we had on hand, we bade farewell to Himari at the apartment and returned to the Mill Valley site.

It was evening, and we were crouched, soaking wet, in the tall grass outside the grounds, preparing to breach the outer wall. Our faces were covered with black nylon masks to protect us from being identified once we breached the headquarters. Cody connected Himari to the drone control interface, which would allow him to remotely monitor the exterior of the building and give us a heads-up on any unexpected arrivals. The front-facing outer wall of the headquarters was made entirely of glass, so he would also be able to see into the main lobby and track the movement of the guards who were stationed there.

Once we'd tested our comms devices, Cody slipped a spectral cloak around his shoulders and practically disappeared as the technology built into the lining of the plain cloth filtered the full visible spectrum of light around him. In the darkness, it rendered him nearly invisible to the naked eye, and, with luck, to the cameras on the perimeter wall. The cloak worked well in situations where visibility was low, but there was a discernible shimmer present when the wearer was in motion that made it unsuitable for occasions where someone might notice it and raise the alarm.

Using a set of gecko gloves, which he'd slipped over his hands and feet before donning the cloak, Cody made his way up and over the wall. The gloves employed synthetic setae on the outer base, which were flexible, microscopic, silicone pillars that imitated the process of electromagnetic attraction that the lizards they were named after used to *stick* to walls. On the other side, he secured a black nylon rope and threw it back over the wall for us to use when the time came.

Huddled in the grass outside the wall, Risa and I watched the drone feed on wrist monitors Cody had supplied, silently calculating the remaining distance as he dashed across the grounds on his unseen approach to the building. Sporadic reflections of light where there should have been nothing but darkness were vague evidence of his presence as he ran but would hopefully be disregarded as technical interference by anyone noticing on the monitors inside. No alarm was raised by the time Cody would have arrived at the northern side of the building, leaving us hopeful that the first stage of our process had been completed without issue.

Next, he'd use the gecko gloves to scale the outer wall. We were trepidatious about this stage, since if the wall was overly wet from the rain, it would be a much more difficult task to ascend it safely, but took some comfort in the large eaves on the roof that were helping with the runoff and protecting the walls themselves from becoming overly slick. His destination was a hallway on the fifth floor, close to the control room. He was carrying a small, powerful laser pen that would allow him to draw a hole in the glass of one of the outer panels of the hallway, which he would use to breach the interior. We waited patiently as he climbed, unable to visually verify his progress.

Like the first kernel of corn popping in a kettle I'd been watching, Cody's voice came abruptly through the earpiece, signaling the beginning of the next phase of the operation. "I'm in."

Shortly after, he swore and asked Himari to send him the specs for an IL3850 security panel with biometric access prevention, which Himari located and uploaded to his wrist monitor. Cody studied it for a short while then whispered, "Drilled in underneath. Just fishing for…got it…I should be able to bypass the biometric requirements by shorting out the sensor. If the default manufacturer's password hasn't been changed…that's it. I'm in."

I'd been holding my breath without realizing it and let out a long sigh of relief. With access to the control room, Cody could work his particular blend of magic. If everything went as planned, he'd loop the broadcast feed of the camera monitors in the lobby and security room and disable the motion sensors of the stairwells inside. We still had about an hour until the shift change, but I was anxious to get into the building so Risa and Himari could begin scraping data on the network. There was a long silence before Cody spoke again.

"Sorry, had a friend in here, and they weren't exactly welcoming. We're looped in. You're a go to breach the wall. Stay low and get to the rear service door at the southeast corner of the building. I'll unlock it from here."

I sprang into action, leaping up onto the cement wall and scaling it quickly with the help of the rope. I dropped down to the grass on the other side and moved directly toward the back side of the DFDC headquarters. Risa followed me closely. The service door was unlocked as promised, and we slipped through, closing it behind us. The stairwell we found ourselves in was dark, which was good, since it meant Cody had effectively disabled the motion detection system. Without being in proximity to one of the security bands that were worn by each of the guards, movement in the stairwell would have initiated an alarm had it been active. I used the light from the monitor wrapped around my wrist to illuminate the stairs as we descended toward the B2 sector, where the server room was located. When we were about halfway down the first flight of stairs, I heard the door above us open. We both covered the light from the monitors on our wrists and froze.

"What the…" came the sound of a patrolling guard's voice above. "Ed, I have no lights in the east hallway right now. Nope. Nothing. Yeah, I'm moving around right now, and they aren't coming on."

Frantically, I whispered for Cody to turn the motion sensors back on. The door above us opened again as someone else arrived, and thankfully the lights of the stairwell came to life.

"Looks okay to me?" said a voice I presumed belonged to Ed. "You want to leave and come in again, make sure they are working?"

"Now, that just makes no sense," the first guard muttered.

"Maybe I should check your pulse. Are you feeling all right? These things don't light up for ghosts. You're not a vampire, are you?"

"You're busting my balls? What do you want from me? I'm telling you it wasn't working before. What do you want me to do, ignore it?"

We waited for them to finish their conversation. I hoped once they were satisfied, the patrolling guard would be heading up and away from us, or things were going to get violent quickly. Eventually, we heard the door above swing open then close again as Ed departed, followed by the sound of retreating footsteps up the stairs. Still we waited, frozen and unmoving, unsure what the range was on the safety net of the guard's bracelet as he grew farther and farther away. Listening carefully, we heard someone pass through a door far above us. Trying to move my mouth as little as possible, I requested that Cody disable the system again. He gave the green light, and we let our breath out as one then moved quickly through the double doors leading into the B2 level, which Cody had unlocked.

"We're in. You can turn it back on," I said once through.

This section of the Division headquarters hadn't changed much since I'd last visited. We were in a wide hallway lit by a series of orange lights. There were closed doors down the length of it that led to custodial offices, service closets, electrical access panels, and facility management services, all of which were kept hidden and out of sight down here underground. Risa began moving down the hall, and I followed her as she turned down a similarly lit passageway. It led to the room that was home to the physical network servers. We stopped outside a thick metal door with another biometric access panel. Risa began unpacking equipment until she found the cables she was looking for and connected her tablet to the panel. Typing rapidly, with the tablet casting a thin strip of light across her eyes in the barely lit hallway, she looked like she belonged. This was her world, where she was most comfortable, and she was the master of her domain.

Within minutes, the panel let out a defeated series of beeps, and the doors unsealed, allowing us to push them apart and get inside. The server room was cold. Cool air poured in from vents on the ceiling, causing goosebumps to rise on my arms. Rows of identical servers filled the cramped chamber. They were mounted on standing racks, the outer faces of which were aglow with strips of blue light, giving the entire room a soft azure cast. Physical servers were rarely utilized, since most data was hosted virtually over the Evernet, but in cases of extreme security risk, corporations and government usually opted for the more archaic method because it was more insulated from external threats.

"Are you good?" I asked.

She nodded and connected to one of the machines. I left the room and closed the door behind me so as not to distract her. Back in the hall, I asked Cody for an update on his status to find out if I was needed upstairs.

"The guard in the control booth with me woke up, but I've got him tied, gagged, and blindfolded," he replied.

"Sounds kinky," Risa quipped over the comms.

"I don't think he's feeling sexy," said Cody. "He's got more of a twitchy-struggle thing going on."

"Stay focused," I chided.

"I've brought up tracking on the security bracelets the guards are wearing. I'm keeping an eye on their positions in the building, so I should have some warning if anyone starts moving in either of our directions."

Waiting alone in the eerily silent hallway, with only the dim orange light to see by, I felt the events of the past few days creeping back into my mind. I'd managed to distract myself sufficiently since Pavel's death with the planning of this operation, Risa's body, and the hope I'd felt when Cody had joined us, leaving little time to dwell on what had happened. But the soft, fiery glow and the silence were creating an atmosphere that was giving me too much time to reflect, and before long I found myself wanting to escape. Kama had told me I was unwhole and would be consumed by darkness if I didn't start confronting it, but I didn't think this was the time or the place to start battling my demons. I closed my eyes and breathed slowly through my nose, drawing on the mental images that comforted me to calm and center myself until the anxiety had moved through me.

"I'm in, boys." Risa's voice came through the earpiece. "Himari, the conduit is open now. I'm sending you credentials that will get you onto the network."

"What should I be looking for?" asked Himari.

"Anything related to something called Operation Dreamreaver."

I had no idea what that was, and regardless of how this ended, I was definitely going to have some questions for Risa later. My thoughts were interrupted suddenly as an alarm began to blare throughout the basement.

"Cody?" I shouted over the noise. "Do you hear that where you are?"

"One second," he said. Moments later he continued, "The network monitor is flashing red here. I think opening the conduit triggered some sort of hidden failsafe. Risa, you two are going to need to work fast to find that data. I have security coming my way, and three more are moving from the lobby toward the stairwell."

"Someone's logged remotely into the server I'm on," said Risa. "They're trying to terminate my access. I'm going to need to concentrate on preventing that. Himari, find that data. I'll keep the conduit open as long as I can."

"I'm shutting down all DFDC drones, cameras, and motion sensor security. I'll hold this room for as long as I can. If they take it, they'll lock us down and bring the perimeter defenses back online from here," said Cody.

"I'm on my way," I said. "Once I'm through the door from B2 to the stairwell, lock all of the doors leading to the level to give Risa more time."

"Roger that, Captain."

I dashed back down the hallway, through the door into the stairwell, and began rushing up the stairs. As I reached the landing of the first floor, the doors flew open and three guards barreled through. The sensors were off, so no lights activated, but they could see the glow of the monitor on my arm, and they stopped, confused. I took advantage of their momentary surprise and struck first. I didn't want to hurt these men, who hadn't done anything to deserve it, but my desire to keep from being arrested for trespassing and cyberterrorism outweighed my more noble inclinations. I rained several blows down onto the head of the first man, aiming to knock him unconscious quickly. He raised his arms, but I hit him hard in the gut, and he grabbed at his stomach reflexively, which gave me the opportunity I needed to land a shot on his chin that caused him to go limp and topple over.

In the time it had taken me to reduce the number of

opponents to two, they had both gathered their wits enough to understand they were being attacked and charged me in unison. I dropped to the ground and dove aside then came up from a roll in a corner of the landing. One man had overestimated the distance of his charge and toppled down the half-stair to the platform between levels. The remaining guard got it the easiest. As he approached me in the corner where I crouched, I prepared a stun patch, and with a lunge, slapped it on to his face. He collapsed immediately, and after a quick kick to pacify the man who'd fallen on the stairs, I continued ascending the landings until I reached the fifth floor.

I burst through the door and charged down the hallway toward the control room. Much of the fifth floor was comprised of corporate cubicles. I raced through a large, open office space and then passed a series of conference rooms. Thankful that I knew my way around the building, I cut through several doors and hallways until I neared a locked door that led into a more secure wing of the floor. In the hallway outside the door there were several men. Two of them held flashlights on the panel by the door, illuminating it for a third who was kneeling and attempting to bypass the lock.

The alarm continued to sound. It was a discordant, obstreperous clamor that made it difficult to think. I centered myself and tried to commit my focus to the men ahead. One fell to a spring-loaded electric cartridge from my wrist as I approached. His flashlight tumbled from his hand and skittered across the floor. The light from the second flashlight adjusted its direction to see what had happened. I came in from his left side, out of the light and with the sound of the alarm covering my approach. He was taken completely unaware as I slammed my elbow into his temple and knocked him to the floor. The final man grabbed his fallen flashlight and came up from his knees, waving the light in every direction. It eventually came to rest on the mask covering my face.

"Who are you? What do you want?" he asked in a shaking voice as he fumbled for the gun at his side.

I dashed in his direction then slid to the ground as his hands came up with his weapon, allowing my momentum to carry me the remaining distance. I wrapped my legs around his like a pair of scissors, squeezed, and twisted to my side, bringing him to the ground. Then I struck the side of his head with my elbow hard enough to daze him. He grabbed his head with both hands, which allowed me the time I needed to prepare a second stun patch and slap it on his neck to put him under.

"Status report?" I asked, raising my voice to be heard over the blaring siren.

"Are you okay?" asked Cody. "Looks like you ran into just about every guard on this wing of the building."

"How much time do we have before guards from the other wings arrive at your position?"

"I can't say for sure; there are a few scattered groups from the other wings that are trying to access this floor from the other stairwells. They probably aren't sure what the threat is, exactly. The only way they'll be able to know for certain is by getting access to this control room, but I expect they'll be busy with trying to bypass the doors I've locked in their way for a bit longer."

"They'll be mobilizing a response right now from the barracks up the road. Those guys are going to show up armed and ready for a fight. We don't have much time. The last thing we want is to be here when those soldiers come to break this up," I said.

"I've got something here," said Himari. "It's a hidden folder with the operation name Therisa gave me. Inside are a series of documents, photographs, and what looks like a mission summary. It's all heavily redacted, but so far, it's all I've found."

"Do you see a list, Himari?" asked Risa. "We're looking for something that indicates members of our unit."

"Not immediately, but there's a lot of information here. I need more time to know for sure."

"We're about out of time," I said.

While we'd been talking, I'd roamed back through the halls to the central balcony of the fifth floor. It was open to the entire front lobby, as was every floor beneath it. Through the glass of the front entrance I could see perimeter lights on, illuminating the entire estate. A transport truck had just arrived through the front gates and was approaching quickly.

Steeling myself for the inevitable confrontation, I said, "Get us a copy of everything in that folder. Risa, as soon as he's got it, leave. Cody, do we have any control over the lights outside? They've got the place lit up like an Alaskan summer."

"Those lights operate on the independent backup system. I can't shut them off from here," he replied. "I'm going to have company here in a minute, Captain. Those boys just managed to get through the door from the northern stairwell."

"Turn off all of the lights in the front lobby. Do what you can to hold them off for as long as you can, and then get out," I said. "I'll try to distract our friends outside."

I unlatched a clip from my utility belt and snapped it onto the balcony railing then rolled over the side into the lobby below.

The cable reel at my side controlled the speed of my descent until I hit the floor of the front lobby, and at the same moment, the room went dark. I hit the release mechanism for the clip, which fell from above and retracted back into the reel. From one of the pouches on my belt I pulled a small, cylindrical tube and popped the lid off. When I tilted the tube toward my hand, several small silver spheres rolled out to gather in my palm. One by one, I tossed the spheres out into the lobby, and upon impact, the foglets, true to their name, began to rapidly emit walls of mist that merged and spread throughout the entire lobby, blanketing the room.

"Himari, I don't think I can maintain this conduit for much longer," said Risa. "I've got multiple people working to shut me out."

"It's nearly complete," he replied. "Stand by…"

On the wrist monitor, from the perspective of the drone that was hovering over the grounds, I could see men being deployed from the rear of the truck. They were armed with body armor and assault rifles and were moving in on the main entrance.

I heard gunfire upstairs, and Cody whooped excitedly into his mic. "They're shooting into a metal door! Where's the Division hiring security from these days? That's my cue to vacate the premises. The gas in the room should keep anyone from getting in here for the next five or ten minutes, but after that, everyone needs to be off the estate grounds, or the perimeter defenses will probably be live and back under DFDC control. I've unlocked the basement level doors for you, Risa. Good luck, everyone."

Cody had brought a burn ring along with him and planned to use it to escape the control room by creating a small hole in the floor that he'd use to cable down to the room beneath him. A burn ring was a malleable hose filled with water and flammable components that were activated when the rip cord on the hose was pulled, which drained the liquid and exposed the white phosphorus to oxygen. When the phosphorus lit up as a result of the exposure to air, it would ignite the thermite in whatever shape he'd placed the hose and burn through the floor. The gas he'd mentioned, which was a toxic byproduct of burning the phosphorus, would linger and prevent anyone who gained entry to the control room from following him or making use of the facility for a short while.

"Dammit. I'm completely locked out of the system," said Risa. "Himari, tell me you got the file?"

"I've got it," he replied. "I just hope it contains what you expected."

"I'm heading to the southeast stairwell now. Where are you, Jacobi?" Risa's voice had urgency to it, and I knew she was probably berating herself for having tripped the failsafe with the conduit. The way she saw it, whatever happened to us now was on her. I knew the feeling well and sympathized but didn't hold her responsible. There were layers of security that just couldn't be predicted; unforeseen variables that reared their ugly heads in every planned engagement. We'd made the best plan we'd been able to with the information we had and were adjusting on the fly.

"Just doing what I can to slow things down up front," I said and fired several rounds into the ceiling. Through the eyes of the drone, I could see the soldiers out front spread out. Just as they'd been trained to when under fire, they posted up behind whatever cover they could find and trained their rifles on the lobby, which was now completely obscured by a thick fog.

I dashed out of the room toward the stairwell and the service door we'd originally come in through, and found Risa waiting for me at the exit.

"Ready?" she asked.

At this point, we'd have to scramble across a well-lit lawn and get over the wall somehow without being shot at by the men around the front. Since neither of us had spectral cloaks like Cody, it wasn't a particularly encouraging scenario. Instead of heading right to the side of the wall we'd entered over, we'd need to run straight back, opposite the front lawn where the troops were situated, and hope we were fast enough to avoid detection. I nodded, and she threw the door open. We broke into a run but came to a halt immediately when we heard the sound of someone behind us shouting over the alarm.

"Stop! Put your hands into the air, or you will be fired upon!"

We both complied and turned to see that three uniformed men had come around the corner of the building and had trained their rifles on us, ready to fire.

I looked at Risa, who gave a slight shake of her head. There was no way we could close the gap quickly enough to disarm the men. If I tried to throw a cartridge, I'd be full of bullets before I completed the motion, and even then, it would only hit one. It was over. We'd done everything we could.

"Close your eyes," we heard through the earpiece. It took me a moment to process Himari's request, but I realized what was happening when Cody's drone came down between us and the soldiers. I squeezed my eyes shut just in time to avoid the intense flare of the flash capsule it released.

"Get back inside!" I shouted. We utilized the few moments

of sightlessness and disorientation they'd be experiencing to dive back through the door into the building. Risa was rubbing her eyes, which she hadn't closed in time to avoid the blinding light. The effect would soon fade, but I put my arm around her waist to help guide her down the stairs until we'd reached the door to level B3. We passed through and began winding through the corridors beyond.

"Where are we going?" asked Risa.

"The bunker tunnel," I answered. We'd been drilled several times throughout our time at the Division in how to evacuate in the case of an imminent threat to the headquarters. The escape route we'd been trained to use was a tunnel that began here on level B3 and supposedly led to a nearby bunker underground.

"Right now," I continued, "there are no lights and no cameras. Any minute now they're going to have the control room back. All of those things are going to come online, not to mention the perimeter drones. We don't have a very long window to get out of here, and we can't hide. This is the best shot we have."

We reached the bunker tunnel doors. Similar to other doors we'd encountered in the building, there was a biometric access panel that would need to be conquered in order to get through. Risa connected to the door and began attempting to crack it. After a few minutes, she shook her head.

"Everything is in a heightened state of lockdown. I can't utilize the same method I did earlier to get us through this door. If we could drill under the panel, like Cody did to access the control room, we might be able to disable the sensor, but I don't really know how, and I don't have those kinds of tools."

"Cody or Himari, could either of you walk Risa through

disabling the sensor on this panel if I find a way to get access to the wires inside?" There was no response. "Cody? Himari?" Nothing. We were either too far underground, or communications were being blocked somehow.

I heard a door open from back in the direction we'd come from and tensed, reaching reflexively for my gun before remembering I couldn't or wouldn't use it on the people guarding the building. Instead, I loaded a cartridge into my hand and prepared to hurl it at whoever came around the corner in search of us. A familiar voice called out to us from out of sight, down the hall.

"Slate? Don't kill me. I'm coming out." A figure approached in the dull red light of the hallway with his hands raised, and as he neared, I recognized the features of Sam Winston.

"What the hell are you doing here, Sam?"

"I work here, Mr. Slate. What the hell are *you* doing here?"

I stammered for a moment, having subsequently realized both the audacity and absurdity of my question.

"Don't bother answering," he said. "I know why you're here. I've come to help, but we need to move quickly."

He walked to the panel and rested his hand on the surface. Several lights activated on the screen as the biometric scanner evaluated the temperature of his hand and compared his fingerprints with the records in the database. When the process was complete, the door opened, revealing a cement tunnel that led away and was quickly swallowed by darkness.

"Wait," I said, regaining my composure. "How do you know why I'm here, Sam?"

"We don't have a lot of time here. Why don't we hold off on

the questions and answers until we're out of danger?" He held his hand out toward the tunnel and raised one eyebrow.

I nodded grudgingly and passed through the portal into the tunnel beyond, followed closely by Risa and Sam, who pulled the door shut behind us. The tunnel sloped slightly downward. Sam had a flashlight and guided us deeper underground. We arrived at a door identical to the first. Sam opened it, and we passed through into a chamber with low ceilings and metal lockers lining the outer walls. On the opposite side, a doorway led deeper into the bunker.

He led us directly through the door into a larger chamber. In the center of the chamber, a ladder led from the ground into a tube in the ceiling. He began climbing, and we ascended after him. After several dozen meters of climbing, he stopped above me. I heard the sound of sliding bolts and then the affirmative confirmation beep of another scanner. Fresh air filled the tube as Sam lifted the hatch above him, and we each crawled out onto a cement panel surrounded by a barbed wire fence. I became very still suddenly when I noticed the perimeter turrets positioned at each corner. Sam noticed and followed my gaze to the defenses. He held his wrist up. He wore a security band similar to those the guards back at the headquarters had been wearing.

"Even if you'd gotten through the door, things wouldn't have ended well for you here," he said. "Stay close to me." He walked to the gate and slid it open, then closed it behind us when we were through.

"Himari? Cody? Can either of you hear me?" I asked.

Cody responded. "We got you, Captain! Lost you there for a little while. Is Risa with you?"

"I'm here," she said. "Are you out?"

"I'm in the vehicle now," he answered. "Send me a beacon, and I'll come to you."

We were at the top of a hill. A thin dirt service road led away from the fence toward the base. I led us down, away from the entrance to the bunker and the gun turrets defending it. The dirt road intersected a paved one at the bottom. Risa sent a beacon to Cody.

"To answer your earlier question, Mr. Slate…" began Sam.

"Your card," I said. I'd been mulling over the possibilities since I'd first seen Sam in the basement of the DFDC headquarters. For him to have known what we were doing there, he'd have to have been monitoring us. "Right?"

He nodded, looking slightly embarrassed. "Yes, the card I gave you when I dropped you off that evening. There is a chip built into it that I've been using to monitor your situation."

"You've been using me. You put us onto Richard Robbins and the Phoenix Coalition. Why?"

"I needed outside assistance. Someone in the Division has been blocking my efforts to open an investigation into their activities, which has, as of late, increasingly begun to fall under the purview of Domestic Crisis."

"We almost died up on that mountain, Sam!" I yelled, then lowered my voice and said, "You put us at ground zero for a shit show we had no intel and no background on whatsoever."

"Because you're the best at what you do, Mr. Slate. I had every faith you'd come back down that mountain. Don't pretend it didn't serve your purpose as well. Our goals are aligned right now. You want to get to Mason Robbins, and I want his father."

He was right about that, but I was having a hard time moving past having been spied on and the fact that without Jack's help we probably wouldn't have made it off that ranch. I'd had a suspicion the DFDC had been monitoring my progress, but I'd wanted to believe Sam hadn't been involved.

"I've never lied to you," he said. "I've also been cleaning up the bodies you've been leaving in your wake to keep the heat off. And if I hadn't been monitoring you, I wouldn't have been able to get you out of the situation you landed in tonight. I think it's important we move beyond hurt feelings right now and focus on how we can help one another to move forward. How badly do you want to get to Mason Robbins, Slate?"

This was no time for emotional baggage. Lives were on the line. I let out a sigh and said, "Tell me what you know."

Sam nodded and seemed to relax as well. "When my investigation into Robbins' organization was blocked, I knew something was off. I started digging in, under the radar, and discovered that someone in the executive branch of the DFDC was providing the Phoenix Coalition with funding. I followed the money trail to the ranch in Colorado, then on to several Colombian accounts, which were outside of my ability to investigate more specifically."

"Accounts in Colombia? What's the money being funneled there for?" I asked.

"I can't be sure," said Sam, "but it's a lot of money. I'd wager a guess it has something to do with that powder he's been using to get to your unit."

"How long have you known about that? You could have warned me."

"I only know what I've heard you talking about," Sam said

defensively. "I didn't know there was a connection between Richard Robbins and what was happening to your unit until you asked me to look into Mason. I only suspected."

"So it was just a coincidence you picked me up and brought me to Ben?" I asked incredulously.

"Not exactly," Sam replied. "When the people in your unit started experiencing those tragedies, the same thing happened. I sent it up the chain and was subsequently told to back down. They were sweeping it under the rug. That's why I planted that card on you. I wasn't sure what was going on or who I could trust. But I think it's pretty clear now that someone at the Division contracted Richard Robbins and the Phoenix Coalition to run trials on that drug in order to get real-time data on its efficacy. I don't know why you and your friends ended up as the test group, but it looks a lot like that's what's going on."

I heard the sound of an approaching vehicle. Cody flashed the lights of his truck as he neared.

"I can't come with you now," said Sam. "I need to head back and tell them I looked for you in the bunker but didn't find you. Tomorrow, I'll come to you. If you're interested, that is. Will you work with me on this?"

I looked at Risa, who shrugged. If Sam could provide us with DFDC resources, even in a limited scope, it could aid our efforts enormously. And if I were being honest with myself, I had a vested interest in bringing Richard down as well. Whatever they were planning, I wasn't going to let the horrors the people I cared about had experienced be unleashed into the world at large.

"Tomorrow then," I agreed and entered the vehicle when Cody pulled to a stop in front of us.

As we pulled away into the night, I thought back to what Kama had said at his restaurant. Maybe I *was* like the Baku, eating the nightmares of others so that they were spared the pain. Maybe I *had* grown overly full on the darkness. But I could only do what I knew. I'd never had an easy time swallowing the bitter taste of change. Whatever it took, I'd have to find some more room down there to get this last meal down.

Chapter 11

During the ride home, Risa asked Himari to transfer the stolen data to her. She alternated between sifting through what he'd found and sneaking concerned glances at me when she thought I wasn't paying attention. I was anxious to understand her reasons for pushing us toward the risk we'd just taken, but I'd waited this long already, so I decided to refrain from trying to solicit information from her until she was ready to share what she'd discovered.

Back in the apartment, we all slumped down onto the furniture, exhausted, and reflected on the events of the evening. We joked about the absurdity of what we'd accomplished, chided ourselves on mistakes made, and celebrated having gotten away with it all somehow. Eventually, Risa asked me to step onto the balcony to talk. We stood for a time, listening to the rain and watching the lights of the city below. I was beginning to wonder if it would ever end. Over the last several decades, climate change had impacted the weather patterns drastically, and although we'd made a global shift toward relying on cleaner energy, we'd moved too slowly, and unpredictable weather events had become all too common.

Risa turned to me and broke the silence. "Jacobi, what I need to talk to you about is important and complicated. I'm not sure what the best way to do it is, so I'm just going to be upfront with you and hope you're able to accept what you're hearing."

"I'll do my best," I said lightheartedly, though her demeanor and tone were making me nervous.

"About six years ago," she continued, "there was a FDEES raid on an Iranian compound in the Zanjan province. The team was sent to neutralize or capture a man named Ghazi Khadem, an officer of the Iranian Armed Forces responsible for the deaths of thousands of American and British civilians by acts of terror. He was brilliant and had managed to plan and execute his attacks undetected by our finest minds for years during the war. Do you remember him?"

"Risa, of course I know who Ghazi Khadem is. His name was on every major news network for half a decade. I personally led several attempts to bring him into custody, but he'd always been one step ahead. You were with me on some of those raids. Why are you telling me this?"

"I'm not certain about the timeframe. I mean...*merde*, please, just let me continue."

I nodded and held my hands up apologetically.

"The night of the raid, Khadem was killed. When he became cornered, he blew himself up and took a man and a woman who'd raided the compound out with him," she continued.

I frowned, since I'd not heard about Khadem's death. Considering his importance during the war, it was difficult to understand how it had gone unmentioned.

"The team disarmed a series of self-destruct mechanisms that had been designed to eradicate his entire network and uncovered a treasure trove of intelligence. Deep within that data, hidden behind cascade encryption, they located the plans for a coordinated strike on the United States. It was a list of twenty-five sleeper agents and the details for a plan that would use the agents to cause mass destruction by way of chemical warfare throughout the most vulnerable American cities."

What Risa was describing was effectively America's worst fear come to life. I had questions about how she could possibly know this when I, as her commanding officer at the time, had been unaware, but I remained silent and allowed her to continue.

"Secretively, the DFDC brought each of the people on that list in and questioned them extensively, probing for any signs they were complicit in the plan that had been outlined by the data. They found nothing. Not one shred of evidence the people on that list were somehow sleeper agents in disguise. The Division had no way to prove it and no legal capacity to hold them, and one by one, they were released."

She paused then and turned away to gather herself. Her hands were gripping the railing of the balcony so hard her knuckles were turning white.

"Are you okay?" I asked.

"It wasn't good enough for the Division executives," she said, her voice growing angry. "They were convinced the people on the list had just been trained too well, been too careful, and that the threat was imminent. You remember how it was during the war, Jacobi. Everyone was so afraid the next bomb was going to go off in their city; afraid the next attack would kill another person they loved. They decided they couldn't take the risk, and Operation Dreamreaver was their solution."

I could see where this was going, and I didn't like it.

"A whitewash operation," I said. "Eliminate the sleepers."

Risa nodded, and her eyes began to water. "They assigned the same unit to the mission that had located the data to keep the number of people who were aware of the situation minimal. Over the next five months that team systematically eliminated those civilians. Accidents, all of them. In ways that could never be connected."

"What does all of this have to do with Mason?" I asked, still confused.

"After the operation was complete, the Division received a message. It was from a well-known Iranian hacker who'd worked closely with Khadem. He was laughing at us. It mocked the killings and claimed the entire list had been a fabrication. The whole thing had just been concocted to get us to kill our own people. Innocent lives, taken by our own military, the same soldiers who'd killed Khadem. It was a carefully constructed revenge mechanism. The hacker released the information on the Evernet. There was enormous public outcry, but the DFDC denied it vehemently."

"I don't understand…" I said, trying to connect her story to ours in my mind.

"Jacobi," she said, and took my hands in hers as she faced me and looked into my eyes. "The unit that carried out the raid and the orders from Operation Dreamreaver was disbanded. Honorably discharged. As a parting gift, the Division offered each of them an opportunity. Memory reduction science had made significant leaps forward in the years leading up to those events. They offered each member of that unit the opportunity to have the memories surrounding the killings, and the entire Operation, removed from their minds."

"What…what are you saying?" I asked, fearful I already understood the truth.

She smiled at me warmly but with great sadness in her eyes.

"We were that unit, Jacobi. It was us."

I let go of her hands and turned away, reeling. I felt nauseous and confused. My mind was trapped between two realities, the one I knew and the alternative one I was being presented. I closed my eyes and tried to concentrate, but waves of uncertainty crashed repeatedly into the wall of calm I was trying to erect, slamming against it like an angry mob at the gates of my consciousness. After some time, I felt Risa's hands on my back, and I turned to face her.

"I chose to do this thing? I agreed to have these memories wiped from my mind?" I asked, desperately trying to comprehend. "And you didn't do it."

She nodded. "You were under a lot of pressure at the time. You felt responsible, and it broke you, Jacobi. Many of the others felt the same and simply wanted to forget so they could move on with their lives."

"But, so much time...just gone. How is that possible?"

"It's built into the science of the reduction. They found that the mind could be coaxed into passing over gaps in the memory it can't explain. Your mind effectively jumps from the last memory it had before the procedure to the most recent one that doesn't conflict with the gap and disregards everything in between. The fact that I'm telling you this now is dangerous. In some cases, the pressure of trying to recall and understand that gap has overtaxed the mind and caused dementia, or worse, madness. But I think what's happening to us is related to these events."

I was having a hard time concentrating on her response. I felt trapped and discombobulated, like I was a prisoner of someone else's truth. But something in what Risa had just said pulled me back to the conversation at hand.

"The list…" I said, "Ben's list."

Risa nodded. "I couldn't be sure, because none of us were told who chose to undergo the procedure and who didn't. Those of us who chose to forego it were specifically ordered not to bring these events up or mention the reduction, in order to avoid the potential harm it could cause, both emotionally and mentally. But I saw the data tonight, and it matches exactly. Everyone on that list had their memories of those events removed."

"Mason," I said as clarity surged like a rising tide. "He remembers, and he's holding us accountable."

"Jack said Mason had been put in charge of the trials. If he needed a test group for this drug and was harboring resentment against the people in our group who went through the procedure, it does add up," Risa confirmed.

I thought back to everything Mason had told me. He'd called me a coward and said I wouldn't have been able to understand his motivation. It all made sense.

"None of this helps me find him," I realized, discouraged.

"We have Sam now," she said. "And we understand why it's happening. That's more than we had before." She paused and studied me. "Jacobi…"

I said nothing, lost in thought and staring down at the streets of the flooding city. I was silently comparing the state of my emotions to the encroaching ocean surge. Where once I had felt like the stone of a solid foundation, now I was underwater, gasping for air and being pummeled by waves of doubt.

"Jacobi," she repeated more harshly.

Dejectedly, I turned and met her gaze.

"This has to stop. We *need* you in order to finish this. I know you want to drown in your sorrow right now with everything that's happened. But you can't. You have to get yourself together. Find your fire. Whatever you have to do to find your way out, do it soon. People have died. But there are people in there," she said, pointing inside, "and right here, who are still alive, and those people are counting on you now."

It was outside of my character to be conquered by my emotions. As the events had piled on over the last couple of weeks, I'd lost touch with the part of me that could just set it all aside and press forward despite the pain. I felt tired and defeated, but I knew Risa was right. I didn't have the privilege of slipping away into depression and self-pity. Not while the danger was still present. She'd asked me to find my fire. I needed to stop feeling sorry for myself and get back to focusing on all of the lives that had been irrevocably overturned by the actions of Richard Robbins and his son. My fire was born from the simmering rage lying dormant in the pit of my stomach, but I was disconnected from that rage. It had been fueled by certainty and righteousness, and the stores of both had been significantly depleted by this latest revelation.

"You're right. I'm sorry," I said. "I'm trying. I've been struggling, trying to understand this fear I have of losing control. Trying to understand why this fear of being manipulated and used has been waking me up at night, sweating. After what you've told me, I think everything that's happening has just been pushing on some subconscious sore spot that I didn't even know existed."

"That makes sense," said Risa. "The reduction probably only partitioned out portions of your memory, not the unconscious response mechanisms that would have been associated with them. It must be extremely confusing."

I laughed suddenly, realizing Kama had seen this in me too. He'd likened me to a ghost who wandered, unwhole, and warned me I wouldn't have the strength to combat the darkness he saw within me until I'd found what I'd been missing.

"Risa, could my memories be restored?"

"I don't know," she said, shaking her head slightly. "But right now, I think you should decide how much of this you want to share with Cody. I'll leave that up to your discretion."

In the end, I decided Cody deserved to know the full truth and asked Risa to repeat her story for the others inside. He seemed to take the news well enough and nodded thoughtfully when we tied in our theory that Mason was looking to hold us accountable for our role in the assassinations, but he said nothing. Since I was still having a difficult time processing the information myself, I didn't have much to offer by way of encouragement and left him alone to consider what he'd heard.

As I prepared to retire for the evening, Himari approached me.

"Jacobi-san. May I speak with you for a moment?"

I nodded.

"This must be very hard for you — to learn what you have about these innocent people who were killed."

"It's late, and I'm tired, Himari. I'll be all right."

"Perhaps, yes. I do not wish to add to the weight you are

carrying." His brow furrowed, and he looked as if he were trying to decide whether to say more. After a moment, he placed his hand on my shoulder. "Before you go, consider this. You are a warrior. Death follows the warrior like a storm. Innocent or guilty, death cares little. The repercussions of the choices we make can resound throughout the rest of our years. You allowed yourself to be trained and used as a weapon. I have no doubt you did so out of a desire to see the greater good prevail. But do not fool yourself into believing you are *ever* innocent. That is the consequence we who choose to take life in the name of a greater good must always face."

"What do you mean?"

"Innocence and guilt are not always evident. You must accept that these deaths, and all of the deaths you have ever been involved in, are a result of your choice to be embroiled in conflict. Honor the warrior within you. You will not always be right. Death will not always be justified by righteousness. And all of it, right and wrong, is the path the warrior must walk. You must accept that when you choose to take a life, even that of a base criminal, that someone loved them and someone will miss their presence when they are gone. A mother. A sister. This is the cost of war — the pain we carry. If you are not willing to take it on, then you must part ways with death and find a new way."

He had given me a great deal to consider. I thanked him for his words and returned to my room, anxious for a respite from my own jumbled and chaotic thoughts that only sleep would provide.

The following day, we coordinated with Sam and invited him up into our lair. We discussed the details of Operation Dreamreaver with him, of which he'd been unaware. While he agreed it seemed a likely motive, he was less interested in why Mason had chosen our unit as the trial group and more focused on how we were going to put an end to the Coalition's efforts.

"Mason is the dog here, Slate," he said. "His father is holding the leash. We get to Richard and we can shut this whole thing down permanently. If you really want to flush his son out, we should hit the source directly."

I asked him what he had in mind. He outlined a scenario in which he'd provide me with transportation and gear, and I'd supply a team of operatives to raid the ranch outside of Boulder. Sam could appropriate Division resources under the guise of using them for an unrelated operation, but he didn't have the authority to reassign an FDEES unit. Even if he could have, he'd have to brief them on the objective. Without knowing who he could trust, he wasn't willing to get anyone else involved, which was what made him so interested in me and my team. I could provide him with a group of trained operatives who could accomplish the mission that no one at the DFDC would condone. What he wanted was to capture Richard and force him to testify against DFDC collaborators in exchange for leniency. He also proposed that with his father in custody and the operation jeopardized, Mason would have no reason to continue the trials.

I didn't tell Sam, but I knew that wasn't true. I'd heard the vitriol in Mason's voice, filled with malevolence and a desire for revenge. Whatever the mission had meant to him when he'd been placed in charge, it had since become something much more personal, and he was going to see it through to its poisonous end. I did, however, agree Richard Robbins needed to be stopped and thought poking the hornet's nest might provoke Mason into acting with imprudence. So far, he'd been meticulous in his planning, and that had left me with very little to exploit to expose him. If I could rile him and trigger an emotional response of some sort, it might goad him into acting hastily and making a mistake I could take advantage of.

There were families at the ranch, and heavily armed militia, many of whom had military experience, so it wouldn't be a simple extraction. We'd agreed that our best odds lay in getting to Robbins and abducting him quietly, to lower the chance of a shootout with his private army. I had some ideas and told Sam I'd begin preparing our team.

In the middle of the day, I received the damaged file Pavel had mentioned recovering from a deleted state on an old, retired DFDC Evernet site. It arrived from an unidentified source, likely whomever he'd instructed to follow up with me. Risa and Himari did what they could with it, but neither could crack the encryption. I passed the data package along to Sam with an explanation of its source and a warning he should be careful who he turned to for help breaking it open.

In return for our assistance with Richard, I had another request. I wanted a direct and secure line to Ben so I could update him on the investigation. I didn't plan to share any information about Operation Dreamreaver with him, but I wanted him to know he wasn't responsible for what had happened with his wife and that I was getting closer to finding justice for Mary. Sam told me he'd do what he could to make it happen and left to start sorting out the details for providing us with what we'd requested.

Later that afternoon, he contacted me to tell me the call I'd asked for had been arranged. I was nervous as I waited on the line for Oaks to connect. It was partly that I wasn't sure how he'd take the news, but even more than that, I wondered if my quest to understand what had happened to him was the only thing he had to hold on to right now. There was a possibility that bringing the investigation to fruition would leave him so empty he'd just give up. When the call finally connected and Ben appeared on the wall monitor, my heart sank. He looked ten years older than when I'd last seen him. His eyes had lost the spark of vigor that had been so vivid throughout our friendship, his hair was matted and unwashed, and his beard had grown even more wild and untamed.

"Ben," I said. "It's good to see you. Are you all right?"

He cleared his throat. "I'm still here." His voice was hoarse, as if he hadn't used it in days.

"Oaks, I know what's happened to you. You were right. What happened to Mary wasn't your fault."

The mention of his wife's name seemed to hit him like the lash of a whip. His eyes flashed with anger, but I thought I saw a hint of hope in their depths and understood it was a hope for a potential end to the maelstrom of confusion and guilt that thrashed with furious intensity inside of him.

"Tell me," he said, stirring to life.

I told him about how the Phoenix Coalition had been contracted by someone in the Division to test an unknown substance and that our disbanded unit had been selected as the trial group. I explained that once the drug was in your system, it became impossible to resist the instructions of others, and that Mason Robbins had been giving orders to him through a remote earpiece he'd likely been told to hide or destroy before the police arrived at his house. I told him about the other members of our unit and how many of them had experienced similar tragedies. Finally, I assured him Risa, Cody, and I were working together to bring justice to the people who were responsible.

Oaksley listened, and as I feared, I saw the enthusiasm slowly leave his face as he learned the truth about what had happened to him. The understanding of it brought no solace, and the pain hadn't been eased by knowing. Still, the final chapter of his story wouldn't truly be over until Richard and Mason had paid for their part in Mary's death, and though I doubted it would bring him lasting peace, I promised him to see it through.

"They're evacuating us from the island," said Ben. "Tomorrow, or the day after, perhaps. They're taking us somewhere else, safe from the flooding."

"I'll find out where you're going and contact you again when we've ended this."

"Jacobi," said the admiral with a solemn expression, "I'm an old man. And I'm alone now. If I thought Mary wouldn't judge me for it, I'd have ended my life by now. I don't see a road ahead. It's just a dark, empty canvas, and I was never any good at art."

"You're not that old. Not really. I'm going to find a way to get you out of this. You don't deserve to be in a cell. I have a contact at the DFDC, and he knows about what's going on. As soon as we can prove your innocence, we're going to get you out of there."

"I don't think that's how it works," he said, smiling tightly. "And what then, anyhow? What am I going to do without her? No, it's over for me. I wish I had the strength to do it, but she'd never forgive me."

"I can't imagine your pain. I'll do whatever I can to help."

"Is that an offer to take care of it yourself?" He chuckled. His dark humor had a ring of legitimate curiosity I wasn't entirely comfortable with.

"I'm not going to kill you, Ben."

"Pity," he said. "It's the kindest gift you could give me now."

"We'll figure something out. You're going to be okay," I said, more to convince myself than Ben.

"Thank you, Jacobi. Thank you for what you've done."

"Oh, I almost forgot. I've been taking care of Nautilus as well. I think he's doing okay. He just, sort of…floats, but at least it's right side up."

"Can I see him?" he asked. Nodding, I wandered into the kitchen, grabbed the fish bowl, and brought it back to hold up in front of the monitor. Ben smiled as he watched Nautilus floating in the bowl, but before long his smile faded, and he shook his head. "That old fish has been floating in there for too many years. You should set him free or put him out of his misery."

Too late, I realized the similarities between their situations. The fish was a reflection of Ben, imprisoned in a never-ending state of solitude with no purpose, and I could tell from the sound of his voice that he'd made the connection. Inwardly, I scolded myself harshly for not having predicted the effect it would have.

"Once you're out of there, we'll find somewhere beautiful and set him free," I said sadly.

We locked eyes, and Ben replied, "I'll hold you to that." And I understood we were no longer talking about the fish.

After my conversation with Ben, I needed time to myself to think. I ended up floating in the pool, listening to the water running in off the rocks, for what felt like hours. The others must have intuitively understood my need for space, because no one interrupted my meditative state. During the time I lay floating on my back, soaking my physical and emotional bruises, I focused my intention toward freeing myself from the web of negativity I was caught in. I started by accepting that I was very much in pain.

Himari had been right the night before. I was responsible for the decisions that led me to being involved in the deaths of the civilians who were assassinated during Operation Dreamreaver. I was responsible for the decisions that led up to killing Jack, and for what happened to Pavel. The choices I'd made about what defined me and what I wanted to contribute to the world were the underlying cause, despite my inclination to play the victim and avoid responsibility. I couldn't honor the warrior inside of me, as he'd put it, if I wasn't willing to acknowledge that my violent lifestyle would forever have dark consequences. He'd suggested the pain of those consequences was a weight that must be carried to be truly at peace with the path I'd chosen. It was a terrifying thing to think about. I'd been running away from accepting all of who I was. I'd even stopped asking myself if I was happy with whoever that might be.

The elevator door opened, and I opened my eyes to see Matvei Kamenev, followed closely by Boris and a tall, thin blonde. She wore an elegant white dress and had the lustrous black fur of an animal I couldn't identify thrown over her shoulder. The glare she gave me as I stood gave me the impression she thought I'd just pissed in the pool. Matvei was trying to keep his expression neutral, but I could sense an underlying tension there.

"Mr. Kamenev," I said as I pulled myself from his pool and grabbed a towel to dry off with. "This is unexpected."

Having heard the elevator opening, Himari and Risa wandered into the room from around the bend of the tube-shaped outer hallway. Himari bowed, and Risa remained silent, but I could tell from the way she was standing she was vigilant and prepared.

"I wouldn't have interrupted your stay here, but it recently came to my attention that Pavel Volkov is dead. Is it true, Jacobi Slate, that Pavel died in your presence?"

The question took me off-guard. I had neither anticipated the news of his death traveling so quickly nor the potential impact it could have as a result of his connection to Matvei's organization. I wasn't exactly sure what Matvei's stake in this was, and that left me hesitant to respond, but I nodded.

"I was with him when he died. Yes."

"Did you kill my brother?" The woman in white stepped out in front of Matvei and hissed the question vehemently. The words carried with them a promise of vengeance that hinged on my response.

"I would never hurt Pavel," I said, keeping my voice calm. "He was my friend."

She seemed to relax slightly, but her anger lingered in the distrustful stare she continued to throw my way like a sharp knife.

"But," I continued, "I am responsible for his death."

"*Zasranec*," she spat out in Russian, pulling a small pistol from an expensive handbag at her side. I saw Risa tense but extended the fingers of my right hand, signaling her to wait. Before the blonde could raise it in my direction, Matvei held his hand up and gave her a reproachful look, as if to assert dominance and remind her he was in control.

"*How* are you responsible?" he asked me.

"I hired Pavel to investigate the background of several individuals who were on a list. I suspected they had been targeted by someone, but I underestimated the precautions in place, and Pavel was compromised. He became a target himself. If I hadn't asked him to look into those people, he would still be alive."

Matvei took Pavel's sister by the arm and pulled her aside for a moment, whispering into her ear. They argued, but eventually her intense anger began to dissipate into something akin to defeat. She put the gun back into her purse, and after one last spiteful glare over her shoulder, she stepped into the elevator and departed.

"I am sorry," said Matvei, turning back to me. "She is very upset, and she is looking for someone to blame."

"I understand," I replied. "I feel the same way, Mr. Kamenev."

"You will do this thing then?"

"I'm doing everything in my power to bring Pavel's killer to justice, I promise you that."

"Justice," he said, "is relative. What you might find just, Lena, that's his sister, might think is only a good start, yes?"

I said nothing, waiting for Matvei to decide how he wanted to proceed.

After a short pause, he continued. "Jacobi, I want to help you. I've done what you asked me to, have I not?"

"You have, Matvei. And I thank you for the generosity you've shown to me and my associates."

"I can't have you running around here, shooting people outside the building. There can be no more of that. You can stay here for as long as you need to. But when this is over, we're going to have a long talk about clearing the debt you're incurring."

I nodded. "I'm truly sorry about Pavel. He was a good man."

"Eh, people die," said Matvei, "I'm more worried about what I'm going to do about Lena. They were twins, and she is ruthless and thirsts for blood. Her mother is a very important woman, highly placed in the structure of Sokoly Zimoy. They both need closure. You will let me know immediately when *justice* has been served. If there is anything I can do to expedite the outcome, call me."

"I will."

With that, Matvei Kamenev turned and left with Boris, who shot me a wink as the elevator door closed.

Risa approached with her head tilted slightly, her insinuated question evident without words.

"It happened a few days ago. You were asleep. I met him across town, and Mason or someone Mason was controlling got to him when he stepped outside for a phone call."

"Why didn't you tell me?"

"I'm not sure," I answered, which was the truth. It had just been another tragedy to throw on the pile. It hadn't changed anything. "It felt personal. Pavel wasn't on the list. I got him involved. Mason had him blow his brains all over the wall in front of me to prove a point. I guess I just needed some time to process that."

"Jesus, Jacobi. I'm sorry."

"I'm okay now. I know what I have to do."

"Okay. What?"

"Himari," I said, "I need to see The Blacksmith again. I need to talk to him about a trade."

I went alone. After warning me The Blacksmith was not going to be pleased to hear from me, Himari consented to giving me the old man's direct contact information. There had been no answer, but I left a message detailing a proposition and received a return call within the hour, which included instructions for connecting with a transport to the *Forge*. I felt the fewer people that accompanied me, the less chance there would be that he'd feel pressured or intimidated, and I wanted this to be an amiable agreement, without the uncertainty and distrust that had beleaguered our last encounter. I'd walked to the nearest landing pad and was waiting there for a passenger drone he'd sent to pick me up and take me to the ship.

Before long, it floated in quietly from the skies. It was dark-red and made from a lightweight carbon, fiber-reinforced composite. The four propellers at the base adjusted their angle downward to soften the landing as it touched the ground. The door slid open, and once I'd buckled myself in, we were away.

The ride was brief, though the ship had moved from its last location and seemed to be holding its position farther south. Stepping out of the drone, I was received by The Blacksmith and two of his apprentices. One held an umbrella over his chair. The other moved forward to provide me with the same courtesy, which I thanked him for as we made our way off the deck.

The Blacksmith led me to one of his workshops, where we spoke at length about an idea I'd proposed in the message I'd left. He confirmed the concept was sound, but as to whether or not it would be a viable solution to his problem, he remained skeptical. He was willing to accept that what I was offering was a fair trade for my request, which was for him to try to restore the memories I'd allowed the DFDC to hide. According to him, memory reduction didn't actually remove any memories. It only prevented the conscious mind from accessing them, and he assured me he could tear down the walls that had been put in place. I promised him I would deliver on my part of the deal in exchange for a procedure to roll back the reduction I'd undergone at the Division.

Risa and I had spoken before I'd departed, and she'd warned me that knowing what we'd done might be difficult, but remembering would be far worse. She'd spent five years of her life working to come to terms with her part in what had happened and struggled with it still. I understood her concerns. The events of the last several weeks had left a few scars, and despite my burgeoning acceptance of the things that had transpired, I was still in a vulnerable emotional state. Remembering the assassinations we'd conducted, and the horror of discovering we'd been manipulated, would undoubtedly add more weight to the burden I was already hauling. But one thing Mason had told me kept coming back into my mind, and ringing true. He'd told me I couldn't hide from the consequences of my choices, and after digesting Himari's advice, I agreed.

The memories of everything we'd done were inside my head, even if I couldn't access them. My subconscious was being triggered by trauma I couldn't even identify or relate to, and I was tired of being confused by the reactions of my own mind. I was ready to stop hiding. I wanted to be whole again, and I was prepared to pay the price, even if the price was bearing the full shame of what we'd done.

As I lay there, strapped to a gurney, several of The Blacksmith's apprentices moved about the room, checking monitors, testing equipment, and working on connecting me to sensors in preparation for the surgery. He had explained it would mostly be conducted via electromagnetic manipulation coupled with a simple, invasive process to remove a microscopic conductor that had been put in place in the hippocampus portion of my brain. The blue light of the operating room began to swim as the anesthesia was administered and took effect. My eyes slipped shut, and I welcomed the darkness, bidding farewell to the ghost as the exorcism began.

Dancing. Laughter. We were spinning and ended in a graceful dip. Our eyes connected, and I held her there. Her smile radiated warmth. I'd never been looked at that way before, with such love, such understanding. In just months, our lives had shifted so drastically. We killed, we fought, we brought justice to those who would bring terror and death to innocents, and now, we loved. And that changed everything. It was almost impossible to envision a future of violence and danger when I was surrounded by so much light. I just wanted her to be safe.

My eyes flickered open. The memory had been fresh. Vivid. I

moved my head slowly from side to side, trying to get a better sense of my surroundings. I was lying on a gurney. The straps had been removed. I was alone in a dark room. I remembered then, I was on the *Forge* and I must have been waking from the procedure. As I lay there, once-forgotten memories drifted aimlessly into my thoughts, kicked up like freshly disturbed dust off of relics in a long-abandoned attic.

Cody raised his glass in celebration. Tom, Katy, Aaron, James, Risa, Wendell. They were all there. It was my birthday. Ben had spilled the beans and given up the date to the unit after years of secrecy. He'd been bribed with a bottle of 2025 Scotch whiskey. At least he was sharing. They all joined the toast. I was grateful for their friendship, but we were all becoming closer than I was comfortable with. They trusted me to make decisions their lives depended on, and those decisions were made more complex by relationships with emotional stakes. I'd need to pull away.

Something was beeping incessantly. Apprentices arrived, filing into the room to investigate the noise, check the readouts on the equipment I was connected to, and update documents on their tablets based on the results.

"Can I leave now?" I asked weakly. My throat was sore, and my ears were ringing. They ignored me and carried on with their work. They must have injected me with something, because I drifted in and out of consciousness for a time, alternating between a dreamless slumber and a turbid delirium through which it was difficult to discern my place in time. In my waking moments, the memories flooded in, and I relived them, partially from the darkness of the recovery room and partially as if I were experiencing them in the present.

They finally found him. I need you to plan the operation. You're taking your team in. He leaves that compound in our custody or not at all. We finally have him, Jacobi, after all these years. This is everything we've fought for. Make it happen, I believe in you. Understood, Ben. We'll bring him in. After months of careful planning, turning informants, satellite surveillance — it was all coming to fruition. He wouldn't be a step ahead this time. Every bomb he'd built, every civilian he'd murdered, we finally had him.

"Not getting away this time, Khadem," I muttered into the darkness. He'd done *so* much harm. The world would be a better place without him. I'd be damned if I was going to let him slip through my fingers again.

When this tour is up, I'm done. Four more months. Fourteen years of my life I've given. You'll come away with me. We'll find some land and build a home. We'll raise some animals. Oregon? I do love the ocean. Wherever I can wake up to you staring at me like this. Come take a shower with me. Marry me? Of course I'm joking.

"Why not?" I asked the emptiness. "We're perfect together." I'd never find someone who understood me better than her. No one else would ever look at me that way. Once again, I fell into the dreamless dark, waking to the sound of...

Ghazi Khadem. Exploding. His parts, and parts of Tom and Katy, strewn across the floor. Such sorrow. We'd lost too much. The price we'd paid was too high. Exchanged for intelligence locked behind cascade encryption. Torture. We had the ciphers. Sleepers. An activist. A banker. An artist. So many potential threats.

"Was it worth it, Ben?" I wondered aloud, but there was no reply. "You know I'll follow your lead on this." This wasn't my call, and I thanked the universe for that. We should have found something. We should have been able to get at least one of them to crack...

I opened my eyes to find The Blacksmith seated in his wheelchair beside the gurney. His hands were folded in his lap, and he seemed to have been patiently waiting for me to return to consciousness. He said nothing, allowing me the time I needed to adjust to waking. Once I felt fully cognizant, I raised my head and noticed all of the sensors that had been connected to me had been removed. I attempted to sit up and was happily surprised to find my strength was sufficient.

"The procedure is complete," he said. "When you are ready, the drone is waiting to return you to the city. Do you...remember?"

The sensation was different than I'd expected. It didn't feel like a river of memories had rushed in to fill a void. I wasn't overwhelmed by confusing, unfamiliar experiences. Instead, it was more similar to the experience of rubbing a limb that had fallen asleep back to life. It wasn't unlike forgetting a small thing, like a line of poetry, and then being reminded of it. It had always been there, but out of reach and inaccessible until the reminder triggered a process of recollection that began to add clarity and detail. The more I thought about the things that had been blocked, the clearer the events became.

So when I considered his question and thought back to the experiences I'd had regarding the assassination of innocent civilians, it was no surprise I was immediately overcome by an urge to vomit. The look on my face must have signaled the inevitable purge of guilt and disgust, because The Blacksmith passed me a metal bowl from a nearby counter.

When finished, I held my head in my hands, rocking slightly, utilizing the movement to distract myself from feeling the full horror of what I'd done. I remembered everything. More than anything, I remembered why I'd chosen to have the memories blocked. I'd set an example for the people in my unit. Through my own behavior, I'd encouraged them to follow orders and commit acts of atrocity they might have otherwise refused. They had looked to me as a leader, and I had led them down the wrong path. It was that, more than anything else that twisted my gut with regret.

But I'd also known this was coming, and in the six years since the events had occurred, I'd grown stronger and wiser. Despite having just been unblocked, the memories felt distant and removed. The anguish was dulled by the time that had passed between then and now. I'd agreed to hold this pain. Until I found a way to process it and work through it like Risa had done, it was going to be a part of me. But I wouldn't let it own me. I wouldn't let it interfere with holding the people responsible for this accountable. I raised my head and nodded.

"You've done your part," I said. "Give me some time, and I'll get you what I promised."

I got up slowly and changed back into my clothes, which were neatly folded nearby. The Blacksmith escorted me back up to the deck, where the passenger drone was waiting.

"I'll begin my research in order to be prepared for when you return, Jacobi-san. I must admit, I'm excited about the potential of your solution. In the meantime, I hope you find the peace you are seeking. We will speak again soon."

"If I do find peace," I replied as I entered the drone, "it'll be in the aftermath of a fair bit of conflict, I expect."

He adjusted his glasses and raised his hand to wave goodbye as I boarded. The drone departed, and the *Forge* fell away behind us, adrift on the massive waves of the Pacific. As we flew, I closed my eyes, lost in thought.

I threw a left hook, which Cody danced away from. We were sparring in the ring at the gym in the DFDC headquarters. He shot a straight kick forward, but I grabbed his leg and dropped to the ground, taking him down with me. He tapped the mat and stood, wiping off his forehead.

"You're always ready for that one, Captain."

"So stop using it," I said, grinning. "One more?"

"That's it for me," he answered. "I've got to head out. Got a date."

"Oh! Big man on campus! Who's the unfortunate lady?"

We slipped through the ropes and hopped down onto the floor as we talked. I noticed Mason watching us from the wall near the entrance to the locker. He had his arms and legs crossed and looked agitated. Cody took a long squirt of water from his bottle.

"A gentleman never tells," he said, grinning.

"Cody, a gentleman never tells whether or not he's sleeping with someone. He doesn't keep their name a secret."

He paused and frowned, then said, "Oh."

"Listen, I'll catch up with you later, all right? Enjoy your date. Don't let her take advantage of you."

As Cody walked into the locker room, I approached Mason, who hadn't taken his eyes off me.

"Something on your mind, Robbins?" I asked.

"Can we sit, Captain Slate? Talk somewhere?"

"Sure. You want to go a few rounds?" I asked and gestured toward the ring.

327

He shook his head.

"Yeah, okay. Let's just take a seat here then." I parked on one of the nearby benches and Mason joined me there. He was avoiding eye contact and clearly uncomfortable. "So, what's up?"

There was no one in the gym but us, but Mason lowered his voice anyway. "It's this operation. Are we seriously going through with this? Not one of those people showed any sign of being a threat. Not one."

"We're not in a position to make decisions about what we're going to go through with and what we aren't here, Mason. What are you suggesting?"

"You can talk to Oaksley and tell him he's making a mistake. He'll listen to you."

Ben and I were friends, but our professional relationship had never been marred by either of us sharing our doubts with one another about the missions we undertook.

"Can you guarantee that?" I asked, lowering my voice to a whisper as well. "Can you guarantee there's no danger? Because I can't. That's why I leave those kinds of decisions to the people getting paid to make them."

"Give me a fucking break, Slate. You're not a fool. This is too perfect!" he said, growing aggravated. "We found every landmine, got past every tripwire. One day in the can, and the guy we grabbed spits out the cyphers to the encryption. This is bullshit. It's a setup."

I could feel my temper flaring. It was partially because he was being insubordinate, but also because there was truth in what he was suggesting. But I wasn't in a position to convince the executive leadership otherwise, and recognizing that only served to frustrate me further.

"Robbins," I said, my voice growing more intense. "I've been listening to your bullshit since you got recruited into this unit. You're always questioning me, always pushing back. Can't you just get on board with the rest of the team for once? You think this is easy for them? For me? It's not going to be

328

easy for anyone, but it's our goddamned job. We're soldiers. We go where we're needed and do whatever needs to be done, because we're at war, for fuck's sake."

"Even when that means executing American civilians, Captain? Twenty-five people, not a single crack in any of their profiles. Not one actionable discrepancy to investigate. They're not well-trained, sir — they're innocent!"

"You don't know that. When twenty-five explosions erupt throughout twenty-five cities next year, or ten years from now, and each takes five thousand lives, that'll be on us. You do the math, Mason. Do you want that weight on your back? You should consider yourself fortunate you don't have to make this decision. It's not up to us. You need to tighten up, because if you start spouting these doubts off to everyone else, it's only going to make what we have to do that much harder. Are you on this team? Can we count on you? If not, then pack your shit and head home, because this is happening with or without you."

The disdainful way he looked at me made it clear he thought I was, in fact, a fool. He shook his head but said, "Yeah, Captain Slate. I'm on the team." He stood up and backed away, smiling that fake smile he was always putting on, then turned and walked away, leaving me sitting on the bench alone.

I knew I should have handled the situation better, but the stress of what we'd been asked to do was wearing on me as well, and I was thin on patience. When I'd first been briefed by Ben, I'd brought up similar concerns, but he'd told me the executives had made up their mind on the subject and it was our job to comply. The truth was it didn't matter what we wanted or what our opinions were. We were tools. Weapons, deployed to eliminate threats against our society. Ben knew that and expected me to understand, without complaint, and I wasn't going to let him down.

I opened my eyes as the drone landed on the launch pad. Walking back to the apartment, I wondered how many people were still in the city, the streets of which were now under nearly a foot of water in some cases. Ground vehicle traffic had completely come to a halt downtown, and passenger drones like the one I'd just ridden were a rarity afforded only to the wealthy. It was only drizzling slightly, but the wind was strong and the sky remained totally overcast. I realized I wasn't even sure what time it was. It was too light out for it to be the same day I'd left to meet with The Blacksmith, which meant I must have been there overnight. I pulled out my CUBE to confirm and discovered it was late in the afternoon. I also noted I'd missed a call from Risa. I had no idea what I'd say to her when I got back.

"How could you do that to us?" she asked with tears streaming down her face. "How could you ever do that?"

"Risa," I said gently. "It has nothing to do with us. I hate what it will mean for us. But I can't live this way. It's too much. The rest of my life? I'd be throwing away the chance to live a normal life, without this feeling, for..."

"Love?" she asked. "For love, Jacobi. Yes. For me. What happened to us was not your fault. It hurts now, but I want to remember this. I want to remember us."

"We can start again," I pleaded. "We can start over. Without the guilt. Without the fucking pain we see every time we look into the mirror. Without the ghosts of twenty-five innocents standing behind me, reminding me I'm a goddamned murderer!"

"Every war has casualties, Jacobi. Every war has innocents that die,

people who don't deserve their fate. What we did, we did because we believed it was the right thing to do. We believed in a greater good. We were wrong, but we're only human. You have to let this go. I don't even recognize you anymore. You're just carrying all of this darkness with you."

"I can't. I can't let it go, Risa. I can't sleep at night. I can't think about anything else. I have to do this. I have to forget."

"Everything we've shared," she said. "Everything we've come to understand about one another. Gone. You'll throw that away because you can't move beyond your guilt? I'm not going to do it. I won't forget. I'm going to get through this, and so will you, if you just trust me."

"I don't have a choice. I can't do this."

"You could. You're stronger than you think. Please, Jacobi, for me. Stay with me."

"If you're not going to do this, then you can come to me," I said. "When it's over. I'll fall for you just as easily as I did five months ago. I don't want to lose you, Risa. Promise me you'll come to me."

She didn't answer. She held her face in her hands, and her body shook with sobbing.

I walked into the living room of the penthouse and found everyone, including Sam Winston, gathered around the dining room table. There were maps laid out across the surface. I noticed green cargo containers stacked up against a nearby wall, which presumably held the gear we'd requested. Everyone looked up as I arrived.

"Where the hell have you been, Mr. Slate?" asked Sam. "We've got a goddamn operation to plan here."

331

I said nothing. My eyes were locked on Risa as I approached her. As I neared, I saw what looked like a mixture of hope and trepidation in her expression. When I was close enough, I threw my arms around her and pulled her tightly toward me. She buried her face against my chest, and I could feel her body shaking as she quietly wept.

"I'm sorry," I whispered into her ear. "I'm so sorry."

Chapter 12

With the help of a trusted colleague at the Division, Sam managed to crack open the data package Pavel and his team had salvaged from the deleted voidspace communications hub. I wasn't entirely surprised to hear the software locking it had been designed by the DFDC. Shortly after they'd started combing through the data, the file began to immolate. Someone on the Division's internal network had been aware of his efforts to reveal whatever had been in the package and had shut them down. This only served to infuriate Sam, who redoubled his efforts, more convinced than ever that one or more high-level executives were in collaboration with Richard Robbins.

In their brief exposure to the data, he'd seen references to Mason Robbins and his father, the name of one of the executives on the board of the DFDC, and the name of a small town in Colombia, Mitú. The executive named in the file was a man named Simon Branch. Branch had been integral in the formation of the agency. He was extremely powerful and equally well connected. Though the evidence against him was incriminating, the file had been destroyed, and Sam had nothing tangible to take to the remaining members of the council as proof of Branch's involvement with Richard Robbins and the trials.

The day before the raid on the ranch, everything changed. Sam had managed to pull enough strings to get imagery from a satellite passing near the ranch, and what he'd seen there was a massive mobilization. Richard was knee-deep in the middle of a major exodus. Trucks were packed with supply crates. Men were armed and fully uniformed aboard transport vehicles. Sam didn't believe for a second that this deployment was unrelated to his recent discovery of the location in Colombia. We moved our focus from the ranch and adjusted our strategy to prepare instead for a foray into the jungle of the Amazon Basin.

There were no roads that led to Mitú. It had an airstrip running through the center of town, but we'd elected to fly down on a tiltrotor Osprey. It had meant stopping once to recharge, but using that type of craft would allow us to avoid the highly visible airstrip and land, more privately, in one of the small hamlets across the river to the southwest of town.

I was light another ten thousand credits, but we'd added Gray back onto our roster of misfit soldiers for the mission. After he'd invested his earnings from the previous job back into his shop and gotten his mortgage payments settled, his wife had decided to take him back. He said he'd have taken just about any work to get out of the house and away from her, but he looked happier and more content. I hoped his skill with a rifle wouldn't become necessary, but I was going to be glad to have him with us if it did.

We were on our final approach after the four hour flight from California. I'd asked the team to use the time to get some rest, but most of us had managed a couple hours of sleep at best. The horizon wasn't showing signs of light yet, but dawn was fast approaching.

Risa was asleep with her head resting on my shoulder. I noticed the others beginning to stir, sensing the end of our journey as the two pilots adjusted the speed and elevation of the vehicle. I wasn't sure where Sam had recruited them, or what he'd told them about the mission, but they hadn't asked any questions, so I returned the courtesy.

I'd spoken with Sam at length about the strategy we'd adopt upon arriving at Mitú. We'd try to integrate quickly, find a source of information, and a place to lay low and plan. The hamlets on the west side of the Vaupés River were remote. We estimated we'd have a chance to contain any knowledge of our presence for a day or two before word got back to town. Since we were heading into this situation blind and uninformed, we'd need that time to scout the area and to determine exactly what Richard's operation here entailed.

Red lights popped on, indicating imminent touchdown. The team popped fully awake at the sign, adjusted their gear, and prepared for deployment. I heard the tiltrotors angle for landing and felt the slight impact of the Osprey hitting the dirt. The rear hatch fell out to create a ramp leading down, and we unstrapped then quickly exited the aircraft, which took back to the sky immediately and quickly became lost to view.

Looking around, I saw we'd been dropped off in a large, open field at the edge of the river. Across the water to the east I saw a few lights in Mitú, but the area was mostly dark. In addition to a sparse line of palms along the bank, I could see a small cluster of buildings to the south. There was a light approaching us from that direction. I gave a low whistle and pointed.

The others evaporated into the surrounding landscape, but I remained. I pulled out my CUBE and directed it to translate between English and Spanish. Afterward, I put my weapon on the ground at my feet and held my hands above my head as the light neared. When whoever was holding it noticed me, they froze and shouted a question in Spanish I couldn't understand. I couldn't see much past the light of the lantern, but I could barely make out the outline of a woman holding a long rifle of some kind.

The CUBE translated the questions to English and asked, "Who are you? What are you doing here? What was that noise?"

I replied, "I'm American. There are others with me. We don't intend any harm to you or anyone else. We're looking for some bad men. Other Americans. Can you help us? We can pay you. Credits."

The CUBE repeated my question, in Spanish, and the woman looked around nervously.

"American?" she asked cautiously. "I speak little English."

"Can you help us? We need a way to cross the river and someone who knows the area to guide us."

The woman looked extremely mistrustful once the CUBE had completed translating my request. I guessed the promise of payment was all that was keeping her from kicking me from her property, or worse, pulling the trigger.

"How much credits?" she asked, her curiosity overcoming her suspicion. We began to haggle, and before long we'd reached an agreement. Once she'd lowered her gun, the others appeared from the shadows they'd lain in, popping up from patches of tall grass and slipping out from behind nearby trees.

Daniela, as she introduced herself, had tangled hair that was graying at the roots. She was somewhere in her fifth decade of living off the land we stood on. It was her son, Luis, who would be tasked with taking us across the river, but not before she'd welcomed us to Colombia properly by taking us all back to her home and boiling water for fresh coffee. I was grateful for the translator, because Daniela had a wealth of information to divulge. She was an herb farmer who made her living growing and collecting both medicinal and traditional herbs on the land her family had owned for generations. Her husband had passed over a decade before, and she'd been left to raise a son and a daughter alone.

I'd been surprised by how little she'd been impressed by all of the weaponry our team was carrying, but the more she told me about the history of the land, the more I realized armed troops were no uncommon sight in Mitú. The history of the town was rife with incidents of violence and guerrilla warfare related to gaining an advantage in the rubber industry. Over the last three decades, the skirmishes had intensified as the Amazon Basin became more heavily forested and Brazilian forces pushed more forcibly at the Colombian boundary.

She spoke of more recent violence as well. Mitú had been under the control of an arm of the Suarez-Giraldo cartel for the past fifteen years. Its proximity to the Brazilian border and the natural shipping lane the river provided made it an ideal hub that the cartel had recognized and taken advantage of. As we enjoyed our coffee and waited on her son to wake, Daniela told us the local leadership of Suarez-Giraldo had not been cruel or violent to the villagers, as long as they had ignored their business. In fact, they had provided employment to many of Mitú's residents, and the local economy had boomed as a result of the various industries the cartel controlled.

I asked her what had changed, and she told a story about American soldiers that had arrived in the town over a year ago. The soldiers had asked a great many questions about the Suarez-Giraldo cartel and had behaved violently in some cases when their questions had not been answered honestly. Over the following weeks, minor skirmishes had played out between the Americans and the cartel, but on one bloody day, the conflict had erupted into total warfare. In a series of brutal incidents, the cartel distribution offices had been attacked, their members massacred. A similar act of violence occurred on that same day at a place Daniela described as *fortaleza de la jungle*, the jungle fortress.

When I asked, she couldn't tell me how to get there but said she'd been given an account of what had transpired by a woman who had worked on the land and seen it firsthand. Daniela claimed the woman, and many other civilians, similarly employed, had been allowed to escape into the jungle with their lives to spread the news of what had happened throughout the town. The Americans had warned them never to return. Since then, the soldiers had occasionally returned to Mitú in small groups for supplies and resources but were otherwise exclusively found at the complex they'd taken over from the cartel.

I pressed Daniela to connect us with the woman she'd heard the story from. I hoped she could either guide us to her old place of employment or mark it on our map for us to investigate. The herb farmer didn't believe her friend would be willing to do so and told me as much.

"She won't take the risk," the CUBE translated. "Why should she risk her life for you?"

"Daniela," I said. "We want to make these men return to America. If your friend helps us, they won't be here to threaten her or anyone else any longer."

She shook her head and said, "You are Americans. They are Americans. Same. No trust."

"Please consider asking her," I replied. "We can't stop them if we can't find them. If she helps us, I'll give her double what I paid to you, and double your credits as well. We only want to help. Think it over."

I felt better knowing the Coalition didn't have a noticeable presence in town. And if the first woman we'd met had known someone who had been employed at the jungle fortress, then we'd almost certainly be able to track down someone else with similar information. We needed to get across the river to situate ourselves with supplies and secure a command center of some sort, even if that meant renting a cramped hut with a palm frond roof. Anywhere we could stay out of sight to formulate a plan would be sufficient.

A lanky teenage boy arrived in the kitchen, barely awake. He was shirtless, wearing only a pair of canvas shorts and scuffed sandals that had remained functional long past the point they probably should have. Reasonably, he seemed concerned that there were five armed soldiers in his mother's kitchen. Before he had time to vocalize his distress, she began barking instructions to him to escort us across the river and assist us with finding accommodations. He didn't seem happy about it but appeared sullenly resolved to comply.

Without words, he led us through the fields to the river, where there were several longboats pulled onto the shore. If the boy was nervous about escorting five armed soldiers, it didn't show. He rolled a cigarette before motioning us all to get into one of the boats and puffed it while he rowed us across without ever taking it from his mouth. The river was wide, and the black water was slow-moving as it flowed to the east. It was transparent but stained, like a cup of English tea. As we neared the opposite shore I noticed the sky was brightening and people were beginning to move about their business in the town.

We reached a grassy area between two copses at the bank, and Luis hopped out of the longboat to drag it ashore by a rope at the nose. Without pausing, he waved for us to follow him up the small hill leading into town. Daniela had instructed him to assist us in finding a place where we could set up our equipment and sleep, but I had no idea how exactly he planned to accomplish the task. I was concerned because if American soldiers had recently terrorized Mitú's civilians, they weren't likely to be very welcoming of new ones arriving fully armed.

We followed the boy as he wound his way through dirt alleyways, over fences, and behind dilapidated storefronts until the structures thinned out and became sparse toward the edge of town. There he stopped before a large building with weeds overrunning the entrance. It was an old brick church, abandoned and forgotten by time. The bricks were tan, and charred near the windows, suggesting a fire of some kind had taken place long ago. A bell tower stood outside, disconnected from the main building, but the bell at the top was gone. A huge cross hung above the massive double doors leading into the building, and a statue of a woman holding a child, once white but now tarnished and gray, stood silently in the plaza outside. I doubted the use of the building to plan a violent assault on our fellow man was in line with whatever belief structure the original occupants of the place had in mind, but I hoped they'd agree the evils we planned to prevent outweighed the blasphemy.

Though it was hardly erased, Catholicism had begun to decline, both in America and around the world, as science continued to expound upon the fundamental questions many had looked to religion to answer. Once scientists could effortlessly construct embryos via somatic cell nuclear transfer or induced parthenogenesis and create human beings with science alone, it had become more difficult to deny their claims of understanding our evolutionary history and future. The old guard dwindled as the children of a technological age came to power. Science was on pace to kill God, just like they'd always feared it would.

Risa nudged me and nodded toward Luis, who was staring at me questioningly. I'd been lost in thought and hadn't heard whatever question he'd asked but took a guess and told him the place was perfect, hoping he'd attribute any confusion to the language barrier. He seemed to accept my response and nodded, relieved his work was done. Without a farewell, he left the way we'd come.

"Let's find a way inside," I said. "Cody. Change up your outfit and disarm then head into town to see if you can get the list of supplies we went over earlier. Try to seem as…un-American as possible."

He put on his best Australian accent and said, "I'll see what I can dig up, mate."

Risa pulled on one of the double doors, which grudgingly opened after a few solid tugs. Inside, dust and cobwebs covered tables and pews. We were fortunate there were so many windows to allow the daylight in, since there was no power or internal light. I helped Himari rearrange the furniture to clear a central area we could unpack our equipment into. We rolled out several maps of the region and began pinning potential locations for the *fortaleza de la jungle* based on satellite imagery Sam had provided before we'd departed. It was guesswork, but at least we'd have some potential targets to recon with Cody's drone. Risa uncovered a metal box filled with old candles, which she put into sconces on the walls to provide more light.

Since we weren't sure how long we'd be settling in for, we did what we could to make the space more livable, and before long it had shaped up into a functional command center. It wasn't very secure, considering the doors didn't even lock, but my hope was that we wouldn't be there long enough for that to be an issue. Gray kicked through the rotted wooden doorway into the bell tower and ascended the brick stairwell to the loft. From there he could see out in all directions and provide advance warning in the case of company.

In the early afternoon, Cody returned carrying a crate of goods. He'd traded for blankets, purified water, food, and other assorted goods that we'd discussed. Since none of us had eaten in hours, we were grateful for the sustenance. I had stepped away while the others finished eating to fill Sam in over the comms on what we'd managed to accomplish while he'd slept when Gray alerted us that someone was approaching.

I looked out from one of the front-facing windows of the church and saw that two women were drawing near. Recognizing Daniela's wild gray hair, I stepped outside to greet them. Fortune was favoring us, it seemed. She introduced Mayra as the woman she'd mentioned who had previously been employed at the cartel complex the Phoenix Coalition had usurped. For twice the credits I'd promised, Mayra was willing to lead us there, with the condition she didn't have to go inside. We settled our debt with them both, and Cody agreed to meet Mayra that night at the landing where Luis had pulled the boat ashore. Because of his spectral cloak and the drone he kept folded in his kit, it made the most sense for him to scout the area alone. Any more of us out there with him would just increase the odds Coalition surveillance would pick someone up and spoil our advantage of surprise.

Late that night, Risa, Himari, and I were fiercely engaged in a game of poker we'd been using bottle caps to bet on when Cody returned from the expedition.

"How bad is it?" I asked, dropping my cards and thankful for the opportunity to get away from yet another hand I'd been about to lose to Risa.

We joined him at the table we'd spread the maps out over. He removed many of the pins that we'd placed to denote potential sites but left one down in an area about four miles to the southeast, across the river. The satellite imagery showed a series of buildings, but the footage Sam had gathered of the area had been broad in scope and lacked detail.

"It's here," he said. "It's a fenced-off compound with a castle-like structure, a barracks, and a third building that has some transport trucks out in front of it." As he described what he'd discovered, he loaded up the footage the drone had collected. We gathered around the only holo-display we'd brought to watch.

"They have some sentries," Cody continued, "but I didn't notice patrols. I didn't see any stationary or drone turrets either. Didn't have the impression they're expecting an attack. But there are over thirty armed mercenaries there, at least, so I don't blame them for feeling comfortable."

"What is this building?" I asked, pointing to the two larger structures.

"Mayra called it the laboratory. If they're cooking this shit up, then it's happening in there. I see ventilation stacks there," he said, indicating an area of the roof, "and this looks like a backup power generator on the ground outside."

"Did you see Richard Robbins?" asked Risa.

"Negative. But I couldn't get the drone near the main residence without risking detection. They're more heavily concentrated in that area. If he's here, that's probably where we'll find him."

"Everyone get your gear prepped and rest up tonight. Gray has been in that tower all day, so I'm going to go relieve him and take a shift at watch. Himari will relieve me in three hours, and Risa will take the shift after him. Tomorrow, we settle up here and get our game plan straight to hit the compound."

The night passed without incident, and the next morning we began preparing in earnest for the attack. In the early afternoon, Sam contacted me on a private channel and asked me to step away from the others for a moment.

"Mr. Slate, I have some unfortunate news," he said. "One of the transport vehicles that were being used to evacuate Alcatraz Island prisoners went down this morning over the bay."

"Ben?" I asked, desperation rising in my chest.

"Admiral Oaksley was on the flight. With the extreme ocean activity, it's been difficult to conduct a proper search and rescue. No bodies have been recovered. I'm sorry. I know the news comes at a hard time, but I thought you'd want to know."

I wanted to scream in frustration, but instead I said, "Thank you, Sam. Thanks for letting me know."

I felt the fight taken right out of me, and I sat down on the dusty floor of an old storeroom in the church. This had all been for Ben, and now he was gone. With everything we'd gone through together over our years in the service, for him to go down in a transport crash seemed like someone's sick idea of a joke. The only thing that comforted me in that moment was that

Ben had always been a man of the sea, and it had been the sea that ultimately claimed him and took him home. I must have sat for a while lost in thought, because eventually Risa came to check on me.

"You okay?" she asked as she entered. "Cody thinks the explosives will be sufficient if they're planted inside…Jacobi? What's wrong?"

"It's Ben," I said, my head hung low in defeat. "Some sort of transport accident. They haven't found any bodies."

She sat down beside me and put her arm around me.

"I'm all right," I continued. "Ben…didn't really want to be here anymore. Not after Mary. But I thought I could make it right. I thought I could fix it. It was a long shot, but I thought I could fix it."

"Whatever it was," said Risa, "I know you had the best intentions. You were a good friend to him, and he loved you. Listen, I know you don't want to hear this from me, but it's just one more thing you're going to have to stow away for now so we can focus on getting this job done."

"No, you're right," I said, standing. "I want to get this bastard." Ben might have been the catalyst for my initial involvement, but Mason and his father were inevitably going to come after me, whether he'd asked me to look into the details surrounding Mary's death or not. This was as much a fight for my own safety and survival as it was something I'd been doing for Ben. Richard Robbins was going to pay for his part in what had happened to Oaksley and everyone else that had been drastically impacted by these trials. When this was all over, I'd take the time I needed to process the magnitude of loss I'd experienced recently and try to come to terms with my part in

Operation Dreamreaver. But now wasn't the time for processing pain. There were other lives at stake, and I needed to be at my best for them.

Once we felt fully prepared, we retired early for the evening and woke late in the night to pack our gear and depart. We'd decided that just before dawn would be the most opportune time to strike the Coalition because sentries were notoriously less awake and observant just before the sun returned. We didn't have a complicated plan, or nearly the amount of intelligence I'd normally have required to feel confident of our success, but we had a purpose. This was personal for most of us. The fire in each of us was fully ablaze now, and news of Ben's disappearance had been the gasoline. We all understood the chaos that was about to be unleashed, but we were soldiers, and chaos just fueled our adrenaline.

Our faces were painted dark green and black to keep our skin from reflecting any light. We were armed, armored, and spitting fire. Between the five of us, we were also equipped with enough augmentations and gadgetry to bring a small city to its knees. Thirty men seemed a paltry amount to stand in the way of justice for every life that had been broken by the Coalition's plans.

We took a longboat down the Vaupés for a mile before dragging it ashore and heading west into the jungle. Cody led us along a well-traveled trail through heavy brush and a dense forest of rubber trees. The path eventually opened onto a larger road, which we followed, without light, for about a half an hour. The moon was bright in the eastern sky as Cody signaled we were getting close to the compound. The foliage along the road began to thin and open up, and I saw lights ahead through the trees, coming from buildings beyond a tall barbed-wire fence. We left the road and cut through hanging vines, hacking our way toward the perimeter.

As we neared, we stopped to listen and make sure our approach hadn't been noticed. There was no commotion in the compound, but the sounds of the Amazon poured in from the jungle around us. Insects and birds I'd never heard before joined in chorus to create a cacophony of unfamiliar night noises. It was exhilarating but also emphasized the sense of being far from home. I knew we had arrived at that moment of calm and clarity before the avalanche would break from the mountain and begin to thunder downhill, frenzied and unstoppable. It was the point of no return, and none of us were strangers to the anxiety that inevitably accompanied it. But as much as I felt trepidation, I felt an impatient excitement growing. I was hungry for vengeance. They'd tried to use us like dogs, but they'd soon discover we were wolves.

"Mr. Slate." Sam's voice came through my earpiece. "I wanted to relay a final reminder that without Richard Robbins alive, we'll have no proof to bring to bear against whoever is responsible for this at the Division. I urge you to show restraint in the light of the unspeakable tragedies he is responsible for."

"We know what our mission is, Sam," I replied. "I'll do everything I can to make sure he's still warm when he gets to you."

Gray cut the wire of the fence, and Himari slipped through first. Cody had lent the spectral cloak to him, since Himari's particular objective was going to require the most secrecy. Within seconds, he had become nearly impossible to detect as he loped through the darkness to take up a position near the main residence. From there he would infiltrate the stone fortress where we suspected Robbins was residing. He'd be alone, but we'd synced our augment applications so I could monitor his video feed via my own retinal display and give direction if needed.

Gray went through next. There were two sentry towers near the gate of the compound. His objective would be to eliminate the threat there and then take up position in one of the towers to provide cover. Risa had already left, skirting the fence to the west to breach at a location closer to the barracks. Cody and I were responsible for the laboratory. We kept low, making our way toward the building, where we meant to plant a series of explosive devices inside to collapse it.

The estate was overrun by tall grass and weeds. It wasn't difficult to maintain a low profile as we moved from structure to structure. Near the lab, there were three dark-green box trucks parked next to one another in a line. I ignored them at first, but curiosity ultimately prevailed over common sense, and I took a detour to the rear of one of the vehicles while Cody worked on the access panel at the entrance. Pulling aside the canvas to look within, I saw that it was partially filled with square, wooden crates. I hopped up into the truck and kneeled to examine the boxes. A thin line of sealant held the lid on tightly, but I easily cut through it with my knife and opened it up. Inside were neatly-lined, wrapped kilos of a coarse, white powder. A quick check of the other vehicles revealed one to be identically loaded, while the last was empty.

I guessed we'd uncovered the reason for Robbins having brought the remainder of his forces to the manufacturing facility. He was defending his shipment. With this much product, he'd be in a position to begin distributing on a major scale back in the States. The trials had been successful, and now he knew he had a product governments would pay for. This was far more than whoever he'd been working with in the Division could possibly need. I didn't believe Richard Robbins would stop at providing this substance to the American government. In the hands of special-forces units from agencies around the world, assassinations and inexplicable acts of sabotage would become commonplace. No one could question another country's involvement if the acts were carried out by someone respected by their own people. Those in power would begin to question the motive behind every decision or occurrence and wonder who was actually to blame. It would lead to distrust, misinformation, and strife on a global scale that might ultimately lead to retaliation with catastrophic consequences — exactly what Robbins and his group of doomsday preppers were counting on.

Resolved to end any chance of that coming to fruition, I left the trucks and regrouped with Cody, who had successfully disengaged the locks on the doors. We explored the hallways of the building until we rounded a corner and spotted a lone sentry pacing back and forth before a wide doorway. Timing his approach, Cody quietly slipped down the length of the hall and wrapped his forearm around the mercenary's throat. The guard struggled, but was quickly incapacitated and lowered to the floor.

I caught up to Cody and pushed open the doors, which swung inward into a large, open room filled with scientific equipment. In the center, there were long tables covered with the same powdered substance we'd seen in the trucks outside, but in various stages of being processed and filtered. Three men wearing biohazard suits were busy separating seeds from a pile of long white flowers at the end of one of the tables. One looked up and noticed me.

"*¡Jesús, ponte una maldita máscara!*" one yelled at me as I stood in the doorway. "*Máscara!*" he repeated, pointing to my right. I turned my head and saw a shelf with several face masks with filters. I quickly grabbed one and threw it on, realizing the danger of my situation. I'd been under the influence of this drug once before and never wanted to experience the effects again. Despite our face-paint, the men didn't seem adverse to our presence, and carried on working once we were masked. As there had been a recent influx of new arrivals from the ranch, I thought it possible they were just assuming we'd arrived with Richard. I took out my CUBE, set it to translate, and approached cautiously while Cody stayed behind to guard the hallway.

As I grew near, I lifted my gun and instructed the men to raise their hands into the air then shouted a series of questions to ascertain the extent of their involvement. When they realized I wasn't with the mercenaries they began begging me to help them. I asked them to slow down and speak slowly for the translator. One of the men, a Dr. Bosko from Poland, spoke English well, and was more than happy to give me a complete explanation of their circumstance.

The men were scientists. They'd been abducted and manipulated into working on the compound by way of threats of violence against their families. Robbins had demanded they genetically alter seeds from the flowers of the Borrachero tree, which they called Burundanga, into a more streamlined product that was less dangerous, more effective at breaking down the user's ability to resist instructions, and easier to administer into the system. Richard had recently kicked production of the product into overdrive, and the exhausted men had been forced to work through the night to prepare the product for transport out. Dr. Bosko had a flurry of information to volunteer, but I told him it would have to wait.

I'd need to shift gears somewhat to adjust for a hostage escort scenario. It wouldn't be difficult, since we hadn't had a very specific plan to begin with. We just needed Richard, but if we could shut down his operation while we were there and get these men to safety, all the better.

They waited while I planted the explosive devices from my kit. Cody assisted me with identifying key load-bearing areas of the building. I grabbed the remaining masks from the shelf, suddenly aware that when this place went up, we'd all need to be protected from the smoke of the burning drug. Upon leaving the lab, we escorted the scientists to the hole in the fence we'd created on the way in and instructed them to hide somewhere off the road nearby. Cody and I returned to the trucks. As we used our remaining explosives to rig the two vehicles that were carrying product, Gray's voice came through my earpiece.

"Gate towers belong to us now, amigos. I've got vision throughout the compound. Sentries outside the main residence are gone. I assume that's your work, Himari?"

"Yes," Himari responded. "I'm inside now."

I brought up Himari's augment feed on my right eye. The image came to life on the lens, imposed over my view of the compound like a ghostly holograph. Closing my eye allowed me to focus on his broadcast without the distraction of my own environment, and I saw that he was moving down a dimly lit stone corridor toward a staircase that spiraled upward.

Remembering how much larger his quarters on the ranch were than the homes around it, I said, "Himari, look for the most opulent room — something that would set him apart from the others."

"*Hai*," he replied.

"Risa, are you in position?" I asked, toggling Himari's

broadcast for the time being.

"I'm in cover outside the entrance to the barracks. When this kicks off, I can give you a minute or two, but after that they're going to get organized and start breaking through."

"One more thing," I said. "You all need masks. If we're nearby when the labs go up, you're each going to need something to filter out the smoke. Cody will bring one to you, Gray, and take up position nearby. I'm coming your way, Risa. We'll cover the barracks together." Himari would be fine, since his toxin filter modification would be more effective than any face mask.

I hoped we'd be long gone before we triggered the explosives. If Richard could be extracted from the main residence without the alarm getting raised, we could blow the labs from a safe distance and be gone, leaving the rest of the mercenaries without leadership and scrambling to figure out what had happened. But we didn't have a clear sense of exactly how many mercs were in the stone, fortress-like structure he'd infiltrated, so we needed to be prepared for the potentiality of his discovery and buy him time to finish the job.

Cody and I separated and moved into position with the others respectively. Risa waited, barely breathing in the darkness, crouched behind the low cement barrier she'd chosen for cover to overlook the barracks. I handed her a mask and took cover with her behind the makeshift barricade.

The camp was still quiet, but I couldn't shake the feeling the anthill was about to meet the boot. The front of the massive stone building looming behind us looked like something out of a medieval fairy tale, with two crenelated towers rising up just beyond the highest story on the front corners. The rest of it had been renovated and updated with newer, cleaner cement blocks, but the original front face had been maintained. I wondered what purpose the building had served and thought perhaps it had been another church or a small Spanish fort that had been repurposed by the cartel. It lay dormant now, the unlit rooms beyond the barred windows revealing nothing of its past or of the efficacy of the subterfuge transpiring within its walls.

To that effect, I closed one eye and activated Himari's feed to check on his progress. I tensed, suddenly immersed in the action of the close-quarter combat he'd been engaged in. I was grateful I'd trained with this technique so frequently during my time as a captain because the two simultaneous inputs could be disconcerting and difficult to follow without practice. He was in another hallway, just outside of a large set of wooden double doors. Two of Richard's mercenaries were sprawled unconscious on the floor. A third man was wildly throwing blows at Himari, who gracefully moved away from the contact point of each one as they came in.

With a sudden lunge, Himari moved inside of his assailant's attack, caught his outstretched arm, and flung him over his shoulder into the wall opposite the doors. The Coalition mercenary fell to the ground and writhed in pain, clutching at what were likely several broken ribs. Himari silenced his groans with a quick kick to the head before turning back to the doorway.

He tried the handle and pushed on one of the doors, but it didn't budge. Another kick from his hydraulic enhanced cybernetic leg threw the door open. I opened my eye as a muffled blast rang out in the night around me and Risa, barely audible from within the fortress walls. We froze, but there was no immediate activity from the mercs in the barracks. The ghostly holograph of Himari's broadcast was still playing out over my reality. He'd immediately taken cover after kicking open the door and avoided Richard's shot.

Closing my eye again, I watched him charge into the room. Richard was half-naked, standing behind a lavish, canopied bed, aiming a semiautomatic shotgun at the entrance to his chamber. He fired twice more, but whether it was the spectral cloak or Himari's inhuman speed, both shots missed their target as we darted evasively across the room toward him.

He was snarling as we collided with him, tackling him to the floor. The fight was brief but intense. Richard was well trained and seemed to possess more strength than I'd given him credit for, since he landed several savage blows that caused Himari to grunt in pain, even behind his armor. Through his broadcast, I could hear yelling from within the fortress as more men, undoubtedly alerted by the shotgun blasts, began to move on his position.

Himari, now positioned atop Richard on the ground, batted his arms aside and slapped one of the stun patches I'd given him onto Robbins' neck. It worked quickly. Richard's face, contorted by violence and anger, began to relax as his eyes fluttered closed. Wasting little time, Himari moved to the doorway and prepared himself to engage the mercenaries coming down the hall.

Waiting outside, I felt helpless. I shut off the feed and rose, then began moving toward the entrance of the fort to help him. Behind me, Risa hissed out a warning as two men came running out of the front door of the fortified structure. They were moving in our direction, toward the barracks. I ducked back down behind the barrier beside Risa, hoping I'd been quick enough to avoid notice, but I knew they were certain to see us when they got closer, since we were positioned between them and the barracks on the wrong side of the wall.

Gray's voice came through the earpiece: "Left."

Cody responded, "Affirmative. Right."

Both mercenaries fell simultaneously as the silenced shots from my team in the sentry towers hit their marks.

I threw Himari's feed back up to check his status. He was running, carrying an unconscious Richard Robbins on his shoulders. He grunted with each step as he ascended a spiral stone staircase. It ended abruptly at a ladder, which led to a hatch in the ceiling. I shut the feed off.

A moment later, a dark shape emerged at the top of the closest tower. I tapped Risa on the shoulder to get her attention, pointing. The limp form of a body was being slowly lowered to the ground by the shadow at the top. When it reached the ground, the figure lowering it leapt from the top of the third-story tower and landed gracefully in a roll. I crouched and moved out of cover toward where they'd landed. Himari noticed me as he untied the cable reel he'd wrapped Robbins' unconscious form in, picked the body up, and followed me back into cover next to Risa. I clapped him on the shoulder, grinning and shaking my head. The man truly was superhuman.

The duration of the patches he'd applied to Richard was unreliable and could vary from person to person, depending on factors like tolerance and weight. Because of that, I intended to leave the compound as quickly as possible. We had what we'd come for.

Although the mercenaries here were complicit in terrible acts of violence, they were acting at the behest of driven, powerful men. I guessed it was likely they'd cease functioning without direction. Based on what I'd learned from Jack, we could cut off the head of the snake, and the body would eventually wither.

"Signs of life?" I asked over comms.

"Crickets," replied Gray.

"All right, let's get…" I froze. Richard Robbins had awoken and was staring at me with extreme malice.

"Robbins," I said calmly. Kneeling down beside him, I lowered my face until it was next to his and whispered, "This place is locked down. You're leaving here with us, one way or another. Come quietly, and no one else has to die here tonight. If you cry out, everyone here that trusted you, every kid you fooled into believing your bullshit, is going to die. If that happens, it's on your conscience, not mine."

I watched his eyes as he processed my plea for cooperation. For a moment they were distant as he weighed the value of their lives against the potential of his own freedom. Then the corners tightened and his pupils focused with the angry determination of a man who would sacrifice anything to see his ends achieved. I knew in that moment what he had decided. One hand shot forward to clamp over his mouth, the other with the patch I'd been fumbling to open while trying to distract him. I wasn't fast enough. He let out a desperate shout, loud enough to alert the men in the barracks, before the patch landed and put him back under.

I swore loudly and said, "Everyone dig in. I guess we're all-in on this."

Spotlights from the roof of the laboratory came to life and were turned in our direction. The shouts of alerted mercenaries could be heard echoing throughout the camp. Lights went on in the barracks as men began responding to the rising state of alarm.

"Gray! The lights!" I shouted.

As quickly as they were turned on, the searchlights were shot out by Gray, perched in the tower near the front gate. Men returned fire from the rooftops, but without the light they were firing blind. The barracks doors flew open, and Risa opened fire, dropping three men who had rushed out to the ground. Muzzle flash from within the doorway caused us to duck back behind the cement barrier. I noticed Himari was gone, having wrapped the cloak around himself and disappeared when the alarm went up. I had little time to wonder where he'd gotten to, since behind us armed men were appearing on the towers of the main residence. I realized once they pinpointed our position, Risa and I would be caught in the crossfire between them and the men in the barracks.

"Get your masks on," I said, pulling out the detonation device for the explosives we'd planted. "We have what we came for. Conduct a fighting retreat from the compound."

Bullets hit the wall next to me, ricocheting away into the dark. Someone from one of the towers had seen us. Risa was concentrating on returning fire into the barracks to keep the men inside suppressed and hadn't noticed. I took a grenade from my belt, pulled the pin, and lobbed it toward the men on the nearest tower. The blast sent bodies hurtling over the ramparts. Men from the second tower had seen the exchange and began taking shots in our direction as well. I grabbed Richard Robbins' unconscious form and began pulling him away in an attempt to get out of the line of fire.

"We have to move!" I shouted.

She fired another burst at the entrance to the barracks then fumbled at her side for a familiar cylindrical tube, emptying the contents into her hands. She hurled the foglets at the entrance, and a heavy mist began to issue forth from inside the building. She turned to help me with Robbins by grabbing one of his arms but cried out suddenly and fell to the ground, clutching her leg. She'd been hit. I dropped Robbins and ran to her side, positioning myself between her and the shooter on the tower, then returned fire. The man on the tower had the advantage of higher ground, and with him crouching behind the ramparts, my shots had little chance of hitting him from the angle I was firing. I knew this was a losing battle, but if I moved, Risa would be exposed.

"How bad, Risa?" I yelled.

She didn't answer immediately, and I turned to see her face contorted in pain as she clutched at her thigh. I fired several more shots toward the tower and ducked as bullets rained down at us. The men in the barracks seemed to be unwilling to chance moving through the fog Risa had summoned, but I knew we didn't have much longer before they'd build up the nerve to take the risk. Leaving Robbins, I picked Risa up and carried her, dashing out of the line of fire from the tower and setting her down once we'd reached the wall of the residence. Sweat was beading on her forehead, and her breathing was rapid, but she began fumbling through her kit.

"I think it went through," she said through clenched teeth. "I have a bandage in here. I can wrap it. Go get Robbins. I'm okay." I wanted to stay with her and protect her, but I knew the best thing we could do at this point was to get Robbins, and get out of the compound so we could treat her wound properly. I left the cover of the wall to recover Richard, and began taking fire immediately as I raced back toward the cement barrier we'd initially been positioned behind.

"Cody!" I called out. "I'm taking fire from the far tower of the residence."

I thought about throwing another grenade, but the far tower was much farther away than the first, and I had little chance to land the toss. I ducked again as bullets hit the road barrier I was crouched behind. A bright flash of light went up next to the tower, and I recognized it as one of Cody's drone's flash capsules. In their confusion, the two men firing at me from the roof of the tower stood up from the cover of the ramparts. I took aim with my rifle and fired twice, and both men collapsed. I picked Richard up, anxious to get away from the entrance to the barracks, which would soon have the bulk of the mercenaries pouring from it to join the battle.

Gunfire rattled through the night behind me as men from the rooftops of the laboratories continued engaging Cody and Gray in the towers by the gate. As I reached Risa, I dropped Richard again and knelt beside her to check on her wound. It was fully wrapped, but the bandage was already soaked with blood. She didn't look well.

"Can you walk?" I asked.

She shook her head and said, "I don't think so. You need to go, Jacobi. Get Robbins out of here."

I laughed. "If you think I'm carrying this piece of shit out of here instead of you, you're delirious."

I heard the shouts of men from the direction of the barracks and looked up to see that several figures had begun to emerge from the blanket of cover the foglets had provided. I positioned

Risa's arm around my shoulder and began to pull her up, then froze in place as a group of mercenaries turned the corner and discovered us there, vulnerable and incapable of defending ourselves. They raised their rifles, but the air shimmered behind them and a katana flashed wildly, the molten red flat of the blade leaving trails in the air as it struck. Four men fell as one. Himari's face appeared as he lowered the hood of Gray's spectral cloak.

Releasing a sigh of relief, I asked, "Still think you owe me?"

Himari said nothing, wiped the blade of the katana on one of the mercenary's uniforms, and returned it to its sheath. Then he picked up Richard and slung him over his shoulder. With Risa hanging on to my neck, I took the detonator out and triggered the explosives in the lab. The laboratory and the two loaded trucks out front went up like a solar flare. The resulting explosion shook the ground, while the building collapsed in on itself, sending a massive cloud of smoke and dust into the air. With the men on the roof neutralized, Gray and Cody would be free to disengage. I carried Risa as Himari and I made our way to the fence behind the residence, which he ripped open for us to pass through. The explosions had created enough confusion in the compound that we were able to slip away without further harassment.

The night sky was red behind us from the flames of the burning laboratory. Whatever hopes the unconscious man strung across Himari's back had held for the vile substance he'd been producing, we'd brought an end to them tonight. I had Mason's father in custody, and we'd shut his production down. I knew it wouldn't be the end of Mason's efforts to bring justice down on those of us who had chosen not to endure the pain of the mistakes we'd made during Dreamreaver. I hoped, however, that once he discovered what we'd done, it would be enough to provoke him into acting impulsively and making a mistake I could capitalize on. It wasn't over, but we'd struck a violent blow against the objectives of those responsible for the events that had impacted us, and the people we loved. With the fall of Richard's plans, a small piece of my hunger for justice had been fed, but the feral wolf inside me was not yet sated. I felt it pacing, teeth bared, anxious for Mason to show his hand so it could lunge and bite.

Chapter 13

We rendezvoused with the rest of the team farther down the road to the east. The scientists had seen Cody and Gray when they'd approached and come out from the jungle. The three of them were huddled just off the road, looking terrified. Risa was barely conscious in my arms. I knew we desperately needed to stop the bleeding from her thigh. I set her down and removed the bandage to reveal the wound. Blood gushed both from an entrance and exit wound. From what I could tell, the bullet had grazed her femoral artery but hadn't transected it completely. Stitching the wound would take too long, and the hemostatic gauze she'd used when she'd wrapped it wasn't clotting her blood effectively enough. The others gathered around me.

"Pass me your firepen?" I asked Cody. He dug through his kit and handed me a thin cylinder. I removed the cap, and the wide, flat tip began to glow hot. I waited for the color to fade then applied it to Risa's wound, and she cried out as it was cauterized.

"One more, Risa," I said and then applied the tip of the firepen to the exit wound. She squirmed but didn't cry out this time. With both bullet holes cauterized, I applied disinfectant and wrapped her leg back up then told Cody to keep it elevated while I stepped away.

I was aware the remaining mercenaries in the camp could come looking for us at any moment, and we had no way to carry

Risa safely for miles back to the extraction point, so I beckoned Dr. Bosko over.

"Do you know if there are any open areas nearby? Any places clear enough for a vehicle to land?"

"I'm not sure," he replied. "We weren't allowed to leave the compound. I know there are fields to the north. They were recently cleared to create an orchard of Borrachero trees. The Angel's Trumpet flowers the Burundanga seeds are extracted from blossoms on those trees, so they clear entire areas to grow them."

It was our best hope, and I decided to take the chance. I connected with Sam over the comms to let him know we had Richard in custody and request a redirection of our extraction point. I activated a beacon for the pilots and informed him we'd fire a flare when we reached the orchard, assuming we could locate a suitable place for the Osprey to land.

We set out through the jungle to the northwest. Cody and Gray carried Risa together, doing what they could to keep her leg elevated. The morning light was beginning to break through the darkness. Hacking through vines and searching for paths through the dense growth while carrying Risa and Richard slowed our passage significantly.

Along the way, Robbins woke and began to struggle with Himari. We'd cuffed his hands earlier, but he started flailing so hard, I became concerned he was seizing as a result of one of the suicide pills his man in the Starlight Hotel had used when I'd subdued him. We set him on the ground to check on him, and he spat at me from his knees. He stopped flailing once Himari put him down, and I was relieved to see there was no foam coming out of his mouth. In retrospect, I supposed he placed too much value on himself to die for a cause, even his own.

"You idiot," he said, the words dripping with caustic disdain. "You just pissed off some very powerful people."

"Good to see you again, Richard. I wish I had time to settle up with you right now," I said, crouching and looking into his eyes, which were still filled with spite. "You've caused a lot of pain."

He sneered at me derisively but had nothing to say in his own defense.

"You see all that smoke over there?" I pointed to the southwest. "That's coming from your laboratory and your trucks. If I were you, I'd be more worried about all the people *you* just pissed off, seeing as there's no way you're delivering any product now." I cut a strip of cloth from a bandage and wrapped it through his mouth then tied it off tightly behind his head. He grunted and stared fiercely at me. Himari pulled him back up onto his feet and pushed him into motion then took up a position closely behind him to prevent any chance of escape into the jungle.

We skirted the flames of the compound and kept well north until the rubber trees thinned and fell away, revealing a series of open clearings. There were trees laden with the same white flowers I'd seen piled in the lab, in various stages of growth. One of the clearings looked to have been recently planted. The Borrachero plants were small, like shrubs. The small field was barely big enough for the Osprey to land in, but with good piloting, they could make it work. I fired off a flare. It was going to be a race now between the Osprey arriving to extract us and the remaining men at the compound, who'd certainly notice it as well.

"Take up defensive positions," I said, pointing. "Here and here. Himari, put that cloak back on and move a bit farther in. Try to give us some advance warning if you see anyone approaching." He nodded, wrapped the cloak around himself, and pulled the hood over his head. "Put Risa down in as much cover as you can find over there, away from the field."

"No. Fuck that," she said, shaking her head. "Put me down right here, I can shoot."

"Risa…" I began to argue.

"No."

Sighing, I submitted to the power of her defiant will once again. I instructed the group of scientists to fall back to the edge of the field and lay low. Then we waited. The Angel's Trumpet flowers smelled sweet and alluring. It was almost difficult to believe something so catastrophic could be produced from the Burundanga seeds when the flowers themselves were so enchanting. But humankind had always had an inclination for taking beauty and warping it to our own design, often turning it ugly in the process. As far as I could tell we were capable of just about any imaginable atrocity if it led to power — monetary, political, or otherwise.

While I scanned the jungle to the south for mercenaries that might come to investigate the flare, I heard the rotors of the Osprey closing in from above. Whether the remaining members of the Phoenix Coalition had not seen our flare, chosen not to investigate, or simply lacked the leadership to organize an effective counterstrike, they did not come. I wondered if, without masks they had simply been overcome by the toxic agent when the buildings burned. Whatever the reason, I was grateful the fighting was over for now. The Osprey pilots gracefully navigated the small extraction zone and successfully landed the vehicle. The rear hatch opened, and we ushered the scientists inside before carrying Risa in and laying her down on some blankets we spread across the floor near the pilot's cabin.

I sat across from Richard, who was looking increasingly weary as the fight slowly left him. Reaching across the aisle, I pulled the strip of cloth from his mouth.

"Who are you working with at the DFDC?" I asked as the Osprey lifted into the air.

He looked away and remained silent.

"Was it Simon Branch?"

He tensed subtly but held his silence.

Across from me, one of the scientists had brought an Angel's Trumpet onto the Osprey with him. He was staring at the flower, twisting the stem between his fingers. I imagined his thoughts were probably similar to my own reflections earlier, comparing the beauty of the thing to the horror of his experience over the last many months. He looked up, noticed me watching him, and held the flower out before him.

"*De la trompeta del ángel al aliento del diablo,*" he said sadly.

In an attempt to translate with the minimal Spanish I understood, I said, "From Angel's Trumpet to—"

"The Devil's Breath," Richard interrupted gruffly. "That's what they call it down here."

I looked up and nodded. "Devil's Breath. Fitting name. I suppose that makes you the Devil."

He snorted and said, "Look around you, Slate. Technology, robots, war — take your pick. We've got too many mouths to feed and too many minds to agree on any one solution. We're not long for this world. Am I the Devil because I see things for what they are? If the end is inevitable, is it evil to help wipe the board clean? Is it evil to put an end to the suffering so we can rise from the ashes and make things right?"

"You don't know the future, Robbins," I replied. "You might think it's inevitable, but you don't get to decide the fates of others based on a hunch and call yourself a hero for it. You're no hero. You're a murderer. Who are you working with at the DFDC?"

Again, Richard turned away and said nothing. Cody passed me a rag and a small container of water for washing the paint off my face.

As I was finishing doing so, my CUBE vibrated. I pulled it out to see who was attempting to reach me. Stunned, I stared, confused and suspicious, at the contact, Benjamin Oaksley. I unfolded the device and approved the connection request, but it wasn't Ben's face that appeared. It was Mason Robbins, smiling disingenuously. From what I could see of the background, he appeared to be standing in the dining room of Ben and Mary's house, right where she'd been killed.

"Captain Slate," he said. "We have unfinished business. Might I suggest a rendezvous?"

For him to be standing in the place where Mary's life had been taken from her was almost more than I could bear. I could feel my blood beginning to boil. "Why don't you wait for me right there? I'm on my way back from a business trip, but I'd be happy to stop by for a visit as soon as I land."

"I had something else in mind. More of a reunion for old times' sake. You, me, and our mutual friend here. Say hello,

Admiral." He turned the camera, and there was Ben, cuffed and gagged on the floor. He looked at the camera and shook his head, as if telling me not to come. "I found him swimming in the bay. Apparently his prisoner transport drone ran into some technical problems."

My mind raced to process this new information. Mason had brought down the transport drone to capture Ben. I could only think of one reason he'd want all of us together, and it wasn't to catch up on old times. My concern that Mason's endgame was for me or the admiral to harm the other was tempered by the knowledge Ben was still alive. Despite the darkness of his current situation, he was still with us, and beyond the initial blanket of horror I felt at seeing him as the prisoner of a madman, there was hope.

"I'll be there," I said. "I wish your father could join us too, but it looks like he'll be in solitary lockdown until this whole situation with the Devil's Breath and the DFDC gets sorted. It's a shame about the laboratories down here and all the men who had to die protecting them. But you can ask your father about that." I angled the camera toward Richard, who stared back defiantly.

Mason seemed taken aback for a moment, but contrary to the rage I'd hoped to induce, he broke out into laughter. "Looks like that crazy son of a bitch won't get to watch the world burn after all. It changes nothing between us. Give him a message for me. Tell him he deserves everything he gets. Be ready for my beacon, we'll be waiting for you. Come alone and unarmed. And, Slate...don't test me."

The connection closed. We had four hours until we'd arrive back at DFDC headquarters. I was trusting Sam on his word that with the evidence he'd collected and Richard in custody, he'd have the traction he needed with the Division council members to prosecute and convict the man. It would be up to him to bring the relationship between the Coalition and whoever had hired them to run these tests into the light. My team had done their job, and our part in that battle was over.

"Everything okay, boss?" Gray asked, watching me from his seat across the aisle.

"Just a loose end I need to clean up back home," I said.

"Anything I can do to help?"

I shook my head. "This one's on me. Get back to that lovely wife of yours, Gray. If that rain is still coming down in the city, the water taxi business has to be booming."

"The place is a ghost town. Everyone evacuated. If you hadn't called me, I'd have been gone too. You're not going back in there, are you? The city is practically underwater."

"No choice," I answered.

He nodded. "Best be careful, then."

I rested my head back against my seat and closed my eyes. I was tired and still struggling with processing the memories I'd unblocked. The man I'd thought I was had turned out to have a different moral code than the person I really had been. It was taking time to unravel the twisted yarn of emotion that accompanied that understanding. Before we'd left, I'd told Cody there were ways to remove the memory wall, if he decided to. He'd told me he was content and lived a happy life. He'd said whatever he'd chosen, he'd done it for a reason, and he didn't care to unlock whatever was hidden back there.

I respected his choice but wondered what it meant that the opposite was true for me. I hadn't been able to entertain the idea of moving forward without remembering or understanding that darker side of myself. In the end, it boiled down to control. The deceit our unit had endured during Operation Dreamreaver had caused me to feel entirely powerless and instilled in me a psychological revulsion to losing control. The constant, subtle panic I'd been feeling throughout this ordeal had been being triggered by my lack of understanding and an inability to stop the events that were transpiring. Reclaiming those memories had been an act of attempting to reclaim control. Control of myself, and control over a situation I'd never fully comprehend otherwise.

I'd been tricked into killing innocent civilians once, and my subconscious had been reeling at the possibility of it happening again. And then it had, and I was still wracked by the guilt of what I'd done to Jack, and nearly Risa. It had, because of Mason. He'd chosen us to be the trial group, because of what I'd made him do and because of what I'd turned him into by forcing him to participate in a series of assassinations he'd believed were unnecessary. The worst part was not being sure if he was even wrong. We deserved to live with what we'd done. Forgetting had been a dishonorable act against the memories of the people who'd had their lives wrongly taken.

The weight of that acknowledgement rested heavily upon my shoulders, but whether he'd been right or wrong about our role in this, by his actions, Mason had perpetuated further violence against innocents, and that was unforgivable. His hatred for me and the resentment of the position I'd put him in might have been valid, but it hardly justified the suffering of others. This was about me and him and always had been.

We were in Annette Kalowsky's kitchen. She was face-down at the table. Mason reached a gloved hand in to check her pulse. The cold glance of aggression and blame he cast in my direction was all I needed to know we'd achieved our goal. I'd accompanied him because I hadn't been convinced he'd go through with it otherwise, but I'd watched him stun her and apply the aconite patch, which had induced the cardiac arrest. He pulled the patch and turned to face me.

"There's no going back now, Captain," he said. "You'd better be right about this."

I prayed that I was.

The recollection was painful, but with what could be the final confrontation with Mason looming, such memories were coming in unrestrained and unbidden. I could have distracted myself, turned my attention to the present and shut them out, but I wanted to remember. I owed it to our victims.

Mason had become an instrumental part of the operation. After the first few sleepers he'd neutralized, he'd changed and drifted even further from the unit. He'd begun requesting the assignments and bragging about his role in the deaths of the sleepers, his cynicism rising to levels where he seemed to be intentionally throwing the terrible acts we had been asked to commit back in our faces. Something had shifted within him. Something hidden just below the surface had been unleashed, and I'd begun to recognize that it was what he'd actually been resisting all along. It wasn't the act of potentially harming an innocent he'd been so afraid of. He'd been afraid of how easy it might be for him.

I opened my eyes and stared across the way at Richard Robbins, silently questioning how much of his own madness he had instilled in his son. Mason had tried so hard to be someone better, someone noble. In the end, he hadn't been able to escape the legacy his father had always wanted for him — the perspective that human beings had no real value, weren't worth saving, and innocent or otherwise, might as well be put out of their misery. Looking at Richard, understanding the extent of his lack of empathy, and having personally witnessed his inability to see value in the lives of those surrounding him, I felt pity for his son. But I also felt anger. I was angry at the weakness Mason had revealed by being incapable of overcoming his conditioning.

When the admiral called us all in to be debriefed, I'd sensed something was wrong. It was a waver in his voice I'd never heard before, accompanied by an unfamiliar note of regret. Later, he'd played the transmission the DFDC had received, which revealed Operation Dreamreaver had been a setup. The unknown Iranian hacker sent us time-stamped videos of himself planning the entire thing and carefully choosing the victims, but it was the peals of laughter at the end of the transmission I remembered most vividly. We'd been manipulated and used. We were wrong. As we'd sat there, horrified and stunned, Mason joined in the laughter. In a fit of hysterics reminiscent of a mangy hyena, he pointed his finger directly at me and walked out of the room.

That had been the last time I'd seen him until I'd found the photograph he'd used Wendell to deliver to me. I'd conveniently forgotten everything, but he'd been simmering at a low boil for half a decade, despising me — holding me responsible for the man he'd become. No amount of discussion or reasoning would resolve our differences now. I wasn't happy it had come to this, but the moment he'd targeted our unit, he'd set the stage for one of us to fall. Though I pitied him, he'd killed my friends, and I'd do whatever was in my power to ensure he wouldn't be able to hurt any more of the people I cared for.

The Osprey set down on a landing pad near the DFDC headquarters. Sam was waiting for us there with several other agents, who took Richard into custody. There were trained medical officers as well who gently moved Risa into an ambulance Sam had requested. I walked beside her and held her hand while they transported her on the gurney. She looked weak from the blood loss, but she was smiling. I'd sat with her for some time on the return trip and told her about Mason and Ben. She'd been ready to come with me, to limp along if she had to, but it ended up being the first argument I could recall winning.

"Be careful," said Risa as the gurney was loaded into the vehicle.

"I'll see you when it's over," I replied, hopping up beside her to hold her hand.

"Jacobi, what you've done...remembering these things. I just want you to know I understand. I remember. And I went through what you're going through. I spent years learning to live with the shame and also mourning the loss of you."

"I can't imagine what that must have been like. You didn't deserve to go through that alone. I should have been there."

"You don't deserve to go through it alone either. And I am here. I'll be here, when you finish this, if you're ready to pick up where we left off. I love you."

I bent and kissed her, determined it wouldn't be the last moment of intimacy we would share.

"Thank you," I said, "for everything."

When the scientists' feet hit the ground, they embraced one another with tears of relief. As they were ushered into a military transport, I reflected on how their testimonials regarding the forced labor they'd endured to genetically enhance the Burundanga seeds would throw the final pile of dirt on Richard's grave. We'd stumbled into a goldmine when we rescued them. They could provide detailed information regarding the effects of the modified strain of Devil's Breath and on Richard's intention to distribute it for nefarious purposes. The council would have no choice but to recognize the legitimacy of Sam's work.

I'd spoken to Dr. Bosko at length about the drug on the flight home. The more I learned about it, the more disgusted I was. It had been used in Colombia and other parts of the world where other species of the Borrachero tree had grown for centuries, from luring innocents into mass graves in precolonial times to robbing or raping civilians in present times by slipping the powder into someone's drink. The enhanced substance they'd created together over the last year could simply be inhaled and produced a stronger and more reliable effect. Horrified by what they'd achieved, they each swore they'd take the information to the grave. I hoped for their sake that no one else with the knowledge of their part in this would be cruel enough to coerce them into providing their formula, but we'd yet to prove the identity of whoever it was on the council that had funded the trials. With something this powerful, all bets on people in power behaving civilly were off. I trusted Sam would do everything he could to keep them safe.

The flooding had become much worse in the city, and my car refused to pick me up when I requested it, on the basis of *no available route*. That left me stranded, so I approached Sam to request a lift south back into the city.

"I've got my hands full here, Mr. Slate. The city is under two to three feet of water right now. Can't you wait this out? I don't even think they're letting vehicles back over the bridge."

"Believe me, I'd love to. But it's Mason. He contacted me on the flight home. I need to get into the city today, and I need to go alone."

"I'm surprised to hear that, considering how things turned out the last time you tried to do this on your own. You've got a full team here. Why not utilize them?"

I didn't want to tell Sam that Ben was alive. The fewer people who were aware he hadn't drowned when his prisoner transport had crashed into the bay, the easier it would be for him to begin a new life somewhere without the legal hassle of trying to prove his innocence. Sam knew Ben wasn't responsible for Mary's murder, but he was a man of the law, and I wasn't sure where he'd land on letting Oaksley slip away if we made it out of this alive. On top of that, if Mason suspected I'd involved the others in any way, I was sure he'd kill Ben and disappear.

"You're right, Sam. It didn't go well before. He caught me off-guard, but that's not going to happen again. I have my reasons for doing this alone. You'll just have to trust me…and provide a vehicle that can navigate those streets. I think you owe me that, considering what I've just given you."

He considered my request for a short while, eyeing me with the disapproving frown I'd come to expect from him when things didn't line up the way he'd like to see them. I hadn't known Sam Winston long, but I'd come to appreciate his stalwart pragmatism, perhaps due to the fact that it counterbalanced my own frequent lack of common sense.

"Fair enough. I'll arrange for a unit transport to take you into the city and drop you off wherever you need to be. I owe you that, and more. You did good, Captain." He radioed in for a vehicle to pick me up then began to walk away to assist the agents handling Richard. Turning back suddenly, he shook my hand and patted me on the shoulder then said, "Good luck, Mr. Slate."

I gathered the others and explained that I had urgent business in the city. Gray offered Himari and Cody a place to wait out the flooding, but Sam had already arranged accommodations for them at the barracks nearby, and they wanted to remain close to Risa to keep an eye on her. I said farewell to them all and thanked them for their role in what we'd accomplished. "I couldn't have asked for a better team down there. You should all be proud of what we did. You each deserve a few days of rest. If all goes well, I'll be back tonight, so get those cards ready and hold on to your bottle caps, because I'm coming for them."

As I prepared to depart, Cody pulled me aside, away from the others.

"What if it doesn't go well?" he asked. "Whatever it is you're doing."

"It has to," I answered.

"It's Mason, isn't it? You're going for Mason."

As Fades, we'd undergone rigorous lie detection training, and keeping the truth from Cody now would only serve to further frustrate him.

"He's got Ben, man. I need to do this alone, or he's going to kill him."

"The admiral didn't drown after all," he said, shaking his head in wonderment. "Still, this is stupid, Captain. We could keep our distance or set a trap. We could take him down together!"

"Cody, I appreciate the enthusiasm, but you're not thinking this through fully. Mason has the same training we do. If he thinks even for a second I'm not alone, he'll put Ben down and rabbit. I can't have that. I know this is your fight as much as it is mine, but I'm asking you to trust me here. I can end this tonight."

"I've always trusted you. If you say this is how it has to go down, then so be it. Go get this bastard so I can get home to my kids."

"What did I tell you?" I asked, grinning. "Domesticated."

"I just spent two nights in the Amazon Basin hunting private military company mercs. I think that's about as far from domesticated as it gets. Seriously, though, Jacobi, is there anything you need? How can I help?"

"No toys for this one, I'm afraid, but thanks for the offer. You've done so much more than I could have asked already, Cody. Keep watch over Risa. I'll see you on the other side of this." We shook hands and clapped one another on the arm.

What I couldn't explain to Cody was the side of my argument that was completely irrational. Because of the choices I made during Operation Dreamreaver, innocent civilians had died. That was going to weigh on me for the rest of my life. Everything that had happened over the last several weeks was a result of that failure. As I had become a direct representation of those mistakes for Mason, he had become a symbol of resolution and atonement for me. It wasn't real, but I couldn't shake the idea that this felt like a trial — that whoever prevailed from this confrontation would feel justified in their perspective. If there was some hope of beginning to heal the open psychological wound I was bleeding from, I needed to take that chance.

I saw the troop transport arrive at the gate and made my way over. It was massive, with armored tires that wouldn't have much difficulty traversing a couple feet of water. With one last wave to Sam, I jumped up into the passenger side and we pulled away.

"Where to?" asked the driver, a middle-aged man with a finely trimmed handlebar moustache.

I gave him the address to Kamenev's building, and he grunted then got us on our way. Before we drove to the beacon I'd received from Mason, I needed to change out of the clothes I'd been wearing for days and stow all of my weaponry. Mason had told me to come alone and unarmed, and he'd been trained too well for me to risk not complying. This would have to play out another way. I just hoped the idea brewing in my head wasn't as suicidal as it felt right now. I had to trust my gut and see it through.

We were stopped briefly by the police, who had set up a roadblock on the north side of the Golden Gate Bridge. My driver flashed his identification, and they waved us through without issue. As we drove into the city, I could see that the elevated sections weren't being hit terribly hard, but rain and the overflowing sewage systems were running downhill into the areas closest to the shore, which were now completely flooded. The massive truck navigated the streets with ease, though slowly, and we reached the apartment without incident.

The driver agreed to wait outside while I ascended the tower as quickly as possible to get what I needed there. The front doors were locked, but after a quick scan of my palm, they opened. The lobby was quiet and empty. The lights were dim, since the building seemed to be operating at some kind of low power capacity. I was thankful to discover the elevator was still working.

Once back in the penthouse, I removed the heavy ballistic vest I'd worn to the jungle and the sweat-soaked shirt underneath, replacing them with a dark, long-sleeved shirt that would allow me more maneuverability. Looking around for my suede jacket, I realized I'd left it at my apartment, since it had been covered in Jack's blood. I threw on the loose cotton overcoat I'd worn the night I went to see Wendell at the Ares arena instead. If I was going to die, the least I could do was go out comfortably and looking sharp. I briefly considered taking Sam's business card from where I'd secured it in an insulated drawer, but pushed through the momentary lack of resolve. I could beat Mason alone, without putting anyone else in danger. I'd convince him he was wrong about what happened, and maybe by doing so, begin to forgive myself for my role in it. It was the only way. I needed this.

The drive across the city was treacherous and painstakingly slow. We hit a few areas where the tires were almost completely under water, but the transport truck proved to be up to the task and delivered me successfully to my final destination. I was standing knee-deep in water at the entrance to the San Francisco Zoo, watching the truck depart. A part of me wanted nothing more than to be on it, heading back to where my friends waited. I took a deep breath and locked that part of me away. There was no avoiding this confrontation, and wishing otherwise was just a distraction I couldn't afford. I began to cycle through my usual mental exercises as I climbed over the gates and hopped down the other side onto the grounds of the zoo.

A small reconnaissance drone fell in beside me as I made my way toward a walkway that looked as if it would take me in the direction I needed to go. I could see others hovering in the distance, patrolling the perimeter. Mason was dug in like a tick, just like I'd suspected he would be. As I walked, the drone pacing began to emit a thin, blue line of light as it initiated a weapons and augmentation scan that ran from my head to my feet. I ignored it and kept moving.

Because it was so close to the shore of the Pacific, the storm surge had had a heavy impact on the area. There were empty pens everywhere. The animals had been evacuated. I followed the flooded walkway toward the beacon, which appeared to emanate from a large, two-story cement building in the distance. The wind was so intense, it was creating small waves on the surface of the flood water I was wading through. Outside the building was a sign indicating that I stood at the entrance to the House of Primates. The front doors were unlocked. Mason's doing, I presumed. The drone followed me inside, trailing a few yards behind as I entered the lobby. It was a spacious atrium with high wooden ceilings and several hallways stretching away from it that led farther into the building. I was close enough now that I could see the red outline of Mason's beacon about thirty yards away, so I took the passage that led in his direction.

The hall was glass on both sides and looked out into open pens that would normally have housed monkeys of various breeds. After passing through another open atrium at the end of the hall filled with trees and flourishing plant life, I arrived outside a set of double doors, beautifully carved with depictions of mangroves. The sign outside informed me I was at the entrance of something called the Primate Playroom. I took another deep breath then opened the doors and stepped through.

The heat on the other side was oppressive. I was in a huge, artificial eco-habitat, similar to the lobby of Kamenev's building, but the environment was more akin to tropical grassland. The air was dry and smelled of earth and musk. A ring of stone benches surrounded a central area segregated by a tall, wire mesh fence. Inside the fence, a circular area was filled with acacia trees, boulders, and knee-high grass. There was also an assortment of wooden structures that reminded me of ones you might see on a children's playground. There were balance beams running between towers with ladders on them, long sets of hanging bars, and ropes dangling from the trees.

Above the fenced-off area, a massive, dome-shaped skylight revealed dark clouds moving beyond the glass. The red outline of the beacon was positioned on its knees beyond the wire mesh. I turned my augment lens displays off and saw it was Ben, not Mason, who I'd been tracking. His hands were cuffed behind his back, a gag ran through his mouth, and his head hung low, like he'd fallen asleep sitting up or just run out of energy to keep it upright.

Beside him, Mason sat atop a small boulder holding a gun aimed directly at Ben. A holo-display set up next to him showed what looked to be a grid based map of the grounds and multiple drone feeds broadcasting simultaneously.

"Finally, the hero arrives," he said. "Looks like he's still your little lapdog after all, Admiral. We've been waiting so long I was beginning to think you might just let him die alone here tonight."

"He's dead either way, if you get your way. What's the difference?"

"The difference is you'd have had to live with that on your conscience. And you don't handle guilt well, Captain. Come in through the fence, there." He pointed to a gate with the gun.

I did as he ordered. Once I was through he directed me to stand near Ben.

"I bet you're curious what this is all about," he said, looking smug. "Care to know why I brought you both here to the monkey cage at the zoo?"

"I know what it's about, Mason."

"Is that right?"

"I know what it's about because I had the memory block removed. I know about Operation Dreamreaver. I remember you trying to stop us from making that mistake, and I know you hold me and Ben responsible for not listening to you. I remember how you changed with every kill, growing more and more callous, and how it shaped you into the sad, bitter man you are today."

His eyes shot back and forth as he processed the information.

"Sorry," I continued. "Did I spoil the big reveal?"

"I didn't want to be like this," he said, his voice rising. "You made me this way!"

I nodded and said, "You're right. I'll take responsibility. We pushed you into doing something horrible. We were wrong, and innocent people died because of our mistake."

He looked confused, as if my acceptance of his accusation didn't fit into the perfect picture of whatever revenge fantasy he'd planned. I pressed him a bit further.

"But you know what I think, Mason? I think down beneath the surface, you know as well as I do I'm not the one who made you this way. I think you know you always had a choice."

"Choice? What choice? I was just a soldier. We follow orders, remember? Isn't that what you told me?"

"That's right," I said. "We were *all* soldiers. Soldiers doing what we'd been ordered to. You. Me. Even Ben. Our orders came directly from the council. Someone gave the go-ahead on that operation, and we couldn't have changed that decision any more than you could. Not without refusing our orders outright, and that's not the choice any of us made. You're holding us responsible for making the same decision you did."

"I wasn't in charge!" he yelled. His anger was mounting.

"If you refused, you'd have been kicked out of the service. You would have gone home to Daddy a failure. A washout. You couldn't live with that, could you? Imagine Richard's surprise at learning his kid couldn't hack it because he wasn't willing to kill."

"I tried to stop it. I tried to tell you! It was so obvious, but you were both too *stupid* to see." Mason had jumped down from the rock. He began pacing back and forth, and waving the gun to accentuate his words. I kept talking to try to keep him off balance, hoping to provoke a mistake.

"No. The truth is that you didn't care about the sleepers. You just didn't want to be like him. But you *are* like him, Mason. You're a sociopath and a murderer. You can blame Ben and me for whatever you want, but in the end we just accidentally pulled the mask off the devil underneath. It was always hiding there, whispering things you refused to accept, wasn't it?"

"Shut the fuck up!" he yelled and pointed the gun at me. "You shut your fucking mouth, right now!"

I said nothing, and kept my hands raised above my head.

"No," said Mason. "No, you fucked me. I was someone else.

383

I was someone better until you refused to listen to me and made us go through with Dreamreaver. But each of those people you made me kill was easier than the one before. Everything my father wanted me to be grew in strength with each of those murders. Everything he'd tried to instill in me about humanity's lack of worth was coming out. And you, the hero, the savior — ordering me to kill those people. You just made it all true."

I was beginning to understand the source of Mason's disgust with me. My decisions had been so reprehensible in his eyes that they had validated his father's madness. He'd resisted for a lifetime, only to be shown irrefutable evidence that even heroes were fallible and capable of wanton disregard for the sanctity of life.

"You're leaving out the context, Mason. What we did, we did because we thought we were preventing a much larger act of violence."

"*You* thought. You thought that. I never did. I tried to tell you. You wouldn't listen."

"It was a mistake. Easy to judge in hindsight."

"Oh, you say that," he said. His burst of laughter carried the same insincerity as his smile. "But if you really believed that, you wouldn't have just run away. All of you! You just made it go away."

"I'm not running now, Mason."

"I never ran! Rose..." His voice cracked. "She couldn't know how much pressure I was under. She didn't understand what you'd done to me and how hard it became to disagree with everything my father was teaching us. She paid the price for that."

There was a wildness churning in his eyes. It wasn't madness. It was strain. He was remembering the man he used to be before he'd broken, and the memory was painful.

"Your father won't be pushing those beliefs on anyone outside a prison cell for a long time."

"It's too late," he said softly. Then his voice turned to ice. "Drink the water in that bottle." He pointed his gun to a glass bottle of water on the ground near Ben.

"It's not—"

"Drink the fucking water, Slate! Or the admiral takes a bullet in the knee!"

I knelt and picked up the bottle then twisted the lid off. Looking directly at Mason, I took several deep gulps. The moment of truth had arrived. On the Osprey, I'd discussed potential counters or neutralizing agents with Dr. Bosko, who'd been working on altering the Burundanga strain. There were none that he'd been certain of, but he'd given me a theory to work with. He'd said the amygdala, an area of the brain that detects potential danger, was targeted and shut down by the Burundanga, and this was a part of why people under the drug's influence didn't have the good sense to refuse instructions dangerous or harmful to others. He suggested a sufficient rush of cortisol could potentially convince the body's cells that they were, in fact, in danger, and should react accordingly.

My pituitary gland modification did exactly that, enabling a fight-or-flight response that gave me a surge of adrenaline, releasing cortisol that traveled through my blood, activating cells. I didn't want to crack my pinky knuckle too early, but I knew if I waited too long, I could lose the impulse to do it at all. I decided I couldn't take the chance and cracked it. All I could do was hope it would interfere enough with the drug that I could retain some semblance of self-control. If at any point I felt I was going to cross over the threshold and lose the ability to resist Mason's commands, I planned to activate my kill switch and rob him of his glorious finale.

We waited, and before long I could sense the edges of my conscious mind starting to dull.

"Kick him," said Mason, who had determined enough time had passed that I would be under the full effect of the substance.

I didn't feel any compulsion to do as he'd asked, but I didn't want him to see that. I kicked the admiral in the side and tried to make it look worse than it was. Ben grunted and keeled over.

"Look at me Captain, and admit it's your fault I became what I am."

"It's my fault," I said.

"Tell me how sorry you are," Mason commanded, laughing.

"I'm sorry."

"You're just a trained monkey, Jacobi. You can only do what your masters tell you. Just like the ones that perform here in this cage."

Mason was pacing again, and appeared to be convinced he was in full control.

A gray fog was gathering at the boundary of my conscious thought. It was getting harder to tell whether or not I was saying these things to fool him or because he'd told me to. I wasn't sure how much time I had left. I cracked my knuckle a second time, activating the remainder of the adrenaline in an effort to shake off the encroaching haze. It helped a little, but I could tell it wasn't enough. The Devil's Breath was in full effect now, and the cortisol coursing through my cells just wasn't sufficient to keep me lucid. I was losing myself quickly, but Mason was taking his time, making sure I was fully under the spell of the substance.

"You did the right thing, though. At least you had the strength to get rid of that memory block. At least you know what you did. I'd say Captain Slate's courage has earned you a quick death, Admiral. You should be grateful." Mason finally stopped pacing and said, "Take my gun, Slate."

I walked to him, careful to keep my eyes vacant and devoid of any hint I might still be at all cognizant.

"It didn't need to be like this, you know. You should have listened to me. None of this would have happened." He wasn't wrong, but I needed him to stop talking and give me his weapon. I could feel my awareness rushing away like air evacuating a vacuum and I wasn't sure I had the strength left to resist.

He handed me the pistol. This was it. I tried to summon the will to lift it and pull the trigger right there, but couldn't. I was barely able to retain my sense of self, let alone articulate the compulsion to kill the man in front of me. The fog was surrounding me now, and deep within I could see the glowing red eyes of the nightmare watching me as control began to slip away. It hadn't been enough.

"Shoot him."

I raised the gun to Ben's head. There was barely enough fight left in me from the cortisol surging through my body to resist his command. Ben's eyes were wild, but he held his chest high, ready to meet death with his honor intact. With everything I had left in me, I reached up with my left hand and pulled the gag out of Ben's mouth.

The admiral spat the words out like venom from a viper's fang. "Kill that son of a bitch, Jacobi."

I turned the gun on Mason to comply with Ben's command, but he reacted too quickly. He hit me in the gut with a straight kick that sent me flying backward. The gun flew from my hand and slid under the fence into the surrounding stone benches. The darkness was closing in around me. I was lost in the fog. I heard the frantic neighing of the mare and looked up to see it galloping straight at me. Mason was running at me, and for a moment the two were one: a hybrid horror both equine and anthropomorphic in nature, furious and full of hatred as it charged.

The admiral lurched to his feet. His hands were still cuffed behind his back, but he threw himself into Mason, and they both toppled over.

"Jacobi!" Ben yelled as he and Mason struggled on the floor. "Help me! Try to resist it!"

His instructions spurred me into action. I rose and moved toward the two grappling men, throwing my hands into the pockets of my coat along the way to see if by some miracle I'd left a stun patch there. There was no patch, but my fingers came across something else. I pulled out the vial of Blu I'd taken from the dealer at Ares the last night I'd worn this coat. Oaksley's order to try and resist was echoing through my mind, a cacophony of noise that resounded chaotically amid the ensuing chaos, so I complied.

Without hesitation, I pulled the cap and pressed the vial to my skin. It made a soft *pssft* as the hit of Blu was injected into my bloodstream. One wasn't enough. If anything, I began to feel more confused and sluggish as the first hit ran through my system. The world slowed as I watched Mason raining blows onto Ben, who was unable to defend himself. I pressed the injector to my arm again. *Pssft.* I needed to move beyond the drug's phase of numb pleasure, even beyond *riding the wave* on the edge of ecstasy and energy. I needed to be so jacked up that my adrenaline would spike up to levels that would produce the cortisol I needed to keep the fog at bay. *Pssft.*

An erratic rush surged through me as the third hit entered my system like the rising ocean tide. The world was spinning and out of focus, but I was high with clarity of purpose. Mason was atop Ben, trying to put the gag back in his mouth. I rushed forward, snarling, and wrapped my arm around his neck. I fell backward, pulling him away from Ben, and squeezed. His face began to turn red as he struggled, but I held on tightly.

An elbow crushed into my side, causing my hold to let up slightly, but that was all he needed to squirm out from underneath. He landed several more blows to my body as he fought to right himself and stand.

Through a fit of coughing, Mason yelled, "Stop!"

But I wouldn't. There was an animal inside of me now. I was a wolf, gnashing its fangs and tearing into Mason with my claws. We fought savagely, with everything we had. I barely tried to avoid his strikes, so intent was I on lashing out with murderous fury. All of the sorrow and loss I'd felt over these last weeks was caught in my throat like a scream that couldn't escape. I knew only rage, and I channeled it into every strike. Whatever pain I felt was drowned out by the torrent of delirious violence I was lost within as we traded blow after blow.

Over time, the resilience of our battered bodies was depleted, and we began to slow. As the adrenaline drained from my system, it was replaced by the pain I'd been ignoring. The fog was creeping back now, too. It hadn't been enough. He was going to win. We circled one another, panting, each too exhausted to throw another punch. I collapsed onto my knees to catch my breath. The world was pulsing, breathing, closing in around me. Knowing the end was finally here, the emotional blockage in my throat cleared. A mournful howl escaped my lungs. It was born from the frustration that evil would triumph over good, the woeful sorrow that innocent lives would go unavenged, and the belated recognition that once again, I'd made a grave mistake by trying to do this alone.

"Get up," said Mason, breathing heavily. I stood. The sick expression he disguised as a smile returned to his face as he realized my ability to resist his commands had ended. "Kill him. Strangle him if you have to, I don't care."

As the fog thundered toward me like charging cavalry, I had only enough awareness left to be horrified that I was doing what he'd requested. I had a fleeting recollection there was something I'd wanted to do. There was something I needed to activate…but the thought was gone before it could fully manifest. I approached Ben, and the final crest of the wave of Blu I'd been riding collapsed, dispersing onto the shores of total surrender. It took with it the depleted reserves of my will to retain awareness, and the dark fog rolled over me like a storm. As it overcame me, the last thing I remembered was the rain. It was a shower of glass, falling all around me as the ceiling shattered and dark figures descended from above.

When I came to, I was surrounded by familiar faces. They were gathered around me, smiling, but I was confused. I was unsure where we were or how I'd come to be there. I'd been dreaming of something hopeful, and with waking, the sensation felt less distant, more tangible. Despite my disoriented state, the presence of my friends brought me comfort. Slowly, the muted sounds of the world around me came into focus. Soft, garbled words abruptly gained volume and clarity, and I became aware they were being directed at me.

"It's over, Captain." It was Cody speaking. He was crouched beside me. I began to recognize the faces of the others around me as well. Gray, Himari, Sam Winston.

"Over," I said, repeating what he'd told me but not understanding the context. I sat up. The bioengineered eco-habitat we were gathered in was hot and dry, but a strong wind from outside was ventilating the room through several openings in the ceiling. It looked like a simulation of the tropical grasslands of West Africa. I was leaned up against a rock. Glass littered the floor. It wasn't until I saw Mason, cuffed, unconscious, and leaned up on the boulder across from me that my surroundings began to make any sense.

"I gotta say," said Gray, "you were high as a kite, Boss. We've been here a solid two hours, and they were two of the most entertaining hours of my life. Before you passed out, you'd do anything we told you to, and I won't lie to you, we told you to do some stupid shit. Even Himari got in on that fun."

I tried to concentrate and put the pieces of the story together. Little by little, everything leading up to when I'd drunk the water was coming back into focus.

"It was a smart thing you did, taking the card along, Mr. Slate." Sam was talking to me now. He was standing several feet away, looking concerned.

Bewildered, I said, "What? I didn't...I didn't bring your card."

"Of course you did. How else could we have tracked you and listened in? Are you sure it's not there, in your pocket?" He pointed to my right pants pocket.

I slid my hand in and came out with one of Sam's cards. The sly son of a bitch had planted it on me back at the base.

"Oaksley—" I said, remembering.

"Is dead," Sam finished, smiling slightly. "Isn't he?"

"Tired, and extremely confused. But not dead yet." Ben's gravelly voice piped in from outside my field of view to the left. I turned and saw he was lying on the floor with his head resting on a medical bag.

"Let's keep that to ourselves, though, shall we?" Sam asked.

We waited for another hour or so while Ben rested the concussion he'd received as a result of Mason's beating, and I regained my faculties. Sam told me that within moments of my leaving the DFDC barracks, he'd begun to organize the team to follow, despite my determination to face Mason alone.

"I understand that you were concerned for Admiral Oaksley's safety," he said, "but you've been out of the Division for over half a decade. I think you've forgotten just how capable we can be in these situations. We listened in through the transmitter on the card and moved into position to breach as soon as we knew the admiral wasn't in immediate danger."

I started to interrupt, but he raised a hand and cut me off before I could speak.

"Whatever you're going to say, if I hadn't done what I did,

you'd both be dead. You might not like—"

"Thank you, Sam." I wrapped my arms around him. "I was going to say thank you." Tentatively, he put his hands up and returned the hug, patting me on the back.

"Quite right, Mr. Slate. You're welcome."

We did disagree when it came to what we'd do about Mason, though. He wanted to bring him in and have him testify against his father. I knew Mason wouldn't cooperate with us, regardless of whether or not Sam thought it would seal Richard's fate, and I had a different justice in mind for him. He was too cunning, too well trained to be out there somewhere, imprisoned or otherwise, plotting revenge. I wanted to move away from all of the killing, but when a dog went rabid, you had to put it down.

We argued, but in the end I wouldn't budge, and Sam had to be content with the fact that we'd retrieved Richard and the scientists for him. He'd have to make his case with what he had.

"What will you do?" he asked. "Kill him here? I won't be an accessory to murder."

"I have something else in mind for Mason," I said.

"Oh? And what is that? Actually, don't tell me. I don't want to know. If I was here as an agent and not as a friend...Well, in any case, Admiral Oaksley and Mason Robbins have something in common. Legally, they're both already dead."

I could see the concession was difficult for him as a man of integrity, but the premise of our working agreement had been helping one another get to our respective adversaries. I'd delivered, and now he had as well. I stepped away to make a call that would seal Mason's fate.

Shortly afterward, when it was time to leave, I walked the

team to the Osprey they'd dropped in from, which had landed in a large plaza outside. Ben stayed behind to keep watch over Mason. Himari and I walked together.

"Just out of curiosity," I asked, "what sorts of things did you guys make me do when I was out?"

"Don't worry," he said.

That was a relief.

"Gray recorded it all so you'll have the chance to see for yourself."

I groaned. "Himari," I said, growing serious. "Whatever debt you think you had with me, it's been paid, and then some."

"*Hai*, I agree," he said.

"You do?" I asked, surprised. "Good…"

"Yes. The debt was cleared some time ago. The rest I did because I chose to help a friend. You would have done the same."

He stopped walking and turned to face me. "I have not been entirely honest with you, however. I hope you will forgive me, because I know that my dishonesty has caused you great pain. Do not blame Therisa either, because I asked her to become complicit in my lie."

"What are you talking about?" I asked. Dishonesty was out of character for Himari, so I half expected another joke.

"You'll soon find out. If you are able to forgive me, then call me. I'll cook for all of you. Please understand that I was only doing what I promised I would." Then, without another word, he turned and boarded the Osprey.

Sam approached and shook my hand. "I suspect we won't have much cause to meet again anytime soon, Mr. Slate. At least, despite my predilection for working together, I hope that is the case."

"Oh, I don't know, Sam," I said, "I still have your card. Whenever I'm feeling lonely, I might just whisper sweet nothings into your ear."

"I think we've had enough of that to last a lifetime." He chuckled. It was the first sign of a sense of humor I'd seen from Sam Winston since we'd met. "In any case, you might as well tear it up. I won't be on the other end of that transmission any longer."

"Listen," I said, "can you keep me in the loop regarding Richard Robbins? I'd say I'm invested at this point. I'd like to know how it turns out."

"Yes. We'll see about that," he said. "Someone funded that project, and one way or another he'll help identify the people at the Division who were involved. I suspect Simon Branch was involved, if not the sole collaborator. He has a long history of unethical behavior, but he's powerful. It will be difficult to bring charges against him without getting creative." It was a bit cryptic, but I decided not to push him further. "Good luck, Captain."

Waves rippled across the flooded plaza as the Osprey rotors came to life. Cody gave me a nod and a final salute as the rear hatch began to close. He'd be heading home to his family now. I made a silent promise to myself that this time I wouldn't allow so much time to pass before making an effort to connect with him again, and under better circumstances.

I returned to the Primate Playpen. Ben was sitting up, watching Mason intently. He had the gun I'd almost shot him with in his hands and wore an expression of disgust as he studied the man responsible for the death of his wife.

"Tell me I can shoot him," he said. "Let me end this bastard, Jacobi."

"Could you do it? Would it help?"

"I could. God help me, I could kill him right here, in cold blood." His voice cracked as he said it, and his hand had started shaking.

I placed my hand on the barrel of the gun that Ben had raised and trained on Mason's chest and pushed it down.

"I promise you, there will be justice. But let's let someone else carry that weight. Killing Mason isn't going to fill the void you have inside."

"No, but it would feel damn good." He handed me the pistol.

"For a time, perhaps," I said.

"A short time is all I'm likely to need, Jacobi."

Studying Oaksley, I could see he was no longer the man I'd once seen as a living monument to stalwart will. It was obvious that these last weeks of living with what he'd done to his wife had taken a vast toll. The only sparks of emotion in his eyes were ones of anger or regret. It would be a long time before he would be able to feel hope or joy again. I looked at him with deep sympathy and said, "I need to talk to you about something. If you really mean what you're saying, and you're serious about giving up, there may be a better way."

I laid it out for him. Ben had been opposed at first. He didn't see the point. But after a lengthy discussion in which we explored the alternative and what was ultimately at stake, he agreed to participate in the experiment I'd proposed to The Blacksmith. I reached out, and they sent the passenger drone from the *Forge* to retrieve him. I knew it might be some time before I'd see him again, but I felt confident that if my theory held up, he would ultimately be better off than he was now, struggling to press on in a world he no longer cared to exist in. Mason and I had hitched a lift on the drone and got dropped off on a landing pad down the road from Matvei's penthouse suite.

As we parted ways, I gripped Ben's hand and pulled him into a tight hug. "Just promise me you'll fight."

"I'll try, Jacobi," he said. His eyes were wet with emotion.

"I'll come as soon as I can. This is going to work."

"It will. Or it won't." He smiled. "I'll be okay either way."

The drone departed, and I watched it fly away. I wanted to be with Ben to support him through what was to come, but there were things I needed to resolve before I could join him on the *Forge*.

We trod through the floodwater toward Kamenev's apartment. I pushed Mason in front of me and kept the gun trained on him. The rain was finally letting up. By the time we arrived, it had come to a stop altogether. Once again, the dark glass building towered above me, harkening back to the day this all began.

"What is this place?" he asked. "Why are we here?"

I didn't bother responding.

"You can't even kill me yourself," he said, laughing. "You're weak, Captain."

I did feel weak. It wasn't because I couldn't bring myself to kill Mason. Bringing him here was no different than committing the act personally. I understood that now. Knowing the suffering he would likely endure brought me no joy. This was for Wendell Hamilton and his brother. It was for Aaron Watts and his best friend, Philip Holsted, Tucker Rogers and his family. James Turner. It was for Ben and Mary Oaksley. It was for Jack, Rose, and their unborn child. It was for Pavel. But it wasn't for me. I felt weak, because as much as I wanted to be done with the killing and begin to change my relationship with death in the way Himari had suggested, I couldn't allow him to live. It was too dangerous. I felt weak because although I understood Mason was as much a victim of circumstance as he'd made the rest of us, I held no mercy for him in my heart. This last time, I'd turn a contract over and absolve myself of guilt for whatever happened in the aftermath.

I was pleased to see the main lights were back on in the lobby. Boris was behind the front desk with several of his comrades, and he stepped forward to greet us as we entered.

"Welcome back, Mr. Jacobi. They are waiting for you upstairs." He spared a glance at Mason, but there was no malice in it. If anything, he looked sorry for the man.

Boris and two of the others escorted us up to the penthouse suite. They led us into the main living area, where Matvei waited with several more of his syndicate goons. He wore a pressed tuxedo, and his thinning hair was slicked back across his head. He'd also trimmed his moustache and beard. They were less wild and more refined. The effect was that he appeared a bit more menacing than what I remembered from our past encounters.

Pavel's sister, Lena, sat beside him, wearing a red dress, equal in extravagance to the one she'd worn on her last visit to the apartment. As we entered, her gaze was drawn to Mason, and her expression darkened.

"Ah, Jacobi," Matvei said, rising. "We left the celebration we were attending in the city of angels to get here as quickly as possible when I received your call. It was a coming-of-age ceremony for the son of one of my men. That is how important this is to Lena."

"This is the man who killed my brother?"

"This is him," I said.

She approached and put her face right up to his. Mason twisted his lip into a sneer. Lena smiled. It was perhaps the only smile I'd seen someone give that was more disingenuous than his own.

"Take him," she said.

Several men took him from my possession and began dragging him out of the room.

"Wait," I heard a voice say from the balcony above us.

"Ah, your friend is finally up. Not to worry, the doctor has cleared him," Matvei said to me.

The goons stopped, and I looked up. Jack stood with both hands on the balcony railing. His eyes were locked onto Mason's. I watched, mouth agape, as he slowly made his way down one of the spiral staircases, clutching at his bandaged side. As he passed me, I said, "Jack…"

He held up a hand and shook his head but didn't take his eyes off Mason. "This wasn't your fault, Jacobi. It was his. All of it." He shuffled the rest of the way over to stand eye-to-eye with the man who had killed his love and the child she had carried.

"It was me, Mason. I was the father."

Mason snarled and lurched toward Jack, who stood unflinching as the syndicate men restrained their captive.

"You beat her to death and burned their bodies. You call yourself a victim, but what could ever justify that? No. You're a monster, and you deserve what's coming. I just wanted to look you in the eye and tell you that before you were taken away. Goodbye, Mason."

With that, Kamenev's men pulled him toward the hallway leading to the elevator. We stared at one another as he was taken away. The sneer never left his face, but at least he wasn't laughing. Watching him disappear around the corner, I felt unresolved. I knew he would die and that his death would be painfully drawn-out, but as I'd warned Ben, it didn't fill the void left in the wake of the trials he'd conducted. There was no way to right the wrongs he'd been responsible for. He'd pay in blood for the blood he'd spilled, but there would be no real justice for the innocent lives that had been taken. I could only take solace in the fact that with Mason's death, he wouldn't be able to bring harm to bear against anyone else, and there was some small satisfaction to be found in knowing it was over at last.

"He's a dangerous man," I said, turning back to Lena and Matvei. "Trained, like me. Don't take any chances, and don't give him the opportunity to escape. That's the agreement. We understand one another?"

Lena nodded. "Of that you can be sure, Mr. Slate. I promise you." As she walked past me on her way to follow them out, she placed her hand on my arm.

"Thank you for this. Wherever he is, I'm sure that Pavel is grateful also." If there was a heaven for each of us, unique to our own vision of bliss, I had no doubt Pavel was currently much too distracted by beautiful women and gambling to take any notice. I nodded my thanks regardless.

"Well, Jacobi," said Matvei, "again, you've done me a great service. She has been nothing but sullen and morose since her brother's death. And her mother! Oi! I've not heard the end of it since Pavel died. For a time, I thought you might have to take the fall for it just to shut her up. I hate to say it, but I believe this settles the debt between us."

"No Moscow?" I asked.

"Of course, you are welcome to join me when I return! There would be no end to the work I could provide you with there, but no. The place is a mess, but I think you have paid in full for the time you spent here, and the medical bill."

"That's good," I said. "I'm not sure my heart is in the contract retrieval business any longer."

"Oh? What will you do instead?"

"I was thinking about becoming a private investigator."

Matvei erupted into deep-bellied laughter. "That's rich! You. A policeman!"

I started to argue that they weren't cops, but decided not to bother.

On his way out, he turned back and said, "Oh, I almost forgot to tell you. I'll be returning in a few days. I expect the place to be empty then. It would be quite awkward otherwise."

Boris clapped me on the back as the two of them walked past

me.

"Jack…" I said again as I turned to him. Words were failing me. He'd been alive this entire time. I'd given Himari a directive to protect Jack, and he'd chosen to allow me to think I'd killed him in order to keep the fact he'd survived a secret. After what I'd done, I understood why he'd kept it from me. Since I hadn't known, there was no way I could be used to harm him again. I was filled with conflicting emotions. A part of me felt betrayed, and I was angry Risa had known but allowed me to suffer through the guilt, but more than anything, I was relieved. I felt extremely grateful Jack was alive and that I could begin to let go of the pain I'd been harboring.

"In the flesh," he said. "Well, most of it."

"I shot you…"

"You sure did, you bastard! Got me pretty good, too. I'm told it was touch-and-go there for a while, but those Russians in the lobby called in some crazy doctor to look after me. He scares me, honestly. But I'm alive, thanks to him. I've been holed up somewhere on the thirteenth floor recovering all this time. Himari's come to visit me a couple times, but god, it's been awful dull compared to hanging out with you."

"I'm so sorry for my part in what happened."

"Hey now!" he said, his face growing stern. "It's okay! I know this wasn't your fault. Besides, you got the bastard."

"I got him, Jack. I got him."

We stayed up deep into the night, and I recounted the story of everything that had happened since our last fateful encounter. I spoke about the lessons I'd learned about taking the world on by myself. I'd thought bringing Mason down alone would help

me atone for the sins of my past, and the lives I'd destroyed —
that if I could persevere against him and his belief that
everything had been my fault, it would somehow prove him
wrong and justify the decision I made. Somewhere along the line,
I'd realized the path to absolution wasn't through him. I think it
was right about when my plan had failed, and I 'd been about to
murder Ben with my own hands.

No, If my soul had any chance to be saved, it would be
because of the good advice and incredible support of the people
in my life who were there for me. Kama had tried to warn me
not to swallow any more of the darkness. I thought he'd meant
the lives I'd taken to protect the greater good, but maybe there
was more to it. Maybe solitude and loneliness were also
ingredients in that meal.

Himari helped me understand that I was responsible for
every life I took, innocent or guilty. Death surrounded me as a
result of choices I'd made, and the only way out now was to turn
away from who I'd become. It was true that I'd been used and
deceived, but as a soldier and a killer, I'd chosen to be in a
position where I was vulnerable to it. Those were the
consequences of that choice. I could live in misery for what I'd
done, or accept accountability and begin to try to heal.

Risa was here to show me how to do that. She'd been
through it and had both the experience and compassion
necessary to guide me to the other side. She was a shining
example of what strength and love could achieve — a buoy I
could use to stay afloat on the sea of confusing emotions that
were laying siege to my self-confidence. She was a beacon I
would use to find my way home.

I had Jack, with his boyish innocence and kind heart, to
remind me that even experiencing the darkest things couldn't

break your spirit if you wouldn't let it. Cody and Gray, with their humor and loyalty. Sam, with his sensibility and integrity. I had all the tools I needed to come back from this at my fingertips, if I was willing to use them. The path to absolution wasn't through Mason. It was through accepting that we were stronger together, and that I couldn't always be in control. As much as I prided myself on my independence, I wasn't going to make it as a lone wolf. Maybe the baying of the pack would keep those nightmares away.

Epilogue

The following week, Risa and I visited Ben aboard the *Forge* to check on the progress of The Blacksmith's work. We interrupted a game of chess that was taking place between them when we arrived, which, according to the crew, had become a daily occurrence everyone looked forward to. He was in unusually good spirits. It seemed life aboard a seafaring vessel had been good for him, particularly one with the modern accouterments this ship offered. But the real reason for his prolonged stay here had been the idea I'd proposed when The Blacksmith had assisted me in regaining access to my blocked memories.

Himari had said that based on the projected results of the simulation he'd uncovered, if he'd gone through with the integration process with the Anvil artificial intelligence, it would have eventually dominated his conscious mind and taken over. The Blacksmith had wanted to observe that process and was convinced he could inevitably reverse it with enough data. I was no scientist, but I'd given that some thought, and during my earlier visit I proposed that the conflict between the Anvil's consciousness and the mind of the person it was integrated with could be directly related to a sense of perceived rivalry between the two. I had offered a theory that if the Anvil could be modeled after a particular personality by using data from memory and then integrated with someone with whom a deep bond had been shared, it might bypass the perception of rivalry that was responsible for the conflict. The basis of my proposition was that if the Anvil had been modeled after someone who cared deeply for the person being integrated, it might nurture and protect the consciousness of that individual, rather than seeing it as an enemy and attempting to dominate it.

The Blacksmith had been intrigued and agreed to test the concept, if I could provide a willing participant. Since Ben had lost the will to carry on after what he'd been forced into doing to his wife, I had encouraged him to try this approach and suggested it was a way for him to still be with her. They were just finishing up the initial stages of the process. Ben's memories of Mary had been downloaded and analyzed then programmed into the Anvil's personality routines. It used her voice, had her demeanor, and shared his memories of her. In every sense, it believed it was Mary Oaksley.

One of the first things they'd done was to use the same procedure that had blocked the details of Operation Dreamreaver to remove Ben's memory of ever killing his wife. Now, fundamentally, he understood she was gone, but his mind simply skipped over the lapse in his history, landing just beyond the block, and remained oblivious to the discrepancy in order to maintain its logical integrity.

I was glad to see him happy and to know he was being cared for here. Since he'd be the first recipient for AI integration, the members of the organization on the ship treated him with reverence and respect. Despite our inability to predict the efficacy of the experiment, I took comfort in knowing that if the procedure didn't work as I had theorized, and Ben's mind was ultimately dominated and erased, it wasn't far from what he'd wanted to begin with. A chance at success had been better than the alternative of giving up without a fight.

Months later, we met with him again. His time was split between being analyzed by The Blacksmith on the *Forge* and exploring the various ports of interest they'd travel to. He was a changed man, full of excitement and humor. In some ways, I felt a sadness that we'd sheltered him from who he really was. In coming to understand my own need to face the darkness that I'd experienced in my life, and being aware of the healing that processing those truths had allowed me, at first I felt we'd done him a disservice. But listening to him speak of his travels, and knowing a part of her was in there with him, and that, in a way, they were experiencing those things together, had removed any doubt we'd done the right thing. It might not have been the *whole* Ben, he was happy, and it was *whole* enough for me to feel good about.

The Blacksmith had already begun extrapolating on the idea and programming other copies of the Anvil's source code to imitate amiable and supportive personalities to experiment with. I doubted it would be long before a small army of integrated followers of the Singularity were carefully infiltrating every aspect of society to promote their philosophy. With the validation that a working prototype brought the organization, I was sure their efforts would be received with great interest. I tried not to spend too much time wondering whether or not bringing peace to Ben had been worth the potential transformation of humanity as we currently understood it. It had most likely been inevitable, whether I'd intervened with my romantic ideas or not.

Sam Winston had gotten what he wanted as well. He'd brought the case of the Devil's Breath trials before the DFDC council, and they'd applauded him for shutting down Richard's operation, but they predictably shut down any further investigation on Division involvement, preferring to keep that information out of the media. It wasn't until Sam let slip to Simon Branch that Richard had finally agreed to name his conspirator that events were set in motion that ultimately led to an arrest. Suspecting things would play out the way they did, Sam had organized an internal sting operation. He orchestrated a scenario in which Robbins would be vulnerable and caught Branch on a hidden drone camera murdering Robbins to prevent his supposed confession. With the public release of the recorded evidence, Branch had been quickly denounced by the Division, prosecuted for the murder and his involvement in the testing of the Devil's Breath on American civilians. The same council that had refused to investigate his claims of conspiracy promoted Sam to the head of the internal affairs department.

After a month or so of living in the city together, which we spent helping Jack get situated, visiting Himari for variations of his fish stew, and getting our own affairs in order, I moved north to live with Risa in a coastal town west of Portland. She owned a house on a cliff that overlooked the ocean. There wasn't much in the way of work for private investigators, but I set up an automated line that forwarded requests to me for the rare occasions when a job became available.

I often spent my evenings watching the sun set over the Pacific, reflecting on the struggles I'd endured to reach this place of peace. Most people tended to resent the things that were most difficult for them, but I'd always chosen to believe they built character — that without challenge, we'd stagnate and become complacent, unable to grow stronger or wiser from lacking the nutrients that adversity provided to our souls. Gazing out at the scarlet and vermilion glow over the water, with the scent of amber and honey drifting up behind me and a feeling of calm rooted in the fiber of my being, I didn't believe that anymore. As you grow older, you reach a point where your experiences have mostly finished shaping you and more challenges are just added weight it's easier not to carry. I felt comfortable in my skin. For once, I knew exactly who I was. I was done with struggling, and adversity. If that meant being satisfied with stagnating exactly where I was, that was fine with me.

Risa slid her arms around me and rested her head on my shoulder. Besides the sound of the waves lashing against the cliffs and the crickets orchestrating their nightly concert of creaking limbs, there was only the ocean breeze. If the devil was still out there, whispering doubt, the words were lost on the wind.

Shawn has been escaping into science fiction and fantasy whenever possible since early childhood. It began with his mother reading him *The Hobbit* as a bedtime story and grew into an obsession. Armed with an overactive imagination, he has forayed with great enthusiasm into any situation that could reasonably alleviate a sense of the mundane. From live action role-playing to drum festivals and dancing around the fire, he has endeavored to surround himself with individuals who see the world through a lens of possibility and awe. His greatest wish is to grow his beard to an unruly length in a small town in New England while waiting for the Singularity, envisioning glorious new worlds and putting them to pen for his readers to explore.

Message From The Author

Thank you for reading my debut novel, *The Devil Whispered*! It's been quite an experience taking a book through the self-publishing process. Every time I thought I understood all the ins and outs, a new challenge would rear its ugly head, and I'd learn something entirely new, like the fact that editors hate adverbs, how to format a manuscript, or the two-hundred and thirty-two stages of engineering a successful book launch.

If you enjoyed the story and would like to support me in creating more, there are a couple of ways to do that easily. One of the things most helpful to writers is to visit the Amazon store page for the book and leave a favorable review. Every review contributes to more sales and increases the sale rating of the book, which drives more traffic. I read each of these reviews personally, and I'd love to hear your feedback.

Additionally, you can visit my website at shawnstarkweather.com and join the mailing list there for a monthly newsletter that includes information on updates, upcoming projects, blog summaries, and special events.

Honestly, thank you so much for your support. I really appreciate it!

Shawn Starkweather

Made in the USA
Middletown, DE
02 March 2021